ALREADY AT RISK

already at risk

WILDFLOWER SERIES
BOOK 4

AMELIE RHYS

Published by R. H. Publishing

Paperback ISBN: 979-8-9933877-0-3

Ebook ISBN: 979-8-9893446-9-7

Cover Design: Caitlin Russell

Character Art: Alie Reighard at alies_artwork

Editing: Sandra Dee at One Love Editing

For more information about Amelie's books, check out her website:

www.amelierhys.com

content notes

This book is intended for an 18+ audience.
Already at Risk *includes explicit sexual content, references to emotional domestic abuse in a former relationship, references to grief as it applies to the death of a parent during childhood, mentions of car accidents, medical trauma and emotions stemming from it, and details of a child custody battle.*

To ensure that the topics listed above have been handled with the care they deserve, I collaborated with sensitivity readers during the writing and editing process.

Please note, I am not a lawyer. And while Cameron & Natalie's custody case follows the legal process as closely as possible, some liberties have been taken for the sake of the story.

playlist

a little more time - ROLE MODEL
The Smallest Man Who Ever Lived - Taylor Swift
Woman - Mumford & Sons
Riptide - Vance Joy
The First Time - Damiano David
I Just Don't Know You Yet - Absolutely
All over me - HAIM
Invisible String - Taylor Swift
Man I Need - Olivia Dean
Your Eyes Tell Stories - Bo Staloch
Hands - Hylynd
Constellations - Jade LeMac
Forever - Noah Kahan
Let It All Go - Birdy, RHODES
Means I care - Tate McRae
All This Love - Cat Burns
dirty little secret - Artemas
Almost, So Close, Maybe - Mercer Henderson
Tears - Sabrina Carpenter
Sunflower, Vol. 6 - Harry Styles

To anyone who is learning to find themselves again and can suddenly breathe. I hope the air is sweet. You deserve it.

And to Zorro -
A girl couldn't have asked for a better canine writing companion all these years. Whenever I think of Cameron & Natalie, I'll think of that last summer you lay next to me in the grass in our new backyard while I finished their story.

Miss you, big guy.

six months ago

NATALIE

I was always envious—and happy for—women who emerged from a divorce and had that group of friends who took them out to celebrate, forced them to get back out there, made them a cake that said he wasn't good in bed anyway *or something.*

At this moment, in particular, I was wishing I had a larger social circle than my best friend who lived across the country, my nine-year-old daughter, my coworkers who saw my face enough when we were clocked in at the hospital, and, of course, my brothers.

In other words, I wished I had any *kind of social circle.*

Instead, it was just me and a little black dress against the world tonight. I'd almost talked myself out of this ten times, but it had been one year to the date since I'd filed for divorce, and that deserved commemoration, right?

I strode into the divey Irish pub, sliding onto a barstool with more confidence than I felt.

One drink—I'd just have one drink to honor the occasion, and then I'd head home.

"What can I get you?"

The bartender threw a coaster down in front of me, ready to place something on it.

"Whatever it is she wants, I'm paying for it," a deep voice cut in.

"Oh, that's—"

I turned to my right, where a man had suddenly appeared.

A handsome *man, who grinned at me, his expression both soft and teasing. There was something about the combination of dimples and a jawline that could cut through the hardest exteriors.*

My *exterior.*

"Okay," I finished.

"Yeah?" he prompted, like he knew exactly what had just happened. "It's okay?"

I sucked in a breath and shook my head. "I don't need you to buy me a drink. You're welcome to sit there, though."

He chuckled. "Thank you for the permission. I'm Cam."

CHAPTER ONE

cameron

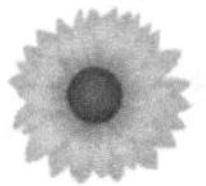  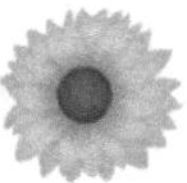

I COULD THINK OF a million moments when I'd wished I could pick up the phone and call my dad, but this one had to be at the top.

So many years had passed since I'd heard his voice, but I tried to imagine it: that bit of rasp and deep timbre. There'd be hearty laughter, jovial congratulations. He had this way of making everything seem like a big deal, even when it was a small one. I'd spend entire summer baseball seasons barely making it to first base, and he'd hype me up like I was the star of the Little League show, even when I was shit.

But this *actually* felt like a big deal.

Or, it was certainly on its *way* to being a big deal. Something Dad would appreciate, anyway.

All I'd ever really wanted was to be like him, to fill the shoes he'd left behind. And what Daphne Gardner just told me...it felt like the closest I'd ever come to fitting into them.

I was going to be the youngest junior partner at Gardner Law.

God, that thought felt good. *Really* good.

There were only two bitter parts about it. One, that I couldn't share it with the one person I really wanted to, and two, it wasn't a sure thing. Yet.

But I was only a case or two away from making it happen; that was what Daphne had just insinuated in our meeting, when she'd started by asking if junior partner was something that interested me, that twinkle in her eye because she knew the answer. I kept replaying the conversation in my head as I walked out of her palatial office, with its towering bookshelves and boxy Styrofoam couches. I wanted to make sure I hadn't misunderstood.

But there was no doubting it: partner was going to be mine—as long as I didn't fuck up. As long as I kept my clients, kept winning, and kept going.

I bit down on a grin, staring at my feet as I walked, finally feeling like I was moving in the right direction.

Hell, I wasn't much of a resolutions kind of guy, but I had made two goals for myself this year, and junior partner was one of them. Honestly, of the two, it was the more attainable target, had a clearer path to success, and therefore, it had become my priority.

As for the other one? Well, I didn't really know where to start with it, but after only a few seconds of celebration, my brain wandered there anyway, like it did every day. Without fail.

I should be thinking about clients. About the cases I could close, and how I could do it faster. I should be thinking about how best to convince Daphne that I was absolutely ready for this promotion in the firm. I should be thinking about what I was going to say to Julian when he stopped me in the hallway in a matter of minutes, lying in wait to pester me about the meeting like the meddlesome, supportive friend and colleague he was.

But no, all I could think about was *her*.

Because why think too long about anything practical when I could spend all my time thinking about a woman whom I'd probably never see again?

Truthfully, it was a damn miracle Daphne was recognizing my work at the firm, considering I spent about half of every day with my head up in the goddamn clouds, fantasizing about what I'd do if I got a second chance with the woman of my fucking dreams. It had been six months, and I hadn't stopped thinking about that night, couldn't stop thinking about the way I'd let her slip through my fingers, on the precipice of a kiss.

It would have been the best kiss of my life, I just knew it. But something had clicked in her brain as I'd pulled back and searched her eyes for consent, causing her to flee instead of giving in to me like I'd been hoping.

I wanted to find her. Wanted to *apologize.* Had it been something I'd done? Had I misread the signals? Misunderstood the soft moans leaving her lips as I trailed mine up her neck? Miscalculated the way her pulse had thumped—*raced*—against my open mouth?

I had no idea. No idea who she was or what had gone through her brain. But I wanted to know, was dying to find out all of it. And besides going back to Mulligan's whenever I had a free night, hoping to see her again, I had no idea where to start. But I was determined to figure it out. Sparks like that didn't ignite often. And when they ignited in a place that meant as much to me as Mulligan's did? *Fuck.*

She was my second goal—the unattainable one.

First, make partner.

Then, get the girl.

It would likely help if I knew her full name. Or maybe her phone number. A general location I could send a pigeon carrier? I'd take literally *anything* at this point.

But I had nothing. Absolutely fuck all.

Sighing, I checked my watch. Only a few minutes to go before my meeting with the Londons—a meeting that Daphne had just surprisingly mentioned. It seemed to be of particular interest to her, creating suspicion that *this* was the case that hinged on me making partner.

Fine by me. Actually, more than fine. That would be ideal, honestly.

This meeting was the least of my worries. Daphne must have forgotten, or maybe she'd never known, that I *knew* the Londons.

Well, I knew Noah London. I'd never met his sister before—who was my actual client in this case—but it was the relation to Noah that had Daphne wringing her hands. We weren't usually the type of firm that dealt with high-profile clients. That, and I had a hunch that she was a bit of a fan.

But while he might be a national-level sports celebrity as the quarterback for the New England Knights, Noah London was also just someone who moved in my circles. Had been for years since he went to college with my sister and was one of Julian's best friends.

Julian, who was staring at me from the doorway of his office as I strode down the narrow hall of Gardner Law, crystal clear conference room windows passing me by.

"Can I help you?"

Julian raised one auburn eyebrow. "How'd it go?"

I shrugged. "Good."

"Man of few words today, huh?"

"She was...encouraging," I added. There really wasn't much else to say. Nothing concrete to share. *Yet.* "I think she wants to meet Noah."

Julian laughed. "Daphne's a Knights fan? Never would have guessed."

"Or something," I muttered, not really sure if it was the football she was a fan of or just *Noah*. Hopefully, it was sports-related, considering Noah was very much taken. By Julian's sister, Gemma. And I had a feeling Julian wouldn't want his sister kicking his boss's ass.

Reading my mind, Julian asked, "My future brother-in-law coming with today?"

My brows tugged together. "Did they get engaged?"

"Nah, but they will soon."

I nodded, not surprised. "I think Noah's coming. And Blake, possibly. Natalie included him on the initial email she sent me. I think he's been helping her work through things."

Julian nodded, but I could see the gears in his head moving, and I knew he was thinking what I was.

Natalie having the support of her brothers was great; we always wanted to see that clients had a good support system in these types of situations. But because of what her ex had claimed in his recent filing, it was going to be important to balance Natalie's family support with her stance that she could provide for her nine-year-old daughter, Chloe, on her own.

"Have you met Natalie?" Julian questioned, curiosity in his gaze.

Shaking my head, I checked my watch again. Five minutes until our appointment. "No, have you?"

"Yeah, a couple times." He leaned his shoulder against the door frame of his office. "Gemma is Chloe's figure skating coach. Before her maternity leave, I went to a couple of her shows, so I've seen Natalie there. She's great; Gemma loves her."

I crossed my arms, taking mental notes. "You ever see her ex showing up for his daughter at those shows?"

"God no," Julian snorted. "That piece of shit? Not a chance."

For Natalie's daughter, who deserved to have her dad show up to things that were important to her, that wasn't the answer I wanted to hear.

But for our *case*...it was good news, exactly the type of anecdote I needed to compile more of.

We were going to win this thing. I'd give Daphne the kind of results she wanted to see. I'd put Natalie London's ex in his place. And I'd help a single mom get back to focusing on her life without any interruptions. From what I knew about Natalie and her job as a trauma surgeon, she was busy enough without dealing with a custody battle.

I wasn't worried.

At least, not until I left Julian behind and headed toward the front of the office, walking up in time to see Noah London open the glass doors, sandy-brown hair, broad shoulders, slightly bleary-eyed from late nights as a new dad. Another man followed behind him, his hair darker, his face a little slimmer than his brother's, his expression serious. He held the door, allowing his sister to slip in front of him.

Sparkling green eyes met mine, ones that almost matched Noah's but were brighter, more dazzling. Her honey-colored hair was swept up in a clip, but several strands framed her face. *That face.* That beautiful fucking face that had been haunting my dreams for months, ever since she sat beside me in a bar and then abruptly disappeared into the night a few hours later, like a princess who had to make it home before the clock struck twelve.

The woman I'd been trying to figure out how to find?

The woman I never got to kiss?

The woman I'd been *thinking* about kissing ever since she slipped away?

She was standing right in front of me. Her name, apparently, was not what she'd told me that night. No, it was Dr. Natalie London.

And she was my newest client.

CHAPTER TWO

natalie

WITHIN TWO MINUTES OF meeting my new lawyer, I knew two things to be true.

One, he did *not* remember meeting me six months prior in an Irish pub. He didn't remember the drink we shared or how it had turned into two drinks, then three drinks, then *maybe* four.

Admittedly, that was probably why he didn't remember.

But two, it *bothered* me that he didn't remember. It annoyed me that when we approached him in the lobby a few minutes ago, he introduced himself as though we'd never met before. When he held out his hand for me to take in a firm shake, *he* didn't blush or react like his skin was on fire. And if there was any flicker of recognition in his system, he sure as hell didn't let it show.

I didn't typically let the behavior of men get under my skin. After years of enduring my ex-husband's emotional abuse, gaslighting, and—the cherry on top—affair, I didn't let men affect me.

Except...he had that night. Affected me, that is.

So shameful to admit, honestly.

I really shouldn't let my brain wander into the details, not right now as he led me into his office, my brothers flanking me on either side.

I definitely should *not* be thinking about the way he'd pulled me onto the dance floor.

Or how he led me into the hallway next, outside the single stall bathroom that had one too many dicks drawn on the walls and a toilet with the handle you had to jiggle three times and cross your fingers to get to flush.

I didn't need to think about the way he'd pushed me against the wall or dragged his lips up my neck until they hovered over mine, *waiting* for permission.

He never got it.

He'd given me a second to think, and then reality had cut through the alcohol haze, reminding me who I was: a single mom who had made a promise to herself *not* to do this. I'd only gone out for a short celebration, something I'd wanted to do for myself but also had done at the behest of my daughter and my therapist, who both told me, in a different array of words, that I needed to *loosen up*.

But instead, I'd spiraled and then locked up in a handsome stranger's arms. It had been the consequence of a surge of arousal and then the crash of awareness that I was out of my depth when it came to casual, sexual encounters in the twenty-first century—because yes, it did feel like my failed marriage lasted for an entire century and then some.

Now, that stranger was here, in front of me. And he wasn't a stranger anymore.

Cameron Bryant, Attorney at Law.

My Attorney at Law.

Shit. *Shit, shit, shit, shit.*

"Dr. London."

His deep voice brought me back to reality, out of the memories of that drunken night that he was acting like didn't exist. I glanced up at him to find a passive expression, patient as he waited for me to respond. Again, no...awareness. No curiosity, no trying to puzzle out if maybe I was a face he'd seen before but couldn't place. His gaze was steady. Professional. No hint of recognition.

"I—I'm sorry," I stuttered. I couldn't *believe* I'd just stuttered, but I wasn't used to talking to men this attractive, certainly not ones who knew the sensitive spots on my neck. And I especially wasn't used to men who called me Dr. London in contexts that had nothing to do with medicine. "Can you repeat the question?"

Mr. Bryant—if he was going to be respectful and formal, then so was I—flashed a generous smile that made heat rush to my cheeks.

God, what was *wrong* with me?

Actually, I knew what was wrong with me. He had dimples, perfect indents in his light brown skin that made me want to melt. Everything about him was warm, just like I remembered, and despite how he was acting, he felt oh so very familiar. His smile was still kind, still picture-perfect, and his suit remained tailored precisely. The only thing that was different was perhaps his insistent professionalism and his short, black hair, which had grown a little since I'd last seen him, enough that there was a bit more curl to it now.

"Of course. I just wanted to confirm the information from your email. You have full custody of Chloe at the moment?"

I cleared my throat. "Legal, yes."

And I'd naively thought that after our initial custody proceedings ended last year, that wouldn't be contested. But here we were.

"Which is, of course, the only acceptable arrangement," Noah muttered beside me.

Cameron glanced at him, a twitch of his lips. But then he directed his attention back to me, ignoring my brother.

They were friends. Or friends of friends, I guess. Noah went to college with his sister, as I understood it. And one of Noah's other friends from college, Julian, also worked at Gardner Law Firm. But clearly, my brother and Cameron weren't close enough for us to have ever met before.

Not that I met a lot of my brothers' friends, considering how busy work kept me now and how isolated my ex-husband made sure I was for years.

"And joint physical?" Cameron checked with me.

I nodded. "He gets two weekends a month."

Blake, my oldest brother, muttered something under his breath about how it was two weekends too much.

"And a full week during winter and summer breaks," I added.

"And you'd like to maintain this?" Cameron checked with me.

"Yes," I confirmed. "I mean, I wouldn't mind if it was less. Which, I think, is what got us into this mess in the first place. When Korey had to request permission to move a few hours away, I suggested that maybe we consider reducing his visitation or that he should be the one who is doing the driving." A heavy sigh fell through my lips. "Which, of course, pissed him off. I should have known better. Because now he's gone way off the deep end and is trying to turn the tables, so Chloe lives with him instead."

Cameron nodded, taking that in. If he was surprised by Korey's unusual, slightly extreme behavior, he didn't act like it. "Do you think Chloe likes the schedule as it is now? Is there anything she talks about wanting to change?" he asked, adjusting his tie a little.

"Sometimes she grumbles about having to leave for the weekends with her dad, but I'm not sure she'd want to give them up, either." I cocked my head to the side, considering. "She wants to see him, but she doesn't love having to leave. If that makes sense?"

Cameron nodded, his voice understanding. "It does."

"Abrams doesn't give two shits about his daughter," Noah added, but Cameron kept his attention on me, dark brown eyes flicking around my face, looking for something. A reaction? I wasn't sure. "He only began showing up for things in the last few weeks, when he started this whole mess. It's like he's playing a game."

"And what does he get by winning?" Cameron asked me, almost like Noah wasn't in the room.

"Control," I said. I'd been thinking about this question since I learned what Korey was trying to do. "He regains some semblance of control in our lives. He didn't like losing it. All of his other reasons are just excuses, and I suspect he knows it. But he's trying to spin it to sound like it's in Chloe's best interests. He's saying that she'll be close to his hometown, so his parents are nearby, along with the rest of his extended family, a big network of support. That the schools are better there. That they have great skating programs for her. That his work schedule is more predictable and less intense. All this shit, just because he knows if he controls Chloe and brings her into *his* world, he'll control me, too."

"He's a narcissist," Blake grunted from my other side.

Cameron nodded thoughtfully before leaning back in his chair. "Noah and Blake." His eyes flicked to my brothers for the first time since we'd entered the room. "Could you please give me a moment alone with your sister?"

Both my brothers hesitated. I felt their eyes shift to me, looking for some kind of implication that I was okay with the idea of being left to my own devices. It wasn't until I nodded that they pushed out of their chairs and strode from Cameron's office. The door clicked behind them, but I still felt their presence, lingering.

Sure enough, when I peeked over my shoulder and through the slim window that ran the length of the door, Noah and Blake could be seen leaning in the hallway just outside, arms crossed, looks of concern on their faces.

"Noah's a great guy, and I've always liked him," Cameron said without much preamble. He leaned forward across his desk, pinning me with a sincere look. "And I'm sure I'd feel the same about Blake if I got to know him. But your ex-husband is claiming that you rely entirely on others to support Chloe, and having your brothers too involved in this process is not going to make it any easier to combat his narrative."

"Doesn't that make him a hypocrite?" I wrinkled my nose. "*His* support system being nearby is in Chloe's best interests, but having *mine* be involved in her life means I'm not a good mom?"

"He's absolutely a hypocrite," Cameron said calmly. "I'm not denying that at all. I'm just looking out for the optics of the situation so we can set you up for success."

"I understand," I said, and I did. Truth was, I *did* rely on my brothers too much; I knew that. Being a trauma surgeon meant that my day-to-day was unpredictable and often long—incredibly long. I was lucky enough to have Noah, who immediately stepped up to help with childcare after my divorce from Korey. During the off-season of his football career, Noah welcomed Chloe to spend so many days and nights at his apartment. And then, when his girlfriend recently gave birth to a baby girl, making Noah too busy as a dad to call in for uncle duty, Blake had shown up in Boston to take over. I knew there were other reasons why Blake moved to the East Coast, but it didn't matter. He was here, and I couldn't thank him enough. "I'll talk to them."

"I can say something, too," Mr. Bryant said. "If you think it would help them to hear it from me."

I shook my head. "I wouldn't want to subject you to that."

Blake and Noah were not going to take the concept of *backing off* well, but they'd do it if it meant there were better chances for Chloe.

He shrugged. "I'm a lawyer. I'm no stranger to having difficult conversations." His eye contact suddenly intensified, and I realized that his declaration about difficult conversations was actually more of a warning. "But I don't have to be *your* lawyer."

I blinked.

And then blinked again.

"If it would make you more comfortable for me to pass along your case, I can," he added.

"Why would that make me more comfortable?"

He raised a brow. "You really want to keep playing pretend? During the night that we spent together, I didn't exactly get the impression that you were the kind of woman who did that. Outside of the fact that you lied about your name, that is."

My jaw dropped, both in surprise and automatic defense, and Cameron seemed satisfied by my reaction. I must have made it clear that I remembered exactly who he was. That I *had* been playing pretend. Something I'd only been doing because *he* was.

As mortified as I was, I also felt relief. He *hadn't* forgotten me.

But we needed to clear some things up.

"We did not *spend the night* together." I lowered my voice in case my brothers could hear our conversation through the door. Construction companies these days used cheap-ass materials. "We shared a few drinks, that was all. Are there rules about lawyers sharing drinks with prospective clients?"

Cameron's gaze flared at my words, my choice to reduce the evening to drinks. But I didn't need him to know that I'd been thinking about that night, replaying the hot touches and heavy breathing in my head for weeks now, wondering if I'd done the right thing by pushing him away. I didn't need him to know that it was the closest I'd come to a man in so very long, and it *did* something to me. Whereas to him, it was probably just another night at the bar. A man as good-looking and educated as Cameron Bryant probably had his pick of the litter when it came to last call at the bar.

"There aren't any rules against it," he answered, no longer seeming amused. "Especially if they don't...do it again."

I nodded and clasped my hands in my lap. "Then I think we are fine to proceed as is, Mr. Bryant."

He perused my face for a moment. Finally, he replied, "Okay, Dr. London."

I cleared my throat. "I appreciate the sentiment, but it's fine to call me Natalie."

"Natalie," he repeated, emphasizing the name that *wasn't* the one I'd told him the night we met.

"*You* told me your name was Cam," I countered, realizing how ridiculously childish I sounded a little too late.

"It's a nickname," he said in a deadpan. "It's a shortened version of my name. And you're welcome to call me that or Cameron, either one."

I sighed, feeling like I owed him an explanation and hating that I felt that way. But I didn't want this client-lawyer relationship to have a rocky start. Well, *more* of a rocky start, anyway.

"I've learned from my mistakes, and I don't give things away freely anymore. Not even my name, if I don't feel like giving it," I said. The intensity of Cameron's eye contact unnerved me slightly, so I looked around the room instead, taking in the certificates on the wall, the photographs of his family on the bookshelf, and the orderly way he aligned his pens on his desk, like they were silverware beside a dinner plate.

Cameron huffed a laugh. "And you shouldn't."

I frowned and looked back at him. "I apologize if you feel I deceived you or led you on, but—"

"No, that's not it at all," he interrupted, shaking his head.

"For the purpose of the case, I just don't want you to think that I'm always like that," I explained.

"Like what?"

"Like the kind of mom who regularly spends the night away from her daughter, going to bars, getting drunk, pretending I'm someone else, and dancing with strangers."

The corner of his mouth tugged upward. "Ah, so you admit there were drinks *and* dancing."

I pursed my lips. "That is not the point here."

There were drinks and dancing and his hands in my hair, but that wasn't *me*. I'd wanted it to be me, wanted to be ready for it to be me, but I wasn't quite there yet.

"I don't think that," Cameron said with a sigh. "Trust me, Natalie. It could not have been more obvious that you don't normally do that."

"Right."

I flushed, heat once again rising to my face. Of course it was obvious that I was inexperienced and out of practice. I knew that wasn't exactly my fault, but still. It didn't feel like great encouragement, considering I'd been contemplating all day whether I should accept a date with some guy I matched with online. *Josh* had been pestering me for over a week. And like I said, I really *wanted* to try the dating scene again, longed to be ready for it. I didn't need men to make my life into a fuller version than it was because Chloe and I—we were happy. But I wouldn't mind dipping my toes back in the water.

To make matters worse, Cameron seemed to have clocked my embarrassment, a sympathetic expression overcoming his handsome features.

"Natalie—"

"So, what are the next steps?" I interrupted. "For the case."

Cameron mulled over his response for a moment, a muscle jumping in his jaw as he assessed me. I had no idea what he was looking for, but eventually, he came to some sort of internal decision. He stood, walked around to the other side of the desk, and leaned back against it.

"When you originally reached out, you mentioned that Mr. Abrams has been sending you emails with some of his demands," he said, crossing his arms over his chest in a way that made it very hard not to look at the way his crisp, tan suit stretched across the muscles in his upper arms.

I nodded, unable to talk as I looked up at him. He felt larger than life, taller than Noah or Blake. And without his desk between us, I felt like another layer of my defense had been stripped away.

"Can you send them to me?"

"Of course." I scrambled to get my phone out, opening my email and—

"Oh my God."

The room filled with the sound of a woman's moan, followed by a man's grunt, and then a high-pitched whine. And panting, there was panting, too. Right before the distinct slapping of two people's bodies while—yep, you guessed it—fucking.

Holy shit, holy shit, holy shit.

"Oh my God," I echoed in a gasp, but it was anything but sexy. Terrified would be more accurate. Humiliated. *Again.*

My fingers shook as I tried to swipe up on the video, trying to get it to disappear. But it took way longer than I should have, and I sank lower in my seat, wondering how the hell this day could get any worse.

"I am *so* sorry," I impressed, beyond mortified. I attempted to find the emails from Korey, refusing to look at Cameron. My body was so hot, it felt like I might melt into the chair, become one with it. "I made the mistake of telling my friend about my therapist's suggestion to become more *in touch* with myself before trying to date again, so she started sending me all these videos. I don't really think that was what my therapist meant, but my friend, she's a real free spirit, and—"

"Natalie." Cameron's calm voice interrupted my rambling. "It's okay."

It was *not* okay.

At the moment, I wanted to strangle Ellie. Even if it wasn't her fault, but mine for not closing out of that properly.

I found the emails I was looking for, forwarded them to Cameron's address, and then looked over my shoulder, checking on my brothers.

"They didn't see," Cameron assured me.

He seemed to be right; Noah and Blake stood facing each other in the hallway, talking. Not really paying attention.

"And even if they did, I'm pretty sure they've watched equally...descriptive things in their lives," he added, obviously trying to make me feel better.

"Maybe," I huffed, not wanting to think about my brothers and their porn-watching habits. "But if they have, I'm sure it has nothing to do with their lack of a sex life, considering they're both with the women of their dreams."

Blake eloped with his best friend about a month ago after pining over her for *years*. I was happy for him, for both him and Noah, but couldn't help wondering why I couldn't get their luck in the dating department. I was more on par with my younger brothers, longing for things I couldn't have.

I finally looked up at Cameron to see him staring at me funnily. And that was when I realized that, on top of everything else, I'd admitted to having a nonexistent sex life.

Excellent.

I crossed one leg over the other, trying to look nonchalant even though I felt anything but. I wore a dress today when I rarely wore dresses. It was usually sweats or scrubs for me. *Maybe* a pair of jeans and a top if I was feeling ambitious. But I'd wanted to appear professional, somewhat put together, for our meeting.

I was afraid that was *not* the impression I was making to Cameron.

His eyes flicked to my lap, where the slit in my dress seemed to have widened when I repositioned, exposing my bare thigh. I felt the warmth of his gaze on my skin and took a shaky breath.

Clearing my throat, I said, "If *you'd* rather pass me off to another lawyer, I'd understand."

He lifted his gaze again, but it felt more like he dragged it, like his eyes could do what his hands did that night, touching every inch of me and creating a path of heat. When he spoke, his voice had a surprising roughness.

"That would depend on why you think I want to do that."

"Just so you don't have to deal with me." I waved my hands around, very nondescript-like. "This."

He looked over me another time, his lips forming a slight frown. "What if I want to deal with you?"

My stomach did a little flip, interpreting things that weren't really there.

"Then I would appreciate any help you are able to give me," I said sincerely. His gaze burned and then cooled a little when I added, "And Chloe."

"Of course." He clapped his hands together and strode to the door, opening it for my brothers. They immediately filed back inside. "Then I would be honored to help you kick your ex's ass in court."

"Fuck yeah," Noah cheered, dropping down into his seat again.

"I've been waiting to kick his ass *somehow*," Blake muttered dryly, drawing up on my other side.

Cameron just met my gaze with a slightly amused expression.

"I'll talk to them," I mouthed.

But he just flashed an understanding grin.

And I almost collapsed on the spot, struck dead by his dimples.

This was probably a mistake.

But there were a few more facts I'd discovered today, compounded with what I'd already learned about Cameron Bryant the night I met him.

He was respectful, but didn't appear to coddle. Not only did he understand boundaries, but he followed them once they were laid out. And he had enough of my brothers' trust that they willfully walked out of the room without causing a scene.

I needed a new lawyer. The one I previously worked with was good, but he was no longer practicing. And I couldn't afford to take the time to find another one.

So now all I had to do was forget how close I'd been to kissing Cameron Bryant.

And never, ever think of it again.

CHAPTER THREE

cameron

THE MOMENT JULIAN'S THROAT cleared behind me, I knew that I'd watched Natalie London walk away for just a beat too long after our meeting.

Fuck, and I thought I had the art of subtlety down.

I turned back to my friend and colleague with the air of someone who was *not* going to admit that they'd just done anything wrong.

But Julian sensed it, raised a brow, and then muttered, "She has *four* brothers, Cam."

"I am very aware of her brothers, Julian."

Very aware, considering two of them were *very* present today. Which was fine, though it did make it more difficult to have a candid conversation with her, forcing me to follow her lead when she pretended to have never met me before.

There was just a split second when I'd believed her act, and it felt like a kick in the goddamn gut. Because of course, the one woman I couldn't get out of my fucking mind didn't even remember who I was.

But then she avoided my eye contact in a way she never *once* did that night in the bar, and I knew she was just trying to hide. Like she'd been hiding from me for the last six months.

I hadn't known her real name, her number, the street she lived on—nothing.

And here she was. Noah London's *sister*. My newest client. Completely off-limits.

Fuck me.

Julian shrugged and fell back into his office. "Just thought you should know."

I followed him and for some reason asked, "And why's that?"

"Because of the googly eyes you were making when she walked away."

"Juniper." I turned to Julian's wife, who happened to share an office with him. A terrible decision that no one seemed willing to rectify. "Please tell your husband that I was not making, and have never made, googly eyes."

Unfortunately, Juniper just flashed me a pained smile.

"You know how much I love to tell Julian that he's wrong, but..."

"I was just...admiring her," I tried to salvage. Julian snorted as he sat in his desk chair, and I added, "Not like that. I'm just appreciating what she does to save lives and fight for her daughter."

There. Neither of them could argue with that statement.

"Did you just realize that intelligent, hardworking women are hot?" Julian said with a raised brow. "Fuck, I could have told you that, man."

He turned his gaze to his wife, whose face was suddenly flushed.

"Okay, I'm done with this conversation," I muttered. I spent too much of my time at work watching these two flirt with each other.

"Wait, Cam." Juniper snapped out of the longing look she was giving her husband to stop me. And because it was Juniper, I paused my movements and waited like she asked. Wouldn't have done it for Julian, but I'd do it for Juni.

"I just..." Juniper pursed her lips in thought. "You *could* hand off her case to someone else."

Oh, I know, Juniper. I was very aware that I could do that. I'd definitely *considered* doing that. I'd *offered* to do that. But Natalie hadn't taken me up on it, and considering Daphne had made it clear she was counting on me to handle this case, I didn't push it.

"So you don't have to worry about...professional boundaries," Juniper added, and internally, I sighed. She had no fucking idea how much I was going to struggle maintaining professional boundaries with Natalie London. No idea how I'd memorized the sound of her breathy gasps, the way they felt against my skin, how my lips felt pressed to her racing pulse, the intoxicating and heady scent of her perfume, so sweet, a touch of vanilla combined with something else I couldn't put my finger on. I'd been ready to let her ruin me that night, ready to give her everything I owned just for a taste of her lips.

I'd *still* give her everything I owned for a taste of her lips.

So yeah, I was fucked.

Externally, I choked on a laugh and said, "Professional boundaries, Juni? I don't know if you can really talk to me about that. What you two are doing in here when the door is closed is not something I want to know."

I looked around their office, at Juniper's side filled with trinkets: plants with names I couldn't pronounce and photos in bright frames and a colorful arrangement of pens and office supplies. All very innocent-looking, like a third-grade teacher's desk instead of a lawyer's, except I knew half the books she had stashed up on her top shelf were the opposite of innocent, considering I borrowed them sometimes.

And then I turned to look at Julian, finding him with a ridiculous smirk, his auburn hair rumpled, and the slightest hint of red on his normally pale complexion. Was he...*blushing*?

Jesus Christ, what had these two just done.

"Just remember you encouraged this," he said with a shrug and then kicked his feet up onto the corner of his desk.

He wasn't wrong about that. I totally told him to get his head out of his ass where Juniper was involved.

"Well, it wasn't like it was any *more* professional when the two of you couldn't get through a meeting without insulting each other. Even if I now realize that was your own personal brand of flirting."

Juniper sighed. "This isn't about us. This is about you and Natalie London. From what Gemma tells me, she could use a nice guy like you, Cam." Juniper poked me in the chest like that would help get her point across. "Maybe let someone else be her lawyer, and ask that intelligent, hardworking woman on a date."

Julian just shrugged his support of the idea, but I shook my head.

"I don't think Natalie London wants me to ask her out on a date, Juni. She just wants a guy who is going to crush her ex-husband in court. Which is something I'd personally really like to do."

If dating Natalie wasn't an option, I'd take being her lawyer as a close second. I really did want to help her. Based on the emails she sent me alone, her ex was clearly a narcissistic asshole, just as the Londons had described, and I already fucking hated him. Especially because I wondered if *he* was to blame for the switch in Natalie's mood that night, the reason her confidence had morphed, and suddenly, there'd been anxiety in Natalie's eyes when I'd pulled back to look at her. She'd seemed so sure of herself, and then it had disintegrated in front of my eyes. I didn't like that a woman as assertive and perfect as Natalie could lose even a tiny bit of her shine because of something a man did.

Possibly did, but still. I had my theories.

"Okay, I'm here for that, too," Juniper conceded with a nod. Seeming happy enough with my answer, she turned back to her desk and closed the cupboard above it that housed her secret little library. Then she smoothed her polka-dotted skirt and seated herself primly in her desk chair.

Julian, on the other hand, was looking at me with scrutiny. Like he'd caught the hint of possessiveness in my statement.

Yeah, so what if *I* wanted to be the one to tell Korey Abrams to fuck off in the courtroom? In legal terms, of course.

"Sounds kinda like you'd like to crush her ex outside of court, too," Julian murmured. "Wonder why that is."

"Because he's an ass," I said succinctly.

Better to keep it at that.

God, I wouldn't mind landing a punch to his face.

"Mhm," Julian hummed but then kicked his feet off his desk and turned back toward it. "Don't get me wrong, Cam. I'm here for it. Just...you know. Be careful."

His words weighed heavy. There was a lot to be careful about in our line of work. We held people's futures in our hands, and I was well aware I needed to be levelheaded enough to be able to pull through for Natalie. I also had my own career to consider, and Julian knew how close I was to climbing up the ladder.

But I was careful. I always was. I kept my head down, worked hard, and got things done. And this would be no different.

"Always am," I said solemnly, and Julian nodded with acknowledgment. Because he knew it was true.

"Is Collins still coming this week?" Julian asked, switching the topic of conversation now that we'd sorted through that.

"Yeah, she's already landed, I think. I'm catching her art show tonight, and then we have plans to get dinner later this week."

"Say hi to her for me."

"Will do."

It had been a few months since I'd seen my sister, so I was looking forward to seeing her. Collins lived in California with her real estate investment mogul husband, Beau, but they both traveled to the East Coast when time and circumstance allowed.

She had an exhibition tonight, but they planned to stay at their Boston home for the rest of the week, which was probably good. Seeing Collins and Beau would help take my mind off work and clients.

Or, more realistically, how badly I wanted one particular client.

"Your brain is anywhere but at this dinner, Cam. I'm beginning to think I should have gone with Beau to his fancy client dinner."

"Fuck, I'm sorry." I dragged a hand down my face, trying to shake myself out of it. But I knew it was no use; it had been this way all week. Ever since Natalie showed up at Gardner Law days ago. "It's just this case."

"It's always a case," my sister said with a sigh. "Sometimes I worry about you, you know."

"Every job has its challenges." Like the woman of your dreams becoming your client and then not being allowed to touch her. "It comes with the territory of being employed."

When Collins gave me a disbelieving look, I doubled down and tried to focus on our conversation.

"You really mean to tell me that you don't obsess over a painting for hours on end? That you don't stress about your sales? That Beau doesn't worry over numbers at his desk?"

"Have you met Beau?" Collins shook her head with a chuckle, her tight curls bouncing around her face. "Beau doesn't understand the concept of stress."

"When you let your phone die after that art show in Brooklyn and didn't bother checking in with anyone, Beau called me like forty-seven times. I'm not even exaggerating."

"Stress about work," Collins clarified.

"Fine, ignore the Beau example. Your husband is an anomaly. He doesn't count."

I'd tried to be more critical of the man taking care of my sister when she first introduced us, but I quickly realized it was an impossible task. He gave her everything and more *and* was annoyingly nice about it.

Collins' lips pressed together in a sheepish way that I recognized from any situation where Beau came into the conversation. And then her expression morphed as she began to drive home her point.

"Painting and art is my passion, though, Cam. I obsess over a painting, but I love it."

"Who says I don't love my job?"

"I don't know." She gave me a scrutinizing look. "Maybe those bags under your eyes."

Rude, but okay.

"These bags mean that I got shit done this week. Every time they get bigger means I've won another case."

I probably should invest in a good eye cream, though. My thirtieth birthday just passed, so I had no illusions that the bags would be going away anytime soon.

Collins sat back in her chair with her wine. "I'm proud of you. Don't think I'm not."

"I know you are. You're just being you."

Sometimes it seemed like Collins grew up too quickly, became an adult too fast. As her older brother, I felt guilty about that. I should have shielded her more in the aftermath of Dad's accident and death, shouldered more of the responsibility so she didn't feel an ounce of it. We were both young, but she was younger.

It was one reason I was glad she had Beau in her life, though. He was successful and smart, but also fun and adventurous, and he breathed life into her while she brought him back down to Earth every once in a while. They were perfectly complementary.

"I'm the only sister you've got." She pointed an accusatory finger at me. "I have a job to do, and I take it very seriously."

"It's appreciated, Lins."

"And you know it's a part of my job to grill you about your dating life."

Excellent. Great. Just what I needed.

"There really is no dating life," I admitted before my gaze wandered around the outdoor patio we sat at—one of my favorite places on Tremont Street. Ivy covered the brick exterior of a century-old building that didn't have enough seating inside to fit the busy flow of patrons that visited daily, and for good reason. They served stiff cocktails and knew how to make a good lobster roll, among other things.

"To be determined." Collins flashed a smile when I looked back at her. "I'll believe it after I ask my twenty questions."

"That sounds like a waste of perfectly good dinner conversation."

She ignored me. "Any dates since I saw you last?"

"None."

"Match with any special guys, girls, people on a dating app?"

"You know I don't have dating apps."

I preferred to meet people in real life.

Like in little pubs.

And then drag them onto dance floors and into back hallways.

"I was hoping you'd give in and download one." She drummed her fingers on the wooden tabletop. "We could use an addition to the family, give Christmas a little bit of excitement this year."

"I'm telling Mom, Uncle Tony, and Pops that you think they're boring," I said, lifting a brow.

"I didn't say that." Her lips quirked. "I just don't understand why you never bring anyone home."

"Because there's never anyone *to* bring home."

"What about that hot actor that you went home with after Beau's bachelor party? Mom would *love* him."

My mom had worked in theater her entire life, so yes, she likely would. But that was *not* the point here.

"First of all, I can't believe Beau told you about that. Second of all, that was *years* ago, Collins."

"So?" She shrugged. "Nothing wrong with rekindling a one-night stand. Shooting your shot."

True. But I didn't want to. There was only one late-night meet-up I wanted to rekindle, and she was off-limits.

"Oh, one of Nessa's backup singers recently split with her boyfriend, and she's *gorgeous*. Super sweet, too. Her name is Bryn. Maybe I should set you up?"

"Isn't Nessa on tour right now?" One of my sister's best friends was the wildly popular singer-songwriter, Wednesday Elevett. "That sounds...complicated."

She shrugged. "Doesn't have to be."

No, thank you. Not interested.

"No, Lins. Dating's just not my priority right now, and you know it."

Collins rolled her eyes. "It *is* possible to have a good dating life and a good career, you realize that, right?"

I considered her for a second, taking in her concerned expression. "I know. You're proof of that."

"Aw." She brightened. "I'm going to take that as a compliment."

"As you should. But drop it, Collins. I'm focused on work, and I'm fine with that."

Especially because my work right now included a very pretty trauma surgeon who was just a little bit distracting whenever she appeared in my brain. Which happened to be a lot. It was likely concerning, especially since she was apparently *so* permanently in my head that she seemed to be materializing right now, before my very eyes.

Oh my God. What was *wrong* with me?

That couldn't really be—

"What are you—who are you *staring* at?"

Collins twisted in the direction that I'd been looking, but I'd already ducked my head to stare down into my gin martini.

"No one," I said, taking a swift drink of it.

Fuck, I needed to get my shit together.

I took another sip. Downed the whole damn thing, actually.

And then forced myself to look up again, not really sure if I was hoping to learn that I'd been seeing things or if I wanted it to be real—wanted *her* to be real.

But before I made up my mind, our eyes connected, and I knew, without a doubt, that there was nothing *not* real about the way Natalie London made me feel when she stared straight into my fucking soul from across the restaurant patio.

CHAPTER FOUR

natalie

MY THERAPIST. ANY ONE of my brothers. All *four* of my brothers. The teacher in high school who told me I'd never make it past my freshman year of college. The professor who said I'd never make it through med school. The charge nurse on the fourth floor of SCMC who kept us all on our toes.

All of the people I'd rather see right now than Cameron Bryant.

His brown eyes, filling me with the kind of warmth that could easily be from embarrassment or awareness—take your pick—trailed over me once, lingered, and then traveled to the man sitting across from me.

Right.

My date.

Cameron's lips dipped into a frown. And then his entire expression pulled tight. I watched as his fingers flexed around his drink as he brought it to his mouth, not taking his eyes off the man across from me.

I realized that I'd probably given him the impression that dating wasn't in my wheelhouse, what with the explosion of explicit content in his office and the subsequent insinuation that I had no sex life. All that, combined with the way I'd shut him down and pushed him away that night at the bar, probably led him to believe I didn't go out much.

And I didn't, really.

But it wasn't that I didn't *want* to date. Or have sex. I was just trying to be careful about how I approached the topic. Even if I wanted to brazenly push forward on both fronts, I knew I had to be mindful of the damage my previous marriage had caused. I would be irresponsible to ignore it—proof I *had* learned things in therapy—and the uncertainty that had filled my entire body when Cameron sought that kiss six months ago told me I *couldn't* ignore it.

I just needed a little practice.

Time to warm up, if you will.

And the way I'd felt with Cameron, it hadn't been warm. It was *hot*. Burning. It had felt uncontrollable and frantic, heading straight toward something I just *knew* I wasn't ready for, not after the last time I'd experienced a rush of emotions like that and the decisions I made from it. It wasn't the kiss that I'd been afraid of; it was what I knew the kiss would lead to with the chemistry flaring between us, undeniable and indescribable.

I needed to be responsible about dating. About what I exposed myself to. What I exposed Chloe to. I needed to be responsible about how I took care of myself when I finally had life going in a direction that I wanted it to, when I'd finally created something good for us—for Chloe and me.

So tonight's date was as simple as that; it was just practice.

With someone safe, who caused no feelings of rampant desire or urges I couldn't control.

Because Josh, my online date, had barely stopped talking. He was explaining some kind of tech that his start-up was designing, a new socials app that he was *sure* would blow up. He hadn't asked me a question once. I found it hard to believe that he took a look at me and thought I didn't have one interesting thing to say, but what did I know? At the very least, he could ask about my job. What trauma surgeon didn't have a good story or two to tell? Or my daughter. I personally thought my nine-year-old was the most interesting person on the planet.

I sighed, wishing Cameron would stop scrutinizing him. Even though that was exactly what I was doing, too.

So I stopped and looked at *his* date instead. She was a gorgeous woman with brown skin and a bright smile. Curly shoulder-length hair. A coral fitted dress that probably cost the same amount as one of my paychecks. Which was, well, a decent amount. Just saying.

Something hot turned in my stomach, and I internally chastised myself. I was *not* going to be jealous that he was on a date with another woman when one, he was my *lawyer*, and two, *I'd* been the one to reject *him*. That would be so very unreasonable of me.

"And then when my friend filed for the patent..."

I flicked my attention back to Josh, trying not to focus too hard on how poorly he'd arranged his tie. It might have been endearing if he had kids and his four-year-old had tied it, but as far as I knew, he was childless.

He kept talking. For so, *so* long. I'd finished my meal, and he'd still only taken a few bites of his, simply because he didn't seem to want to pause his boring story long enough to put food in his mouth.

I tried, more than he was probably worth, to stay engaged with what he was saying and not focus on the heat that kept warming the side of my face, coming from where Cameron sat. It felt like his eyes were on me, but that would be ridiculous, right? For him to *keep* looking at me when he had his own date right there in front of him.

Picking up my gin and tonic, I took a long sip, hoping that maybe I'd find an escape from this situation at the bottom of it.

"Dr. London, it's so nice to see you."

I looked up in surprise to find that Cameron was standing beside our table. Right there. Next to me.

What was he *doing*?

I thought during our mutual once-over we'd also mutually, silently, decided not to acknowledge one another.

"You're a doctor?" Josh said from across the table, coming to an abrupt halt in his story.

Thank God.

Cameron's gaze turned sharp as he looked toward my date. His brows pulled together as if he couldn't quite understand what was wrong with this man.

"Yes," I said with the kind of patience I usually used on my daughter. "That's why I said I worked in the emergency department at Suffolk County Medical Center."

"I mean, yeah," Josh said with a shrug. "I just didn't know that meant you were a doctor. I assumed you were like a—"

"Do yourself a favor and *don't* finish that sentence," Cameron cut in.

"I'm a trauma surgeon," I said kindly. Too kindly, I think. I watched Josh's eyes grow wide before I turned to Cameron. "It's nice to see you, too, Mr. Bryant." And because I didn't know what to say after that, I decided introductions were the best course of action. "Josh, this is my lawyer."

For some inexplicable reason, Cameron's jaw, which was covered with a light scruff I had the strange urge to run my fingers over, ticked.

This was going *great.*

So great that I could not have been happier to see the waitress approach our table, giving us all a distraction that we needed.

"Are we ready for the check?" she asked.

I nodded. "Yes, please."

"Will that all be on one?"

"Two, please." Josh held up two fingers. "But I'm happy to take the appetizer."

The waitress could not have walked away faster.

Damn, I needed her.

"Ah, I thought this was a date," Cameron said, his voice like a caress. I hated that it made me feel things, that all he had to do was speak a few words to send my pulse haywire, when after listening to Josh for what felt like hours, I still felt *nothing*. "Since it's not, I'd love to steal Natalie away after dinner. I have a few things I'd like to discuss."

Josh choked on air.

Finally, some speechlessness.

"Sure," I said breathlessly, not really knowing what else to say. I tried not to feel satisfaction that Cameron had put Josh in his place so effectively, but it was impossible. And while I'd been kind to Josh, I didn't feel kind enough to stick up for him. Because while it *had* been a date, it had been a *very* bad one.

Cameron winked at me once before walking away.

And I tried very hard not to trail my gaze after him.

It took me another twenty minutes to escape Josh, and I assumed that by the time I exited the restaurant, Cameron would be long gone, considering I'd seen him leave with his date some time ago. But the moment I walked out the door and turned to my left to start my trek home, I ran head-on into a wall of muscle. A suit-covered chest.

Two hands gripped my bare shoulders, steadying me and unraveling me all at the same time. Because a man was touching me. And I knew exactly who he was—the only man who had ever made me feel this way from a simple brush, a mere taste of skin-on-skin contact.

His breathy chuckle made me shiver, and I leaned into his warmth for just a second, until the sound of his voice, so very close and masculine and husky, made me jump away again.

"We seem to like the same restaurants and bars," he commented, sounding thoughtful. "I'm surprised we haven't had more run-ins over the last six months."

I shook my head. He had no idea how many times I'd been tempted to go back to that pub, to see if he might still be there. Because while one part of my brain knew what I needed, the other part knew what I *wanted*.

"That would mean I'd have to go out more than twice in one year," I said before finally looking up at him, just in time to see the sparkle in his eyes dim slightly at my words. "What are you doing?"

"Waiting for you. Wishing I'd just plucked you from that man before I walked away." His features tensed. Was he impatient to leave? "I should have realized he'd try to hold you captive longer."

"But what about your date?" I looked around for her, but Cameron was alone. "She was very pretty."

Cameron looked over his shoulder in the direction that I assumed she'd left.

"She is." His lips spread in an amused smile. "Probably because we share the same DNA."

Oh.

Heat returned to my skin, and *shit*, he could probably tell. My cheeks felt it the most. But that was okay, as long as he didn't realize that I was also, admittedly, relieved.

"She's your—"

"Sister," he finished for me. "You couldn't tell? We have the same eyes, same nose, same complexion."

I shrugged, feigning nonchalance. "She doesn't have dimples."

Cameron's smile grew, his eyes glittering as he let the words sit between us.

"No," he finally agreed. "She doesn't have dimples."

"Did you have a nice dinner?" I asked, wanting to push the conversation away from the fact that I was very aware of this man's dimples.

He nodded. "Yeah, it's always good to see her. She's visiting from out of town. California. Her husband picked her up." Cameron cocked his head to the side, considering me in a way that made me feel bare. "And how was your dinner, Natalie?" He raised a brow. "Or should I say, *Sunny*?"

I shook my head at his usage of the name I'd given him at the pub that night—a homage to finally seeing the light after a too-long divorce process and the dark marriage that had preceded it. It had felt fitting for the occasion.

"Josh and I matched on a dating app, so he knows my real name."

Cameron looked disapproving. "*That* man earned your real name, and I didn't? I'm all for making men work for you, but you need to make them work harder than that, Natalie."

"I..." I started, but I didn't really have anything to say to him, because truthfully, he was right. Josh hadn't proved he deserved any bit of me. "I know. He's the first guy I've tried meeting up with from an app, but maybe I'll have to adjust my process in the future. Since that was *not* a success."

He stared at me for a long moment, and I refused to back down from the eye contact. "Just don't tell anyone else your name is Sunny."

"Why?"

Cameron leaned closer, a brief whisper in my ear that tingled my insides. "That's *my* fake name," he murmured.

I was starting to feel more than warm. Once again, something closer to *hot*, and I knew I needed to take a step back. But *God*, it was hard. Especially because I agreed with him. Cameron could have that name to himself. I liked that idea, actually. He could keep it—as a memento of a night that I thought about all too often, a reality that I wished I could pursue.

"Can I get you home?" he asked, pulling back like he hadn't just made me feel more than my date had all night.

I shrugged off the question. "I was just going to walk. I live over on Liberty, so not far."

"Then I'll walk with you."

"I'm more than capable of walking myself home."

I'd been living as an independent, single woman for longer

than he likely realized. Longer than my divorce had been finalized. I was comfortable navigating the world alone.

"I know you are," he allowed. "But you disappeared on me that night. And I've been spending the last six months wondering if you made it home okay, Natalie. Please don't make me go through that again."

His husky words made my breath hitch, requiring a second to recover. Or several seconds, longer than it usually took me to formulate responses.

"Well, it won't be six months until we see each other again," I pointed out. "You'll only have to wonder until Monday morning. That's when our next meeting is, right?"

Cameron just stared at me, his jaw hard. "I can walk you home, or I can call one of your brothers to do it. It's up to you."

"When I told Blake I was meeting someone from a dating app, he made me share my location with him. He's probably sitting at home, wondering what I'm doing standing outside the restaurant."

Cameron shucked his hands in his pockets with a nod. "See, I knew we'd get along."

I rolled my eyes and started walking in the direction of home. Without missing a beat, Cameron picked up his stride beside me.

"So you didn't like him?" he asked.

"Who?"

"Your date."

"Who says I didn't like him?"

I had no idea why I was trying to lie through my teeth.

"You said yourself that the date wasn't a success. But even if you hadn't, I know how you look when you like a guy, and that wasn't it."

My steps faltered, something that seemed like it was becoming a regular occurrence around this man. His lips twisted at my reaction, like he was enjoying it far too much, and then when I opened my mouth to try to protest—a silly idea, really—he cut me off.

"Don't lie about it, Sunny."

"I wasn't going to lie," I lied.

He lifted a brow.

"Maybe I *should* call Blake," I muttered, even though I knew I wouldn't.

I'd been trying not to bother my brothers as much as possible this week. Blake was in newly wedded bliss, having just returned from his honeymoon, and Noah was in new dad trenches, and I knew that what Cameron had told me the other day was right. I shouldn't rely on them so much.

Cameron put his hands up in mock surrender. "I'm sorry. I'll stop."

I shook my head because I wasn't entirely sure I *wanted* him to stop. It certainly would be a *good idea* if he stopped, but...

"Is Chloe with Blake?" Cameron asked, veering the conversation in a different direction, like he promised.

I shook my head. "She's at a friend's house, working on a project for school. I was going to pick her up on my way home. They live just a block over from us."

He nodded. "Okay, lead the way."

I did, deciding not to argue with him about it. The tone he'd used was firm, but gentle, letting me take the first steps, and telling me he'd follow. Cameron somehow knew how to say things that didn't bring out the fight or flight in me; he didn't talk like Korey had, whose commands were snappy and harsh and made me feel trapped in a corner, *unable* to flee.

If I'd been with Korey that night at the bar, he wouldn't have *let* me leave. He would have held on tight, the same way he'd tried to do with our marriage. And the same way he was now trying to do with Chloe.

Control—it was all about control.

Now that I had it in my grasp, I loathed the idea of giving it up.

But I didn't feel like I was giving anything up while I walked side by side with Cameron until we made it to the Hillsons'.

The birds chirped, a sign of spring blooming into summer. I loved this time of year, if just for the cherry blossoms that lined this street, filling the air with a sweet scent that carried above the smell of the city. The Hillsons had a particularly large tree at the bottom of their steps, but most of the pink petals had fallen to the sidewalk. I stepped over them as I walked up to the door of their brownstone, and Cameron leaned against the railing at the bottom of the steps, waiting, looking effortlessly attractive.

"We're just around the corner from home," I said. "You don't have to stay."

Cameron's lips pressed together for a second before he said, "Imagine what your brothers would do if they found out I didn't make sure their sister *and* their favorite niece got home safe."

"Careful," I said. "There's another baby in the family now."

"*Oldest* niece, then," he amended.

I shook my head and knocked on the Hillsons' front door. "Are you afraid of my brothers, Mr. Bryant?"

He lifted a brow. "Did the way I kicked Blake and Noah out of the room the other day make it seem like I'm afraid of them?"

"No," I admitted.

Korey had definitely been intimidated by my brothers. The reason I suspected he cut me off from them for most of our marriage.

"You haven't met Sully or Theo, though," I added.

My two youngest brothers lived in Minnesota, where we were raised. Theo was a professor at the U, while Sully was a software engineer, and they couldn't have been more polar opposites. Theo was a man of few words, while Sully would never shut up, if he were given the option. But the one thing they had in common? They'd always stick up for their family, especially Chloe. Even if they weren't as present in her life as my other brothers.

Cameron was unfazed. "I'd be happy to meet them sometime. And then I could kick them out of the room, too."

The door opened before I had a chance to respond to him, which was probably for the best.

A woman with silver-streaked black hair and a kind smile opened the door. Mrs. Hillson, or Jill, was one of my favorite moms on the block. We met the first night I moved here with Chloe, still a little shell-shocked from the divorce. She'd brought over dinner and left her number, and sure, sometimes it seemed like she looked at me with a bit of pity in her eyes, but I chose to believe it came from a good place. That it was more compassion than anything else. She told me her mom was an ER nurse when she was growing up, so she knew the hardships and the horrors that we saw, and how it could take a toll.

"Natalie," she greeted with a smile. "You look so lovely."

I tried to ignore the surprise in her voice, the reminder that I didn't get dressed up often. Jill's eyes drifted down the steps to Cameron, her brows rising to match the lift in her tone. She glanced back at me with the not-so-subtle look of a woman telling another woman, *Nice catch*.

Ah, shit. I'd have to correct her about that one, but it wouldn't be now.

"Thanks, Jill." I grinned back at her. "I appreciate you having Chloe over to work on the project. Is she ready?"

Before Jill could answer, my little tornado of a daughter came bounding out of the house, yelling back to her friend inside.

"Bye! See you Monday!"

"I see that she is," I chuckled and then waved to Jill before trying to catch up with Chloe, who had already made it to the bottom of the steps, stopping short at the sight of Cameron.

"Are you Mom's date?" she asked without any hesitation, and I wished I could have sunk into the pavement.

"No, honey," I interrupted before Cameron had to find an answer. "This is Mr. Bryant. He's Mom's new lawyer. I met him through your Uncle Noah."

"Hi, Chloe." Cameron crouched a bit so he could be more on Chloe's level. It wasn't very successful; Cameron was a sizable man, and though Chloe was tall for her age, he still had a lot of height on her. "You can call me Cam."

"Hi!" She was more of a ball of energy than normal, bouncing on her toes in front of Cameron, and I wondered how much candy she and Mia had snuck when Jill wasn't looking. Her brown hair that nearly matched mine was falling out of her ponytail with every movement of her jittery body. "Do you know my Aunt Gemma, too?"

Noah's girlfriend was one of Chloe's figure skating coaches, and my daughter *adored* her. I was well aware that she liked her more than me most days, but I was also okay with it. For the most part. I just felt lucky that Chloe had so many good role models in her life.

Cameron chuckled. "I do know Gemma. I work with her brother and her friend Juniper."

"Oh, Juniper has the *best* dresses," Chloe said enthusiastically. "I think Mom should go shopping with her. She doesn't have *any* dresses."

"I have a couple," I protested. "I'm wearing one right now."

I glanced down at the rosy wrap dress I had on, which I'd thought had complemented my complexion nicely. I'd always been told my fair skin had pink undertones.

"Yeah, but..." Chloe gave me a disapproving once-over, and I rolled my eyes.

"I think your mom looks very nice," Cameron said, his voice warm and soothing.

"Yeah, you're right. She does." Chloe shrugged and then turned on her heel, walking off in the direction of home. "So how was the date?" she asked over her shoulder, and then she gave a pointed little look to Cameron and said, "It was *my* idea, you know."

"Was it?" he asked with a tilt of his lips.

"Mhm," Chloe said proudly.

Internally, I sighed.

"It was okay, honey," I answered. "We can talk about it more when we get home."

And discuss how it might be a bit before I went on another

date after that failed attempt. Dating during the custody trial might not be the best option, anyway. That should truly be my focus.

Chloe nodded and took off, running down the sidewalk ahead of Cameron and me. When she got to our house, she jumped up the steps two at a time.

She'd definitely had too much sugar today.

Cameron and I walked in silence as we followed her, stopping when we reached the bottom of the stairs she'd raced up. I turned to face him with a pained smile.

"Thank you," I said. "For the escort. And from saving me the pain of ending that date myself."

He nodded. "Anytime, Natalie."

He sounded like he meant it.

"I'd invite you in, but I need to get Chloe to bed."

Somehow. Might not be possible, but I had to try.

I took a backward step onto the bottom stair, slowly edging away from him. Not because I necessarily wanted to, but because I knew I needed to. Before my daughter said something embarrassing again.

Cameron brushed off my words. "Of course. Don't worry about it."

Another step. "Can I order you a ride or something?"

"Nah, I'm good." He gave a reassuring smile but didn't move.

I was halfway to my front door now. "You're going to stand there until we're inside, aren't you?"

The corner of Cameron's lips twitched. "I'm nothing if not thorough."

"Noted."

His mouth transformed into a smirk, and I tried not to stare at it. Tried not to remember what it had felt like on my neck, how talented it had been, even for those few short moments. I wondered, not for the first time, if walking away from him had been a mistake. Especially now that I knew more about him, knew who he was, that he probably would have been a safe person to rip the proverbial sex Band-Aid off with, even if I told myself that was something I shouldn't do. That I shouldn't be jumping into bed with anyone that fast. But would it have been such a terrible idea if the man were Cameron? At the moment, it didn't seem like it.

But I'd been fooled before.

And it didn't matter anymore, anyway.

"It's a good thing for a lawyer to be," I added.

Because that was all he was to me.

"And I'm a very good...lawyer," he said slowly, his voice dropping on the last word, almost like he didn't want to say it.

"Mom, hurry up!"

I stumbled backward up another step. "Have a good night, Cam."

His gaze glittered. "See you Monday, Sunny."

With a shake of my head, I forced myself to turn around and open the door, disappearing behind it and sagging against the wooden interior of the nineteenth-century entryway.

When I peeked out the window to the side of the door a few moments later, Cameron was still standing there, looking at the sky, pinching the bridge of his nose. But it only lasted a second before he shoved his hands in his pockets and walked away.

six months ago

CAMERON

I'd never in my life sprinted to a seat faster than I did when I saw this woman walk through the doors and sit herself at the bar.

Alone.

But only momentarily. Because now I was here, and I didn't really plan on leaving, not unless she asked me to.

"I'm...Sunny," she said slowly, like she had to consider whether she wanted to give me her name.

That was okay. Maybe it was the lawyer in me, but I liked a cautious woman.

And Sunny seemed absolutely an apt description for her.

She flashed me a smile, and suddenly, we weren't in a divey Irish pub with dim lighting on a cold November night, but somewhere warm and maybe tropical. This woman was a blast of fucking sunshine. I could almost feel my skin heating just from the exposure to her.

"It's nice to meet you," I said, giving what I hoped was an encouraging smile. "If I can't buy you a drink, can I at least offer a bit of conversation?"

"Maybe." She pursed her lips in consideration. I tried not to look at them. "Will it be interesting? I can't stress enough how much I don't care about whatever workout you did at the gym this week."

I had to stifle a laugh. "What if I told you I didn't go to the gym this week?"

Her gaze swept over me, hot and assessing. Because yeah, I had a body that required maintenance.

"I'll allow the lie," she said and then immediately took a drink of the beer the bartender placed in front of her.

"Unfortunately, though, I'm not very interesting," I admitted with a chuckle. "But I bet you are. What do you do for work?"

"I'm a trauma surgeon," she said casually, as though I wasn't supposed to be blown away by that.

I settled deeper in my chair, determined to never leave.

"You must have a lot of stories to tell."

Her eyes shone as she looked at me, like no one had ever asked her to tell stories before, like no one had ever cared.

"So many stories."

CHAPTER FIVE

cameron

AFTER A BUSY MONDAY morning full of meetings and prep work, I walked into my office to find Natalie London standing in it, staring at my bookshelves. Or, more specifically, at the pictures framed on it.

I had a few sitting there, scattered amongst textbooks. A photo at my law school graduation with Julian's arm slung around my shoulders, grins on our faces, my diploma in hand. One of me with Beau and Collins at a Wednesday Elevett concert. Another when I was about ten, at a baseball game with Pops, Dad, and Uncle Tony. But the photo Natalie was staring at with a soft smile on her face was my favorite one.

I hadn't been sure if she heard me come into the room, but then she glanced my way and asked, "Is that you?"

She nodded at the thirteen-year-old version of me, standing with my family on a beach.

"Sure is," I murmured, coming to stand beside her. I pointed at the young, curly-haired Collins whose face was scrunched next to mine in the picture. "And that's my sister, who you saw on Friday. And my mom." I moved my finger to the white woman with strawberry blonde hair and a smattering of freckles. "And my dad," I ended with, feeling that familiar deep ache in my chest as I brushed my fingertip over the tall Black man with my same brown eyes. He wore a familiar blue ball cap, the one I still had, that was worn and fraying by now.

"You were such a cute kid," Natalie said, the corners of her mouth upturned. "Where are you in this picture?"

"On Cape Cod," I answered, feeling my throat tighten as I dropped my hand. "It was my mom's birthday."

I paused, and when Natalie didn't say anything, seeming to wait to see if I had more I was going to add, I decided to keep talking. Because it felt good.

"When we were younger, my mom liked to make vision boards, collages. She and my sister have always had that sort of artist eye. Their crafts and projects could usually be found scattered throughout the house.

Anyway, Mom had made a board dedicated to places she wanted to go, and it included the vibes of a coastal New England escape. So my dad recreated it for her birthday, surprising her with a weekend getaway. We stayed in this tiny cottage by the beach, ate at quaint restaurants with Mom's favorite foods, swam a lot. The swimming was my favorite, but I also remember going to this little bookstore, where each of us picked out one book to read for the weekend."

I felt Natalie's eyes shift to the side of my face, but I couldn't tear my gaze away from the picture. "What book did you get?"

"*The Lightning Thief*," I answered.

I still had the tattered copy of it.

"Chloe loves *Percy Jackson*," Natalie said, delight in her voice at the mention of her daughter. "The new show is her absolute favorite."

"A nine-year-old with good taste." My chest warmed, and my lips twitched with a hint of a smile before sobering. "It's the last picture of the four of us together before my dad passed."

Natalie's breath audibly hitched. "Oh, I'm so sorry, Cameron." Her words punched me right in the gut with how genuine they seemed to be, like it truly broke her heart that the family in the picture didn't quite exist anymore. "It's such a lovely photo," she added, her voice gentle.

"Thank you." My throat was a little scratchy, and I cleared it before taking a step away from the bookshelf and forcing myself to sound casual. "But we're not here today to talk about me."

"I wouldn't *mind* talking about you," Natalie said, a threadbare laugh escaping through her lips.

I shook my head, knowing that was likely true. I was sure a part of her dreaded these conversations that all revolved around the one person she was trying to escape. I heard her heavy sigh as she followed me toward my desk. Rounding it, I sat in my chair, facing her.

"I just want to let you know before we get started that I'm on call today," Natalie said as she sat down across from me, and I got a good look at her for the first time since she'd arrived.

And *shit*.

Somehow, I'd temporarily forgotten how goddamn gorgeous she was.

The thing about Natalie was that it all seemed so effortless. She wore a simple white tee and jeans, her hair thrown up in her usual clip, but she radiated beauty. And fuck if I wasn't going to struggle to keep my shit together. Even more than on Friday, when she'd been wearing that pretty pink dress, something she'd put on to go out with a guy who wasn't fucking me.

"I apologize if I get pulled away," she added. "I usually do shift work these days because it's better for Chloe, but I still had this on-call on my calendar. And I tried to switch—"

"It's okay, Natalie." She didn't need to justify herself this hard, not with me. "I don't mind working around your schedule."

"Thank you." She gave a perfunctory nod. "I appreciate it."

I sucked in a breath, trying to focus on anything that wasn't how good she looked today. Every day. Always.

"Let's start by chatting about Chloe," I said, flashing a smile I hoped was reassuring. "Okay?"

Natalie nodded again, folding her hands in her lap. She sat

straight in her chair, her shoulders back, her chin held high. Her guard was up today, almost like she was practicing for court. And while I found Natalie's strength and determination attractive as hell, I wish she didn't think she needed to use it as a shield *all* the time.

"Why don't you tell me a little more about her?"

Maybe talking about Chloe in a low-stakes way would help her relax a little.

"Well..." Natalie started, her lips pulling into an inward grin, something I doubted she realized she was doing. "She's really smart, and I'm not just saying that because I'm her mom." Natalie gave a light laugh before adding, "Her teacher tells me that she thinks Chloe gets bored quickly at school because the pace is a little slow for her, so they're working on finding some enrichment to help with that."

"That's not surprising," I said with a smile, and Natalie gave me a funny look, like she couldn't understand why I'd say that. So I added, "Her mom is a literal trauma surgeon. If she inherited your genes, I'm sure she's brilliant."

Natalie blushed and shook her head, not wanting to acknowledge the compliment.

And I quickly decided all I really wanted to do in life was feed Natalie London compliments like candy.

"Come on, Natalie. I might not have a medical background, but I know you've gotta be one of the youngest surgeons on staff. I know you're older than Noah, but not by that much."

"I'm thirty-two," she admitted, her cheeks still pink. "I...graduated high school with a lot of college credits under my belt already. Not a big deal." She was a very big deal. "Chloe loves to learn, too," Natalie continued, doing a quick dive into talking about her daughter instead. "I never thought she liked it when I talked about medicine or work, but apparently, Blake has been helping her memorize all the names of the bones. He's a doctor, too, if you didn't know."

I did know. I'd recently decided it was important to know

everything I possibly could about the London family. For work purposes.

"Cardiologist, right?"

She nodded. "I'm sure he sprinkles in little heart facts along with the bones."

"There are worse influences." I leaned back in my chair, crossing one leg over the other. "What other things does Chloe like?"

"Animals. She *loves* them," Natalie answered, and a look of warmth spread over her face. "I think she gets that from my mom, who runs a pet rescue organization in the Twin Cities. And Noah adopted a puppy last summer, Winnie. Chloe's absolutely obsessed with her." Her expression dimmed slightly as she added, "As you can probably tell, she spends a lot of time with adults, being an only child with no other kids her age in the family. Which I think is why she relates to adults a lot better than other kids. Sometimes she struggles with making new friends, and I blame myself for that. For not giving her more opportunities with her peers when she was younger. But I think being in figure skating has really helped."

"Chloe seems very well loved and cared for," I said, reassuring her. I suspected that Natalie put a lot of pressure on herself to be perfect at everything, including being a parent.

"Yeah." There was a softness to her exterior now, her guard lower, not as noticeable. "She is."

I took a deep breath, knowing we had to deepen the conversation, get into the bits that might be less comfortable for her.

"The judge will want to know why it will be in Chloe's best interests for you to keep full custody," I said. "So I think it's important to consider your answer."

A flash of emotion crossed Natalie's face, but she stayed silent. I let her think on it for another moment before encouraging her. "You can just say what you're feeling, Natalie. We're not in court yet. My job is to help you prepare for it, take your thoughts, and frame them into responses you can use."

"I have a lot of feelings," she said with a shaky breath. "And thoughts."

"Any parent in your shoes would, I'm sure."

She crossed her arms over her chest and nibbled on her bottom lip. And since that caused a visceral reaction inside me at literally the most inopportune moment, I lowered my eyes to my computer screen, watching the blinking cursor as I waited for her to answer.

"Korey has never been a present father," she finally said, and I lifted my gaze again. "Even when he lived with us. In some ways, I think with the visitation he has now, she sees him more and has a better experience than she ever did when we were together."

"Can you explain that?"

"Because she has her expectations set. Versus her always *thinking* he should be there and him never being home when we were married."

"Where was he?"

"At work, mostly." She sighed. "I know that I work long, odd hours, and it isn't ideal for this case. But I promise you, Korey was worse. And if he tries to say he's cut back on the time he spends at the office, it's only because he no longer has to stay late to sleep with his receptionist. You know, now that he's free to have her over whenever he wants. She might have even moved in with him. I've been trying to figure that out because I want to know who is spending time with Chloe when she's there."

I'd suspected that her ex cheated on her, but I didn't have confirmation until now, and it physically pained me to keep a straight face for her benefit. For our benefit. Because I was a *professional* who was not emotionally attached to this case *in the slightest.*

"That's a question we'll get an answer to," I said. "The judge will want to know who would be living with or involved in Chloe's life in both potential households. So romantic partners will come up."

She deserved to have a warning about that. It fucking sucked that she was going to have to relive the facts of his affair and their relationship *again*, but it would work in our favor to have those details.

"I figured." Surprisingly, Natalie just shrugged. "And that's good, fine. I came to terms with his affair a long time ago. It pushed me to get the divorce. I don't know if I would have woken up and gotten out if it weren't for that. It was a blessing in disguise."

She was being a hell of a lot more mature than I wanted to be right now.

"They'll want to know about you, too," I added cautiously.

"Me?"

That put her off-kilter a bit. And if I were being honest, it put me off-kilter, too.

"If you've had any romantic partners who have lived with you or been a part of Chloe's life," I clarified.

Natalie recovered and snorted like the idea was ridiculous.

"You saw my date the other night."

"I did," I acknowledged. "And it might not have gone well, but I also saw you *on* a date, which tells me you've been dating."

"I also told you that I only go out twice a year," she shot back. "I prioritize Chloe and work. Not dating."

"So the only other—"

"Was you," she confirmed, those green eyes blazing. "And, of course, that wasn't even a date."

I gritted my teeth, experiencing a wave of conflicting emotions. Fuck did I like the idea that other men *hadn't* been taking her out, touching her where I wanted to touch her, kissing her in places I had kissed her. But I also hated every time she minimized our night six months ago. Even though, yeah, she was right. It hadn't been a date. Natalie had taken me completely by surprise, whereas a date was something planned, something purposeful, something I wasn't allowed to take her on. Not anymore.

"And before me?" I asked.

It was a logical follow-up question, I told myself. From the information Natalie previously shared with me, I knew that her marriage had ended a year and a half ago. Which meant there was almost a year unaccounted for between when I saw Natalie at Mulligan's and when her divorce was finalized.

But Natalie just shook her head.

"I'll be very clear. Besides last Friday night, the only other time I've spent time with a guy who wasn't a colleague or my family, the only person I've shared drinks with, the only man who has so much as put his arms around me since my divorce...was you, Cameron. And that was just—" Her eyes wandered away again, and she huffed a humorless laugh. "Well, you know what it was."

I did, but I had a feeling I was thinking something different from what Natalie was. And I couldn't pass by this moment without being honest with her about it and clearing the air.

"Natalie, for what it's worth, I had a *really* great time with you that night."

Understatement of the century.

Her breath hitched. I watched it sort of disappear for a moment before she shrugged it off. "Until I ruined it."

"Nat—"

"Anyway, it's really for Chloe's sake." Natalie wouldn't meet my eyes as she spoke, which made me think that wasn't entirely true. "That I went on that date last week or have even been thinking about seeing someone. She's been really stuck on me dating recently. I'm not sure why, but I think it's because she recently watched Noah get into a relationship, and she loves Gemma, and now they have a baby and—" She pressed her lips together.

"And?"

I shouldn't press her for more details, I really shouldn't. But at the same time, understanding Chloe's perspective when it came to their family dynamics was important.

Natalie sighed. "She wants a sibling. Badly. And I don't know how to just tell her that it's not going to happen, not that simply, anyway. She doesn't understand that Gemma's baby is not actually Noah's child biologically, and things don't normally happen that quickly in relationships. She doesn't know that Noah is stepping up to be the dad of a child who isn't *technically* his and that Gemma was pregnant for several months before they even started dating. But at least I can show her that I'm trying. Dating is far from my priority, but *she* is."

That was...a lot to wrap my head around. But it also made perfect sense. Natalie hadn't seemed all that enthused about her date on Friday, and Chloe had mentioned that it was her idea.

"Do *you* want another child?"

The question was out before I could stop it. Now that Natalie was talking, I really didn't want her to stop talking, even though this was pushing beyond the scope of questioning that was required for my job.

"One day, maybe. If the right person came along."

I bit my tongue, forcing myself not to ask for more information about what *the right person* might look like and if she could ever see herself having a thing for lawyers with brown eyes. And dimples.

"You're a good mom, Natalie," I said because that was the safer choice. "But Chloe seems like a good kid, too. And I'm sure she just wants her mom to be happy, even if that means she isn't interested in dating."

"It's not..." She hesitated, and I willed her to keep going. To say it, admit aloud what I expected was true. "I said it wasn't a priority, not that I'm not interested *at all*."

I tried not to let my expression change.

"I just need some more practice at it, I think," she added.

"I would disagree, Sunny."

"Stop."

"I'm serious." I sighed and pressed forward before she could change the topic again. "Earlier, you said you ruined our night, but that's not true. And I owe you an apology."

Her brows furrowed, and it was a little adorable. Natalie London rarely looked confused, I'd learned. "What are you talking about?"

"*I* ruined the night. I pushed you too far, too fast, and that's on me. I'm sorry for doing that and for making you feel like you did anything wrong."

She frowned. "You didn't, though. You stopped. You waited to see if I was ready, and I came to my senses, realized that I wasn't."

"And that's okay," I said slowly. "It's okay not to be ready."

"I kind of wish I was, though," she groaned in a moment of vulnerability that I hadn't expected. Her walls were suddenly down, like *completely* down, and I had a feeling what I was glimpsing right now was special, something people didn't usually get to see. "Sometimes I wish I could just say fuck it and—" She broke off, shaking her head. *Shit.* "I'm sorry. This conversation isn't what you were probably looking for. We got off track."

No, no. I liked this track. Definitely more than I should, but still. I didn't want to switch it, not yet.

"I think clearing the air about what happened between us is better than not speaking about it. It'll only help our working relationship."

Working relationship, I reminded myself.

Work-ing.

Natalie stared at me, words on the tip of her tongue.

"You can say it, Natalie. Whatever it is. Now's the time."

We would have this one conversation, and then we'd never look back, I told myself. We'd move forward and stay on the right track with this case.

"What—" She cut herself off at the sound of loud voices passing by in the hallway, and I gritted my teeth in frustration. I recognized one of the voices as Julian, talking about where they should grab lunch from. Natalie's eyes popped wide with the realization, the reminder, of where we were and why we were here. She drew in a breath, slow and shaky. "What else should we discuss pertaining to the case?"

Her voice was calm and measured, reflexing back into her original tone.

I, on the other hand, did *not* feel calm. I struggled with my response for far too long, searching my brain for something relevant that I could say.

"You said Chloe is in figure skating?" I asked—the first topic that popped into my head.

Natalie nodded numbly.

"Has Korey ever attended her lessons? Shows?" When she shook her head for both, I asked, "Are there any other extracurriculars Chloe is in that he's been a part of?"

Natalie shook her head again, and I made a note of her answers.

This was good.

Facts.

She was probably right. We should stick to the case. Facts and only facts.

And for the rest of our meeting, that was exactly what we did.

CHAPTER SIX

natalie

"DID YOU WATCH THE video I sent you?"

My childhood best friend asked the question beneath her breath as though someone would automatically know that the video in question was, in fact, like watching a *Magic Mike* show where they didn't even start with clothes.

"I did, El," I huffed as I trudged through the parking lot at work, pushing my legs to go faster than they wanted to move. "And then I didn't fully close out of it, and it started playing in the middle of my first meeting with my new lawyer."

She gasped. "Oh my God, *Nat*."

"Tell me about it," I grumbled.

"What did he do?"

"Nothing, actually." Which I would forever be grateful for. "He acted like it wasn't a big deal."

"Oo," Ellie cooed. "A mature man who is comfortable in his sexuality. We like that."

"I think that's a bit of a stretch to be able to confirm, but—"

"I don't think so," she cut in. "I've decided I like him. Approval granted."

"I didn't realize I needed your approval."

"You always need my approval, didn't you know?"

I rolled my eyes with a laugh, holding the phone away from my ear as Ellie sneezed three times in a row. She'd always had terrifying seasonal allergies but also refused to get the medication I told her to take for it. "Listen," I said when she seemed to make it through the burst of sneezes. "I'm headed into work. Is there another reason you called aside from the video?"

Aka the very thing that had created the most mortifying moment of my life.

"Yes!" Ellie exclaimed, and I could easily envision the way her eyes lit up. "Work is sending me to Boston in a few weeks, so I get to come visit."

"Really?" My heart leapt into my throat. I could *really* use some time with my best friend right now. "Oh my God, that's amazing, El. What are the dates?"

"Um...third weekend in June, I think."

"That's—oh."

Shit.

I could really use a visit from my best friend any *other* weekend than that one.

"What?"

"Nothing." I shook my head with a grimace, wishing I'd played it cooler so as not to risk the chance that Ellie wouldn't come. The timing could definitely be better, but I'd still make it work. "We'll figure it out. It'll be great!"

"Natalie," she said, a warning tone in her voice.

Damn.

"My family will be in town that weekend, too, that's all," I admitted.

A slight pause.

"Family, meaning..."

"Yeah." I cringed. "My parents and Theo and...Sully."

Ellie was silent on the other end of the phone at the mention of my youngest brother, the one who just happened to be her ex.

And not only were they exes, but they'd also broken it off on terrible, rotten, no-good terms. Mysterious ones, too. No one in my family really seemed to know what happened, not even me. Before their split, we'd all assumed they were going to get married; *that* was how perfect they were together.

Sighing, I went on to explain, "Noah bought Gemma a house, is going to surprise her with it, propose, and then invite everyone over for an engagement party. It's a whole thing."

"He bought her a *house*," Ellie repeated.

"I guess they're outgrowing his penthouse," I said with a laugh, even though I understood why Noah wanted to have a yard, more space for his daughter and dog to play.

"If the penthouse is up for grabs, you should take it."

"Pretty sure he's keeping the penthouse, too—oh, shit." My phone buzzed in my hand as I walked into the hospital, and I glanced down to see Cameron's name on the screen. I frowned. "My lawyer is calling me, El. I gotta go. We can figure something out for June. I promise. Talk soon?"

"Yeah," she said, sounding slightly subdued. "Talk soon, Nat."

I switched over to Cameron's call and breathlessly answered, "Hey."

"Hi, Dr. London." God, I wish his voice didn't sound *quite* so good when it said my name. Even if it was overly formal, like he was trying to prove a point.

"Natalie," I corrected.

"Natalie," he said, and I immediately regretted what I'd done. Because now he sounded even better. "I'm sorry for bothering you, but there's a mistake on the paperwork you signed yesterday."

"A mistake?"

That was absolutely not what I needed to hear right now when I was minutes from starting a shift.

"You, uh, signed the wrong name," Cameron answered. "I apologize that I didn't catch it before you left."

I stopped in my tracks in the lobby of the hospital. "I signed the *wrong name*."

"Yeah." Cameron sounded sympathetic but also uncomfortable. "You signed as Natalie Abrams."

"Fuck, I'm sorry." I shook my head, irritated with myself. Clearly, my head was elsewhere after our conversation yesterday, the one that had taken a turn into territory we really shouldn't explore.

"It's okay," Cameron reassured me.

It seemed like he was always reassuring me, and I both hated that and appreciated it all at once. I wished I didn't *need* the reassurance.

"Muscle memory," he added lightly. "It happens."

"Yeah," I said, but I was still annoyed. I didn't want any part of my body to remember any part of my marriage, preferably.

"But listen, I'm going to need to grab another signature from you so I can file our counter-petition," he said, moving the conversation along like usual. "Any chance you could swing by today?"

I put a hand to my forehead, rubbing it in anticipation of a headache. "Cameron, I'm so sorry, but I just got to work."

"Maybe I could come down there?" he offered.

But I shook my head. "I have rounds, and then I'm scheduled for a surgery. I really have to go, actually. I can maybe meet you when I'm done, but it will be late. And tomorrow—fuck. I'm chaperoning a field trip to the zoo at Chloe's school."

"Just call me when you're off work. We'll figure it out." Cameron's voice could not have been calmer; I had no idea how he did it. "It'll be fine, Natalie. Don't worry about it."

I was worried about it.

I knew we were getting down to the wire with our time limit to be able to file that counter-petition, and I didn't want *anything* to go wrong when it came to this case.

When I was silent, Cameron added, "I promise everything will be okay, Natalie. Call me later, no matter the time. Okay?"

"Okay," I whispered because it was all I could really do, and then I hung up and switched my brain over.

Rounds, first. I could do this.

It was eleven o'clock when I got off work. I stared at my phone in the parking lot, knowing that Cameron had told me to call but wondering if that was a good idea. He probably hadn't realized when I said it would be late what exactly that meant. I knew lawyers worked a lot and had extensive hours themselves, but not usually this late. Right?

I settled for shooting him a text instead.

Hey, I'm done with work.

He responded within seconds.

CAMERON: I'll swing by your house to meet you.

I shook my head, not willing to let him do that for a mistake I made.

I can come to you. It's okay. Chloe is at Blake's tonight.

It wasn't *Cameron's* fault that I signed the wrong name on paperwork that was crucial to me maintaining custody of my nine-year-old.

CAMERON: You've been on your feet for fourteen hours. You shouldn't be driving around more than necessary.

This was actually a shorter shift for me.

CAMERON: I'll be there soon.

Not having the energy to argue anymore, I headed home. And sure enough, Cameron was there, waiting for me, leaning against the railing on my front stairs just like he had a few nights ago. He still wore slacks and a dress shirt, sleeves rolled up to expose his forearms, making me wonder if he really had been working this late. A five o'clock shadow layered his jawline, adding to the effect.

"I'm so sorry about this," I started before he could say anything.

He waved off my apology. "It's not a big deal," he said as though it wasn't almost midnight and he wasn't standing outside my house because *I* fucked something up.

"You make a lot of house calls in your line of work?" I asked with a humorless laugh.

The corners of Cameron's lips curved, but it wasn't enough for his dimples to show. "I do whatever needs to be done for my clients."

I pushed past the immobilizing sensation of guilt and got myself to open the door, walking through it and then holding it open for him to follow me.

It was, unfortunately, a disaster inside.

"Sorry for the mess," I apologized. "Usually, I take care of all this—" I waved around at the pile of shoes and the dirty laundry basket by the bottom of the stairs just off the entryway. "—on my off days, but yesterday, I was—"

"At the office with me. I understand," Cameron cut in. "You don't need to apologize."

"I can tell you're very tidy, though," I said before maneuvering through the living room that was, thankfully, cleaner than the entryway. I usually *did* have things clean and organized, but I also had a sort of system for when and how I took care of things, and the last week or so had not gone as usual, what with visits with lawyers and unsuccessful date nights.

"Oh?"

"Like you just said...I've been in your office, Cameron."

"I have the time to be tidy," he said with a shrug. "I don't judge people who don't."

I narrowed my eyes at him over my shoulder. "Do you have flaws?"

He looked taken aback. "What?"

"Like things wrong with you." I stepped over Chloe's skates, which were, for some reason, sitting in the middle of the hallway. "There must be something, right?"

"Trust me," he laughed. "There are things."

I turned and walked backward into the kitchen while giving him a once-over, not believing him. Especially not when he showed up at my house looking like *that*, with his collar unbuttoned and those veiny forearms on display. *Jesus.*

It was at this very moment, when my feet were so sore that they were a little numb and my back felt like it might break in half from standing so still in surgery, that I realized how goddamn long it had been since I'd gotten laid. *Years*. And properly laid? Even longer. I couldn't even remember it. *That* was how long it had been, and Cameron looking the way he looked was really reminding me of it.

"You're not going to find them by staring at me, Natalie." Cameron's voice was suddenly deeper, causing me to snap my eyes back to his face.

"What?"

"The flaws," he said, and if I wasn't mistaken, a tiny smirk slid onto his face, all while his heated gaze roamed *my* face. It didn't go any further than that, though. It was like he'd created a barrier; every time his eyes dropped lower, to my mouth or neck, they immediately bounced back up, like an automatic rejection. Probably because the last time he'd stared at my mouth a little too long, *I'd* rejected him.

I could feel myself flushing, hot and aware—oh, so very aware. Of Cameron and of the fact that I was no longer moving. I was stuck in a standstill, some kind of trance until Cameron cleared his throat, and I broke out of it.

"Can I get you anything?" I offered. "Something to drink or eat?"

"Natalie." Cameron said my name with such clarity—a tone that almost hedged on disappointment. "Please don't think you have to play hostess for me right now."

"I just feel bad that you came all the way over here."

He shook his head. "I actually don't live that far from you, as it turns out."

Great, as if we needed more circumstances to pull us closer together.

I lifted a brow. "I'm starting to think it's surprising that we haven't run into each other more."

Cameron didn't respond for a second, waiting until we were both in the kitchen, on opposite sides of the island counter. "Same," he said, his voice soft, his eyes wandering over me again. If he could see the exhaustion on my face, he didn't mention it. Which I appreciated. People always seemed to remind me that I *must* be *so* tired, even on days when I felt pretty good. And then I'd start to feel...not so good. "Do you have a pen?"

"Right." I shuffled to find something to write with. "Yeah, of course."

We weren't, I reminded myself, here to just ogle each other.

I found a pen in our junk drawer and returned to the kitchen island just as Cameron was placing a stack of papers on the counter. He separated the ones I needed to sign, which were already marked by a little sticky next to each line that required my signature. I focused this time, making sure I wrote the right name.

My name.

Cameron cleared his throat after the last signature, and I looked up to see him shifting on his feet.

"Can I ask you—" He cut short as he watched me launch into the biggest yawn I'd ever yawned.

I covered my mouth and flashed him a sheepish look. "Sorry."

"No." He shook his head, running a hand over his short, black hair absently. "I'm sorry. I've got what I need. I'll head out."

I walked around the island, grabbing a mug from the cabinets next to the refrigerator. "It's okay. I like to take a little bit of time to wind down after a shift." I filled my electric kettle and then started it. A whirring sound filled the air. "Tea?" I offered.

He'd told me not to play hostess, but I couldn't make some for myself and *not* offer him any.

"I'm okay, thank you," Cameron said politely. He looked too *big*, standing in my small kitchen. His shoulders were too broad, his hands too all-encompassing as they splayed across the granite counters. "Why don't you sit, though. I'll make it for you."

"You don't have to—"

"Sit, Natalie."

I sat.

Something about his voice forced it into existence. I didn't know how to *not* sit when he spoke like that, but I also didn't really mind. In fact, I was entirely too tired to care, sliding onto the barstool across from him. Heaving a sigh, I dropped my head, rubbing my temples, trying not to think about the chemical burn patient whom I'd been treating right before I'd left for the night.

"Want to talk about it?"

I shook my head.

No, I didn't want to talk about work. I didn't want to think about it. The only way I survived in my line of work was to compartmentalize and switch my brain into different modes. Which was why I *needed* this time before bed, to make sure my mind had fully shut out the things I'd seen at work today before closing my eyes. I didn't need any visitors in my dreams.

It wasn't necessarily a bad shift, not today. The surgery had gone well, and there was nothing that should haunt me. But there were always things that snuck into my synapses that I didn't want to be there.

"Can I ask why you decided to become a trauma surgeon?" he asked, and suddenly, a mug of tea appeared in my line of vision, steam rising into my face. I breathed it in, the scent of chamomile calming my senses. I hadn't even told him where to find the tea packets.

"Thank you," I murmured.

"You're welcome." His voice had a steady timbre. I bet he could make a killing recording those audio stories that put people to sleep. "It was a lot of work."

I laughed into my cup, blowing air over the top of it. And then I looked up.

"I knew I wanted to be a doctor very young. It fascinated me, I think. My parents got me a doctor play set, and I'd dress up in scrubs and run around the house. I took the game *Operation* way too seriously." I chuckled at the memories of sitting on the floor and forcing my brothers to play with me. "I didn't decide on my specialty until medical school, though. I quickly realized how much I enjoyed emergency care and how good I was at it—the quick, complex thinking, the interdisciplinary aspect of it all, the dynamic. And I decided I wanted to learn all the tools I could to save as many lives as possible."

Cameron was listening so intently that I forced myself to take a drink of my tea and drop my gaze.

"It's pretty amazing," he said quietly, and I just shrugged, not good with compliments. There were so many talented people working in healthcare, and I was just one of them.

"Some days feel more amazing than others. Those are the days I work for."

"I can understand that."

I nodded and then decided to switch the subject. "What were you going to ask me earlier?"

His lips pressed together, a momentary consideration. But then he just said, "It can wait until later."

I looked at my watchless wrist. "Later, I'm going to be sleeping."

"Another day, I mean," Cameron said, the corner of his mouth pulling up.

"Okay," I sighed and drank more of my tea.

If I had a little more energy, I'd probably press him about it. Just because I was curious. I was curious about a lot of things when it came to Cameron Bryant, actually. It seemed like, at this point, he knew a lot about me. But there were so many things I didn't know about him. That didn't seem fair, right?

"What else do you usually do to wind down when you get home?" Cameron asked before I could formulate any of my own thoughts. A shame, really. Now he was going to know even more about me, and I was going to still know next to nothing about him.

But I answered him anyway.

"I give the cat her nighttime treats."

"You have a cat?"

"Yeah." I yawned again. "We just got her. I finally caved to Chloe. Well, sorta. She wanted a dog after Noah got Winnie, but a cat is much more our speed. She's a little shy around new people, though, so she's probably hiding. She's downright terrified of Blake, for some reason. Loves his wife, Delaney, though. Maybe it's a man thing. Her name's Annabeth."

I realized I was babbling, so I shut myself up by taking another sip from my tea and then staring into the brown liquid.

"Annabeth? Cute."

There was something about hearing a man like Cameron Bryant—all business and suits and that dangerously deep voice—calling my cat's name *cute*.

"Like from *Percy Jackson*?" he asked, like he'd just made the connection, and I warmed all over.

"Exactly like that," I confessed.

"Excellent choice." Cameron's low chuckle preceded the sound of a cupboard closing, which drew my attention. I glanced up to see that he'd found the cat treats. He gave the little tin a shake, and within a few seconds, Annabeth appeared, strutting across the kitchen floor like she owned the place.

"Well, would you look at that," I murmured to myself and then watched in awe as she walked right up to Cameron, rubbing her soft orange fur against his ankles. He crouched down to pet her.

Flaws. He *had* to have flaws, right?

With a groan, I put my head down on the countertop.

At the moment, it felt like the most glorious pillow.

"How many treats do you get, Annabeth?" Cameron cooed, and I shut my eyes.

Couldn't see how perfect he was if my eyes weren't open.

"She gets two, and don't let her fool you into giving her more."

"I would never."

The sound of soft meows and cat nibbles filled the room. It was oddly soothing, lulling me further into a sense of calm.

"Anything else?" I heard Cameron ask somewhere in my subconscious.

"Huh?"

"On your list."

"Coffee," I listed. "Wash my hair. Find clothes for tomorrow. You know."

"Well, I can handle one of those, at least," I heard Cameron say.

But barely.

He sounded distant, far away in my brain—where I was currently going through the motions of preparing my coffee, measuring the grounds and finding the coffee filter in the cabinet. I made sure the water was filled and the time set correctly for the morning. Perfect. Good.

Now, upstairs. It was time to head upstairs. Stuck in a semi-conscious state, I made my way up them, hearing the distinct creaking of the old wood beneath feet. Not my feet, though. No, I sort of felt like I was *floating*. That was odd, right?

Maybe, but this felt like the easiest nighttime routine I'd ever had, so who was I to complain?

Strong arms supported me like a guide as I entered a room. Chloe's room first. No, that wasn't right. I backed out and then reentered a different room. *My* room. There, that was better. That was—

"I think it's time for bed, Dr. London," a gravelly voice said, and that was when I realized that I hadn't been doing a damn thing at all.

And now, Cameron Bryant was in my bedroom.

CHAPTER SEVEN

cameron

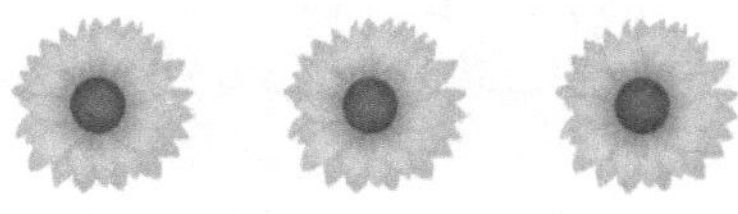

NATALIE FELL ASLEEP ON the counter.

I watched as her body slumped, growing more and more relaxed, until she started to slide. One arm dropped off the counter, and then her shoulder drooped, and I had a split-second decision to make—either let her drop to the floor like an anvil or swoop in to save the day. And like hell was I going to watch her hurt herself.

So I scooped her up off the barstool just in time and tried to contain my fucking smile when she curled into my body, letting me cradle her against my chest. Her weight felt *good* in my arms, like I suddenly realized how empty they were without her.

Natalie barely stirred, unaware of how close she'd been to smacking her face on the floor. And honestly, that was better for everyone. She didn't need to know.

And sure, maybe *now* I should wake her. But then she would have tried to play hostess some more or insist on talking to me when she really should just go the fuck to bed, or at least get a move on with her nightly wind-down routine. She had a field trip to chaperone in the morning.

So I carried her up the stairs, and her head tucked further into my chest. The creak of the floorboards didn't wake her, and neither did the abrupt halt of my body when I walked into a bedroom that looked an awful lot like a nine-year-old girl's. But finally, when I backed up and tried the other available door in the hallway, her eyes flung open.

I suspected it was my voice that woke her, telling her it was time for bed. Now that I had her up here, I wanted her more alert. The alternative was me getting too close to that bed with Natalie. Or too close to Natalie in a bed. It put me too close to any combination of Natalie London and a bed, which I knew to be a terrible idea.

"Oh my God," she mumbled, looking around the room with bleary eyes. She rubbed them, and once again, I found myself thinking she was adorable. "Did I fall asleep?"

"Out cold on the counter."

Almost out cold on the floor, too, but I didn't say that.

She scrubbed a hand down her face. "Ugh, I'm so—"

"Don't say sorry."

"*Fine.*" She dropped her forehead to my chest, and I hope she couldn't tell the way my pulse picked up. "I'm so...mortified?"

The words were muffled against my shirt, and I gave her a little shake to look up at me.

She did, and her green eyes bored into mine, startlingly clear. My breath momentarily vanished, and when I didn't say anything, Natalie bit down on her lip, tugging it between her teeth in a way that was so fucking tempting and seductive. I knew it wasn't on purpose, but holy hell. And then her gaze dropped to *my* lips, and *fuck*—could I kiss her? I just wanted to kiss this woman. At least once. I'd been waiting for six whole months.

But instead, I said, "You don't need to be."

She tore her gaze away from my mouth and whispered, "You can put me down."

My movements were stiff, but I did as she directed, knowing it was for the best. Natalie landed on her feet and then immediately dropped to her bed. I looked away, needing to *not* see her in a bed at the moment, especially one that looked so inviting. It gave me a chance to take in the rest of her room, which was a decent size, considering the narrow hallways on the way up here. It had dark trim that matched the original woodwork in the rest of the townhouse and light walls with other neutral decor that had a calming effect, like Natalie had purposefully made this room as unstimulating as she could, an oasis of sorts.

"If I knew you'd end up in my bedroom anyway, maybe I wouldn't have bothered pushing you away that night," Natalie said thoughtfully, pulling my attention back to her.

She was on her back now, looking up at me. Her honey-colored hair splayed out across crisp, white pillowcases, and I shoved my hands in my pockets to make sure I kept them to myself. Did she even realize what she looked like, lying there like that?

"Why don't you want me in your bedroom, Sunny?"

I needed to know the answer to that like I needed air.

"Because it's a bad idea," she laughed, but it lacked humor.

"I mean, *now* it is," I acknowledged, using that reminder to take a step backward, toward the door. "But why was it a bad idea before?"

She stared up at the ceiling, not meeting my eyes. "Because I hadn't had time to practice yet."

I stilled. "Practice what?"

"Doing all the right things." I was about to tell her that there *were* no right or wrong things when it came to the bedroom, but then she added, "I mean, doing it the right *way*. So it doesn't end up like last time."

"Natalie—"

"I didn't have time to warm up to the idea of you in my bedroom. And maybe it wasn't going to go that far, but it *felt* fast. And last time, it *was* fast. And it ended badly." She flopped her hand over her head. "I'm too tired to articulate myself well, Cameron."

"You don't have to articulate yourself well," I insisted, even though I wanted to let her keep talking. I wanted to hear all the thoughts Natalie kept to herself, wanted to know about the barriers in her head, the ones she put up, the ones I smacked headfirst into that fateful night. I knew she had good reasons, and I wanted to know what they were. "You don't have to articulate yourself at all. I'd actually feel better if you just went back to sleep."

I shouldn't have peppered her with questions. I *knew* now wasn't the right time for this conversation, which was why I'd stopped myself short of asking a question I shouldn't downstairs. *Maybe* we could have it later, when she had the bandwidth for it. Or, more importantly, when she wasn't already lying in bed.

It was so incredibly distracting the way she was stretching out across her sheets. We were already toeing a very dangerous line, and I didn't intend to make it any worse.

"Sleep sounds good," Natalie said with another wide yawn. She stifled it with her hand before turning on her side and peering up at me with that brilliant emerald gaze. "There's a keypad on the back door, if you don't mind going out that way and locking it behind you. The code's 1234."

She collapsed into her pillow then, but I was too busy comprehending her words.

The code was *what*?

"Natalie," I groaned, tipping my head back.

"What?" She looked sleepily up at me.

Adorable. Fucking adorable.

"Please change that code." I sighed. "Tomorrow."

"Why?" Her brows furrowed. "Do I need to worry about you breaking into my house?"

"No, that's just the worst fucking code in the history of all codes."

"Oh, yeah. I know." She heaved an exhale, her lashes fluttering closed. "I can't figure out how to change it, though. I only installed it a few days ago, but now I can't find the instructions. So I was maybe going to buy a new one, but—"

"Okay, okay," I interrupted but used the softest voice I could muster. Her eyes were closed again, and I didn't want to disrupt that. We could deal with the code on the door later. *I'd* deal with the code on the door later. "Don't worry about it right now."

"Deal," Natalie said with a sigh. Her eyes flicked open and pinned on me. "Thank you, Cameron."

"You're welcome," I answered, meeting her gaze beat for beat.

It fucking simmered, and I suspected she didn't even realize. Had no idea what she was doing to me.

It took me far too long to force my feet to move, but eventually, I took a step back. And then another.

And then I was down the stairs and out the back door, taking a picture of the lock before I left.

CHAPTER EIGHT

cameron

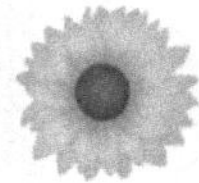 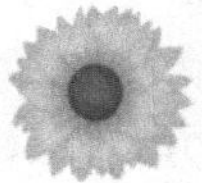 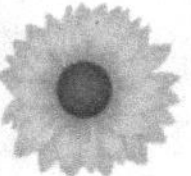

THE NEXT MORNING, HALFWAY through a video tutorial on how to change the code on Natalie's lock, my phone buzzed on top of my desk. And I had to bite down on a smile when I realized it was from my favorite single mom herself.

SUNNY: I woke up and thought I wasn't going to have any coffee ready, but you saved the day.

SUNNY: Again.

SUNNY: Thank you, seriously.

It was the least I could do after not catching the name error and putting extra stress on you.

I wouldn't really mind making Natalie's nighttime routine part of my nighttime routine. I'd happily show up at her place after her shifts just to make her tea, give her cat treats, and carry her to bed.

Maybe one day.

A guy could dream.

SUNNY: That wasn't your fault.

SUNNY: This coffee is going to help me survive twenty-five fourth graders today.

SUNNY: Just kidding. I actually love to chaperone field trips, even if it is a lot sometimes.

I realized that Natalie texted like she talked, in animated spurts. Like she had to get the words out while she had the energy, and then she sort of died away again.

Do you chaperone a lot?

I told myself that this was pertinent information, that I wasn't just trying to continue the conversation. And honestly, that wasn't far from the truth. This was a factual anecdote to support her claim for full custody.

SUNNY: When I can. I try to attend a field trip once or twice a year.

How many do they go on every year?

SUNNY: Like three or four.

So you go on half of all the available field trips?

SUNNY: I guess so? About that.

I really needed this woman to give herself more credit for what she was able to do as a single mom. There were so many parents out there who never went on *any* field trips, her ex likely included.

Which one was your favorite?

Okay, fine, this one had nothing to do with my job.

SUNNY: The planetarium, hands down. You get to stargaze without the bugs? Absolute win. I love it there.

I chuckled to myself and clicked out of the tutorial, feeling confident that I could handle the lock now. Then I pulled up some files that I was actually supposed to be working on. For my job. Where I had other clients outside of the pretty single mom who was my friend's sister.

Right.

I texted her back anyway.

I detect no lies.

I'm going to stop by later to change the code on your lock.

SUNNY: You know how to fix it?

I took a picture of it before leaving last night and found a YouTube video with directions for that model.

SUNNY: You're making me feel silly for not doing that already. Haha I can take care of it, then. Just send me the video?

I can do it, Natalie. I already learned how.

I sent the message before it occurred to me that maybe she didn't *want* me coming over to her house for a third time since this case had started. Maybe she didn't *want* to keep seeing my face when she didn't have to. We were already going to be spending enough time together preparing for her deposition. I couldn't blame her if that was already enough interaction with her lawyer.

I won't bother you or Chloe. You won't even know I'm there. I'll just fix it and head out.

Fuck. No, that wasn't any better. *You won't even know I'm there.* What the hell was I doing? Now I sounded like I wanted an excuse to spy on her at her own home like a fucking stalker.

And yep, Natalie stopped responding after that. Of course. I ran a hand down my face, realizing I'd actually overstepped my boundary this time.

I stood, needing to run to the printer to grab a few things. Maybe I could go outside and touch some fucking grass while I was at it.

But as soon as I stepped into the hallway outside my office, I paused, hearing a very distinct, recognizable voice coming from behind Julian and Juniper's door a few paces away. I walked over to it, saw that it was cracked open, and gave it a push.

Beau Bryant, who'd been chatting animatedly, hands flailing, stopped when he saw me enter. He shot me his characteristic shit-eating grin.

"Ignoring me for these two, huh?" I accused, leaning against the doorframe and crossing my arms over my chest. "What a great brother-in-law you are."

"Don't get your panties in a bunch, Cammy," Beau laughed, perching on the edge of Julian's desk, crossing his ankles with a relaxed lean. "I was going to pop into your office after I chatted with Juni and Jules about some business." He wiggled his black eyebrows as though that was supposed to be suggestive, when in reality, I was sure it had something to do with his real estate investments.

My brother-in-law worked for the massively successful company his mom built from the ground up after she emigrated from Tibet before he was born, but he played anything but a passive role in the organization. He was the idea man, as I understood it, always seeking new opportunities. Although why he needed Julian and Juniper's help, I had no idea.

"Don't you have a full legal team for that?"

Beau nodded. "Yeah, but I needed a Boston local's perspective on something."

"What are you planning in Boston?"

He smiled, a gleam in his gaze.

"And why did you ask them and not me?" I continued. "I'm hurt, bro."

I wasn't really hurt. I wasn't sure I had the bandwidth to take on Beau's needs at the moment, not with everything else going on.

And by everything else, I really just meant Natalie London.

"Oh, Collins told me I'm not allowed to ask you. Apparently, you're too stressed." He leaned forward, inspecting me. "It does look like you have a few more wrinkles since the last time I saw you."

"Fuck you." I rolled my eyes. "I'm not stressed." I was a little stressed. "My sister is just a worrier."

"I know." Beau shrugged. "But she says you've got your hands full with a single mom situation?" He cocked his head to the side and then wiggled his fucking eyebrows again.

This was truly just not what I needed this morning.

Julian, who sat in his desk chair next to Beau, chuckled, and I shot him a quick glare. Meanwhile, Juniper made a curious humming noise, and I decided I needed to clear the air. I did *not* need these two thinking that I was going around talking to my sister about clients. Especially *this* client.

"I ran into Natalie when I was out to dinner with Collins," I explained. "All I did was tell Collins that she was Noah's sister and that she was one of my clients at the moment. That was all."

"No, no," Beau cut in with a breathless laugh, like he was trying to hold it in but couldn't, and it just kept escaping him in little wheezes. "Let me reenact Collins' reenactment. Juniper, sit down across from me." Juniper obeyed with a shake of her head and a tiny smile, wheeling her own desk chair to the middle of the office and sitting in it. "You're Collins, and I'm this guy." He jabbed his thumb at me. "And you—" He pointed at Julian. "You're Natalie."

"Beau," I groaned, pinching the bridge of my nose. "We don't have to—"

"Okay, so we're eating dinner, catching up, you know." He pretended to shovel food into his mouth while smiling at Juniper. "And then all of a sudden—*bam*." After an overdramatic double take, he started staring at Julian.

And then kept staring at Julian.

Silently.

Without moving.

This was the reenactment. The entirety of it.

Goddamnit, Beau.

"Okay, knock it the fuck off," I grumbled.

"We get it," Julian laughed. "You can stop staring at me, man."

"That is *not* what happened." I really needed them to know that. "I did not just stare at her like a creep."

"Okay." Beau extended the word to have five more syllables than it needed.

"I'm going to kill Collins," I muttered beneath my breath.

"Hey now, careful." Beau stilled, raising a threatening—but not so threatening—brow. "That's my fucking wife."

My brother-in-law was simultaneously incredibly extra and undeniably chill...that is, until anyone said anything about Collins, my sister and the woman whose last name *he'd* taken when they got married.

Juniper changed the topic, playing peacemaker. "How long are you and Collins in Boston?"

Beau flashed me a slightly apologetic look—like he realized he pushed it too far—before turning to Juni. "We're flying out in the morning. We'll be back in a few weeks, though. For the party."

"Party?"

"Engagement party. Noah's proposing," he said, lowering his voice as though someone might overhear. Then he glanced at Julian, who looked at his shoes and smiled to himself. It wasn't a surprised reaction; he must have already known. Juniper, too, who grinned more openly, clapping her hands together.

I grinned, too. Then my brain once again wandered to Natalie, wondering if she knew about it.

"I'm really happy for Gemma," Julian admitted aloud, sounding a little rougher than normal.

Julian, choosing to openly share his emotions? What a fucking day it was.

I shook my head, imagining what kind of party that was going to be. Meanwhile, my phone buzzed in my pocket, and I pulled it out with the speed of someone who was just a *little* too desperate to hear back from one particular client.

Sure enough, it was her.

SUNNY: Chloe and I decided we're going to order pizza and have root beer floats tonight for dinner because we deserve it if we make it through the entire zoo without getting eaten by lions. You're welcome to join us if you're stopping by to fix the lock.

ME: I happen to love root beer floats.

I was so fucking screwed.

six months ago

NATALIE

I let him buy me a drink.

Sure, I might have said that I was only going out to Mulligan's for one drink. And yeah, I might have already finished that drink.

But that decision was made before I found myself next to him.

And I'd already rejected his offer of buying me a drink once. I couldn't say no a second time, could I?

As a surgeon, I was never the biggest fan of Grey's Anatomy. *You know, something about all the medical inaccuracies and how everyone always died felt a little repetitive. But sometimes, I didn't mind tuning it out and just...appreciating. It was okay to just live in a fantasy land filled with hot doctors every once in a while.*

I felt like I'd slipped into an episode tonight, being that this whole thing was a bit unrealistic and had the potential to end in an emotional wreck. But more importantly, this little pub might as well be a fantasy land. Because while the man beside me said he worked in law, he sure looked like Dr. Jackson Avery. Minus the eyes. Cam had warm, brown eyes that I seemed to be sinking further into with every sip of my beer. I should really, really stop looking at them.

"Have you been here before?" he asked. "They have a hell of a whiskey list, if you like that kind of thing."

I shrugged.

If I kept evading his questions, did that make me seem cool and mysterious and less like I was just a little out of my depth when it came to flirting with handsome men?

"If I said I came here all the time, would you believe me?"

He raised a curved brow. "Why wouldn't I?"

Because I haven't sat at a bar like this in years, *I thought to myself.*

Cam chuckled to himself when I just shrugged again. "I wouldn't. But I'd believe you enough to be coming back here every night after this, anyway."

A breathless laugh left my lips. "Yeah?"

He was being over-the-top. A flirt.

But then his expression became stoic, his eyes flicking over me once and then dropping to his glass.

"Yeah," he repeated into his beer as he took a sip.

And something about it all made me say, "You know, I wouldn't mind seeing that whiskey list."

Cam's eyes shot to mine.

A grin appeared again.

"Coming right up, Sunny."

CHAPTER NINE

cameron

"ALL FIXED," I ANNOUNCED as I walked back into Natalie's kitchen.

She looked up from behind an open pizza box with surprise on her face. "Already?"

Her surprise was warranted; I'd only stepped outside a few minutes ago after arriving at her house.

"It's not exactly a long process," I said with a shrug. "Do you have a scrap of paper or anything I can write the new code on?"

She nodded and then grabbed a notepad and pencil, slapping it down on the kitchen island, where she'd fallen asleep last night. Then, she spun around to start grabbing plates from the cabinets, calling, "Pizza's here!" to Chloe.

Footsteps raced down the stairs, and within seconds, Chloe burst into the kitchen.

"Hi, Chloe," I said as I scribbled the lock code on the notepad, hoping Natalie's daughter was okay with me crashing their pizza night plans. "How was the zoo today?"

"Hi!" Chloe appeared unfazed by my appearance in her kitchen. "It was pretty good. My favorite part was the bird show. A macaw almost landed on my shoulder!"

"It was terrifying," Natalie mouthed before shuddering. Chloe turned toward her a second later, missing her mom's reaction.

"Can we have our root beer floats *with* dinner?" she pleaded, and Natalie nodded, pointing to the freezer.

"Sure, honey. Grab out the ice cream, okay?"

Chloe's face lit up, and I took a second to compare it with her mother's. They had the same shine in their eyes, same sort of vivacity. They both sort of buzzed around the kitchen, coexisting in a symbiotic way. I knew I should probably stay out of their way, but I didn't like not doing anything, so I stepped into the mix, opening a cupboard and finding glasses for the floats.

"Thank you," Natalie said breathlessly, taking the glasses from me and putting them on the counter next to the ice cream that Chloe had grabbed. "What kind of ice-cream-to-root-beer ratio do you like in your floats?" she asked me.

"Can't say that I'm a float connoisseur, but I'm gonna guess a pretty equal one," I said and then opened two drawers before finding spoons and straws. I put them on the counter with the rest of the materials, right as Chloe appeared with three cans of soda in her arms.

"I like *lots* of ice cream," she announced, putting each can down on the counter with more force than probably necessary. "*Three* scoops."

"And I like more root beer," Natalie added, a tiny smile on her face as she started spooning ice cream into each cup, using the appropriate ratios: a lot of ice cream for Chloe, a little ice cream for herself, and a medium amount for me. "I just like a little bit of the creaminess for flavor."

Chloe cracked open a can and started pouring root beer into her cup, and I knew within a second that it was going to fizzle over. Snatching a towel from behind me, I whirled back around just as Natalie was sucking in a breath, noticing the same thing I was. Luckily, I managed to wrap the towel around the glass right as root beer began overflowing onto the countertop.

"You have to go *slow* with that, Chlo," Natalie admonished gently.

"Oops," Chloe muttered, wearing a grimace.

"It's all good." I wiped up the rest of the spilled root beer. "Try again."

She did, watching the glass so carefully this time that I had to stifle a laugh. The pizza might just be cold by the time we got these root beer floats made.

"Oh my God." I could hear the humor in Natalie's voice as she realized what Chloe was doing. "I mean…I told you she was a fast learner," she said under her breath to me, and I shook my head with a smile.

"You weren't wrong." I raised the volume of my voice a notch. "These look *great*, Chloe."

"Why, thank you," Chloe said, pressing her lips together in a pleased-with-herself grin and then dropping into a funny little curtsy after she finished the last pour.

"Now we have to remember which one was which," Natalie laughed.

"This one's mine," Chloe said confidently, snatching one of the glasses off the counter, grabbing the pizza box with her other hand, and running away into the living room.

Natalie turned to me, and there was that spark in her eyes. The one I remembered seeing when she spun to face me in the bar, the first time I saw her. It was like feeling the sun come out from behind the clouds, its heat brushing my skin.

"I might have also told her we could watch the new *Percy Jackson* TV series with dinner," she said, almost sheepishly. Like I would care. "I told you, she's obsessed. We've watched all the available episodes once already."

"Look, Natalie," I said, starting to feel more and more like I was intruding. "I don't have to stay, either. If this is your night off with Chloe, I don't want to interfere with that."

"No, no." She shook her head. "Trust me, Chloe is always excited to share her love of things with new people."

"But maybe *you* don't want to share her love of things with new people," I offered. "And that's okay."

Natalie chewed on her lip for a second, clearly conflicted. I was about to use that to make my exit when she said, "If you don't want to stay and watch *Percy Jackson*, it's really—"

"I very much want to watch *Percy Jackson*," I found myself cutting in to say. "You know, I've always hoped to find someone who loves that series as much as I do."

"Then you should stay," Natalie said with an uncharacteristic giggle, one that reminded me more of the untethered and carefree personality she had when we'd met. And then it vanished again, her expression more serious as she said, "We don't do this every night, of course. I cook. A lot. I'm actually a really good cook. But I miss enough dinners because of work that I try to make them special every now and again, ya know?"

A strand of hair fell out of her claw clip, framing her face instead. I had to shove my hands into my pockets to keep from reaching out and tucking it behind her ear. A second later, she did it herself while blinking up at me with those mesmerizing eyes.

"I know," I managed to say, reassuring her.

She didn't need to prove anything to me.

But I couldn't blame her for wanting to. It actually was, a little bit, her role to prove things to me. Prove why she should keep full custody of her daughter. Prove why she didn't deserve to have any bit of time with her taken away. Prove she was a good mother. All so I could turn around and prove it to a judge.

But every time she made comments like this, I wanted to tell her to stop. Which, I knew, was a problem. Because it was skirting around the role I was technically supposed to be playing.

The corners of her lips tipped up. "Thanks for understanding."

"Thanks for the dinner," I replied and then followed her to the living room to see Chloe perched on the couch, waiting.

"Chloe, if I'd known we were going to watch *Percy Jackson*, I would have brought some blue candy for dessert," I said and then glanced at the root beer float in my hand. "Well, second dessert."

Chloe's head jerked up, her gaze shining knowingly. "You know about that?"

"Sure do, kiddo." I sat on the other end of the couch.

Her jaw dropped, eyes darting to Natalie as though she didn't know what to believe. And then she suggested to me, "Next time?"

I nodded, even though I should really know better than to promise anything to a nine-year-old who I shouldn't be spending more time with than was necessary for my job.

"Next time."

Chloe passed out on the couch halfway through the second episode of the night, and Natalie looked like she was about to do the same.

I should go.

Now.

We shouldn't repeat last night.

I shouldn't end up in her bedroom.

Or anywhere closer to her than I already was on this couch, her warmth pressing into my side as she sat between Chloe and me.

But when I stood to take the dishes to the kitchen and make a smooth exit, Natalie somehow resurrected herself, bouncing to her feet, too, grabbing the plates out of my hands.

"You don't have to do this. I got it," she said and then whisked in and out of the kitchen within what seemed like seconds. "I'm just going to get Chloe up to bed, and then I'll be right back. If there's anything we need to discuss about the case, we can. You can add some...billable hours to tonight or whatever it's called."

I pursed my lips but didn't say anything, not wanting to interrupt as Natalie bent down over Chloe's sleeping form.

It wasn't that I didn't want to stay. It was more that I didn't want Natalie to feel like I was here because I wanted to make money off her. Yes, I wanted her to be happy as a client, but I didn't come over tonight because I was trying to look good on behalf of the firm.

Although that was really the story I should stick to. A professional story, one with intentions that had nothing to do with anything other than being good at my *job*—the very one that was on the line. The very one where I'd been clinging to the possibility of a promotion for months, hoping for some good news I might be able to share with my family, proof that I might be able to succeed in the way my dad always had, the way I'd been *determined* to.

So I stood and waited.

After a bit of encouragement, Natalie got Chloe upstairs, and about ten minutes later, she wandered back down, wrapping a cardigan around her body like a shield.

"Natalie, we don't *have* to talk about the case," I offered against my better judgment.

"We should, though," she said pragmatically. "You're here. I'm here." She cocked her head to the side as she sank back down onto the couch. "Unless you need to leave? I'd totally understand."

I shook my head. She was right. Her schedule was tight, and we should take every available opportunity to prepare.

Natalie grabbed a basket from the side of the couch that housed a bunch of yarn and needles or hooks—whatever you called them. Then she plucked out what appeared to be a half-finished stuffed animal, orange and fluffy-looking, putting it in her lap.

"Is that...your cat?"

A grin split across Natalie's face. "Yes, and you don't know how happy it makes me that you can actually tell what it is." She laughed, lightening the mood. "It's for Chloe. I like keeping my hands busy. I hope that's okay while we talk."

"It's definitely okay," I assured her. "It shouldn't surprise me that a surgeon is good at knitting, but that's impressively good, Natalie."

I thought back to the brief glimpse of Chloe's bedroom I got when I brought Natalie upstairs last night, remembering the pile of stuffed animals on her bed. Had Natalie made *all* of those? Where the hell did she find the time?

"Crocheting," she corrected. Her eyes flicked from the bundle of yarn to my face. "And yeah, I'm...pretty okay with my hands."

Fuck me. I had no doubt she was, but that was the last thing I needed to be thinking about right now.

"So." I cleared my throat. "We went over a lot of the basics the other day in the office. But what we need to dive into is your schedule and how it impacts Chloe's schedule. Because that's a big part of what Korey is using to come at you."

Natalie took a deep breath, absorbing that as I sat on the opposite end of the couch, putting as much distance between us as possible. If we were going to use her living room to do business, then I was going to pretend it was my office, and I wouldn't dare get close to her in my office.

It was really hard to imagine this was my office, though. Being in Natalie's home felt like she was wrapping herself all around me. She was in the warmth of the fireplace, where I imagined flames would crackle on a cold night. There were piles of medical manuals stacked on the mantle above it, sitting alongside a burning candle that smelled like...her: notes of vanilla and something even sweeter.

She was so sweet.

And so off-limits.

Behind her, streetlamps streamed in through big bay windows, illuminating her graceful silhouette.

"My schedule isn't very consistent," she said, sounding regretful.

I nodded. This wasn't news to me.

"Korey's lawyer is going to ask you who is taking care of Chloe while you are at work and how often it happens. And he'll probably probe into the specifics."

Natalie wrapped her cardigan around her tighter, and it physically pained me not to be able to reach out and touch her, even in just a friendly, reassuring way.

This was an office. We were in an *office*.

"It's really just Blake and Noah."

"You'll want to have a specific number of days that she's spent with them, oh, in the last month or few months. He'll probably also ask what their careers are," I added, "and then point out that they also work in high-demand settings."

Natalie bristled a little, and honestly, I preferred that to her feeling like she was losing hope. I liked seeing the fight in her.

"Noah has months every year where his job is *low* demand. It's called an off-season for a reason." She flicked her eyes up in irritation before returning her attention to her hands, and I smiled to myself.

"I thought Noah has historically spent his off-season partying, spending time with women, and ending up in the tabloids?" I countered.

Natalie narrowed her eyes at me.

"I'm only doing what they might," I said under my breath.

She pushed her shoulders back.

"Noah has never been as much of a partier as the media likes to make him seem. He's also in a committed relationship now and has a daughter of his own."

"If he has a daughter of his own, doesn't that limit the time that he can spend taking care of your daughter when you're at work?"

A muscle in Natalie's jaw jumped.

"That's why Blake has been helping me. And while he might be a doctor, too, his position is very different from mine. He mostly works normal business hours, and his schedule is much more predictable. If Korey were to co-parent with me—" She made a face of disgust. "—then he'd be far less available than my brothers. Unless he's made changes to his work schedule that I don't know about."

"Korey's shortcomings are for me to worry about, Natalie. I'll be sure to find out his work schedule when I go to depose him so it's very apparent to the judge."

She looked at me with interest. "You're going to interview him?"

"We arranged a time next week for his deposition. A few days after yours."

"You're not going to go easy on him, are you?"

I shook my head with a low chuckle and then met her gaze, needing her to know how fucking seriously I took this.

"Sunny, I know I seem like a nice guy. But when it comes to my job, I am not the man people want to see walk in the room. I'm probably the *last* opposing counsel they want to run into."

Natalie's eyes blazed, just a tad, at my confidence. I thought for a second I might be seeing things, but then she breathed, "I almost wish I could see that." She shook her head, interrupting our heated eye contact. "But I also want to be as far away from Korey as possible, at literally all times."

"Natalie..." I started, hating how anxious I was to ask this question. "Did he ever do anything to harm you or Chloe?"

She pressed her lips together, and the fact that she didn't have an automatic answer made my stomach drop. It was going to take everything in me not to fucking kill this guy the minute I walked into the same room as him.

"Physically?" She dropped her eyes to her cardigan, picking at a fuzz on it before turning her attention back to her crocheting. "No, he didn't. But he..."

I could barely breathe, waiting for her to go on. But at the same time, I knew I couldn't push her.

"We don't have to talk about it, not if you don't want to."

"No. I'm just...I'm trying to get better at naming it for what it was. It still feels...I don't know. Even when I was leaving him, I didn't see it entirely for what it was. Like I said before, the cheating had been the catalyst for me, and it wasn't until after, until the fog was lifted and I finally began to process everything, that I began to fully realize..." She straightened her shoulders, lifted her head. "I was emotionally abused by Korey Abrams for almost a decade. And Chloe was undoubtedly impacted by that."

God, I admired her strength.

But I hated that she needed to carry it day in and day out... because of him.

I *hated* him.

My jaw clenched, but somehow, I kept my voice gentle. "Do you mind explaining how?"

Natalie returned to inspecting the yarn in her hands.

"Early in our relationship, he started cutting me off from my family. Because of medical school, I didn't have a lot of free time, so if I wanted to use it to travel back home, he would make me feel guilty. At the time, I thought it was valid. Of course I should prioritize spending time with him."

I nodded along, wanting to be supportive. Natalie's hands moved while she spoke, looping yarn, twisting it, pulling it, arranging it in perfect rows. I stared in awe at her dexterity, at how little she seemed to be thinking about what she was doing, all her focus on her words. Which was where my focus should be, too.

"My parents tried to come visit me instead, but he'd come up with excuses about why they shouldn't, why it wasn't a good time. And then it wasn't just trips or travel but *any* sort of plans. He always needed to know what I was doing, and if I didn't tell him, he'd make me feel awful, like I was purposefully excluding him, like I was being deceitful. He started tracking my location, obsessing over it. I couldn't even run an errand after work without being questioned.

So at a certain point, I just stopped...making plans. I didn't see other people. I didn't talk to other people. I didn't do anything. And, of course, it was then, when I felt entirely alone, that he started cheating on me. He'd come home from work later and later. Sometimes never at all. That was usually better because when he did come home, he was..." She drifted off, her voice growing small. "*Awful.*"

"Natalie," I rasped when it seemed like she was done talking. And then all I could think of to say was, "I'm so sorry."

She just shrugged, like she'd gotten over it. But I was sure that wasn't the case. Surviving years of that kind of emotional whiplash wasn't something that disappeared from your reality so quickly.

"Thank you for telling me," I said softly. "I know it's probably not easy to recount some of these things."

"Yeah," Natalie breathed, acknowledging the truth of my words. "It's not, but it's gotten better. My therapist has encouraged me to speak about it. And to not downplay what he did, even though that's still my instinct to do. All the things I used to say weren't a big deal...were. They *are.*"

"They are," I agreed. "I know recognizing that must be hard, but *none* of what you described is okay, Natalie. I know you don't need me to tell you that, but I have to say it anyway. The way he treated you is *despicable*. And I'm so glad therapy has helped you process it." I hesitated but then decided to admit, "It's not the same, but therapy has helped me, too. After my dad's death."

Natalie swallowed hard, looking up. "Do you still go?"

"It's been a while," I acknowledged. "But I try to do check-ins when I need it."

She nodded, dropping her gaze to the yarn again. "It's been good for me. I don't know if I would have made it through the divorce and the first custody battle without it. Leaving was easy compared to the months that followed, when it seemed like Korey wasn't going to let me go. Let *us* go. For a while, I was...*scared.*" She pursed her lips together. "And lonely. My family rallied, of course, but no one really *understood*. My parents divorced not too long ago, but it was amicable. They still love each other, in their own way. Their experience was nothing like mine. But it's gotten a lot better. It keeps getting easier.

Though, sometimes I wonder if I'll ever be rid of Korey completely."

God, I fucking hoped so. The good news was that Korey was moving; yes, he was using that as a part of his custody claim, but I was using it as hope that he'd move out of their lives for good. We just had to win this thing.

"How did the two of you meet?" I asked, wondering how she'd ended up with such a manipulative ass to begin with. "You and Korey?"

"It was..." She heaved a sigh and then looked at me out of the corner of her eye. That look *meant* something, but I didn't understand what. Not until she kept talking. "It was a one-night stand. That, well, obviously became more than one night."

Her words seeped into my brain, slotting into place.

"That was what you meant yesterday. When you said it happened too fast."

Natalie nodded. "Our relationship started in a whirlwind that I'd *thought* was romantic and hot and fun. But it was really just Korey sinking hooks into me and dragging me down as fast as he could, making it impossible to climb my way back to the surface again for a long time." She glanced at me again, a little uncertain, a little shy. "When things started to feel...good the night I met you, it scared me. The last time something felt that good that fast, it had all been a lie. It snowballed into something out of control. And right now, I just want things to be *in* control."

I tried hard not to focus on the part of her admission where she talked about how good things felt between us and more on the part where she said it wasn't the time for it. Especially because I *understood* why she felt that way, given what she'd just told me.

"I get it, Natalie."

She dropped her head against the couch cushion with a groan and then muttered, "It's too bad, though."

She said it so softly, I wondered if I wasn't supposed to hear. But I couldn't help but ask. I *needed* to know.

"What is?"

Natalie didn't move her head, but her eyes flicked up to mine. She examined me from beneath her lashes, her gaze roaming my face, a lazy appreciation, a *want* that was barely concealed. Her breathing seemed to quicken, or maybe I was suddenly just that much more attuned to it, and then her lips parted. I tried not to look at them, but it was too hard. So I watched her mouth form the words "Nothing, Cameron."

Fuck, did I like her saying my name. I liked it *so* much that I wanted to get her to *keep* saying my name. And I wanted the word *nothing* to not have a single thing to do with it.

She knew it wasn't nothing. And I knew it wasn't nothing.

It was something, definitely something.

But we were both going to pretend it didn't exist.

"How long did you say this whole process would take?" Natalie asked after a long beat of silence.

She didn't need to clarify what she meant.

"I didn't."

Didn't really want to think about it, if I were honest.

"How long, Cameron?"

"It depends. Months, likely. Sometimes custody battles can stretch for a year, but I don't think that'll be the case here."

"Months," she mouthed, repeating it to herself.

Months, I reminded myself.

I had months yet to survive.

And it wasn't going to be easy.

CHAPTER TEN

natalie

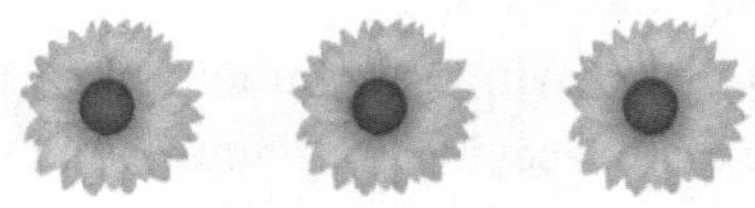

"HOW'S IT GOING WITH Cameron?"

"Cameron?" I repeated, staring at the skating rink in an attempt to avoid Noah's probing gaze. The problem was that the corner of the rink I was so focused on no longer had any students in it, and Chloe had long since skated off to another part of the ice.

"Cameron Bryant," Noah repeated slowly, giving me a funny look, which I caught out of the corner of my eye. "Your lawyer?"

"Right," I said, a breathless laugh coinciding with the word. "It's going fine."

Fine.

It was going so much better than fine and so much worse than fine all at once.

Since the late night at my house, I'd gone into his office on one other occasion in preparation for the upcoming deposition. He'd been considerate with his words. Professional in his mannerisms and the distance he put between us. And absolutely destroying me with his eyes.

The way Cameron Bryant looked at me was something I couldn't even comprehend or put into words, but it made my heart skip beats and my pulse thump in weird rhythms, and I was seriously wondering if I should be making an appointment with my doctor. Or maybe just ask Delaney, who was also a cardiologist and likely more understanding than my brother.

Before I left Cameron's office the last time, he'd asked what my plans were for the rest of the day. When I laughingly complained that I planned to spend it battling wordless IKEA instructions in order to build Chloe a new bookshelf, he offered to swing by to help me.

I should have said no, but I didn't, bringing the total number of times that my lawyer had been to my house up to four.

As it turned out, building furniture was a lot more fun when you got to ogle hot men while you did it.

Just looking.

No touching.

Because we were both being good.

"Fine?" Noah repeated, and I finally tore my gaze away from the empty spot on the rink, looking over at him. We sat side by side in the bleachers that lined the ice. He was busy adjusting the hat on Delilah's head, staring at his infant daughter with the dopiest look on his face. She was strapped to his chest, bundled in probably more layers than necessary for a fifty-five-degree ice rink, and her bright blue eyes blinked at him, a replica of his girlfriend's. "You think the case is under control?"

I blew out a breath, wishing it felt just a *little* more under control.

I couldn't lie; some of Cameron's questioning had rattled me.

"As good as it can be, I think. Cameron's been preparing me for the deposition, getting me ready for all the questions they'll ask. I've gone through this before, but I feel more...unsure of the outcome."

"There's no way he's going to get away with this, Nat." Noah squeezed my knee. "It's going to be okay. Cameron's got your back."

I nodded, agreeing with him on that. Cameron felt like the only reason I was getting through this right now.

My eyes drifted back to the rink to see Chloe skating by. Meanwhile, Gemma paced around the boards, looking a little frustrated she wasn't out on the ice with my daughter.

"She's not thinking about going back to work already, is she?" I asked, turning to Noah, who was staring intently at his soon-to-be fiancée.

"She wants to," he said with a sigh. "And I get it, to an extent. Her leave began at the start of her third trimester because it wasn't safe for her to be on the ice anymore, so she's been away from the rink for a long time. But she's only just started exercising on *land*, and I need her to take it easy. Like I *really* need her to take it easy." He looked at Delilah, worry and adoration mixed in his eyes. "We need Mommy to be safe, don't we?"

Delilah's lips parted in what looked like a smile, though it was probably just a reflexive expression. Either way, it was adorable, and Noah grinned.

"She just wanted to stop by today," he added. "Bring Delilah so she could meet everyone. But she's not supposed to be returning to work for a few more weeks."

"That's good," I said. "She should take her time. Take it easy."

"Trust me, I'm trying to convince her of that."

I gave him a pointed look and added, "She should take it easy *everywhere*, Noah."

"What do you—" He did a double take when he saw my raised brows, understanding dawning. His own brows pulled together as he scoffed. "Who the fuck do you think I am, Nat? Of course we're taking it easy *everywhere*. I'm so scared to cause her more pain after what she just went through, I've barely even touched her."

"I mean." I shook my head, surprised—but also not—at Noah's strong reaction. "Don't *deprive* her, either," I muttered.

"Fuck, can you stop?" Noah grumbled. He grabbed the bill of his hat, tossed it off, raked a hand through his hair, and then threw his hat back on his head again. "I do not need my big sister giving me advice about my sex life."

"I'm sorry." I put my hands up, knowing I was crossing lines. "I'm projecting, and I'm sorry. But I just know..." I sighed, leaning back and propping my elbows on the bleacher bench behind us. "Beyond my personal experience, I've seen at work what can happen when other men encourage it too soon after birth. That's all I'll say, okay? I'll shut up now."

As promised, I zipped my lips after that. And it fell quiet, too quiet, just the sound of skates cutting into ice echoing around the arena. Chancing a glance at Noah, I found him staring at me with a horrified look on his face.

I frowned. "What?"

"Just let me kill him, Nat," he groaned, his eyes searching my face for permission. "Please, I'm begging you. I'll just kill that asshole ex of yours, and this will all be over with."

"*Noah*." I darted my eyes around the bleachers, but luckily, no one else sat too close. We were up high, toward the top of the stands—less of a chance that football fans might find Noah since he'd been trying to keep a low profile since Delilah's birth. "Can you please not talk about murder so loudly at a youth figure skating club?"

Noah shook his head, half ignoring me. "It feels like every day that passes since your divorce, I learn something new that he did to you, and none of us were around to help. It makes me feel sick, Nat. I'm so fucking sorry."

"You weren't around because he wouldn't let you be around," I pressed. "It's not your fault."

Noah loved Chloe, but I also knew that this, right here, was part of the reason he'd been so insistent on being helpful since the divorce. A large part of it was guilt, and I wanted him to know he didn't need to feel that way.

Noah clenched his jaw but didn't push it, changing the topic. "Hey, did you still need help fixing that lock? I can probably swing by this weekend to take a look at it."

"Oh, no." I focused on the rink again, trying to find Chloe. "It's good. Thank you, though."

"You fixed it?"

Goddamnit. He *would* ask for clarification, making me choose between lying to him or just being honest. But why shouldn't I be honest? There was nothing *wrong* with what had happened.

"Cameron fixed it," I said, still averting my gaze, keeping it on my daughter. I'd found her. She was doing something I'd learned was called a forward swizzle while she made her way off the ice. I checked the time, realized that her lesson was over, and stood.

"*Cameron* fixed it," Noah repeated, standing beside me as he cupped a large hand on the back of Delilah's head.

I glanced over to find that my brother's brows had flown way up into his hairline.

Right. *That* was why I shouldn't be honest.

"He stopped by for me to sign some paperwork, and I mentioned it, and he fixed it." I waved it off, wishing this conversation could be over. Noah would look into this, *too* into this. "Not a big deal. Took him a few minutes. Then he left."

After staying for dinner and watching Chloe's favorite TV show with us and then talking far too late into the night.

Yep.

Then he left.

I started down the bleachers, hoping that we could just end this conversation right here. Behind me, I heard Noah mutter something beneath his breath before sighing.

"Well, saves me a trip, I guess," he said louder, following me to the bottom of the stands, where the skaters were lining up to take off their gear. My brother turned to me when we reached the side of the rink, and I prepared myself for a lecture, but all he said was, "We're headed to the Bellflower for dinner after this since we're already out of the house, and that doesn't happen all that often anymore. We're meeting Juni and Jules. You and Chloe should come."

"Come where?" my daughter's voice squeaked.

"Shit, sorry," Noah grunted. "I didn't know she was right there." He pasted a smile on his face and then turned to Chloe, who had appeared at his elbow. "Hey, lil Lo. I was just mentioning to your mom that we're going to get some dinner. But I don't know..." He tipped his chin down, a questioning look. "You might have some homework you gotta get done."

"I don't." Chloe immediately shook her head. "The research on homework does not prove that it is a useful intervention to increase student learning."

For the second time this evening, Noah's brows flew into his hairline.

"Yeah, her teacher is very anti-homework," I said beneath my breath, leaning toward him. "And Chloe has taken it to heart. Might be a little problem when she gets homework from different teachers in the future."

Noah laughed and nodded at his niece. "Noted, Lo."

"Do you want to get dinner with your uncle, or do you want to go home?" I asked her.

Personally, I wouldn't mind curling up on the couch with Chloe and watching another episode of *Percy Jackson*. I wasn't exactly dressed for an after-work outing, still wearing my scrubs since I hadn't had a surgery today. But I also liked the idea of not having to cook, even if it did make me feel a little guilty since there'd been a few times this week I hadn't cooked. Growing up, the Londons were always a "*we have food at home*" household, and I tried to bring that forward. It didn't always work, though.

"Is Aunt Gemma going?" Chloe asked, checking over her shoulder at Noah's girlfriend, who was chatting with one of the other coaches. Since she'd been on maternity leave, Chloe hadn't seen her that much, and I knew she missed her.

"Yep, she's coming," Noah answered.

"Then let's go!"

Chloe took off, running as fast as she could in her skates to grab Gemma.

Noah stared after her, shaking his head. "I think we should both be a little insulted."

"Yeah. But you're not, are you?"

Noah had a glazed look in his eyes as he watched Chloe pull Gemma toward us with the tenacity of an only child who probably got her way far too much. I needed to work on that.

"No, not at all," he breathed.

I should have realized that when Noah said they were meeting Julian and Juniper at the Bellflower Bar, a relaxed restaurant and bar that was only a few blocks over from Gardner Law, there was the possibility of Cameron being there.

I should have thought about that ahead of time and used it as a reason not to go.

But I was almost glad I hadn't realized. Because then I would have been forced to confront reality and admit that I *still* wanted to go. In fact, it only made me want to go *more*. Because while I shouldn't want to see Cameron any more often than was necessary for my custody case, I *did* want to see Cameron. Like, a lot.

Shit.

The Bellflower was crowded for a weeknight. Like a lot of Boston buildings, it boasted exposed, worn brick and historic charm. Gold-detailed frames held black-and-white photos on the wall, and a large mirror sat behind the bar, illuminated on all sides. The atmosphere was lively, the crowd mixed. Most patrons were in business-casual attire, fresh from late evenings at the office. But there were one or two other families, too.

Luckily, we didn't have to wait to be seated. We walked in the door to find that Julian had pushed a few tables together toward the back. Gemma led the way toward them, her bright auburn hair bouncing in her ponytail excitedly. When she stopped, greeting Juniper first, Noah gave her a brief kiss on the cheek before taking Delilah and going to sit by Julian and Cameron.

And, of course, my daughter skipped up to the middle of the table, squeezing her way between Julian and Noah.

Julian looked back in surprise, his expression transforming into one of genuine delight.

"Hi, Chloe," he laughed. "Is your mom here, too?"

"Nah, we just kidnapped her from the rink," Noah cut in. He poked Chloe in her side, making her giggle, and I flicked his shoulder as I walked up behind them.

"I'm here." Julian's gaze trailed to me, and I smiled at him, painfully aware of Cameron's gaze on the side of my face.

"Hey, Natalie," Julian said with a casual wave. "Glad you could come."

"Same," I said, suddenly feeling breathless. My gaze wandered to the rest of the table, and I didn't make it far before I got sucked into Cameron's orbit, our eyes connecting with an intensity I should be expecting by now but caught me off guard every time, causing my throat to close up and my chest to feel tight. Cameron gave me a nod of acknowledgment—like he knew exactly what was happening. The corner of his lips curved slightly.

I opened my mouth to say something. Something innocuous, plain, boring. Something really clever like "Hey" or "How's it going?" But my daughter interrupted before I even got the chance to mutter any of my ingenuity.

"Hi, Cam!" she exclaimed. "Annabeth *really* misses you."

And everyone's expressions shifted.

six months ago

CAMERON

It might have been a mistake to buy this woman a double pour of my favorite whiskey before taking better stock of her alcohol tolerance. Because I was starting to have a sneaking suspicion that she didn't sip shots of neat alcohol often.

But maybe her comfort level was just shifting, too. Her body was looser, swaying toward me, her smile a little easier. Maybe it wasn't just *the alcohol.*

I liked that thought, even if maybe it was wishful thinking.

"Are you originally from the Boston area?" she asked, swirling her whiskey glass as she looked at me with interest.

I shook my head. "New York."

She thought about that for a second before shaking her head. "I don't know about that."

"You don't know about that?" I repeated with a chuckle.

A twinkle appeared in her green gaze. I wanted to figure out how to capture it. Keep it.

"You seem awfully nice," she said.

A louder laugh escaped me. "Well, to be fair, I was born in California. Moved with my family to New York later."

"Ah," she said, as though that explained it.

"And you?" I prompted.

"Minnesota," she said before taking a sip of the whiskey and closing her eyes, like she was appreciating the burn as it went down her throat.

"Makes sense. You're also awfully nice," I said with a grin. "I've never been, but I've heard. I have a friend from there."

"Yeah?" Her gaze darted to me, as though she might know who I was talking about.

Well, she probably would know exactly who I was talking about, considering Noah's reputation in Boston. But I didn't exactly want to risk the chance that she'd suddenly seem more interested in a professional football player than me.

My ego wasn't fragile, but I understood the pecking order of things. And famous athletes—especially the ones at Noah's level—usually came above attorneys.

"Yeah, he's a nice guy," I said, keeping it as vague as I could.

"Mmm." She pressed her lips together. "There are times in life where I wished I was born to be less nice, you know?"

I considered her carefully, undeniably curious.

"Tell me about it."

CHAPTER ELEVEN

cameron

"THAT CAT LIKES YOU?" Noah laughed after an extended moment of silence where no one knew what to say, least of all me. "She hates me."

"She loves me," Gemma piped in. She leaned forward, looking down the table at her boyfriend with a fair bit of smugness.

"Yeah, well, you're easy to love, Em," Noah said, meeting Gemma's gaze with a look of longing that felt palpable.

I looked back at Chloe, knowing that regardless of the awkwardness, I needed to respond to her. It certainly wasn't *her* fault that I'd been crossing the lines of the lawyer-client relationship I had with her mom.

"Tell Annabeth I miss her, too," I said with a gentle grin.

Chloe seemed content with that reply and moved to sit in a chair next to Noah. Although I suspected it had less to do with Noah and more to do with the baby strapped to his chest. Chloe leaned closer to her cousin, speaking in a low hush, her eyes wide with wonder and adoration.

It was easy to see the truth in what Natalie had mentioned before about Chloe wanting a sibling. She seemed enamored of Delilah. It might have also had something to do with her being the only other child at the table, but still. She clearly longed for some kind of connection.

Taking a sip of my beer, I let my attention wander back to Natalie. Her cheeks were pink, either from spending time at the rink or Chloe's blunder. Whatever the reason, it was delightful. Like, really, truly. I couldn't stop looking at how the flush sort of melted down her neck, disappearing into her scrubs top.

"I'm going to run to the bathroom. Chloe?" She looked down the table at her daughter, who perked up at the sound of her name. "Bathroom?"

Chloe shook her head, so Natalie made eye contact with Noah, who simultaneously nodded, confirming he'd keep an eye on his niece while Natalie was gone.

Which meant, with Noah's attention on Chloe, my attention got to stay on her mom.

I watched as Natalie walked around the table toward the back of the restaurant. She fidgeted with her shirt as she disappeared from sight, into the hallway that led to the bathrooms.

It took everything in me not to follow her.

Everything.

Instead, I took another sip of my drink and tried to focus on the conversation around me. Gemma and Juniper sat together at one end of the table, hovering close and chatting about something in low tones that I suspected was Natalie-related. Juniper looked over her shoulder with a concerned expression in the direction that Natalie had gone more than once.

Meanwhile, Julian and Noah were focused on the children. Noah was busy removing Delilah's extra clothes, tossing her little hat and gloves on the table, while Julian peppered Chloe with questions about school and her field trip to the zoo. She recounted the story about the macaw to them, and I sat there pretending that I hadn't heard it before in between checking my watch too many times.

I knew women usually took longer in the bathroom, but not this long, right? It was busy in the Bellflower tonight, but not *that* busy. I doubted the bathroom had a line, and if it did, it couldn't be too long.

When fifteen minutes had gone by and Natalie still didn't return to the table, I excused myself, muttering that I had to use the bathroom, too. Julian nodded absently, but I suspected he was the only one who heard me, which was fine. It was preferable, actually.

I marched to the bathroom at a speed that was probably unnecessary. But sitting for fifteen minutes had been torture enough, and I didn't want to waste any more time before I got Natalie into my line of vision again.

Thankfully, after rounding the corner into the back hallway and getting within steps of the bathroom, Natalie rushed out of it, crashing right into me. She gasped, her palm pressing into my chest as though ready to push me away. But I could tell the moment when she realized it was me.

When my hand flew to her waist, steadying her, her body relaxed, the tension slipping out of her limbs. I pulled her toward me, just a little bit, because I couldn't fucking help it. I'd been so good about not letting this happen, not letting us get this close, but there was only so much I could do when fate intervened. And immediately letting her go when I finally had the feel of her beneath my palms? Hell if I knew how to do that.

"Oh, hi." Her voice was breathless, like seeing me there had knocked the wind out of her. She stared up at me with glittering green eyes that looked the slightest bit watery. Her eyes dropped to my chest, and when she realized her hand was still on it, she dropped her arm to her side.

Damn.

"You were gone for a while, and I was—" I bit down on my words before I could finish my sentence. There was no logical reason to be worrying about Natalie London. It wasn't my place to be worrying about her, but I seemed to be worrying about her a lot lately. Certainly *thinking* about her. In ways that definitely didn't have anything to do with my job. "Everything good?"

"Yeah, all good." Natalie seemed more flustered than normal, but she flashed me a not-so-convincing grin. "I just hadn't expected to be going out after work and wanted to clean up a bit." She fidgeted with the zipper of a light spandex jacket that she'd pulled on, stretchy and white, before looking around me, back toward the table that was out of our line of vision from here. "Chloe's okay, right?"

"Chloe's great," I assured her, forcing myself to drop my hand from her waist and take a step back. "Noah got her a kid's menu, and they're doing the word search on the back."

"Good." Natalie cleared her throat and tucked a piece of hair behind her ear. Then she smoothed a hand down her front, pulling at the bottom of the jacket, making me want to frown. It was unusual for her to act self-conscious. "Good," she repeated.

"You look great, Natalie," I said because I couldn't *not* say it.

"I'm certainly underdressed compared to you." She forced a little laugh, pointing at my suit and tie.

"We're both coming from work," I said logically. "Your work just looks a little different than mine." And again, because I couldn't help it, I added, "You look great no matter what you wear."

"You don't have to say..." She shook her head, averting my eyes. "You don't have to do that, Cameron."

"I know I don't." I also didn't have to fix the lock on her door or put together her daughter's bookshelf or stay over at her house to have root beer floats. "In fact, I shouldn't." I shouldn't do any of the things I'd done or said. "But you do. You look perfect, Sunny."

Her lips parted as she blinked up at me, like she couldn't imagine the honesty I was giving her right now. She looked like she wanted to sink into it, let that reality breathe for a moment, but instead, she sank down to a different place.

"Korey would have been annoyed with me." Her lips twisted ruefully. "He didn't like it when I wore scrubs out."

I gritted my teeth together, trying not to react.

"He can fuck off," I said under my breath. Real professional-like. But I didn't really care at the moment.

"He sure can," Natalie said, also talking in undertones, giving a huff, almost like a laugh but drier and without humor.

Then she flashed me a sweet expression, like she wanted to make sure I knew that her attitude had nothing to do with me. It was laced with kindness and optimism, more than most people in her position would have. I adored her for it, for the sunshine she still carried despite all the clouds and rain that had tried to cover her.

"How was work today?" I asked, deciding to switch the topic. I didn't want to keep talking about Korey, but I didn't want her to walk away, either.

"Great, actually." She brightened even more. "We discharged this burn patient who I'd done an escharotomy on last month. They seem to be doing really well, so that was the best part of my day, probably."

I nodded encouragingly. I had no idea what an escharotomy was, but it sounded important, and it sounded like she did a good job.

She was so fucking smart.

Good with her hands.

Gorgeous.

Fuck.

"That's amazing," I said warmly. "Must be a great feeling."

"It is." She nodded, a little more alive and animated than when she'd come out of the bathroom, which I was thankful to see. Her head cocked to the side, examining me more closely. "How are you?"

"Can't complain." Actually, I could think of a lot of things to complain about at the moment, namely how unfair it was that I was all the way over here on this side of the hallway, and she was all the way over there on that side. "Work was good, everything's good."

I didn't want to talk about me. I just wanted to talk about her. I wanted to ask her what an escharotomy was.

"I'm realizing as I stand here thinking about what to say that I don't know much about you besides that you're a lawyer." She crossed her arms over her chest, mirroring my position. "And you know a million things about me."

"It's my job to know things about you, Natalie," I said steadily. "You have no need to know anything about me."

I admittedly didn't mind her *wanting* to know things about me, though.

"I know, but..." She wrinkled her nose. "Just feels weird, you know? You even know my bedtime routine." A laugh drifted out of her. It was airy and bright, making light of a night that I thought about all too often.

The corners of my lips curled as I lifted a brow. "If I told you my bedtime routine, would it make you feel better?"

She nodded with so much force that a lock of hair fell out of her claw clip. And just like the other night at her house, I had to force myself to keep my hands to myself, to not push her hair back behind her ear for her. "Yes, exponentially."

"It's not very exciting," I warned her.

"You mean you don't read sexy tentacle books before bed?" she questioned, narrowing her eyes in keen assessment of my nighttime activities.

I chuckled. "You know, Juniper does lend me her books. And there's definitely sex. But I haven't found one with tentacles in it yet."

Natalie tsked. "A shame, honestly."

I gave her a look I probably shouldn't, a little pointed, a little heated, because what the fuck else was I supposed to do when faced with Natalie London talking about sex.

"Is that a shame, Natalie?"

She simply shrugged at me, a sparkle of mischief in her eyes as she suppressed a grin.

"So you read *non*-tentacle sexy books," she said evasively, not answering me. "What else do you do at night?"

The real shame was that I couldn't answer that question honestly.

Lie in bed and think about you would be a supreme answer.

In a world where this woman wasn't my client, of course.

"I'm a big baseball fan," I said instead. Baseball was a very safe topic. "I grew up watching it with my dad. My Pops and uncle, too. So sometimes I catch the end of a game or watch reruns. Get a workout in. I like to run. Shower afterward. Read Juni's book recommendations. That's usually about all I have time for."

For some reason, Natalie seemed intrigued by each word out of my mouth. "Baseball, huh?" she said. "I've always thought it would be fun to take Chloe to a game at Fenway. But usually when I do have time to take her to sports games, it's one of Noah's."

"They're a lot of fun," I acknowledged. "But typically when I catch a game, it's in New York with my family."

"You're from New York? Wait," she mused. "I knew that, didn't I?"

A chuckle left my lips, which were curving into a smile, a sort of subconscious thing that happened around this woman.

"I think you know more about me than you may remember."

A little flush rose on her face, not quite as apparent as earlier, but still very much present.

"You're probably right. Some of the details are...fuzzy."

God, I wished I could say the same.

Natalie's eyes detached from mine, wandering to our surroundings. A narrow hallway off the bathrooms in the back of a bar. Double-swinging doors on one end of it, which led to the kitchen, the sound of clanging pots and pans echoing off the walls. From the other end, music—some kind of vibrant pop—and loud chattering of patrons wafted in our direction.

I knew exactly what she was about to say before she said it.

"We seem to have a thing for hallways like this, don't we?" she murmured, eyes flicking over me.

I channeled every ounce of my restraint into not stepping forward. Into *not* pressing her against the wall like I had that night, my arms caged around her. I shoved my hands into my pockets instead, using my eyes to convey the closeness I craved, letting them trace the curve of her neck that I'd tasted and the corner of her smile that I longed to.

"Yeah, Sunny," I breathed, knowing that my voice was the sort of husky mess that gave away too much. "We do."

My gaze flew to hers, and she held my stare. It was the kind of eye contact that made my mouth run dry, my cock twitch in my pants. Hot, heady, palpable. A caress all on its own.

"I should get back," she said, the words falling from her lips in such a slow way, like she'd been trying to keep them in, not wanting to release them.

Somehow, I managed to nod, despite wanting to argue.

Somehow, I managed not to stop her when she pushed off the wall and turned to walk down the hallway.

Somehow, I managed to force my own feet to move, following her footsteps.

Until they were stopped short by the approach of someone else.

Someone who squeezed his sister's shoulder as she walked past and then looked straight at me, gaze cutting right through me.

Fuck.

Noah cocked his head to the side and said, "Hey, man. Got a sec?"

I exhaled a sigh, knowing this wasn't going to be good, and nodded.

CHAPTER TWELVE

cameron

NOAH SHOVED HIS HANDS in his pockets as he walked up to me, and I knew immediately what this was.

His tone hadn't been a passing *hey, man...let's catch up*.

This was a *hey, man...we need to talk*.

"Noah, you—" I started, wanting to get ahead of it.

But Natalie's brother held up a hand, cutting me off, and I stopped, deciding to hear him out. Might as well not expose things that didn't need to be exposed.

"Look, Cam." Noah released a heavy sigh that did not bode well for my future. "I don't know what's going on, but—"

"Nothing is going on, Noah," I said as stoically as possible. "Nothing."

He flashed me an annoyed look. "Just let me finish."

I nodded. Fuck, yeah, okay, I'd been a little too eager to prove my point.

"Truthfully, I think you'd be great for Natalie," he said and then waited, like he was testing my reaction to that. But it wasn't like I was going to say, *"Yeah, man. I think I'd be great for your sister, too."* Not when I was, in fact, her lawyer on an active case involving the custody of her nine-year-old daughter and his niece.

So I settled with, "I have nothing but professional respect for your sister."

Noah dipped his chin, giving me a look that implied he wanted me to cut the bullshit.

"C'mon, Cam. You don't need to do this. Blake and I both clocked it the moment you guys met. And now the *looks* and the *cat* and *Chloe*. Something's up."

"It's because that wasn't the first time we met," I admitted, taking myself by surprise. But I also felt relief flooding me with every word out of my mouth. I hadn't realized how much it was driving me wild to keep that bottled up, not until this moment when I got to let it out. "We met in a bar about six months ago. Hit it off, shared a few drinks, but nothing came of it."

Noah hadn't been expecting that. His expression shifted, stunned. It almost looked like he didn't believe me at first—which I couldn't blame him for, considering Natalie had made it clear she rarely went out—but then something clicked in his brain.

"I...remember that, actually."

"You do?"

"It was in November, right?"

I nodded, and he shook his head with a sort of disbelief, leaning back against the exposed brick wall.

"Natalie doesn't go out often," he said with a humorless laugh, confirming I'd been right about his thought process. "Not just for herself. But it was the one-year anniversary of filing for her divorce. She wanted to commemorate it. Chloe hung out at my place. It made me nervous because Nat was going out alone, but I didn't want to discourage her from celebrating, either. And I was glad I didn't. She came back and seemed..." His gaze raked over me, somewhat assessing, like he was looking at me for the very first time. "It seemed good for her."

"I didn't know who she was," I confessed. "I wish I'd known who she was."

Biggest understatement of my life, for so many reasons.

"Fuck, man." Noah's expression changed from wonderment to sympathy. There was a speechlessness to him as he ran a hand over his jaw, like he didn't know what to do with this new information. "She didn't tell you?"

I shook my head. "Gave me a different name."

For some reason, I found myself not wanting to share with him exactly what it was.

A dry laugh left Noah's lips. "Of course she did."

My brows lifted, and Noah noticed.

"Walls," he muttered. "Natalie has a lot of walls she's put up." He gave me a thoughtful look. "But it seems like you've gotten through some of them already."

I tried to play that off like it didn't affect me, like I didn't care that I was lucky enough to get a version of Natalie not everyone did. "Some of it is out of necessity," I said logically. "I'm her lawyer. There's some information she has to tell me, even if she doesn't want to."

"Right. You're her lawyer."

It was like he'd momentarily forgotten.

I wished to hell I could momentarily forget.

Or permanently.

"Yeah," I said dryly.

"Look." Noah settled his hands on his hips. "I don't have a problem with this. Actually, I think it's fucking great. But I *do* have a problem with this getting in the way of—"

I put my hand up, halting him in his tracks. "Jeopardizing this custody case is the last fucking thing I would do."

"And yet her *cat* is growing attached to you," Noah challenged, leaning forward with the tiniest glint in his eyes. Because while I could tell he wanted to be supportive and chill about this, it was still his sister and niece's livelihood and well-being on the line, and I couldn't *really* blame him for that. "Is Nat bringing her cat to your office?"

"No, it was just—" I sighed. *Fuck.* He was right; I knew he was right. "Chloe is exaggerating. I've met the cat like three times."

"*Three* times," Noah repeated. His eyes grew round and then narrowed, not at all happy by that revelation.

Shit, I should have lied about the cat.

Noah hung his head for a second and then gave me a tired look, like he hated that he had to spell this out for me, that he wished he didn't have to meddle but knew it was for the best. "You have to be careful around Chloe, too. She gets attached easily. And if she gets confused about why you're over all the time—"

"I know," I said, nodding, recognizing the truth in what he was saying. "You're right. I'll do better."

Something in my stomach sank at the thought of distancing myself from them. I'd enjoyed that night on Natalie's couch, watching TV with them, more than I cared to admit. I liked seeing Chloe's excitement about her new bookshelf. Their home was warm and joyful, and I wasn't sure if I'd just gotten too lonely as a recluse who lived alone, if maybe I was simply craving more human connection, to not spend most nights eating by myself, but I didn't think that was it.

Which was why Noah's glare was good for me. I needed this—the reminder. It would help me keep my shit together around Natalie when I felt increasingly like I was slipping, falling, something.

"Good. Okay." Noah sounded satisfied.

But I wasn't done. Because even if Noah was good, I needed to verbalize this—put it into the atmosphere. For myself, for him, for Natalie.

"I don't take this lightly, Noah. It's not just Natalie's case that would be at risk. It's my job, too. If I—" I cut myself off, looking up at the ceiling and knowing I shouldn't spell it out any further, detail what I *wanted* to happen when it came to his sister. "I could lose my ability to practice law, something I've been working toward my entire life."

"And we don't want that to happen," Noah said, gripping my

shoulder. "Because from what I hear, you're pretty fucking good at your job."

"I am," I said, meeting his gaze, reassuring him. "And I'm incredibly close to a promotion I don't want to fuck up."

We both wanted the same things here.

Noah nodded. "Julian told me about that. I'm sure you'll get it." His lips kicked to one side. "Would some tickets to a Knights game help? I heard your boss is a fan."

"I'm not interested in bribery," I said with a lifeless chuckle. "But thanks."

"I want to help." An obvious sincerity rang through Noah's tone. "With anything I can."

"Appreciate it, man."

I really did; it was more than I deserved after the fucking line I'd been tightrope walking with his sister.

With one last meaningful look, Noah strode past me, making his way to the bathroom, and I continued back to the table. I kept Noah's reminders about how much was at stake for me and Natalie tucked into my chest as I walked, preparing to see her again, telling myself that I could do this. I *could* ignore how fucking brilliant she was, how effortlessly beautiful she looked, how much tension simmered between us.

I concocted a plan in my head. It only spanned over the next few minutes, but at the moment, that was all I needed. I'd walk up to her, confirm our meeting time for her deposition, and then I'd walk away, simple as that. I'd leave this little London and Briggs family reunion and head home. Like a fucking professional.

It was a great plan.

Totally foolproof.

At least until I approached the table and found the girls still hovering together at one end of it, but this time with Natalie and Delilah included. Or, more importantly, until I overheard Gemma saying, "I think you just need someone to rip off the Band-Aid, you know? You deserve to get laid, girl."

"I know," Natalie said beneath her breath, confirming they

were talking about her. My senses heightened; my body tensed. I stilled a pace or two behind her and noted the way her attention skirted to Chloe, clocking that she was all the way at the end of the other table, working on a crossword. "I just want to have a little fun and know that it's *just* going to be fun. Nothing too serious. Someone to experiment with. I don't even know what I like. I never got a chance to figure it out."

I don't even know what I like.

The words bounced around my brain, both enraging and inciting me.

I bet I knew what she'd like.

Me.

"Oh, I'm sure we can find someone to fit that bill," Gemma said, a bit playful and impish, like she'd been waiting for this moment where she got to set Natalie up for a long time. "A no-strings-attached arrangement with *you*? There'd be a line out the door."

Natalie swatted Gemma, like she was being ridiculous.

She wasn't being ridiculous.

There would easily be a line out the door.

And fuck if I didn't want to be the first one in it.

I wanted there to be zero competition about who that arrangement would be with, even if my strings already felt a little more than attached. I'd deal with that problem later.

A somewhat nervous laugh left Natalie's mouth before she cocked her head to the side. "Do you know anyone? Preferably someone who doesn't know my brothers." She looked at Juniper across from her, and I felt my jaw harden at her question. "Maybe you're the better person to ask, then. Not this one." She cocked her head toward Gemma.

"I bet Julian knows someone," Juniper said, and I shoved my hand into my pocket, not wanting anyone to see the way it had automatically balled into a fist. Juniper lifted her gaze from the group of girls, searching for her husband. "Maybe..." Her words died in her throat when she saw me standing behind the table, clearly listening. *Shit.* "Cam...does?"

Absolutely fucking not.

She gave me a regrettable expression, like she knew this was killing me, a problem all on its own. But she couldn't have *not* acknowledged me. Not when I'd walked up from behind, and Julian wasn't even paying attention to their conversation.

I cleared my throat, pushing words out of it.

"I'm afraid I can't recommend anyone to you, Natalie." I was a selfish bastard, but I didn't care. The thought of anyone I knew—or didn't know—touching Natalie made me want to choke on my own tongue. "But maybe Julian will be more helpful."

Natalie turned, her expression unreadable. I met her gaze, not wanting to shy away but also not wanting her to see the truth in mine. She swallowed hard, and I gritted my teeth, hating every bit of this.

"I have to go," I said after a beat of silence. "But I wanted to confirm the time for your depo—"

"Nine o'clock Monday, right?" she interrupted breathlessly, like she couldn't wait for this interaction to be over.

Made sense.

I couldn't be upset at her for wanting to experience something better than Korey had given her. God knows she deserved that. And I couldn't blame her for not wanting it with me. It *couldn't* be with me, not right now.

But fuck if I wanted to hear about it.

I gave a curt nod. "Correct. I'll see you at the office."

And then I didn't wait another second before turning on my heel and walking out of the restaurant.

CHAPTER THIRTEEN

BLAKE: Nat, you have that deposition today, right? Need anything?

Yep, I'm heading over to Gardner soon. I think I'm okay.

BLAKE: How about Lane and I drop off some dinner later for you and Chloe?

Sure, that'd be amazing. Thanks, Blake.

NOAH: I should have asked you at the Bellflower, but do you want me to come with you today?

Normally I'd say yes but we're trying to make you seem less involved, remember?

NOAH: Yeah, still not a big fan of that.

I know. But it's just for right now.

NOAH: I hate him.

I know that, too.

SULLY: Don't let anyone try to convince you that you can't be a high achieving woman and a kick ass mom, Natalie Noelle London.

You're such a feminist, Sul.

SULLY: I believe in women's rights and women's wrongs.

SULLY: In case you wanted my permission to just get rid of the asshole in...other ways.

THEO: Love you, Nat.

THEO: Tell Chloe it's been her turn in Words With Friends for like three days.

Will do, Theo. Love you, too.

Anxiety attacked my nervous system as soon as I stepped into the Gardner Law Firm office for my deposition on Monday morning.

Sure, I'd adequately prepared for it. Cameron and I had talked a lot about what to expect, and I'd gone through this before. But right after the divorce, I'd felt so much more confident that the judge would favor me. I'd done everything for Chloe, and Korey had done nothing. I was divorcing him on the grounds of adultery. It all seemed so clear-cut.

And now he was moving further away and trying to make it seem like I didn't have the time or the ability to take care of the daughter that he'd spent years ignoring. He wanted to take Chloe *with* him.

I was so mad.

And so scared.

It didn't help that I couldn't stop replaying the scene from the other night in my head. It flashed through my mind on repeat, specifically Cameron's tight expression when he said that he couldn't *recommend* anyone. The way his eyes had scraped over me, as though he wanted to take a little bit of me with him when he left, like he knew it might be the only part of me he could have, and he didn't like it.

It was the first time I'd seen any emotion on his face that hadn't been laced with understanding and patience. He'd expressed none of that when he'd walked away. It was like a dark cloud had moved over his face, his pupils dilating, his jaw tensing. And it made my whole chest *ache*.

I badly wanted to run after him, but not to ask what was going on. I knew, on the inside, what was going on. What I didn't know was what Noah had said to him, what they'd been talking about in the back hallway. Did that have something to do with his stormy expression?

Cameron met me by the front of the office today, which wasn't unusual. He extended his hand to shake, like any lawyer might when meeting with a client, and I took it, trying desperately to ignore the spark of heat that traveled up my arm. But it was hard, considering I knew Cameron felt it, too. He dropped my hand like it had burned him, said a tight, "Good morning," and then immediately turned, leading me in a different direction than normal.

We ended up in a conference room. Windows lined the outer wall, overlooking Boston's financial district. The opposite wall was also made of glass, a viewing portal to the hallway that ran the length of Gardner Law's office.

"Have a seat, Natalie," Cameron said, his voice calm, maybe a bit subdued. He pointed to the chair that sat across from the video recorder set up on the conference table.

Trying not to feel spooked by that, I sat, smoothing the pencil skirt I wore and folding myself onto the chair. Then I fiddled with my blouse a little, arranging it so the little strings that hung from the collar were straight. It was a sunny yellow color, with little perforated flowers in the fabric that likely weren't visible at first glance. But I thought maybe if I made myself look like a wholesome kindergarten teacher, that might help my chances here.

I glanced up to find Cameron watching me, a glazed look in his eyes, like he was somewhere far away from here in his mind. When he realized I'd stopped moving, looking at him expectantly, he shook himself out of it and cleared his throat.

"You look great, Dr. London. And you're going to *do* great today."

I frowned at the distant note in his voice.

"Natalie," I reminded him.

A noticeable tick appeared along his sharp jawline.

"Is everything okay?" I asked, knowing full well that everything was not, in fact, okay.

Cameron didn't answer for a long beat. I thought he wasn't going to answer at all, until he said, "Everything is fine. Depositions can be stressful, but you'll do wonderfully."

Cameron wasn't stressed about the deposition. I hadn't seen Cameron stressed about his job once in the time that we worked together on this case. He was always remarkably confident, in a way I didn't completely comprehend. He was *still* remarkably confident, unfazed about our meeting today. But he *was* fazed about something. Something else. Something to do with me.

"I saw you talking to Noah the other night," I tried again. "Did he say something to you?"

A vague question that I knew Cameron would understand. I'd seen my brother's reaction when Chloe had brought up Annabeth. I was positive he had, too.

It took Cameron a second to respond, and when he did, his voice was tight.

"It's very important to Noah that nothing jeopardizes your case, Natalie," he said. "And I feel the same way."

"What would jeopardize the case?" I ventured, wondering if maybe we should just discuss this tension between us openly.

Cameron scrubbed a hand down his face, not responding, so I decided to be even more candid. Because like he'd said before, wasn't it best to just get things out there? Be transparent? Wouldn't that be the best for our working relationship?

"Cameron..." I started, tentative, and he dropped his hand. "Do we need to talk about what Juniper asked you at the bar?"

"No, Natalie." He shook his head and pinned me with a steady look. "We don't."

"Are you sure? Because you were either upset about that or whatever Noah—"

"Jealous," he interrupted, causing every word in my brain to fall out of my head. My breath hitched, making it hard to reply, but I didn't have to. Because he was still talking, making everything clear, putting things out in the open just like I'd wanted. "I wasn't upset. I was jealous, Natalie."

Cameron had yet to look away from me, his gaze blazing as he repeated himself.

"And I'm sorry," he added with a sigh. "Really, I am. I swear I'm trying my best here. I don't want anything for you but the best."

I could tell he meant it. He really, really meant it. And that should make everything better, but it made it all worse. *So* much worse.

Guilt seeped into my bones, filling me with so much remorse and regret. If I could have just trusted him a little more from the beginning, if I could have let him in six months ago, we probably wouldn't be here. Or at the very least, I could have walked out of his office that first day I showed up with my brothers and asked for another lawyer.

But I'd wanted *him* as my lawyer, and I hadn't known it would be like this. I didn't realize that a simple attraction would be so hard to ignore.

Cameron seemed to read my mind, like he always appeared to have the capacity to do. He gripped the back of the chair next to me, leaning on it and lowering his voice.

"Look, I don't blame you for pushing me away that night because you weren't ready. And I don't blame you for hiring me as your lawyer because I'm a damn good lawyer." His voice dropped another degree, and there was something so gritty and sexy about it, causing goose bumps to prickle my skin. "And I certainly don't blame you for wanting to rekindle your sex life, Natalie. But I don't think I can handle hearing about you fucking other guys when I am so *viscerally* attracted to you and can do absolutely nothing about it, even if it *was* what you wanted."

My lips parted in surprise while my brain played Cameron's rough voice and the things he'd just said on a loop. I shook my head, trying to comprehend. I knew there was attraction, but Cameron sounded *destroyed* by it.

"Don't look at me like that, Sunshine," he breathed, his voice softer now. "You know it's true; you know I am."

"You've been professional," I said, feeling the odd need to come to his defense. "Mostly."

Maybe we'd been a little more...comfortable with each other than was customary, but there were other factors involved. We had the same social circle. We'd met before. There had been circumstances, like running into each other at restaurants and me signing the wrong name. It wasn't like he was showing up at my house unprompted.

Cameron nodded, like he was agreeing with everything I was thinking.

We'd explored the line, the one we *could* cross. But we *hadn't* crossed it, and that was what was important here. Right?

"And I'm trying so hard to keep it that way, okay?" he assured me. "I just had a momentary lapse of control of my emotions when I heard…" He pressed his lips together like he didn't want to repeat it. "I'm sorry. It won't happen again."

He fell silent, but his gaze was anything but that. He didn't look away, trying to convince me with those deep, brown eyes that he meant every word he said. It made me feel hot from the inside out, causing my breathing to quicken, forcing me to wonder what else might happen if I let this man *more* than look at me, considering what he seemed to be able to do to my body with just a stare.

I wished I could find out.

And I owed it to him to be honest, just like he was to me.

"What if I said it *is* what I want?" I asked, keeping my voice low. "That I wish it could be you?"

Warning flashed in Cameron's gaze.

"Natalie, don't."

I crossed my arms over my chest. "Why can you voice things aloud, but I can't?"

Cameron's eyes fluttered shut, like he was disarmed by my words.

"You're right. But when you say things like that, it chips away at my resolve. And I need…" He released a shaky breath, like he was preparing himself to look at me again. His eyes flashed open, hitting me with heat and want and so many things that felt so good. "I need to hang on to something here."

"I understand, and I'm sorry," I breathed. "I just…" I shrugged, forcing myself to look away, to sever the connection. Except I could still feel it, the heat on the side of my face. Maybe I could convince myself it was just the sun streaming through the windows, the effect of a cloudless day. But I'd know it was a lie. Boston was miserably wet outside today. "I just have a feeling… that I could trust you with this. Like you'd respect me. And my boundaries. And trust is so hard to come by. Hard for me to find."

I looked down at my hands, folding them on the table and twiddling my thumbs in the wake of laying my vulnerabilities out for him to see. Cameron was silent, stewing or something. I wasn't sure. I tried not to care. I glanced up at the glass wall instead, watching as people walked by, unaware of the conversation we were having. I supposed people in law offices had tense conversations all the time, right? This wasn't any different than that.

Except a minute later, Cameron leaned down, so close that his lips brushed my ear and the delicious notes of sandalwood filled my senses, his cologne wrapping around me. "I would take *such* good care of you in the bedroom, Sunshine. I would give you everything that you needed and more. You know I'd be *so* fucking good to you."

And then he stood, so quickly that I almost wondered if I'd imagined the last few seconds.

But then everything became clear when the door to the conference room opened, and in walked a tall man whom I immediately recognized as Korey's lawyer. He was the same lawyer he'd used in the initial proceedings, which did strike me as a little odd, considering those proceedings had not exactly gone the way he'd wanted them to.

Cameron walked over to meet him, shaking his hand. That was good. Distance between us was good. I needed a second to regulate my body after...*that*.

But a second was all I got. Because then Cameron was walking back, taking a seat beside me, once again distracting me with his proximity and how good he smelled and the warmth of his presence. He reiterated the process aloud of what was about to happen, things that were not new to me but felt new to me, especially after that conversation. I took a shaky breath, refocusing on the goal here today.

"Ready, Natalie?" he checked.

His voice was steady, professional. Somehow, Cameron had managed to revert his demeanor in a blink of an eye. He was back to being my supportive lawyer, ensuring that everything about the process would go to plan, impressing me as usual. *Why* did he have to be so impressive?

I drew in a breath, steeling myself. I pushed my shoulders back, spared a quick glance at Korey's lawyer, and then looked into the camera.

"I'm ready."

six months ago

NATALIE

"I'm just not good at saying no," I tried to explain.

Cam snorted into his glass of whiskey. "You had no problem saying no to me."

I nodded. Put a finger up. "Let me rephrase."

He waited patiently for me to go on.

"I'm not naturally good at it. I had to learn how to be good at it because of the mistakes I made in the past."

Cam cocked his head to the side, listening. He was either feigning interest or he genuinely was. Something about the depth of his gaze made me think it was the latter.

"What kind of mistakes?"

"With men." I wrinkled my nose and then amended, "With one man."

I shouldn't be telling him this. I shouldn't even be wanting to tell him this. Shouldn't have my mind on Korey at all, but I was also proud. Of how far I'd come in the year since I'd finally told him no—once and for all.

Cam absorbed my words for a moment before his eyes drifted down, wandering over my hands.

They were bare. I'd never been much of a jewelry girl.

"Don't worry," I said, assuming what he was looking for. "I'm not married."

"Not sure why not," Cam muttered, but I could sense a bit of relief in his expression.

"Divorced," I added wryly. "But I'll spare you the details."

He raised a brow. After a sip from his whiskey glass, he licked his lips, and I found it hard not to stare at his mouth.

It was a very nice mouth.

"Who said I want to be spared?" he murmured.

"I'd rather not talk about the specifics. With him," I said.

"Then tell me about the specifics with you," he countered. "All the details, please." Cam leaned closer, the smell of sandalwood wrapping around me. "Every last one."

CHAPTER FOURTEEN

cameron

 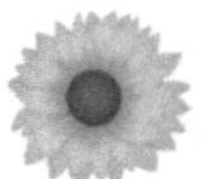 

SHIT.

I got so caught up in the moment with Natalie, with her admission that she wanted *me* to be the one to give her what she needed, that I lost track of time. I got off track. I didn't use the last minutes before her deposition to ground her and encourage her, like a good attorney would have done.

No, I used it to tell her how good I would *fuck* her.

Great.

Excellent.

A clear goddamn example of why this wasn't a good idea.

Yet I still couldn't stop thinking about it, even as I settled in beside her at the conference table. I couldn't stop imagining what it might be like to be the one Natalie let in, the one Natalie trusted with her body and her desires. To be the one she felt comfortable enough experimenting with. I'd let her do anything to me. I'd give her anything she wanted, anything at all. I'd be so good to her. So careful, so cautious, until she asked me not to be. And then I'd give her fucking everything.

Not only did I hate thinking about her with other men, but I also *couldn't*. I couldn't imagine any other man giving her what I would, what I could.

Honestly, it *should* be me.

But that didn't negate the fact that it really *shouldn't*—all at the same time.

I sighed, feeling frustrated as I shifted in my seat. It probably had something to do with how close she was and how good she smelled, how her presence sort of wafted around me, invading every single breath I took, until it felt like I was slowly poisoning myself with want for her.

I looked at Natalie, who had lifted her chin, sitting tall. Even though everything about her outward demeanor portrayed confidence and readiness, I could see the anxiety in her gaze, in the quick flick of her eyes as she looked from the camera to the court reporter next to her ex-husband's lawyer, Mr. Keller, and then finally, to me.

You got this, Sunny.

Depositions were a big step in the discovery process. There wasn't a judge here, but this information would be provided to the judge, giving a lot of the necessary background for the case. Depositions could be long and arduous and emotionally taxing for the client involved, but I had every faith that Natalie was going to do great.

Based on the look in her eye, I wasn't so sure *she* had that faith right now, though.

I opened my mouth to reassure her before thinking better of it. Had he started the recording yet? I might have missed it when I momentarily got trapped in my own head, thinking about Natalie in contexts that had no place here in this room.

Pressing my lips together, I watched as Natalie drummed her fingers on the table, waiting for Korey's lawyer to find the piece of paper he was looking for in the stack he'd brought with.

Her hand shook.

It was slight, likely imperceptible to most, but my brain seemed to automatically catalogue every small detail about Natalie London, which made it hard for me to ignore.

I couldn't imagine that surgeons' hands shook often.

Refusing to just sit there and let her be nervous on her own, I curved my palm over Natalie's knee under the table, giving it an encouraging squeeze. Her breath hitched as she focused forward again, but then she seemed to relax ever so slightly. I didn't trust myself to do anything else, not even a smile, not while other people were watching. Noah had said something about *looks*, and that told me I hadn't been hiding my emotions about Natalie as well as I should have. I needed to work on that. Especially when we might be on camera.

Even this, the touch of my fingers on her bare skin where no one could see, was taking a gamble. Especially when it reminded me of how much heat we could conduct between the two of us, like some kind of goddamn science experiment. And that skirt? The one my fingers brushed as I found her warm skin? God, she looked so fucking good in that tight skirt today. Seeing her walk through the front doors of Gardner Law had been a punch to the gut, Gemma's words on repeat in my mind.

You deserve to get laid, girl.

She did. By me, preferably.

No one fucking else.

I cleared my throat and started to pull my hand back, knowing I needed to keep it to myself, knowing that touching her right now was not going to help any bit of our situation. But Natalie grabbed my hand beneath the table, staying it. She put it back where it was and then placed her palm on top, smoothing my hand down so it gripped the inside of her knee.

Fuck me. She felt so warm, so welcoming.

I tried to keep the pressure of my grasp light, casual, but my heart pounded with a ferality that was anything but. I wanted to ease her trembles, sink my fingers into her flesh and become her anchor, stilling her in a storm.

That was what I did, after all.

Although Gardner Law was on the smaller side, it had enough breadth that it was able to provide specialized consultation in more than one area of law. Family law was what I gravitated towards, though. Families came to me with problems, and I went to battle for them. I became the person they looked to when a part of their world crumbled. And I liked doing it, liked the process, the learning, the fight, the outcomes. It made me feel useful, like I had control in my fingertips.

I wanted to win for Natalie.

But more than that, I wanted to be a man she could count on —and not just because it was my job. I was fully aware that this was different from any other case or any other feeling I'd had about a client.

"Ms. London," Korey's lawyer started, and I already found myself tensing at how he addressed her.

"It's—"

"Dr. London," Natalie inserted, and I watched her rise into a different version of herself. The version that I knew was going to kick this deposition's ass.

"Dr. London." Korey's lawyer made an unattractive grimace as he corrected himself. "Let's get started, shall we?"

"Please," Natalie said, flashing a forced smile as she folded her hands on the table in front of her.

I squeezed her thigh again and watched as the smile shifted.

Suddenly, it felt genuine.

Warm and sunny, like her.

Korey's weaselly-ass lawyer asked Natalie questions for hours, and she handled every single one of them like a pro. I had to cut in a few times to make sure he kept in fucking line, but overall, his lack of ability to rattle her filled me with so much goddamn pride, knowing how nervous she probably was on the inside. Her confidence in her ability as a mother to care and provide for her daughter shone through in an undeniable way, and despite some of the things stacked against us, I had to believe that any judge would see how fit she was to maintain full custody.

We took a break halfway through, and it was only then that I removed my hand from Natalie's leg. She stood, went to use the bathroom, and returned a few minutes later, wearing a hard-to-read expression. She'd put up those walls again, the ones Noah had mentioned. And I couldn't blame her, not after being poked and prodded in all the sensitive parts of her soul for the better part of today.

I gave her space, leaning on the armrest that was on the opposite side of my chair than where she sat. I wasn't sure if she'd want me to slip beneath the guard she'd put up while she was in the bathroom or if she needed it to stay intact to get through the rest of today. I kept my palms firmly on my own knees. If she wanted my hand, it would be there, waiting for her. It was hers to grab, the only part of me I could really offer her right now when we were sitting before a camera, before a man scrutinizing her —*our*—every action, word, inflection. But I wanted her to take it if she needed it.

Natalie dropped back into her chair, pulling herself toward the table. Her eyes darted to me. A flicker of a smile passed over her lips, but it vanished as soon as she trained her attention forward again. She cleared her throat, and I thought that was the end of our brief interaction, but then I felt her.

Her fingers brushed against my pant leg first, like she was searching blindly and couldn't quite find me beneath the table. I widened the spread of my legs, pressing my knee against hers. The contact was...disarming, to say the least. I suppressed a shudder, swallowing hard as I tried to maintain my expression, staring ahead at the camera, which luckily was still off. Korey's lawyer was looking at his phone when I felt Natalie's fingertips brush my knee again. I flexed my knuckles until our hands grazed, finding each other. She hooked one finger with my middle one, giving it the tiniest tug, and I understood what she wanted.

How could I deny her when it was exactly what I wanted, too?

I'd never take touching Natalie for granted, not when it felt like a rare prize, when feeling her like this was forbidden, something that should be out of my grasp.

But she was very much *within* reach right now. I curved my palm over her knee again, sliding it back into the same place it had been before, finding her inner thigh.

Natalie's muscles calmed. I could actually feel the way they loosened beneath my touch, and I tried not to think about what it could be like to do that to her entire body.

Fuck, I just knew I could make her feel so good.

The camera flicked on again, and I gritted my teeth.

The red light on the front of it blinked in our faces, taunting. Reminding.

Natalie cleared her throat, leaning forward with her elbows on the table. Korey's lawyer gave her a once-over, as if to ascertain if she was ready to continue, but I didn't like how he did it with his eyes. And I didn't like the way they lingered. Actually, I fucking hated it.

Whether Natalie noticed or just felt uneasy about the entire experience, I wasn't sure, but I felt her tighten again. A gentle squeeze of my hand on her thigh seemed to help, though, so I repeated it a second time, with a touch more pressure.

"Dr. London." Mr. Keller's voice had a monotone quality that I hated listening to. "We've talked quite a bit about Chloe. Let's talk a little more about you."

Natalie bristled a little but nodded.

I moved my thumb in a circle on her warm skin, a reassuring touch that I hoped she understood. But she squeezed her legs together, like maybe she wanted me to stop, so I did, keeping my fingers still as Natalie answered a question about the medications she was currently taking as it pertained to her overall health, listing a prescription for generalized anxiety and birth control.

"Are you sexually active?" Mr. Keller followed up with.

"Objection, relevance," I cut in. "Natalie, you don't have to answer that."

Natalie's lips stayed sealed, her expression stony.

Good.

Natalie cited Korey's need for control as one reason we were here, and I suspected she was right. I often wondered if this was just a way for him to gain access to Natalie's life again, steal glimpses of her that he no longer got and didn't deserve. He wanted back into her world, and even if he didn't get it through custody, he'd get a taste through this process.

Unfortunately, a lot of that I couldn't help. But sometimes, I could. There were some things Korey Abrams didn't get to know, some things I could put my foot down on.

"She has to answer my non-privileged question," Mr. Keller argued. "If there are new men being introduced into Chloe's life—"

"It's not relevant to a custody case," I pushed back. "We have already determined that my client has not introduced new partners of any kind to her daughter."

"But—"

"If you want an answer, you'll have to get a judge to order it," I said flatly.

Mr. Keller's lips pulled in a thin line, and he shifted his attention to Natalie, lifting a brow at her. "No new partners of any kind?" he asked, looking for her verbal confirmation.

"That is correct," she said.

And then she squeezed her legs together again. This time, it felt more like an urge, a request. So I slowly brushed my thumb in a new pattern, pressing my fingerprints into her skin. I hoped they stayed there, evidence that I'd once been between Natalie London's legs.

When she didn't stop me, I carved a path higher, tracing more of her inner thigh. Her legs parted, her knee pressing against mine again, telling me all I needed to know, telling me that she wanted me there, branding circles on her skin.

When I risked a glance over at her and noted her slightly flushed skin, I should have stopped. But her voice was steady as she answered the next question, and the top half of her body looked unchanged, her elbows still on the table, her hands remaining clasped, albeit a little tightly.

So I didn't stop. I kept touching her.

I knew I shouldn't be caressing Natalie in the middle of the deposition. I knew if someone caught us right now, it might mean I never got that promotion. Hell, it might even mean the end of my career. There were so many reasons I should stop touching her.

But I *couldn't.*

I couldn't deprive my client of something she wanted, something she encouraged with every shift of her body language.

I did hesitate when she squirmed the first time, wondering if I was being more distracting than helpful. But then, similar to the leg squeezes, Natalie readjusted herself in her chair, a nudge. And fuck, for that split second when I'd stopped, I'd missed the feeling of her smooth skin gliding beneath the pad of my thumb, missed the rhythmic connection, missed the spark of heat. And Natalie's light only dimmed when I hesitated, so I took that as a sign. That maybe me touching her was what spurred her on.

Sure, we both knew she didn't *need* my touch. But maybe she liked the idea that she was on camera, that her ex was going to see this, and all the while, she was being touched by another man in a way he never would get to again.

He might get access to this recording, but he'd never get access to her.

Fucking never.

I worked my hand beneath her skirt, wanting to feel more of her skin, needing my hand to palm more of her thigh possessively.

Natalie paused her sentence but played it off like she was just thinking of the right words, and I squeezed, a reminder to keep going. She picked up again where she left off without a hitch.

Good girl.

I kept my grip tight while she continued, thinking about how badly I wanted to feel the rest of her. All of her. How she admitted to wanting it, too. And then my brain wandered back to how she was considering inviting another man into her bedroom. A man who wasn't me.

How the *fuck* was I supposed to let that happen now? How could I honestly just stand by and let Natalie slip through my fingertips? Doing nothing just wasn't a goddamn option. Not anymore. Not when it involved the beautiful fucking woman next to me.

I drummed my fingers, feeling the heat of her core just inches from their tips.

I'd gone too far.

I should stop.

I couldn't.

I didn't.

I just stayed there, torturing her, torturing me.

"Okay, I think that's it."

I'd lost track of time, too concentrated on both making sure Keller didn't ask any more inappropriate questions and on the feel of Natalie's hot skin beneath my palm. I had no idea how many minutes or hours had passed since the earlier break in the session, but the deposition was finally over. Which was good. I only wished I'd *realized* it was about to be over because I would have withdrawn my hand from Natalie's thigh much earlier in preparation.

Because Korey's lawyer was about to stand.

He was going to stand, and the professional, polite thing to do would be for me to stand, too. Shake his hand, all of that. And that would be great, fine, if it weren't for the fact that certain parts of my body were already standing, or well on their way to standing, considering the inside of Natalie's thigh was so fucking soft and warm and perfect and *fuck*.

I breathed in through my nose, willing myself to get a goddamn grip.

"Mr. Keller," I said, needing to postpone this moment just a little longer. "Can you refresh my memory on the details of Mr. Abrams' deposition?"

He gave me a funny look, which made sense, given that I had already sent over a confirmation email for Korey's deposition… this morning.

But he answered me anyway. "Friday morning at nine o'clock."

"Excellent." I gave a curt nod. "I will plan on seeing you and your client then."

The thought of being in the same room with Korey Abrams this week had the immediate effect on my body that I was looking for, and by the time that Keller stood to shake my hand and then Natalie's, effectively ending the meeting, I managed to rise to meet him. *Without* making it known that I had been, for a good portion of that meeting, irrationally turned on.

I would have felt worse about it, guiltier, if it hadn't been a great fucking deposition. Natalie handled the entire thing so incredibly well. I wanted to celebrate, longed to pick her up, twirl her around the room, and then set her down on this table so I could drop my face between her legs and taste what I'd been touching all morning.

She deserved that. She deserved so much more than that, and I *desperately* wanted to give it to her.

Natalie looked at me once Korey's lawyer left, dazed and sort of awed. As though she could read my mind, could see what I wanted to do to her, like my thoughts were written all over my face. Her pupils were blown, her breathing shallow.

"Cameron," she breathed. "I—"

She paused, licked her lips, lifting her gaze to mine. Then she lowered her eyes again, looking at my hand, the one that had been touching her. She stared at it like she wanted to will it back onto her body.

Adrenaline pumped in my veins, and I could see the way it pulsed in her neck, too, right in that spot I'd sucked before, brandished with my tongue that night in the bar.

Swallowing a groan, I shook my head.

Not here.

We couldn't talk here, couldn't even *look* at each other here in this fishbowl of a room.

"Come on," I murmured and took off for my office.

CHAPTER FIFTEEN

natalie

  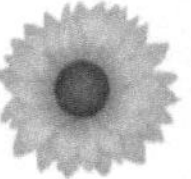

CAMERON WALKED AHEAD OF me to his office, his body tight as he moved through the hallways. His arms were stiff at his sides, his hands flexing and then balling into fists like he didn't know what to do with them.

I was right on his heels, equally jittery. My skin felt stretched too thin, unable to contain the emotions that lived on the surface of my being at the moment. My heart thumped, both from the anxiety of the deposition and the feeling of Cameron's palm on my inner thigh.

His touch had started as supportive. It anchored me, pulled me down to the ground and kept me there when I felt like I was about to float away in a flurry of nerves. But then it became *more*. Explorative, sensual, needy but restrained—like it was killing him not to touch more of me. And now my whole body ached, pulsed with a longing I didn't fully understand. Because I'd wanted him to touch more of me, too. And without getting that, I felt on edge, dangling on the precipice of...*something*.

Cameron burst through his office door, striding into the small space and pacing the length of it once, like he couldn't quite contain his energy enough to stop. Once I'd stepped inside, he made his way back to the door, shutting it firmly before rounding on me.

My stomach flew into my throat as Cameron's large palms cupped both sides of my face, drawing us together. I didn't know what he was doing, but there was not a single ounce of resistance within me, not one part of me that wanted to stop it. He dropped his forehead to mine, his breath fanning my lips as he groaned. It was a guttural sound, dripping with a tangle of emotions that didn't fit into words.

"You did so good, Natalie." His deep voice pierced right through all my defenses and then spread, reaching every part of me. "*So* good in there. I'm so proud of you."

"Thank you." The words came out of me on an exhale. I should say more, do more, but I just let Cameron hold me for a second, closing my eyes as I sank into the moment. His touch, his support, the assurance. God, I needed this.

Actually, no, that wasn't true.

I needed *more*.

Instinctively, I leaned in.

Cameron sensed it. His grip trailed down my jawbone, breathing becoming ragged.

"Natalie." He gasped my name as his lips flirted with the corner of my mouth, and I strained for more, tipping my face in his grasp. "*Fuck*," he cursed beneath his breath. "I've never—I can't—" He broke off, struggling with words that heated my skin, sending shivers down my trembling body.

"It's okay, Cam," I breathed, needing him to understand that I was right here with him, right here *wanting* with him.

He could kiss me if he wanted to. I wasn't going anywhere this time, didn't *want* to go anywhere. There was nowhere in the world I'd rather be right now than here in his grasp.

I opened my eyes to see Cameron shaking his head, his lips once again grazing the upward curve of mine.

"It's not." He sounded tortured to admit it. "It's not okay."

I swayed toward him, placing a hand on his chest. I could feel the pounding of his pulse through his crisp dress shirt, the warmth of his skin. I had to hold myself back from slipping my fingers through the opening between buttons, wanting badly to feel more.

"Why?"

Even as I asked the question, reasons flooded in. He was my *lawyer*. We had the *case* to think about, and—

"You want something slow," he said, a brusque reminder that surprised me. "You want something in control. And that's not how I feel right now, Natalie." His hands dropped to my shoulders, like he was going to force me back but couldn't. They just gripped tight, holding me in place. "Right now...it's not the time. Right now, I feel like if I kissed you, I wouldn't know how to stop."

It took every ounce of restraint in me not to tell him that *right now* I really wanted that—for him to kiss me and not stop. Especially when he said things like that, when his concern for what *I* wanted was at the top of his mind, instead of all the obvious things.

Like we were standing in his office in the middle of the workday.

"God, it's torture, though." Cameron dropped his head to the crook of my neck. His lips brushed my pulse point, sending me back to that night in the back hallways of Mulligan's. I closed my eyes, reeling from the sensation of past and present colliding. "You feel...*fuck*."

The guttural curse vibrated through me, sending another shock wave of heat, and his name left my mouth on a gasp.

"Yeah?" he responded, and I felt the tip of his nose trail up the length of my neck, until his lips were grazing the shell of my ear, the warm panting of his breath hitting some erogenous zone I didn't even know existed. My insides liquified as he murmured, "I'm right here."

"I'm sorry." My fingers twisted in his shirt, feeling moments away from crumbling in his arms under the weight of everything

—the roller coaster of adrenaline, the desire, the want, the *need*. "I'm sorry for making this so hard."

I wasn't sure I'd ever forgive myself, honestly. For messing everything up for us.

"Hard," Cameron repeated, a husky chuckle in the back of his throat. "Yeah, you're definitely the reason I'm so fucking hard right now, Sunshine."

After that admission, he took a forceful step back, an undistinguished growl rising from his chest. I detached myself from his shirt, and he raked a hand down his face. When he dropped it, his gaze flicked to mine, immediately tracking my eye movements, which were trailing down, wanting to see the evidence of what he'd just muttered.

"Don't," he warned, catching my jaw in his grip, tipping my chin up again. "Fuck, Natalie. I don't think I could handle your eyes on me like that right now."

Feeling guilty, I bit down on my bottom lip, tugging it between my teeth in a way that sparked a ferality in Cameron's gaze, which was now trained on my mouth.

"I'm sorry," I breathed again, meaning it.

"Holy hell, what are you doing to me?" The words were barely discernible. He shook his head, trying to bring back some level of awareness, I was sure. And then, said more audibly, "There's no need to apologize, okay?" His thumb trailed from my jaw to my chin to the lower curve of my lip, just barely tracing it.

"Okay," I agreed, even though I wasn't sure I believed it.

"When I can, I want to give you more, want to give you *everything*. I fucking know I could," he said, voice so unbelievably confident.

I sucked in and then nodded, eager for it. "I...I can wait for that." Even as I said it, I wondered how the hell I would ever be able to follow through on that when the tension between us felt this palpable, this *unbearable*. But still, I tried to make it sound believable, doable. "We can wait until this is all over. It'll be..." The little confidence I had in my words quickly trailed away as

Cameron's thumb traveled the edge of my lips, like he was memorizing the shape of them. "Okay," I finished lamely.

"No, it won't." Cameron's lips tugged to the side, and his voice lowered. "But I find it really cute that you think it could be."

My brows tugged together. "What are you say—"

He placed his thumb over my mouth, halting my words. "I'm saying I can't do anything right this second, but that doesn't mean I'm interested in waiting months for you. I'm saying I refuse to miss out on another chance, and I'm not letting you slip through my fingers again."

"But I don't want you to get in trouble. The case..." I tried, attempting to think rationally. It was hard to do when Cameron had let his touch linger on my jawline and then my neck, coasting down it like he was imagining the path he'd take with his mouth later. Or maybe he was reimagining the path he'd already taken. "Can someone else take the case?"

"No."

His answer was succinct, and I thought he was going to leave it there, but he seemed to snap back to reality when I didn't say anything further, silence ringing through the small space.

With a sigh, Cameron took a step back, letting his touch fall away. I felt empty and bare without it, lost and aching, but I knew it was for the best.

He shook his head. "It's too late. I mean, technically, if you wanted a different attorney, you are at liberty to arrange that, and I could help you find someone. But I'd really rather that didn't happen."

"Why?"

"First of all, to say I'm invested in this and you is an understatement." He pinned me with a meaningful look, one sparked with determination. "I would like to personally ensure that your asshole ex has zero control over you or Chloe, and I feel confident I'll be able to do that. Second, I think my boss would kill me." He deflated a little at that. "She's already got her eyes on this case because of Noah, and if I back out of it now, it's going to look that much more suspicious. I've been working—"

He snapped his mouth shut, seeming to rethink whatever it was that he was going to add. Pressing his lips together, he took a few slow strides, closing the distance between us again.

"You said earlier that you trust me. Did you mean that?"

I nodded slowly, in time with the pace of his strides, like he was pulling the confession out of me with each step.

He stopped when there was still a foot between us. He flexed his hand, lifting it like he wanted to touch me, but then changed his mind, dropping it into his pocket.

"I want to acknowledge why that might have happened. I *have* to acknowledge it. And then I want to explain what that trust means for us."

My brow furrowed. "What are you talking about?"

Cameron sighed, and I felt the deepness of it.

"Natalie, part of my job as an attorney is to build trust with clients so I can do my job and I can do it well. My goal is always to make my clients feel comfortable sharing things with me. But I want you to know that I *never* intended to gain your trust for a purpose like this. I'd hate for anyone to think that I'd use the relationship I've built with a client for any kind of personal gain. Do you understand what I'm saying?"

I lifted a brow, pressing my lips together to try to keep a straight face. "I think you're saying that everyone you work with trusts you, and I'm not special."

Cameron's eyes closed briefly as he shook his head. "Jesus Christ. That's absolutely *not* what I'm saying. You're very fucking special, Sunshine. Because you know it goes beyond trust. There's chemistry, too. And I didn't do anything to make that happen. It just *did*, despite all my attempts to stop it, ignore it. Okay?"

I flashed him a soft smile to make sure he knew that I did, that I hadn't really been serious before. "Okay," I said. "There's also the fact that I felt like I could trust you from the moment I met you, when I was just a girl talking to a hot guy in a bar."

Cameron's lips curved, a gentle smile that didn't quite reach his eyes. "Are you sure that wasn't just the alcohol?"

"I'm sure," I answered, giving back the confidence he always showed me. "I wouldn't have stayed long enough to even have the second drink if I didn't. I wasn't planning to, you know."

The shine returned to his eyes. "Alright. Then what I need from you—and your trust in me—is to believe that no matter what, I've got this case handled. I can take care of things in more ways than one, in more places than one, all at the same time. If we do this, it just means you will be my entire focus, Natalie." His words were soft but hard, reassuring but assertive. The perfect combination I'd learned to expect from him. "And I don't mind that at all."

"I don't want to monopolize your time."

It was a protest, but a *very* weak one.

His lips twitched like he thought that was funny. "Trust me. You already do."

"Cam—"

"Natalie, you can decide. The ball will always be in your court," he said, voice firm. Like this was the last he was going to say on it. "Like I said, I'd never take advantage of your trust, and I couldn't imagine ever bringing this up if you hadn't said something first, even though it was killing me not to. It's entirely up to you, but I can't help but at least—"

He paused, rubbing his jawline, stewing on words that I knew were going to destroy me. And sure enough, a second later, his voice dropped to a dangerous degree.

"If you're going to pick someone to teach you what you like in the bedroom, let it be me." The hue of his eyes darkened, turning almost black. "Please."

His words bounced between us, all around the room, echoing. After a long stretch of weighty silence, I breathed the only truth I knew.

"You're the only one I want it to be."

Cameron's shoulders shifted, almost like a weight had been lifted off them.

I wasn't done, though. There were other things I had to say, other considerations. I knew I needed to voice some of my fears, the things that went beyond simply the logistics of our professional relationship.

"But what if we risk this and then it's not even worth it?" I whispered. "What if we aren't compatible? What if we end up not liking the same things?"

"We're compatible, Natalie." Cameron stared at me like he wasn't sure if I was being serious or not. "It'll be worth it."

I knew, from the shaking of my body and the flush of my skin, that he was right. But the rational side of me felt that it was worth discussing. I wanted him to really think this through before committing. Because this wasn't something we could simply take back.

When Cameron still saw the wariness in my gaze, he inched closer, and his proximity swirled around me. There was the smell of sandalwood, the warmth of his body, the husky quality of his voice when he breathed my name again, a slight admonishment to it like he couldn't believe this was even a topic of conversation, that *this* would be the thing I was questioning.

He reached out, his hand curving behind my elbow, tugging me a little closer. His fingers dragged down my arm, stopping at my wrist. A thumb pressed inside of it, like he was taking my pulse, and I knew he'd find it racing. He tapped on it, a sign that he'd clocked me, my body, what he did to me, and then he trailed his hand back up my arm, a gradual torment of touch. My lips parted as I wondered where else he would go, what else he'd do.

"I'm barely touching you, and you're panting." His voice was a sensual caress as he lifted a brow at me. "You know that, right?"

I rolled my eyes, attempting *not* to simply melt at his feet. "I'm a medical professional, Cameron. I'm well aware that my body is either deeply aroused or I'm having a medical emergency."

"Mm," he hummed. His lips twisted while his eyes sparked at

my admission. "Then just think of what I could do if you finally gave me permission, Sunshine."

He took a step back again, letting me think on that as he walked around to the other side of his desk. When I managed to unstick my feet from the ground where he'd rooted me, I tentatively strode forward, keeping my voice low. Because I wasn't quite ready to drop this. I didn't like the idea that we might be risking something when it might not even work out. Even if, yeah, okay, it really *felt* like it would work out.

"What if you like things that I don't?" I pressed.

"It's not going to be about what I like," Cameron said with a shake of his head, also keeping his volume soft. He was looking at his desk, now shuffling things around. "It's going to be about what you like."

"I mean, I still want you to *enjoy* yourself."

Cameron looked up at me, lifting his brows. "You're joking, right?"

My cheeks flamed, but before I could say anything, he cut back in.

"There is not a single situation I can imagine where you and I are involved and I'm not enjoying myself. *Immensely*." He leaned forward on the desk, palms flat. I tried not to stare too much at the way it stretched the fabric of his suit jacket and shirt over his arms and chest. "We can talk about it, though. If you decide you want this, then we'll talk. I promise. Just not here."

His eyes skirted to the door, and I remembered for the first time since we walked in that we weren't alone. That there were people outside that door, walking around. No one would have seen anything, though, right? There was only one window in this room. Just a tiny sliver that lined the door, opposite where we were standing. Someone would have had to look at just the right angle, and even then, they probably just saw my back. Still, nerves traveled up and down my spine, my pulse racing for an entirely new reason.

Seeming to be sharing my thoughts, Cameron added, "If we're going to do this, we'll—*I'll*—have to be a little more careful."

I nodded. "You're right. I'm so sor—"

"Do not apologize for behavior that I initiated."

My lips pressed together at the sound of his lawyer voice, which vanished a second later.

"Today was a big day," he acknowledged. His lips curved, a reminder that beyond whatever just happened between us, beyond whatever *would* happen, there were really good things that came out of today. "It came with a lot of emotions, and I don't want you to feel any sort of pressure after what you went through this morning. So just think about it. It's a standing offer. I'm not going anywhere."

A standing offer.

I couldn't believe that he was really, truly offering me this.

I couldn't believe I wasn't more *embarrassed* about it.

But it was so hard to be when Cameron made me feel so secure in knowing that he wanted this, too. He wanted to help me, and he wanted *me.*

When would I ever get this lucky again? Knowing my track record, probably never.

"What should I do after I've thought about it?" I asked after a beat of silence.

"Call me," he said simply.

"Okay," I agreed and then forced myself to walk away, knowing full well that I'd be calling him later.

Because he was right: we weren't going to survive this case any other way.

CHAPTER SIXTEEN

natalie

I WAITED ABOUT TEN hours to call Cameron, and honestly, I probably would have called him sooner if it weren't for the fact that I had other responsibilities I had to tend to on a Monday, other than going to depositions and making sex arrangements with my lawyers.

But as soon as I got Chloe to bed, made my evening tea, gave Annabeth her treats, and trudged upstairs, I had my phone in my hand.

I hadn't been able to stop thinking about Cameron all day.

I hadn't been able to stop thinking about the things he'd said—with his words, his touch, his gaze, everything. I could almost still *feel* it, a warm, ghostly presence I didn't know how to shake but didn't want to. He'd offered me something I simply didn't know how to turn down.

Taking a shaky breath, I pressed on his contact name and brought the phone to my ear.

"Natalie," Cameron answered smoothly, immediately after the first ring.

Just the sound of his voice saying my name had me sinking lower into the bed, melting.

How did he do that?

"Hi," I replied breathlessly. "I'm calling."

"You're calling," he repeated, and I could hear the faint smile in his voice. Like maybe he'd been waiting for me to call. I *hoped* he'd been waiting for me to call. "Why are you calling?"

"You know why."

"Mm," he hummed into the phone, and it sent a wave of delightful shivers through me. "You're sure you don't want to sleep on this?"

"I don't think I need to," I said, painfully honest. "But I'd understand if you do."

"I don't." He sounded so sure, but that was always how he sounded. "I know what I want, Natalie."

You.

He didn't say it, but I heard it anyway.

My breath hitched as the unspoken word hung between us.

Cameron was right; we had undeniable chemistry. Simple touches and little words seemed to be all we needed to spark heat. As demonstrated at the office, he simply had to murmur my name, and my body felt like it was on the brink of ruin.

We needed ground rules. If we didn't lay down ground rules, this would snowball into something that I couldn't control, and that was the *last* thing I wanted.

Right now, over the phone, was the best time to decide on what, exactly, those rules would be. He couldn't distract me with his touch or wear down my defenses. He had a sexy voice, but I could hold my own against *words*, right?

"This agreement," I started, clearing my throat. "What if we put a limit on it?"

"A limit?" Cameron repeated.

I honestly didn't love the idea, but the anxiety that had been laced into the linings of my heart and soul—thanks to Korey—told me that this was the smart thing to do. So it didn't get too out of hand.

"Maybe five..." I paused, searching for the right word for it. "Lessons?"

That would be enough to grasp what I liked and didn't like, to give me a little taste of sex again. Right?

"Five lessons," Cameron repeated, but something about the stilted tone of his voice had me backpedaling.

"Is that too much? Just one is fine, too. I don't want to take too much of your time or anything like that. It was just an idea—"

"Natalie," he cut in, voice unyielding. "You're not taking too much of my time. Five nights sounds good."

It was too late, though. I was already spiraling, wondering if I was asking too much from him, a man who had already offered me so much.

"Is there something I can do for you in return?"

When it was silent on the other end, I attempted to joke.

"Can I interest you in a crocheted animal, perhaps?"

Cameron sighed heavily through the phone, and I winced, bracing myself for whatever was to come. Sometimes, it was hard to get a read on him, and it was even harder to do over the phone.

"I don't know how I can be any more blunt, but I'll try," he said finally. "I want to fuck you, Natalie. Badly. And you're saying I get to. Possibly five times." He paused, and I imagined him pinching the bridge of his nose like he did sometimes. "Trust me. You don't need to offer me anything more than that. Even though I am positive you make an exceptional crocheted cat."

And because I didn't exactly know how to respond to that when my pulse had taken off like a rocket and my body felt clammy and hot, I murmured, "The one I made for Chloe turned out really good."

"I bet it did." His voice had softened. "Look, Sunshine. I promise I won't pressure you into going anywhere with this that you don't want to. We can keep it to five lessons, but know I'm not going to push you for more than you're ready for. If that's what you're worried about."

Of course it was. Except it wasn't entirely about what I *wanted*. Truth was, I liked Cameron. *A lot*. In another world, where I wasn't burdened by the trauma Korey had put me and my daughter through, I'd be eager to start something with him. Something where we planned to spend time together in *and* out of the bedroom. But knowing what I did now, about how relationships could turn on you if you weren't careful, I couldn't let myself get ahead of anything. Even if I did trust Cameron, keeping this situation secret and experimental with firm boundaries was what I needed.

"I know you want to be careful about Chloe," Cameron added, and my heart lurched into my throat. "So I'll be mindful of that, too. I wouldn't want to confuse her or give her any kind of false expectations if we're just experimenting."

"Thank you," I whispered. Because his words truly meant more to me than I really knew how to express, the fact that he was considering Chloe, that he was prioritizing Chloe the way I did.

"Of course, Natalie." I imagined the way his brown eyes would flick over me when he said my name and smiled to myself. "As for the firm, if anyone *did* find out..." He hesitated, and it was the first time I heard a bit of uneasiness. "It would be best if we could say that this started before the case. If we could say we hooked up the night we met, and it just continued."

"That would be better?" I asked, surprised.

"Still not ideal, but there's less of a strict rule on it if it was a preestablished...relationship of sorts."

"Then we hooked up the night we met," I replied easily, wondering if I dared to ask Cameron what the consequences would be if that *weren't* the case. "It's not...I mean, a *total* lie. Otherwise, I wouldn't know what your lips feel like."

"Not totally, no," Cameron said, his voice a soft hush. "I wish I could say the same, though."

My stomach fluttered at his quiet admission.

"We'll fix that soon," I promised.

Cameron let out a muffled groan, like he'd pressed his face into a pillow.

More flutters erupted inside me. I couldn't remember ever being wanted like this. To be honest, I was having a hard time believing it was real. Before getting my hopes up too high, I should really make *sure* it was real. That this wasn't going to fall apart before it came to fruition.

"Are you positive you want to—"

"Yes," he interrupted. "I could not be any more positive, Natalie."

The words dropped like an anvil between us, leaving no room for any further questioning.

Okay, then. It was real.

My pulse picked up, hammering in my chest, my throat, my veins. I felt it everywhere that he'd touched, like a delayed echo.

"I think this will actually help." I wasn't sure if I was trying to unnecessarily convince him or if I was attempting to reassure myself that we were making the right decision, but I needed to say this aloud. "With the case."

Cameron didn't answer right away. He released a heavy sigh before replying. "I promise you it won't hurt it."

"I just mean...I think we'll be less distracted if we simply let it happen," I tried to explain. "Instead of using our time together at the office to think about how much we *want* it to happen." I paused when I realized what I'd just revealed, suddenly feeling shy about it. "At least, that's how it's been for me. Maybe it hasn't been for you."

"Oh, Natalie." Cameron released a throaty chuckle, and then his voice dropped to a pitch I'd never quite heard before. "You have no fucking idea what it's been like for me."

My stomach flipped. "Tell me?"

"You want to hear about that?" He sounded surprised that I asked, but how could I *not*? "You want to hear how I have to keep my hands in my fucking pockets all the time because the urge to touch you is so strong, I'm afraid I won't be able to stop myself? You want to hear about how just the smell of your vanilla perfume drives me wild for hours, even after you leave my office?" He released an exhale filled with pent-up emotions. "You're absolutely right, Sunshine. I spend way too much time thinking about how much I want you."

It took me a second to be able to respond, letting his words wrap around me, making me feel less alone in this. "Then I think we should free up some of that brain space by giving you what you want," I said diplomatically.

Cameron sighed again, like he didn't believe it was quite that simple, but I didn't understand why. Personally, I thought this would *un*complicate things.

"Again," he started, his voice steady again. "This isn't about what I want. So why don't we talk about some of your concerns you mentioned earlier?"

"Concerns?"

"About our compatibility," Cameron answered patiently. "And the things you're interested in." There was a pause before he added, "In bed," as if wanting to make that point exponentially clear.

"I..." My mind felt like it had been wiped blank. It wasn't like I'd been holding on to a checklist. I just wanted to try *something*. "I don't really know, to be honest."

Cameron hummed to himself, thinking about that for a long moment. Finally, he asked, "Are you in bed right now, Sunshine? Finished your nighttime routine?"

"Yes." A pause before my curiosity took over. "Are you?"

"Yeah." The rustle of sheets while he readjusted proved that. "I'm in bed."

"Reading anything interesting from Juniper's library?"

He laughed softly. "Couldn't concentrate on any kind of reading tonight."

"No?"

"No, Natalie." His voice was like velvet.

"Baseball?"

"Not that, either."

"That's...too bad."

Even over the phone, he somehow had the ability to unnerve me with his directness.

"I think I'll be alright," he murmured. "But I'd rather be there. With you."

"That would be nice," I whispered.

"Yeah?" I imagined him looking at me with a cocked brow and a slight twist of his lips. "Just nice?"

I shrugged, even though he couldn't see it. "Depends what we'd be doing if you were here."

"What a good point." There was humor in his voice, like this was what he'd been trying to get to all along. "What would you want us to be doing, Natalie? If I were there. Right now. In bed with you."

The thought alone overwhelmed and excited me. I tried to imagine Cameron here, beside me. He would take up so much space, in the best way possible. His broad shoulders leaning against my headboard, his long legs stretching across the bedspread, his hands wandering, closing the distance between us the way they did beneath the table today.

I'd want him to touch me. It could be anywhere, doing anything. I wasn't sure I cared, wasn't sure I wanted to dictate it. "I think I'd want you to decide," I answered after a long beat.

"Yeah?"

He couldn't keep the eagerness from his voice, and I smiled to myself.

"I make so many decisions every day. I think I'd like to be told what to do for once." I thought on that for a moment, how I wanted to make sure it differed from what I'd already experienced in the past, and knew there was one major difference. "But also be...prioritized, I guess."

A soft groan came through the phone, making my pulse tick faster.

"You're saying I can do what I want with you as long as I make you come?"

Heat rose up my body at his blunt words. "Yeah, Cameron. That's what I'm saying."

I swallowed past the sudden dryness in my throat, caused by my hot flash.

"So when you say you want control," he continued, clearly trying to piece me and my needs together, "you don't mean you want control over *me*. You just want control over the parameters of what we're doing."

I nodded, happy that he understood and that we were having the conversation so we could be on the same page. Because that was *exactly* what I wanted.

"Yes." The single syllable came out breathless. "If you're up for it, I'd prefer you have control in...teaching me what I like."

"Goddamnit, Sunny."

"What?"

"You're just so fucking perfect." His voice came through in varying degrees of muffled, like he was running a hand over his face. "You were worried about compatibility, but you have no idea how much—*fuck*. Just...yes. Yes, I am up for it. I have every confidence that I can give you what you need."

"I know you will," I said, because Cameron had only ever exuded confidence. "I'm not really *that* worried. I just wanted to be sure."

And he'd only ever delivered on his promises.

I'd only known him a short time, but I couldn't help but feel safe in every one of his reassurances. Every time he'd encouraged or assured me, it made me feel like I was exactly where I needed to be. And I suspected it would feel exactly the same—probably even better—when we explored these new roles.

"You can be sure, Natalie," he insisted. "You can trust in what you felt earlier today when I put my hands on you. You can trust in the instinct that made you drag them back for more."

"I shouldn't have done that," I admitted, knowing that if I were to go back in time, I would probably do it all over again without doing anything different.

"But you liked it." Not a question, but a statement.

"I did," I whispered into the phone. "I liked you touching me."

His hushed "*Fuck*" sent me spiraling.

And it only got worse when he added, "You wanted me to keep touching you, didn't you?"

"Mhmm," I hummed, thinking back to the feel of his thumb tracing circles on my inner thigh, making me want to part my legs, give him access to more of me.

"You felt so fucking good beneath my fingers. All I wanted to do was feel more of you."

An embarrassing whimper left my lips as I thought about it, as I imagined Cameron's hands on me again, as I thought about them touching me in other places, slipping beneath the hem of my underwear.

"Yeah, Sunny? You agree?" His voice was a fucking aphrodisiac, all gruff but smooth at the same time. The most sinful oxymoron.

"Yes," I breathed.

"If my hand slid higher beneath your skirt, what would I have found?" he asked, voicing my exact thoughts.

I slipped my hand beneath the covers, sliding it down my body to my thighs, right where he had been this morning. My skin was warm, probably from the heat of his words. And then I mimicked them, moving my fingers along the inner seam of my thigh.

"Cameron," I panted, unable to say anything other than his name.

"Natalie, tell me." A soft demand.

"Tell you what?"

I already couldn't remember the question.

"What I would have found. If I let my fingers drift higher between your soft thighs, if I dragged them over the fabric of your underwear. Would it have been wet?"

I swallowed a groan. Already in my pajama shorts, I wasn't wearing underwear right now, but I knew exactly what I would have found between my legs if I were. I knew what I *did* find when I left Cameron's office earlier.

"Yes," I admitted on a sigh. "Drenched, actually."

"*Jesus fuck*," Cameron muttered.

The roughness of his voice sent a thrill through me.

"What about now?" he asked, sounding desperate for the answer.

A muted cry left my lips as I slipped a finger between my legs, testing, as though I didn't already know what I would find. My head fell back against the pillows at the glide of my finger over my clit, coated with arousal.

"*Natalie*," Cameron grunted when I was silent. "Tell me."

"Wet," I breathed on an exhale. The only word I could get out.

"I know," he said, more relaxed now. Almost like he was reassuring me. "If I was there, I would do something about it, too. That pretty pussy needs attention, doesn't it?"

"*Yes*." My most transparent confession yet. "I've been needing it all day."

"Needing who, Sunshine?"

"Needing you."

I'd been hot and bothered and on edge since the moment I walked out of Cameron's office earlier. Our conversation, the way he'd touched me, talked to me, all of it made me needy for more. Made me feel like things were unfinished.

"Good girl," Cameron praised. "I need you being honest with me like this."

I nodded, forgetting that he couldn't see me as I stroked my finger deeper, barely withholding a gasp.

"You know I would have spread you out on my desk this morning if I could have," he added, dropping his voice another degree. "I would have taken care of you, Sunshine."

I bit down on my lip, picturing that. Cameron lifting me onto his desk, hiking up my skirt, spreading my legs, and then—

"For now, I need you to do it." His voice sounded tight, barely restrained. "Touch yourself. Pretend it's me."

I was way ahead of him. I dragged a fingertip through my wet slit, letting myself imagine that he was the one doing it, that his fingers had trailed all the way up my thigh and swiped beneath my nonexistent underwear. A pleasure-filled sigh left my lips, the only response I managed for Cameron.

But he didn't seem to mind.

"That's it," he encouraged. "I can already tell you're going to follow directions *so* well, Natalie."

I flushed from his praise, my entire body heating from the inside out. I pressed my lips together, stifling an even louder cry as I circled my fingers around my swollen clit, giving it the attention it deserved.

"Oh, fuck," Cameron cursed, seeming to have heard me anyway. "I wish I was there. I want to see your fingers between your thighs. I want to see you touch yourself while you think about me. I want to see what you do while you're alone in that nice, big bed of yours. How you make yourself come when you watch those dirty little videos. You do that, right?"

"I have." No point lying to him now. I wasn't coherent enough to even try, not as pleasure flooded my body, spurred on by Cameron's words, the images that he was describing, the idea that he might see me, watch me. The warmth of his eyes, I could practically *feel* it.

"You're going to show me." It was a promise and a threat all at once, and my entire body shuddered. "You're going to show me what you like, okay?"

"I thought that was your job?" I countered between panting breaths. "To show me what I like."

"I need to understand you in order to give you what you need, Natalie. You wanted slow and controlled. That's what I'm going to give you. I'm going to take my time, learn you inside and out, and then I'm going to make you see fucking stars."

"*Cameron*," I groaned.

"I'm right here, baby," he said, but his voice sounded more labored. Like this was taking more out of him than he was maybe ready to admit. "Just tell me how it feels. Please, I need to know."

"*So* good."

"Mm," Cameron moaned. "You're soaked, aren't you?"

"Soaked," I assured him. My fingers were coated with my arousal, with the evidence of how badly I wanted him, lost in my dazed imagination.

"Jesus Christ," he grunted and then continued to pant in a way that made me want to know more, wanted to imagine him, wishing I could see him, right now. He was always in those suits, but I wanted to see what he looked like when his shirt was unbuttoned, and his jacket thrown off, and his pants zipped down, bunched around his hips.

"And you?" I managed.

This was a two-way street, and suddenly, I needed to know.

"So *fucking* hard for you," he said without hesitation, his voice cutting through me like steel.

"Are you—?"

"Yes," he bit out before I could even finish the question. "Natalie, I've had my cock in my fist since before I picked up the phone. All I've been able to do all day is think about you and hope you'd call."

Oh my God.

Just the thought of that alone sent me down an entirely new spiral, heat spiking between my legs, my movements becoming more frantic in response.

"You're going to do something for me, Natalie," he continued, gravelly and deep.

"Anything."

I'd do just about anything he asked me to do right now, which was exactly the point. I didn't have to think. All I had to do was listen to Cameron. His voice, the grunts of his movement, his commands. Whatever he wanted, *I* wanted. I had no idea how it worked, but it did.

"You're going to slide your fingers into your sweet cunt," he directed, and I immediately obeyed, letting my hand fall further down between my legs. "And imagine it's me inside you, filling you. Got it?"

I groaned in response, feeling the stretch of my fingers and thinking of what it might be like to have him there instead. It had been so long since I'd experienced any kind of satisfying pleasure from anyone other than myself, and just the thought that he might be able to give me that. No, I *knew* he'd be able to give me that. And *God*, it sent me reeling.

"That's it," he murmured. "That's perfect. You're so perfect." Cameron's breaths were ragged, cutting through me with every inhale and exhale. Palpable, even through the phone. "You *feel* so perfect. It's so good being inside you, isn't it?"

The desperation of his tone made me think that he was close, and fuck, so was I. This pressure inside me, it felt like it had been building for *so* long. So *very* long. And I just needed—I needed a release from it.

All I could do was whimper and pant, unable to form coherent words to respond to Cameron.

"I know, baby. I know it's good."

The sound of his voice, so soft but so knowing and assertive like that, was going to send me over the edge.

I was hanging there, on the precipice, when Cameron cut in again.

"But now you're going to do something else for me, Natalie."

"Yeah?" I gasped, feeling all my nerve endings tighten, seconds from coming undone.

"You're going to stop," he directed, and my lips parted, confused why he'd say that when I was *so* close to reaching something *so* good. "You're going to take your fingers out of your pretty pussy, and you're not going to touch it again until the next time I see you."

He couldn't be serious. I slowed my movements but didn't stop, couldn't quite get myself to.

"But—"

"*Now*, Natalie," he cut in, low-pitched and demanding.

And I stopped, rolling over with a whimper.

"Good girl," Cameron praised, and a different kind of relief washed over me, even while my body felt stuck in a state of confusion.

"I don't understand," I said, releasing a shaky breath. I knew I sounded unstable. I *was* unstable. "You said—"

"I said I'd make you come," Cameron finished for me. "And I'm going to, Sunshine. The next time you come, it'll be because I make you. And as long as you listen to me, it's going to be *so* good, baby. Okay?"

"Okay," I sighed, and as soon as I agreed, a thrill shot through me.

Was my body aching and pulsing and feeling like it was going to explode? Absolutely.

Did I think I could wait much longer for a release? Not at all.

But it was also sort of...*thrilling*. The burst of anticipation and adrenaline was delicious all on its own, along with the resignation of my control, the act of handing it over to Cameron.

"God, you're amazing." There was another rustle of sheets on the other side, like he was also rolling into a new position. And then he asked the question I really wanted to know. "When?"

I smiled to myself, enjoying his directness. I had a feeling I was going to be hearing even more of it from now on, and I felt a flutter of excitement. This introduction of Cameron told me everything I needed to know about our decision to do this; it was the right one. I was still in a daze from how absolutely bone-melting that was, and I hadn't even finished.

"Um..." I started and then frowned, realizing that maybe this was going to be more challenging than I thought. All my excitement dimmed, faced with reality. I hadn't exactly parsed through the details about how a sex arrangement would work while being a single mother and a trauma surgeon. "Well, Chloe is staying at Blake's on Thursday night because I have a late shift."

"I'll pick you up afterward," he said immediately.

"It's going to be *late*, Cam," I emphasized.

"I truly don't care."

And he truly did not sound like he cared.

"Don't you have the deposition with Korey on Friday morning?"

Immediate anxiety swirled in my gut from the idea of Korey and Cameron going head-to-head in a space where I wouldn't be. I trusted Cameron, more than I probably should, but that still didn't mean that my brain didn't go looking for all the things that could go wrong.

"I do." His voice dropped. "And I have no fucking problem walking into that room to question your ex-husband while still having the taste of you on my tongue."

I sucked in a breath, stunned by every bit that he'd just said.

"Sleep tight, Sunshine," he said, his tone softer, like he knew he could talk me to sleep, force me to leave my worries alone for the night. "I'll see you Thursday."

Apparently, the topic of Thursday was not up for debate.

And I was plenty okay with that.

"I'll see you Thursday," I repeated.

Because there was no turning back now.

CHAPTER SEVENTEEN

cameron

 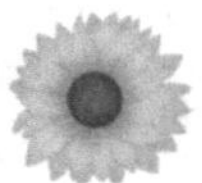 

MY BODY WENT THROUGH a roller coaster of emotions every time I so much as looked at my phone over the next few days, memories of my conversation with Natalie fresh in my brain.

Conversation.

That sure was one way of putting it.

I hadn't intended for that call to descend into phone sex, but as soon as we started to talk about the details of our arrangement, and her voice had turned breathier, and she admitted how much she liked having my hands on her during the deposition, I hadn't been able to stop myself.

And there hadn't been a *reason* to. At the time, I hadn't had the foresight to realize what a distraction it would cause to know what she sounded like when she moaned through a speaker. Or whimpered. Or cried my name.

Every time a name flashed onto the screen of my phone, I hoped that it was Natalie's. And then when it wasn't, immediate disappointment washed over me. Which then sometimes turned to guilt, especially in instances, such as now, when the person who *was* calling me was my mom.

"Hey, honey!" she greeted, and I could hear the smile in her voice. "I don't want to bother you at work, but I just have a quick question."

"You're not bothering me," I assured her extra forcefully, maybe because of the aforementioned guilt. "I was just about to take a break to get lunch anyway."

That was a lie.

I wasn't planning on taking a break to get lunch. I usually ate at my desk and worked through lunch.

"Oh, good." She sounded relieved, which made the guilt worsen. I should really take the initiative to call her more often. "They're not working you too hard?"

Genuine worry wavered in her voice, put there because she knew how hard my dad had worked as a lawyer before he passed. She knew the toll this job could take, but I didn't want her thinking too much about it.

"Of course not," I said.

I'd spent a portion of my morning preparing for the deposition with Korey Abrams tomorrow, but it wasn't my only upcoming deposition, so I'd switched over to review other cases a bit ago.

I was trying to strike a balance, and truth be told, it wasn't exactly working. I badly wanted to prove to Natalie that I had her case under control, especially in the wake of our new agreement, meaning I'd probably spent too much time on it and on her. But the reality was that I still had more than a number of other cases I should be dedicating my time to, cases that Daphne would notice if I let them fall through the cracks.

"How's that production going that you've been working on?" I asked.

"Oh, we don't need to talk about that right now," my mom replied, as expected. Before I could try to convince her that I *wanted* to talk about it right now, she moved on. "Are you free June twenty-fifth? It's during the week, so I know you might be busy, but if you think you could take a night off work, I wanted to surprise Tony and Jay with tickets to a game at Fenway. You guys haven't had some quality time together in a while, and I think it would be good for both of them. Maybe they could spend a night in Boston. You know, get your grandfather out of the house for a bit."

I chuckled because I knew exactly what was happening.

"Is Pops restless and it's driving you up a wall?"

There was a slight pause before she gave in.

"Oh my God, *yes*," my mom groaned, a release of exasperation. "You know I love that man like he was my own father, but I just cannot talk to him about the weather or baseball stats anymore, Cameron. He keeps interrupting my smutty Sundays."

I choked on air at my mom's comment, laughing. I might have gotten my love of books from her, but that didn't mean I wanted to discuss our taste in them.

"He and your uncle still act like they need to take care of me," my mom continued, and I shook myself out of my head. "But I'm *fine*."

My dad's family really took my mom, my sister, and me under their wing after the car accident, and they'd been there for my mom ever since. Sometimes a bit too much, it would seem.

I leaned back in my chair, flicking through my digital calendar, which had already been open on my computer.

"I can clear my calendar that night, Mom," I confirmed. "I'd be happy to catch a ball game and take Pops and Uncle Tony off your hands for a night."

"Oh, good." Her heavy sigh rushed through the speaker. "I'm very grateful for them. You know I am."

"I know you are, Mom," I reassured with a chuckle. "It'd be fun catching a game with them, though. Like old times."

"Thank you, Cameron." The relief in her voice was hard not to notice. "I know you're busy, so I appreciate it. Your uncle and grandfather will, too. You know we're really proud of you and everything you've accomplished, right?"

"I know, Mom."

I stared at my desk, at the pens and papers scattered across it after the morning I'd had. I was scatterbrained, jittery with the anticipation of seeing Natalie tonight. And for the second time in a short while, guilt entered my bloodstream, and my eyes wandered to the photos on my bookshelf—to my parents, Collins, Pops, all of them.

My family had only ever supported me. They were my biggest cheerleaders, and I would never take that for granted.

But they also pushed me to succeed in a way that meant I didn't know how *not* to succeed. I'd been high achieving from the day we took our math minute madness quiz in elementary school and I got the top score in the class. And the more I accomplished, the more it felt like I had to keep accomplishing, so I didn't let them—or anyone—down.

My dad had been so successful in his career, before it had been cut short. And a part of me felt like *because* it was cut short, it was up to me to continue it. And while I knew my family wouldn't disown me or anything like that if I didn't get this promotion, it still felt like they expected me to be the man they lost.

Or maybe *I* just wanted to be the man that they lost, wanted to become everything that he'd been. I wanted to *be there* for my family, like he had been.

A flash of auburn hair out of the corner of my eye told me exactly who'd appeared in my office, slipping in through the crack in the door.

"I gotta get back to work," I said to my mom with regret. "Can I give you a call later?"

Later, between whenever I finished my work and whenever I got a call from the most magnetic woman I'd ever met—the one woman I shouldn't touch but was absolutely planning on it. Tonight.

"Yes, yes," my mom rushed to say. "No need to call back. I don't want to take you away from anything else! Just wanted to check on that date. Love you, Cameron."

"I'll put it on my calendar. Talk soon, Mom. Love you."

Putting my phone on my desk—face down so I wasn't

tempted to see if Natalie had texted me every five minutes—I turned my attention to Julian. He looked a bit sheepish as he dropped into the chair across from my desk that clients usually sat in. "Didn't mean to interrupt, sorry."

I shook my head. "It's fine. She just had a quick question. How can I help you?"

He lifted a brow. "What is this, customer service? I'm here to see if *I* can help *you*."

My lips tugged into a frown as I watched Julian drape an arm over the back corner of the chair and sling one of his long legs across the other.

"With what?"

Julian was a great attorney. I'd known he would be from the moment we connected in law school, thanks to my sister. She described him as the campus big brother at their university in California, said he reminded her of me, especially since we were both law school–bound. Actually, I was already in law school when she first mentioned him, and when she realized he was headed to the same Boston college I was already at, Collins immediately ordered me to take him under my wing.

There hadn't been much need for that. Julian got through law school just fine on his own, but I'd been the one who got my foot in the door at Gardner Law first, after my advisor put in a good word for me with Daphne. And then once I'd established myself a bit, I'd done the same for Julian.

Julian was a big brother. Literally, considering he had five sisters. He was always looking out for people, being overprotective when he didn't have to be, putting his foot where it didn't belong sometimes. He tended to fix problems that weren't his, and sometimes it was annoying, but it was also because he cared.

With me, though?

I was possibly the only person whose problems Julian didn't fix. Our relationship had always been the other way around. Even though I was barely older than him, I'd been a couple of steps ahead of Julian in a life where we had similar trajectories, and he usually came to me for advice.

So it was weird to see him sitting there, asking me if I needed help.

Help with *what*?

Julian shrugged. "Just checking on you. You bolted the other night at the Bellflower. What was that about?"

I leaned on my arm rest, giving what I hoped was a casual shrug. "Just seemed like a family thing going on. I didn't want to intrude."

"Come on." Julian frowned. "You didn't have to leave. You know you're always welcome."

"I wasn't sure if Natalie would be comfortable having her lawyer there," I said, thinking of the thing that might be the most logical. "Didn't want to make anything weird."

"The only *weird* thing was you bolting out of there."

I sighed and leveled him with a look that he delivered right back.

I assumed that Juniper would have told Julian what happened before I left, but maybe she didn't.

I picked my words carefully. "Natalie was talking with the other girls about her...personal life. Specifically involving men." One of Julian's eyebrows cocked. "I didn't think it was an appropriate conversation for me to be involved in, considering I'm her legal representation."

Also considering that the only man who I could stand the thought of her getting personal with...was me.

I knew it was a problem, being that she had instigated a five-night limit on our arrangement. I was well aware that she wanted lessons so she could use what she learned about herself in the future, possibly with other men she decided to date when she was ready. And I was also well aware that *I* wanted to be that man, too.

I didn't really want to teach her what she could have in bed with men.

I wanted to teach her what she could have in bed with *me*.

If it weren't for what she'd gone through with that asshole, I'd be making that very clear. But as it was, I understood her reasoning for wanting to be careful about jumping into anything too fast. I knew why she had boundaries, and I'd respect the hell out of them.

Even if it killed me.

For now, I'd just be there for her in whatever ways I could be.

God, if I didn't just want to take care of her. It wasn't too unlike the internal need I'd seem to have to take care of *everyone* since my dad's death, but I hadn't expected to feel that so intensely with Natalie. I suspected it had something to do with the knowledge that if I didn't show up for her in the few ways she was ready for me to, I might lose her entirely. Before I even had her.

"I see." Julian tapped his chin thoughtfully. "How very professional of you, Cam."

His lips twitched, but I refused to give him the full satisfaction of what he was looking for.

"I'm nothing if not professional, Julian," I said seriously.

God, I was going to hell.

Julian made a little show of clasping his hands, giving me a meaningful look. "I mean, yeah. You usually are."

I narrowed my gaze. "What's that supposed to mean?"

Except I knew what it fucking meant, and today of all days, I did not need a reminder.

Julian lifted one shoulder and glanced around my office instead, not meeting my gaze. "Nothing."

"Did you talk to Noah?" I asked, wondering if there was really a point in beating around the bush.

But Julian gave me a cryptic look when his gaze returned to mine. "You're going to have to be more specific. It's not like I don't talk to Noah all the time, considering he's one of my best friends, the father of my niece, planning to marry my sis—"

"You know what?" I cut in, making a show of returning to my work. "Never mind." I threw a pen at him. "Get out."

He laughed, dodging the pen by one single ginger hair.

Too bad, honestly.

"Okay, okay." He put his hands up in defeat. "I'm just reminding you, again, that I'm here to help if you need it."

I sighed, knowing he was trying, knowing he meant well.

"I appreciate it," I said honestly. "But it's not necessary."

"Noted," Julian said with a nod before he stood, making his way across my small office to the door. "You know I'm always rooting for you, Cam. In more ways than one."

I took a deep breath, feeling the weight of his words on my shoulder. I had all the support in the world, so many people counting on me. And fuck, I knew I should care more about that.

But there was only one person on my mind whom I didn't want to let down.

Someone I refused to give up.

And I told myself it would all be worth it in the end.

six months ago

CAMERON

"Well, I'm a mom," she said, her voice soft, like a confession. But her eyes glowed beneath the bar lights, like she couldn't wait to share more about being a mom. Like that title was the most joyful part of her.

It was possibly the sweetest thing I'd ever seen.

I liked kids. I'd never thought a ton about having them before, but suddenly, I found myself imagining it, thinking about it.

Too fast? I didn't care.

All I cared about was figuring out how to get this woman's number in my phone.

"I have an eight-year-old daughter," she added, her gaze still bright.

She watched my expression carefully, like she wasn't sure how I would react. So I smiled, wanting to reassure her that this didn't deter me. Not a single bit. I thought about asking for a picture—because moms liked to show off pictures of their kids, right?—but didn't want to cross a line or seem overly interested. After all, I was still just a stranger in a bar.

For now.

So I settled with, "She must be pretty great."

One single brow rose. "Oh?"

"I mean..." I shrugged. "With a mom like you."

She rolled her eyes. "You don't even know me."

I leaned forward on the bar and pinned her with a look. "Sunny, I'm really, really trying to change that here."

That got a laugh out of her as she shook her head, like she refused to believe that I was being serious.

"She is great, though," she said when that sparkling laugh died away. "My daughter. She's smart and funny and more perceptive than I'd probably like her to be at times."

I sipped on my drink and tried not to stare too much at her mouth when she did the same.

"I can only imagine."

"You don't have kids?" she asked, and I shook my head.

"Sometimes my sister drops off my brother-in-law for me to babysit when they're in town, but technically, he's twenty-seven." The corners of her mouth indented in amusement, and I added, "Kids are fun, though."

"They are," she agreed and then looked at me curiously, like I was a mystery that needed solving.

I didn't usually like being examined by strangers, but her eyes on me felt like an odd combination of heaven and sin.

And I never wanted her to look away.

CHAPTER EIGHTEEN

cameron

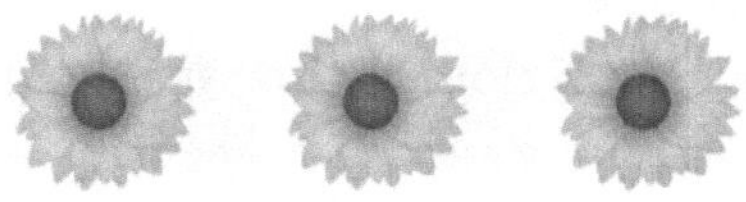

I DRUMMED MY FINGERS on the steering wheel, watching as Natalie crossed the hospital parking lot. I hadn't seen her since she was in the office for her deposition, and I hadn't talked to her since our phone call later that night—the one where she'd touched herself for me, and then I cut her off just before I got to hear the muffled cries of her climax.

Admittedly, part of me wished I hadn't done that. I was so incredibly greedy for those sounds, but I knew the wait would be worth it for both of us, would make it that much sweeter. And the way she fucking *listened* to me? A woman like Natalie London? *God.*

A bubble of euphoria sat in my chest, pressing against my sternum, threatening to burst.

I knew I should have some level of doubt or anxiety, maybe second-guess that I was doing the right thing here, but I couldn't get myself to think about anything but Natalie. About how lucky I was that a woman as amazing as her was willing to trust me with this, was letting me in when I probably didn't deserve it. I didn't deserve to touch her, but at this point, I had no idea how to say no when she was saying yes.

Any kind of doubt was so far in the back of my mind—mostly

because Natalie London was right in front of me. And how could I think of anything else when she was there, giving me the sunniest smile as she walked toward me.

Only she could exude so much brightness after a twelve-hour shift. She must be tired; I could see it in the slight slump of her shoulders and the bit of puffiness beneath her eyes. But she was still so undeniably beautiful, and only eagerness shone in her expression, mimicking exactly how I felt.

I still wore my work clothes after spending all night at the office, but I was so fucking excited to see her. To take care of her, in every way that mattered. She might even let me *hold* her tonight.

"You didn't have to pick me up," she said as soon as she got into the car, unsurprisingly.

"The alternatives were either you getting behind the wheel after a long shift or walking around in the middle of the night." I watched her buckle her seat belt before throwing the car in reverse. "I didn't love either option."

I tried to focus my attention on the road and *not* on how close I was to Natalie after not being able to think about anything but her for the last three days. My hands itched to reach across the center console and close the distance, but I had plans for tonight that involved going *slow*. It was what Natalie needed and deserved, which meant my job was at least to get us home before I touched her. Monday was evidence of our chemistry and how quickly it could spiral out of control.

"It's hardly the *middle* of the night," Natalie argued, and I shot her a look.

Our eyes connected. Only for the briefest moment, but it was effective enough, sending an inferno hurtling through me. Awareness glittered in her green gaze—of us, of what this was, of what we'd said to each other a few nights ago. She tugged her bottom lip into her mouth, chewing on it as she observed me back, and I swallowed a moan as I focused on the road again.

"Your place or mine?" I asked. "Where would you be more comfortable?"

"I wouldn't mind seeing your place," she answered, almost shyly. I bit down on a smile as I took off in the direction of home.

It didn't take long; SCMC hospital wasn't far from Natalie's house, and I only lived a little bit further. When Natalie realized just how *little* of a bit, she burst out a laugh.

"Oh, we do live close," she muttered as I pulled into the parking garage of my apartment building.

"We do," I agreed, glancing over at her. "Convenient, isn't it?"

"I suppose it will be," she said, looking back at me, her tone softer, more sensual. Seductive.

My cock was already swelling in my pants.

I willed myself to keep it together. To *at least* get up to my apartment before losing it.

We stepped out of the car after parking, and I held my hand out to her. "Can I help with your bags?"

"I got it," Natalie insisted, and I let it go. But when the strap of her bulging work tote slipped from her shoulder for the fifth time on our way up to the eighth floor, I swooped it off and carried it the rest of the way.

"Thanks." Her voice came out breathless, and her cheeks flushed red, but it was hard to tell exactly why. She didn't appear nervous, but maybe a little jittery, like she didn't quite know what to do with her body.

I'd fix that for her soon.

Tell her exactly what to fucking do.

"Can't have you wearing yourself out too soon," I muttered as I led her down my hallway.

A brilliant blush spread over Natalie's entire face. "I might be a lost cause in that department, unfortunately. It was a long shift."

I stopped at my door, swiping my key over the lock and pushing it open. "We'll have to see what we can do to remedy that."

Natalie followed me into my apartment, and I noted the way her eyes swept over the interior, from my perfectly stacked shoes to the vintage stadium posters framed on the wall.

"See, I knew you liked things tidy," she said with a click of her tongue.

"Sue me for wanting to clean up in case I brought home a hot single mom tonight," I said with a grin, wanting to make her feel at ease.

I liked my apartment, but it was mostly utilitarian. I had a few touches that made it my own, but Natalie's house felt like a *home*, and she should be proud of what she had done with it since separating from her ex and moving out on her own with Chloe.

"Stop." Natalie stared down at her feet as she kicked her shoes off, meaning I couldn't see the flick of her eyes as she rolled them. But I didn't need to; I knew her well enough by now to read her tone.

"Stop what?" I pressed, stepping close enough to her that when she looked up from her shoes, she had to crane her neck to meet my gaze. Natalie rocked back, her shoulders meeting the wall in my entryway as I crowded her against it.

She didn't seem to mind, though; her gaze slithered over me with longing in it, as though she'd been waiting for this closeness, to once again experience how fucking hot just the simple proximity between us could be. "Stop wanting to impress you? Or stop reminding you how unbelievably attracted I am to you?"

So unbelievably attracted that it was taking everything in me not to immediately haul her off to the bedroom.

I watched the slow shake of her head, unable to take my eyes off her. "You don't have to do anything to impress me, Cameron. And you don't have to compliment me, either." Her voice had lowered, and every word she spoke sent me into a spiral of want. How the hell she did that, I had no idea. "I'm already here, and I'm not going anywhere."

Thank God for that.

"Oh, I know." I pressed a hand to the wall behind her, leaning in. Fuck, she smelled good. She always smelled so fucking good. But I could tell she had just showered, that crisp, clean scent warping with her vanilla perfume. It surrounded me, disarmed me. "I'm not the least bit worried that you're going anywhere tonight, and if you think that's why I compliment you or want to impress you, then you're sorely mistaken."

She blinked up at me, like she didn't understand.

"Is it so hard to believe that I just want to make you happy, Natalie?" I bent my head, letting the tip of my nose drag through her damp hair until I found her ear and my lips grazed the curve of it. "I'm going to make you *so* happy tonight."

I heard the hitch of her breath and couldn't keep my lips from curving in satisfaction.

"I'm already happy," she whispered, and I could feel the bubble in my chest expanding, building pressure inside me. "I'm happy to be between you and a wall again. It's quickly becoming one of my favorite things."

"How coincidental," I murmured, using my teeth to tug on her earlobe and then enjoying the way Natalie sucked in with delight. "*You're* quickly becoming one of my favorite things."

I dropped my mouth to her neck, sucking on that spot, the one I'd been dreaming about, the sensitive hollow above her collarbone that I'd visited before. She tasted just as goddamn good as I remembered. Better, actually. This time, she tasted a hell of a lot more like *mine*. Even if it was just for five nights, even if she wasn't ready for anything more than that, I was going to make sure she knew she was mine each and every time we were together.

Natalie tipped her head back with a groan, letting me take what I wanted, *becoming* mine as she wrapped her arms around my neck, pulling me closer.

Happily taking that hint, I stepped in, crowding my body against hers. Natalie gasped at the collision and then fisted the fabric at the base of my neck, like she needed to hold on to something as I tasted her.

And God, did I taste her. My tongue flicked at her skin as I inhaled her scent, so incredibly intoxicated by it. My teeth scraped, nipping ever so slightly, and the part of me that knew I was giving too much attention in one spot, that I might leave a mark, didn't care. Actually, the thought made my head spin and my cock stiffen in a way I simply wasn't used to.

I'd never been possessive of anyone before, not in the way I knew I was becoming of Natalie.

And I hadn't even kissed her yet.

I needed to. *Oh my God*, I needed to.

"Cameron," she rasped, arching her back off the wall, seeking friction, hungry for it. I understood how she felt; there were too many layers between us, too many barriers keeping us from feeling each other the way we wanted. I hated the restriction of my suit coat and the slipperiness of her light jacket, but I didn't want to stop right now, take time away from anything that wasn't my mouth on hers. Because Natalie was searching for the kiss. She needed it, too. And Christ, did I just want to give in and give it to her.

But I pulled back.

I needed to see her, watch the expression on her face, the shape of her mouth when we redid this moment. Natalie's eyes flicked over me, confused at first, and then realization washed over them. Her lips parted, and I stared at them, breathing heavily.

Wanting, wanting, wanting.

It was just me, her, and this hallway, this wall I had her pressed up against. Six months ago, we'd done this, and it was at this moment that she slipped away from me. And I'd spent every single day, every hour, since then thinking about it, about what I hadn't gotten.

Her mouth on mine.

Her breaths against my lips, gasping for air.

The slide of her tongue when it tangled with my own.

Her body pressed to the wall of my chest.

I fucking needed it—all of it.

And thank the Lord for the bright yearning that painted Natalie's expression, telling me she wanted it, too.

The hesitation I witnessed in her eyes last time had vanished. Her body remained still, not moving even an inch in an attempt to escape. If anything, she pulled me closer, fisted my shirt harder, arched further toward me.

"Tell me I can kiss you," I said, both a pleading request and a command. I needed her to tell me, and I knew she wanted to.

Her nod was slow but sure. "As long as you're sure about this, you can—"

I cut her off before she could even finish, slamming my lips to hers.

I felt the quick intake of Natalie's breath, the surprise in the stiffening of her body. But it lasted only seconds, the same amount of time that she equally disarmed me with the sheer perfection of the kiss and the simple but intoxicating taste of her. And after those seconds passed, after we simultaneously realized what this was, how *incredible* it was going to be, Natalie melted against me.

Her mouth molded to mine, sealing our lips together with a deep moan that vibrated through both our bodies. Natalie sank into the kiss, tugging me impossibly close, as though we could mesh together, as if we could become one.

And I understood why.

It was suddenly crystal clear why Natalie had been so tentative before, in the bar.

Because stopping a kiss like this? When heat erupted inside me and my tongue was already twisting around hers and our breaths collided in harsh pants, desperate for more? When Natalie was whimpering and gasping and tugging my bottom lip into her mouth like she couldn't get enough? Yeah, stopping a kiss like this would be a monumental effort.

There was nothing in the world I wanted more than to drag Natalie down to the ground, right here in my front entryway, and explore and kiss and savor every fucking inch of her. *Holy hell.*

"*Natalie*," I groaned, knowing that while this was beyond perfect, that *she* was perfect, everything I could ever want, it was also dangerously close to unraveling into a territory I didn't have control over. I was so fucking wild for her and this kiss and everything it could be. "*Fuck*, baby."

She gasped my name as I claimed her mouth again, unable to help myself. Everything about this and her and us was just so unbelievably good. I had no idea how I was going to force myself to slow down, but I knew I had to.

"So good." Just a mutter, a reassurance I needed her to hear. "God, I've been dying for this."

I felt her nod as she kissed me back—an almost imperceptible movement that seemed to communicate so much.

"Cam. *Please*." Natalie's murmured cry was almost incoherent, but I heard it, and it only made everything harder. My body was on fire, and everything she did was the fuel.

I cupped her face, roughly holding it to mine, all while continuing to kiss her, over and over until I finally forced myself to pull back.

We stood there panting, lips brushing, breaths mingling.

"Soon, Sunshine," I promised, trailing my mouth to her jawline, refusing to stop completely. "I'll give you everything soon."

Tonight. I'd make her see stars *tonight*.

A shiver of anticipation traveled down my spine.

"Yeah?" Natalie breathed, and I dropped my hands to her waist, still holding her close, still finding bits of her to kiss. Once again, she tipped her head back, welcoming my exploration.

I dragged my palms down over her curves that felt so good, wrapping my touch around her legs instead.

"Yeah," I confirmed and then picked her straight off her feet.

A yelp of surprise flew from her lips, but then she laughed, circling her arms around my neck as I forced my feet to move us out of this hallway. I carried her further into my apartment, weaving to the kitchen and placing her down on the countertop. When I let her go and stepped back, she looked around in confusion.

"You know, I expected a bedroom," she said thoughtfully. "But I suppose if kitchens are what you're into, I'm open to that, too."

I shook my head with a laugh. "For the record, I'm into whatever room has you in it. But also, I'm into making sure you have enough energy for this." She lifted a brow, but before she could protest, I added, "When's the last time you ate something?"

She thought about it.

In my opinion, she thought *way* too hard about it.

"I had dinner around 4:30, I think." She unzipped her jacket, and suddenly, it was hard to focus. She wore a tight white top, which clearly showed the outline of a black bra through the fabric. My mouth fucking watered. "It was just when I could fit it in."

It was almost midnight.

"And what was dinner?"

"A sandwich."

"What else?"

She just blinked at me, and I sighed.

"I'm going to make you something to eat, and you're going to relax and tell me what I need to know."

CHAPTER NINETEEN

cameron

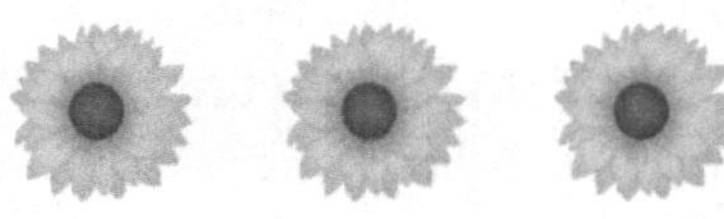

"WHAT YOU NEED TO know?" she echoed while I strode to the refrigerator, grabbing the leftovers of the creamy vodka penne I made last night. "What *do* you need to know?"

There was a reason we'd needed to slow down, and this was it. I wanted to be careful with Natalie, wanted to make sure I understood her. She deserved that, even if I could tell she was impatient right now.

"I assume you're still on birth control," I started, and she nodded, confirming that thought. "What's your stance on condoms?"

She crossed her ankles, staring at them for a second. "I would prefer to use a condom, especially if you haven't been tested in a while."

"I have been tested since my last sexual partner, but I don't have a problem with using condoms," I said, looking at her and hoping she would look up so I could get a better read on her expression.

But all I could see was the slight furrow of her brow, a touch of curiosity, before she opened her mouth.

"When—" she started and then snapped her mouth shut again.

I had no problem sharing, though. "About nine months ago."

"Nine," she repeated, seeming surprised. Her head lifted, and she watched my mouth confirm the number.

"Nine."

No one since you, Sunshine.

She stared at me, and I could see more questions on the tip of her tongue.

"You can ask, Natalie."

No one owes anyone information about their sexual history, but I wanted Natalie to feel as comfortable with me as possible. I wanted her to know that she could open up to me about her own history if she chose to, and if this made it easier for her to do that, then by all means.

But Natalie shook her head in dismissal of the idea.

"The women you've slept with before are none of my business," she muttered, glancing down at her lap.

"Women and men," I corrected and then worked on heating the pasta, tossing it in a pan and throwing the burner on. Once that was going, I took out some of the leftover sauce, coating it over the noodles before giving everything a stir.

When I looked back to Natalie, she was watching me carefully.

"Thank you for sharing that," she said softly and then cocked her head to the side, once again mildly inquisitive but supportive, like she just wanted to know everything about me, about someone's sexual experience that had been different—and likely better, certainly less traumatic—than her own.

But when she stayed silent, I sighed and asked, "What are you thinking, Natalie?"

"Just that—" She pressed her lips together, a pretty blush coating her cheeks again. "It's probably unfair of me to ask you not to sleep with any other partners while we're doing this, but—"

"It's not unfair of you, and I have no problem with that," I replied as I stirred the pasta. Not really a hard ask, considering I hadn't even so much as thought about another person since the moment I laid my eyes on her. How could I when she consumed the entirety of my brain, *all* of it? Every single day. It was exhausting and exhilarating and also slightly mortifying, if I were honest. "As long as I can ask you the same."

Maybe I was a selfish ass for not wanting to share her, but I didn't care.

"Of course," she assured me, and then gave a little chuckle, like the thought of her sleeping with someone else was humorous, like men wouldn't be scrambling at the chance.

But I also knew she wasn't ready to give any of them one.

No, only me.

And I wouldn't be taking any of that for granted. Not at all.

It was quiet for a minute or two as Natalie watched me finish preparing her food. She didn't protest, which told me that maybe she *was* hungry for more than just sex at the moment, but she did ask if she could help. More than once. I shook my head each time, wanting her to get used to the idea that when she was with me, she didn't need to worry about taking care of anything. She did that enough with the rest of her life.

"Let's get some food into you," I murmured, grabbing an empty bowl from the cupboard and filling it up. Natalie eyed me as I prepared it, her lips stretching in a playful grin.

"Are you carb loading me, Cameron?"

I shrugged, stabbing a few pieces of penne with a fork and blowing on them. "Maybe."

"I think you're supposed to do that the night before cardio." Her green eyes glittered. "Not a few minutes before. Don't want to Michael Scott-it."

A laugh burst through my lips. "I think you'll be okay. I don't have anything too strenuous planned for tonight."

More curiosity danced across her face, but before she could ask too much, I lifted the fork.

"Open."

Natalie lifted a brow but did as I directed, letting her lips part.

I stared at them a little too hard, remembering how good they had felt pressed to mine, before sliding the fork into her mouth. Natalie bit it off, humming her satisfaction and chewing. Her eyes watched me carefully, and once she swallowed, she said, "This is really good. But you know, I can feed myself."

"I'm going to make you use your hands later," I said, lifting the fork again once I'd refilled it. Natalie opened her mouth without me asking her to. "I thought I'd give them a rest for now. I bet they've been busy today."

The corners of her mouth curved as she chewed, her interest and amusement shining through her expression even though she didn't say anything.

"And I like it," I said, carefully stabbing more penne. "Feeding you. Do you mind?"

A likely unnecessary question, considering Natalie had already unhinged her jaw for a third time in preparation for more pasta. She shook her head, and I tried to conceal my satisfaction as I slid the fork back into her mouth, watching her tongue dart out, licking it as she took another bite.

"Are you hungry?" she asked after she swallowed.

"Not for food," I answered, and her entire expression lit up. Ravenous, this one.

Soon, baby.

"I'd like it if you shared more of what you're looking for," I continued. "I know you want to experiment with new things. Can you tell me if there's anything specific you want or maybe something you've already done that you want to avoid?"

She shook her head, giving another rueful laugh. "I just want to do something that doesn't involve getting bent over and used until someone else is satisfied."

I froze, my hand hovering midair with another forkful of pasta.

"Excuse me?"

"Yeah." Natalie shrugged, as though what she'd just said wasn't a big deal. "And I always felt like he did it that way because he wanted to imagine it was...someone else? Like he didn't want to see my face. Sometimes it even felt like that when I was on my back. He'd stare at me, but he wasn't there. *I* wasn't there. I mean, of course it wasn't like that at first. But then...well, things changed. You know."

The fork clattered back into the bowl before I shoved it back onto the countertop.

"Fuck, Natalie." I put both hands on the granite she sat on, framing her hips, needing to palm something. I hung my head for a second, not sure I wanted her to see how angry that made me. "God, I really hate him and how he treated you."

"Me too." She forced out a laugh that had no humor to it.

"And I hate that your bar is so low," I said, raising my gaze to find hers avoiding me. I placed a finger beneath her chin, tipping it up so she was forced to see how sure I was that I could change that reality for her. She looked regretful, sad. Like she *knew* her bar was that low but also didn't want to lie about her reality or expectations. "Let's raise it the fuck up, shall we?"

The spark returned to her face as she gave an eager nod.

"I'd like that."

Correction: she was going to *love* it.

I was going to make fucking sure of that.

CHAPTER TWENTY

natalie

AFTER PEPPERING ME WITH a few more questions and making me finish the entire bowl of pasta, Cameron carried me to his room and dropped me onto his bed without ceremony. His apartment passed by me in a blur, and I only got a glimpse of his orderly room before he covered me with his body, pressing my own down into his king-sized mattress.

He shook his head. "You look *so* fucking good in my sheets, Natalie."

I couldn't help a sheepish smile. "Yeah?"

"Mhm," he hummed, nodding as he leaned down, eliminating the space between us. "You'll look even better screaming my name as you come, though."

And then his lips were on mine again, pulling an immediate moan out of me.

Yes, yes, yes.

The tender but dominating way he kissed me was unlike anything I'd ever known, and I *loved* it.

Cameron replied with a gritty "*Fuck*" before he ran his tongue along the seam of my lips, urging them to part. I let him in without hesitating, heat rushing through me as he deepened the kiss. It was all *so* perfect—the graze of his tongue against mine, his heavy breaths mixing with my own, and the warmth enveloping my entire body.

Actually, *warmth* was an understatement. Arousal bloomed inside me rapidly, spreading like an untamed wildfire, leaving me breathless and unsure of what to do. My body had never reacted in such a way to a simple kiss before.

But maybe that was because there was nothing simple about this, what was happening.

Cameron kissed me like it was an *art*.

Instinctively, I wrapped my arms around his neck, pulling him closer, *needing* him closer, but Cameron removed them only a few moments later. He ran his hands from my elbow to my wrists before taking my hands and pushing them back, stretching my arms above my head and anchoring them there. I was trapped beneath him, but in the best way possible. His weight could only be described as delicious and comforting and *God*.

"I just want to explore you tonight," he murmured between kisses. "Learn you. Touch you. See you. Are you ready for that?"

I nodded, eager. He had no idea. Now that I'd given myself fully over to this idea, this desire, I was *beyond* ready to let go. I wanted to hand over any sort of control to him until morning.

"If there's anything you don't like, you tell me." He pulled back so he could look down at me. Our eyes connected in a hazed moment that pulsed with longing. "Okay?"

I nodded again, feeling breathless.

"Aloud, Natalie," he demanded, and I forced a swallow, finding my voice.

"Okay," I vocalized, and Cameron relaxed a little, satisfied.

"Do we need a word for it, or can I trust you to tell me?"

"I'll tell you."

A few years ago, I wouldn't have been as sure of my ability to say no, not with how Korey had trained me to say yes. But thanks to a lot of processing and practicing, I'd unlearned a lot of that. And Cameron had already respected my boundaries more than once, which made me feel that much more confident in my ability to speak up when I needed to, even if he was the one in control here.

"Good girl," he breathed before dropping to press his lips to mine again. *Thank God*. I'd already missed them.

Cameron gave me a hard kiss and then started to travel down my body, dragging his mouth across every exposed piece of skin he could find, igniting sparks everywhere he touched. It felt like so much and not enough, all at once.

When he dropped to my stomach, he pushed my shirt up, exposing my abdomen to brush kisses over it, making me squirm with every inch he lowered. I wanted him lower. I *needed* him lower. I ran my fingers over his hair, over curls that were a little too short to really grab onto, and Cameron groaned, seeming to like having my hands on him, in any way.

"Did you know that this shirt is see-through?" Cameron muttered against my stomach, slipping his fingers beneath the fabric. They slowly smoothed upward, and I arched forward, wanting to help him find what he was looking for. "I've been trying not to stare at the outline of your bra since you took your sweater off."

I smiled to myself because, yeah, maybe I had done that on purpose.

For the most part, I was a practical woman. My closet truly lacked options for sexy clothes, lingerie, or anything that might have been appropriate for a sex arrangement like this. The best I could really do was layer a tight white shirt over a black bra and hope it did the trick.

Apparently, it did.

"Is it?"

I was struggling with coherent thoughts now that Cameron's fingers were tracing the underwire of my bra, skating along my skin. It felt like the path his touch had taken would be seared into my skin.

His smile pressed into my stomach, like he knew I was well aware of how transparent my shirt was.

"Not that I'm complaining," he breathed, nipping at the waistband of my leggings. Meanwhile, his finger was now circling over the cup of my bra, right where my nipple was, sending me reeling from the barely there sensation of him caressing me through the thin fabric.

"You can stare. I don't mind," I said before sucking in, shocked at how such a featherlight touch could cause so much heat within me, how it could shoot straight between my thighs, creating such a strong, undeniable ache. My whole body buzzed like a live wire.

"That's good. I plan on doing a lot of staring tonight."

The huskiness of his voice caused the buzzing to grow louder, my body shakier. I should maybe feel self-conscious about the idea of having Cameron Bryant so entirely focused on me and my body, but I didn't. Nerves had nothing to do with the hammering of my pulse. It was only anticipation, heat, want, *desperation*.

My nipples pebbled, and Cameron groaned in response, immediately taking note. He swiped his finger across one with more pressure, making me arch higher, needing more. And then he gave it to me, cupping his hand roughly over my bra, squeezing me in a way that made me gasp. The quick shift between his gentle exploration and gruff command of my body was *exhilarating*. I loved that I had no idea what to expect from him, that every touch was new, that the possibilities of what might happen were endless. And somehow I knew, from just this very first taste, that they were all going to be *good*. Maybe even great.

Cameron's fingers dipped over the top edge of my bra, and he captured my peaked nipple between them, pinching, causing me to cry out in both surprise and delight.

Great. It was definitely going to be great.

"So responsive." Cameron's raspy voice sounded incredibly pleased as he yanked on one side of my pants and pressed his mouth to my bared hip bone—sucking, teasing, licking.

Heat rushed to my cheeks at his comment. "I haven't been touched for a long time," I admitted.

"A fucking travesty," Cameron growled, dropping both of his

hands to my hips, hooking fingers in my waistband. "This body deserves to be worshipped. You realize that, right, Natalie?"

I looked down to find his smoldering gaze on me, his movements paused as he waited for my answer.

Nodding slowly, I struggled with words. Cameron was poised between my legs, hands ready to rip my pants off completely.

"Don't let anyone touch you ever again unless they're going to do a good fucking job of it. Understand me?"

His voice was brusque while his eyes bored holes into me with their intensity, as though he could barely contain the way he wanted me but was determined to on my behalf, wanting to take things at a pace that would work for me.

But while I appreciated how careful he was being, I didn't need it. Or even really want it. I'd been dancing along the edge of a release for *days*. He realized that, right?

"Will you do it?" I whispered. "Please?"

"Oh, Natalie." Cameron's expression twisted in something akin to pain, but he didn't explain himself. He *did* tighten his grip on my pants, sliding them down my legs in one swift movement. Eager, I helped him, kicking off the stretchy fabric until it was tossed somewhere else in his room.

Cameron found my hips within seconds, kneeling before them like they were his altar. His lips returned to my skin, kissing from my pelvis inward, nipping at the edges of my underwear, like he couldn't decide if he wanted to get rid of them or not.

"Are you wet, Sunshine?" he asked, moving to press open-mouthed kisses to my inner thighs, spreading me wide on the bed for him. "Have I made you ruin another pair of panties yet?"

"Yes," I confessed and looked down to find him staring at me with naked hunger.

He warned me that he was going to do that—stare. But I hadn't expected him to be quite so bold about it, quite so openly transfixed by me, especially considering I wasn't even naked yet.

"I can tell." It was a barely audible murmur. "A drenched little pussy, all for me."

His words—so dirty—and his voice—so deep and gravelly—made me tremble with need.

"For you," I agreed and then held my tongue to keep from asking, *begging* him to touch me. His gaze speared into me, making me feel like I was on fire. My pulse pounded between my legs, a throbbing that went beyond anything that other men had made me feel, and Cameron had barely done anything. I didn't understand it.

I felt his touch a moment later and practically sobbed in relief, pressing my lips together to keep it from coming out. But he didn't go where I expected him to, where I *needed* him to. Instead, Cameron slid his finger beneath the hem of my underwear, sliding it to the side, baring my pussy for him. His touch ran down the side of my slit, skirting away from anything that could give me relief, and I wanted to cry.

I'd never been this turned on in my life, and I had no idea what to do about it.

"So pretty." His awed, raspy voice rolled over me, only adding to my need. "I've thought about this, about you, so much, Natalie. I can't believe—" He swallowed the rest of his words with a low groan, and I looked down to see that one of his hands was fisting the blanket beneath us. "Touch yourself for me. I want to watch."

The command was tight, a slight edge to it. But also reassuring, wanting me to know that this was everything to him.

I slid my hand down my body, tentatively trailing my fingers between my legs.

I'd touched myself plenty of times. It was usually the only way I got off in my later years of marriage with Korey, when he'd either barely touch me or only touch me for his own benefit.

But this felt different. It even felt different from the other night when Cameron talked me through it on the phone. Something about his presence, his watchful gaze, his reassurance. This supervised exploration of my body seemed like it would take me further than it ever had before.

My finger only grazed my clit the first pass through. I

inhaled sharply at the taste of pleasure, and Cameron made a low moaning sound, like I was touching him, too. It only spurred me on, making me increase the pressure the second time, dragging my finger through my pussy with a sensual groan. I bucked my hips, and Cameron's hands moved to my thighs, holding me open, like he was afraid I'd close him off from seeing me.

"Again," he insisted, and this time, I swirled my finger around my clit, tossing my head back at the jolt of fire, from the spreading of heat that spread through my body.

"Is that what you were doing the other night?" Cameron probed, and I nodded, thinking about our phone call, thinking about Cameron's grunts and groans, the rustling of sheets that told me he was frantically stroking himself, too. Would he let me see that? I wanted to see that, wanted to see him. He still wore his slacks and dress shirt, though the top buttons were open and his sleeves rolled up.

"Were you about to come like this?" he followed up with, and I shook my head this time.

The clitoral stimulation—as good as it was—hadn't quite been enough. I'd needed—

"No, not like this," he said softly, answering aloud for me. "You were about to come with your fingers in your cunt, pretending it was me."

"*Cameron,*" I groaned at his words.

"You want it to be me, Natalie?" he asked, a lethal note to his tone, threatening deadly consequences if I wasn't honest. "Want me inside you?"

"Yes," I whimpered.

I'd do *anything* at this point.

But Cameron didn't give in yet. Instead, he murmured, "Were you good this week?" I felt his touch skirt around my clit, grazing my own fingers as he continued. "Did you listen to my directions? Or did you make yourself come?"

I started to nod but then shook my head frantically as I

absorbed all his words. My comprehension was addled, seeming to lag, getting tangled in desire on the way to my brain.

"Which is it?" Cameron made a throaty noise, almost like a laugh, as he circled my entrance. "Were you a good girl?" He slid a finger inside me, causing me to gasp, before pulling it back out. "Or were you naughty?"

"I was good," I promised.

God, I should be mortified by how fast the words fell out of my mouth.

"I know." Cameron's quick confidence in me filled me with a ridiculous amount of pride. So silly, I knew that, but also so *satisfying*. Especially as he began pressing his finger deeper and deeper with every moment that ticked by, filling me with a tantalizingly slow pace. "You're so good, Natalie. I knew you'd listen."

"*Yes*," I sighed, canting my hips to try to find more of him. He was stretching me in a way I barely remembered, and I knew it was only a precursor for what was to come. But already, I felt myself quivering around his fingers, needy for the way he took up space in my body.

All week, I'd been *dying* for this.

"Oh, you're tight, aren't you?" His hoarse voice had a dazed quality to it. "So wet and tight and perfect. *Fuck*."

"Been," I panted. "A while."

"We're going to fix that, Sunshine."

All I could do was toss my head back and gasp as Cameron thrust his fingers into me fully, taking me by surprise and delight. Because it was *so* good—oh, so *very* good.

"Keep touching yourself while I make you come," he demanded, right before he pulled his fingers from my cunt and then pierced them back inside, making me arch up from the perfectly sweet assault of his touch.

Cameron let out a husky, delicious chuckle and used a hand to press me back into the bed, settling right over my lower stomach. He anchored me against the blankets and then fingered me again, rougher, and *oh*—

I could feel him. Inside me. *All* the way inside me. I hadn't felt anyone like this in...*so* long.

"*Natalie,*" Cameron grunted, and I realized I'd stopped my own movements, too distracted by his.

I flicked my finger over my clit again and immediately melted from the combination of Cameron's thrusting and my delicate pressure.

"Mm," Cameron hummed, a familiar sound. "That's my girl."

His praise washed over me, and then he curled his fingers, pressed down harder on my stomach, and found a spot inside me that I'd never been able to reach without help, and oh *God*—

"Cameron!" I cried, and he did it again, harder, more insistent, and my body trembled, feeling unable to hold in my emotions, the pure bliss, any longer. It was...I didn't even *know*.

"I'm here," Cameron answered, sounding so gruff but so comforting, his voice a mix of sin and sweetness. "I'm finally here, baby. You're going to come for me, okay? I've got you."

I gasped as a buildup of something I'd never experienced before pressed against my insides, needing to get out. The hot pressure throbbed, unbelievable and insistent. And Cameron seemed to understand, unrelenting with the precision of his thrusts until something *burst*.

And oh, I *crashed*. I *burned*. I came with an unraveling sensation, powerless to the intensity of it, absolutely decimated with how pleasure erupted inside me.

And *outside* me?

My release was physical in a way unknown to me, wetness flooding Cameron's fingers. More than his fingers. *Oh my God.* His name left my lips a second time, a plea, a thank-you, I wasn't sure what, exactly. But Cameron muttered reassurances as he held me down, demanding that I take the pleasure, all of it. He didn't stop his torments until all my shivers had expired and my body had nothing left to give, until every bit of the orgasm was wrung out of me.

I slumped against the mattress when he was finally done, my

hand flung to the side, my head cradled in blankets. Cameron slipped his fingers from my body, and I closed my eyes, soaking it in.

I didn't open them again until I heard the clanging of his belt, unbuckling.

Cameron stood at the end of the bed, undoing his pants, letting them drop lower on his hips so he could rub his cock through the fabric of his briefs. I stared at the shape of him, exactly what I'd wanted to do on Monday in his office when he told me how hard he was. Because of me.

And now, here was the evidence.

"Still think we aren't compatible?" he murmured, lifting a brow. "I was inside you for less than a minute before you squirted, Natalie."

I choked on a laugh, shaking my head. My cheeks were flushed; I could feel them. Maybe it should be from embarrassment, but I didn't have room for any of that inside of me right now, too drenched in other emotions—yearning, attraction, and an interesting sense of relief, thankful that this was real, that sexual experiences like this *did* exist.

"Is that what that was?" I asked. "Is that what I did?"

He nodded, eyes flaring as he understood the insinuation that I'd never done that before. Only for him, with him. "It was *so* fucking hot, too."

"I—" I was at a loss for words, so I focused on answering his initial question instead. "I never really thought we weren't compatible, Cameron."

"Are you sure?" It was almost a threat. And soon, I figured out why. "I think you might need more convincing."

His fingers—actually, his entire forearm—still glittered with the evidence of my arousal, my climax, almost like he'd purposefully not cleaned them off. And I knew why a second later. He pulled his briefs down, letting his cock free, running a hand over it, dragging his fingertips over his length until it glistened with my cum. He used it to pump his hand, stroking slowly.

And all I could do was...stare.

Cameron was *sizable*, to say the least.

"I think you need to see how hard you make me," he said, continuing to stroke while giving me a half-smile. "I think you need to see how close I am to losing it, just from feeling and seeing you come, Natalie. I almost lost it just now. You have no fucking clue."

I bit down on my lip, eyes fixed on the way his hand wandered up and down, up and down, but softly, without any true intention. Almost like he didn't *want* to take himself over the edge. There was no vigor to it, and for some reason, it fascinated me.

He made a deep, guttural noise, and I looked up to see him staring at my mouth.

His movements quickened, still staring.

I licked my lips, and his throat bobbed.

"Cameron..." I breathed, wondering if I dared to ask. He was in control here, not me. And I liked that. *A lot.* But my mouth was also watering as I watched him.

Luckily, he read my mind.

"You want it," he said, not really a question despite adding, "Don't you? You want my cock in your mouth."

I nodded. I *really* did.

His lips twitched. "I know you're a hungry girl, Natalie."

For him? So incredibly hungry.

"Come here." He crooked a finger. "Sit on the edge of the bed."

I did as he told without thinking more than a second on it, already flooded with arousal from the way he spoke in such a gruff, commanding way.

This was what I wanted. I wanted Cameron to command my body, to make me feel things without making me think about them.

"A good listener, just like I knew you'd be." Cameron's voice was merely a hush, but it settled on my shoulders, and trickled down my back, and made my eyelids flutter shut momentarily. And when I opened them again, I was greeted with the sight of

Cameron's cock inches from my face, his hand still covering it in slow strokes.

I licked my lips for a second time, and Cameron groaned.

His desire shot through me, amplifying mine.

He tapped my cheek with his spare hand. "Open."

Just one word, but it felt so weighty.

I'd never really enjoyed giving head before, but I'd rarely ever had a sexual encounter where it didn't feel like I was being used, where it felt reciprocal. But Cameron and I already had something that felt somewhat symbiotic. A push and pull, a give and take. My pleasure had turned him on, and I felt the same way now that the tables were turned. When a throaty growl emerged from him at the first touch of his erection on my tongue, I had to cross my legs from how strong the ache was.

"Already, baby?" he murmured, pulling back to trace the head of his cock around the shape of my lips, spreading his precum as he did. "I'm barely inside your pretty mouth, and your pussy is already jealous of it, huh?"

I didn't really want to take the time to answer him, not when I had better things to do with my mouth. So I just blinked up at him, curving my lips and leaning forward, urging more of him onto my tongue.

"Oh my—" Cameron broke off with a choked grunt, his gaze fixed on me. "*God*, Natalie."

He slid in further, and I wrapped my lips around him, enjoying the way he swore beneath his breath and tangled his fingers in my hair.

"Suck," he instructed, and I suctioned around him, causing him to tip his head back with another low moan. And because I loved it so much, I sucked him deeper, beginning a steady pace, bobbing my head, swirling my tongue around his cock, noting the taste of my arousal on his smooth skin. Cameron's gaze flew back to mine, watching with heated interest as I worked my mouth around him.

"I imagined being in your mouth like this," he confessed.

Rough. Hoarse. "I know I probably shouldn't tell you that. I know you'll probably think less of me, but *fuck*, Sunshine. I can't help it. I tried, I really did. Until I couldn't. Until you told me this was going to happen, and then I couldn't stop imagining it. It's so goddamn *good*."

His words consumed me, both building me up and tearing me down, reducing me until I was nothing except a woman who wanted to give this man everything I could and make him fall apart. He deserved that for making me feel this way, like I was... good enough. Like I was *more* than good enough. Like I was, for just this moment, everything he wanted or needed.

Gripping his cock in one hand, I started working him simultaneously, with both my mouth and a twist of my wrist. Cameron released a hushed curse and tightened his hold on my hair, encouraging me to take him deeper, work him faster.

I didn't mind at all. I wanted to do and be what he needed. I wanted him to direct me, and he was more than happy to do it, making me suspect that as much as I wanted to be directed, he wanted *to direct*.

We weren't even *just* compatible; we were so much more than that.

"So good," Cameron choked. "My girl's *so* good with her hands. And that mouth—*fuck*."

I tried not to smile. It really was so good, though, feeling him like this, the grip of his fingers in my hair, the tangy taste of his precum, the way he was growing impossibly hard in my mouth.

"Natalie, I'm—" His words got lost when I brought him as far into my mouth as possible. I couldn't quite get all of him—he was so much bigger than I anticipated—but I managed to fit most of him between my lips, choking slightly when he hit the back of my throat. And that was what did it for him.

"Fuck, I—" he tried again, but I didn't need a warning.

I felt him thicken, and I was ready for him, and I *wanted* it, wanted the flood of his cum in my mouth, which I got a second later as Cameron tipped his head back with a cry. He murmured my name, similar in the way that his name was the only thing on my tongue when I came minutes before. I carefully watched his expression, the way he pressed his lips together and clenched his jaw, the way his eyes skirted down to mine, hazy and happy and also dangerous, a glint there.

I slipped him out of my mouth, and the look continued.

I swallowed, and he watched my throat work, as though he could watch his release slide down it.

I licked my lips, and he brought his thumb to the corner of my mouth, wiping cum that I'd missed.

I opened my mouth, and he slipped his thumb inside it, letting me suck and lick it off.

I flicked my tongue over his finger, and Cameron made a noise that caused a rattling in my chest.

"You are..." he started and then shook his head.

But I understood.

Dangerous. This was so good, it was almost *dangerous*, wasn't it?

He pulled out of my mouth again and then stared down my body, noting the way I squirmed. A lazy smile pulled over his face, like he was pleased to see me struggling. I blinked, wanting to beg for something but not knowing what.

Based on the way he was watching me while slowly unbuttoning the front of his shirt, Cameron already *knew* what.

"On your back, baby," he rasped. "It's my turn to taste you."

CHAPTER TWENTY-ONE

cameron

NATALIE FLUNG HERSELF BACK onto the bed like she couldn't get into position fast enough, and I dropped to my knees just as quickly.

I was so fucking eager to make her come again.

The first time had been *mind-blowing.* Hottest fucking moment of my life, working together to get her off, and then having her finally release like that?

We were only getting started, too.

"You can relax, Natalie," I said, feeling the quiver of Natalie's body as I wound my arms beneath her legs, gripped her hips, and yanked her to the side of the bed, tugging her underwear off. I flung it over my shoulder. "I'm going to take care of you."

Lowering my head between her smooth thighs, I spread them open wide and then dropped a kiss to one and then the other, working my way higher.

Natalie squirmed and then choked out stuttered words. "I'm sorry, I just—"

The tone of her voice made me pause, and I looked up to see her lips pursed and her eyes on the ceiling. There was a little wrinkle between her brows, almost like she was confused about something.

"Just what?" I repeated, needing to know what was going on in her brain.

She opened her mouth, but her breath sort of hiccuped, and she had to pause again before pushing herself up onto her elbows, staring down at me.

"No one's ever done this before, and I'm trying not to feel self-conscious about it."

Her confession caught me off guard. I mean, I knew her ex was a loser, but I guess I didn't realize just *how much* of one he was. How could anyone be married to this woman and *not* want to spend days between her legs? I'd been thinking about it pretty much since the moment we met.

Natalie dropped her head back onto the bed and chewed on her bottom lip, uncertainty playing on her features.

"Hey." I said the word like a gentle nudge. "Hey, baby."

She lowered her gaze to me again.

"You have *no* reason to be self-conscious about this. You are so fucking perfect."

A flicker of confidence crossed her face, but she stayed silent.

"Talk to me," I said, needing to get to the bottom of this feeling she couldn't shake.

She could tell me no, and we would stop. In an instant. But I suspected if she really didn't want this at all, she would have said so already. A part of her wanted to experience this, and I badly wanted to show her how good it could be. How good *I* could be.

Natalie cocked her head from side to side before exhaling loudly, deflating. "There must be some reason no one's done it before?"

"Yeah, there is." I leaned forward, wanting to make this exponentially clear. "Every other man you've been with didn't deserve you. They *suck*."

That got a smile out of her, but I wanted more.

"You have the sweetest pussy I've ever seen," I added, struggling not to drop my gaze to stare at it. She was still *so* wet, and I was beyond dying to taste her. "No lie."

Natalie laughed. But the laugh sounded more like she thought I was, in fact, lying.

"I'm serious," I insisted, my voice harder, dropping a few degrees. "You know how you felt a few minutes ago? When you were staring at my cock and licking your lips?"

She nodded, slow, suddenly interested.

"That's how I feel about your hot little cunt." I began lowering my head, keeping my eyes on hers, our connection sizzling. It awed me the way tension continued to stretch between us, even though we'd already broken it to some degree. We'd both already found our release, yet all I wanted was *more*. "And unless you tell me no right now, I'm going to taste it. Because I want you in my mouth so fucking bad."

So bad. She had no idea. I was about to fucking lose it if I didn't get to taste her.

I could see the way Natalie's breath hitched at my words, and I stilled, waiting, giving her a chance to tell me to stop. But she just writhed beneath my hands, almost like she wanted me to hurry up, and I grinned.

Fuck yes.

Her lips parted as she watched me dip my mouth to her pussy, licking a slow path through it, ending on her clit. Natalie gasped, pupils blown wide, an awed, pleasured expression on her face, and I tried to keep my shit together as the taste of her exploded on my tongue. A moan tore from my lips in response.

So. Fucking. Good.

I forced myself to pull away and check in. "Yes?"

She nodded eagerly, her hips doing a little upward motion that made me emit a husky chuckle.

"*Yes*," she said, breathless.

I buried my head between her legs without another word, licking through her pussy for a second time before settling in to lavish her clit with the attention it deserved.

"Cameron," Natalie groaned before collapsing flat onto the bed again. "Oh—oh my God?"

She said it like a question, like she couldn't really believe that it could feel that good. And *fuck*, did that get me going. I couldn't believe I got to be the one who showed this woman how good sex could be when it was done properly, with a partner who cared about your pleasure. *All* I wanted to do tonight was pleasure Natalie London. I wanted to give her so much she couldn't take it anymore. I wanted her crying my name until her throat was raw and her body was spent. *God yes.*

I switched techniques, swirling my tongue around her clit and then dropping lower, exploring her cunt, watching for signs of what she enjoyed, what made her tick.

Natalie loved all of it, but she groaned the loudest when I gave repeated featherlight passes over her clit, the gentle teases working her higher and higher until she was wound tight on the bed beneath me, her body coiled like a spring waiting to be released. She started working her hips, chasing more and more, but I held her down against the mattress, wanting to be the one to give it to her. And as soon as I gave her the pressure she was looking for, she exploded, crying loudly, a sound that washed over my body like a reward. Such a treat. She was such a treat.

"Good girl," I soothed, lifting my head and licking my lips. "Good job coming for me again, Sunshine."

Natalie responded with a babbling of whimpers, trying to turn over on the bed.

Oh, did she think we were done?

"No, Natalie," I muttered, tightening my grip on her hips and holding her in place. "You can take more. You deserve more."

"Cam," she gasped as I returned to my new favorite place and speared my tongue inside her, licking the inside of her walls. "Cameron!"

Her fingers splayed over the top of my head, trying to grip my short hair, but she wasn't saying no, so I kept going, thrusting my tongue in and out. Natalie shivered from the vibrations when I moaned, so fucking obsessed with being inside her that I knew I could do this all night long without stopping if she let me. But I also needed her to come, and I suspected it wasn't going to happen with this alone. I couldn't quite get deep enough, couldn't quite curl my tongue to scrape the right place.

So I returned to her clit, thinking that it'd probably had enough of a break from my teasing. And I was right.

Natalie sighed in a way that I felt in her whole body as soon as my tongue fluttered back over her clit, like she was relieved that I'd made my way home again.

It was so sweet and hot and perfect.

I loved how responsive she was—the way her body twitched and shook with every touch, how her breaths changed depending on what I was doing, and the little sighs and screams that left her mouth, getting louder and louder.

Starting to feel desperate for more of her, I gave my hands permission to wander, sliding one palm up her stomach, slipping beneath her shirt again. Natalie arched into my touch, encouraging it higher, and *fuck*, did I wish I'd gotten her naked before this.

I'd been too busy, too focused on bringing her pleasure as quickly as I could, wanting to prove to her what I could do before she slipped out of my grasp again. Consciously, I knew she wasn't going anywhere. But the pain of having her disappear on me that first night still lingered.

My hands found the gentle curve of her breast anyway, sliding beneath the wire of her bra and cupping her in my palm, enjoying her soft skin, moldable beneath my touch. That, and Natalie's sounds of delight in response, like she was relieved to have my hands on her.

Every single inch of her was unbelievable.

I couldn't ever remember experiencing an attraction as strong as this. My cock ached and pulsed, once again hard as a fucking rock for this woman. It was possible I might even lose it before she did, and she wasn't even *touching* me.

"You're going to come again for me," I rasped, pausing to readjust, bringing my other free hand between her legs. I slid one finger into her pussy with ease because her body was *so* ready for me. Natalie's sharp intake of breath and then following moan told me everything I needed to know, and I added another finger, giving a firm thrust, wanting to pull another orgasm out of her.

"Cameron, I don't know if I—"

"You can," I insisted, because I could *feel* the tension inside her. She was already quivering. "You can give me another one. You come so easily for me, baby."

"I've never—" She paused, crying my name when I sucked her clit into my mouth. Her hips shot up, but I pushed her down into the bed again, moving my hand to her lower abdomen and pressing down.

"Come that many times?" I finished for her, and Natalie just nodded through panting breaths, twitching beneath me. "Oh, honey. We'll be changing that."

Her eyes fluttered shut as my tongue swiped over her pussy, gentle again.

"You've also never had *my* mouth between your legs before, have you?" I added, and she shook her head, her hair becoming a tangled mess.

So pretty like this. She was *so* pretty as my mess.

"You'll come for me because I'm telling you to, Natalie," I insisted, unyielding, not willing to accept another reality.

This was what we both needed.

I drove my fingers deeper inside her and increased the pressure on her stomach, wanting her to feel the way I moved and stroked, mimicking how my cock would one day fuck into her. The thought alone made me *so* goddamn hard, so ready to feel her around me, clenching around my length. But I knew it probably wasn't going to happen tonight, and that was okay.

I had this. I had the feel of her cunt contracting around my fingers, and the sweet-tasting softness that was her clit against my tongue as I delivered those little flicks that she liked. The taste of her, the sensation of her body surrounding mine, it was enough to make my cock pulse and throb, until I was just as on edge as she was. Natalie was a gasping, crying mess, her arms flinging above her head, grabbing at my pillows, and I was bursting at the seams, needing to experience her letting go again.

When she suddenly grew silent, I glanced up to see her concentrating on the ceiling, her jaw dropping, her breathing cut off, and then...a *scream*.

She climaxed with an intensity that shocked even me, her body contracting around my fingers as an earthquake seemed to run through her, breaking her down little by little, crumbling around me. And feeling her like that? *Fuck me.*

I came right after her, cum leaking from the tip of my cock while I still had my fingers stuffed inside her, still had my tongue delving in her pussy. I groaned, sinking into the release, maybe a little shocked, but not really. Because it was Natalie.

"So good," I murmured, slowly extracting myself from her body and brushing a kiss on her inner thigh. "You did so good, Natalie."

I stood on shaky feet, and Natalie stared up at me, looking utterly wrecked and yet so awake and alive, her eyes flaring as she flicked her gaze over my body, getting stuck on the sight of my dripping cock.

"You did that," I said hoarsely.

"You...?" She trailed off, looking stunned, and I just nodded, confirming that thought.

"Yeah, baby."

When she continued to stare, I couldn't take it anymore.

"Come taste it, Sunshine. Taste what you did to me."

Natalie's movements were slower, like all her limbs were weighed down, but she sat on the edge of the bed, dangling her feet over the side and leaning forward eagerly. She licked her lips once, causing my vision to blur, and then parted them. They were glistening wet, puffy, perfect.

I slipped my cock back into her hot, wet mouth, and swallowed a growl when she sucked the cum off the tip.

"That's it," I said hoarsely. "Don't swallow."

She pulled back, releasing me from her mouth, but her throat stayed still, her lips sealed shut.

"Open again."

Natalie obeyed, and I swallowed a grunt at the sight of my cum dripping down her tongue toward the back of her throat. I slid two of my fingers, still soaked in her arousal, onto her tongue, mixing us together.

"Suck me clean, Natalie."

Her gaze blazed as she clamped down on my fingers, licking them off as I pulled out of her mouth again.

"Now swallow," I directed.

Natalie swallowed.

Unbelievable.

"Yeah?" Natalie breathed, and I realized I'd said it aloud.

I nodded, words somehow completely escaping me. I was too busy watching the slight flutter of her lashes and the way her honey-colored hair fell around her shoulders in tangled waves. Her flushed cheeks and sparkling eyes gave color to an otherwise colorless room. She flashed me a soft, shy grin, and she looked *happy*.

A rattling in my chest made it hard to breathe.

"That was..." she started but then just pressed her lips together, the blush on her cheeks intensifying. "Well, you know."

"I know," I assured her. "I know, Natalie."

I knew exactly what it was.

In fact, I suspected I knew more about what it was than she did. But I'd promised her we'd take things at her pace and follow her rules, and I intended to stick to that promise until she realized the same things I did.

"I'm going to clean you up now."

"Oh." She looked away and started to shift, scooting closer to the edge of the bed. "You don't have to—"

I put a hand on her shoulder to keep her from standing. "I'm going to clean you up now," I said again, more forcefully.

Natalie didn't move another muscle until I came back from the bathroom. And then she let me clean her up, using a warm, wet cloth to wipe the inside of her thighs. I took my time, exaggerating the process because I wasn't quite ready to be done spending time with her body tonight. And I wanted her to know that this part was important, too.

After I finally finished, I tossed one of my old T-shirts on the bed for her to put on before I went into the bathroom and cleaned myself up, too. When I returned, I was happy to see that she'd snuggled herself beneath the bedcovers. And she was wearing my baseball tee I'd set out, one from an intramural league I played in back in college.

I tried to ignore the possessiveness running rampant through my veins at the sight, and leaned against the frame of the door with a cocked grin.

"Will you stay here tonight?"

I held my breath as I waited for her to respond.

It was probably bad news for me that I wanted Natalie London sleeping in my bed just as badly as I wanted her in my bed for other reasons, ones we'd just explored. I wanted her tucked under my arm all night long. Just wanted to fucking hold her.

"That sounds nice," she whispered, wiggling her body further into bed. "If you're okay with it."

Thank fuck.

"I'd prefer it."

Massive understatement, but she didn't need to know that.

"When do you need to be home tomorrow? I can drive you." I crossed the bedroom, pulling back the covers to slide in behind her. "And I'll set an alarm for the morning."

"Need to be at Blake's by seven forty-five, so a bit before that," she mumbled as I wrapped an arm around her middle and pulled her back into my chest.

Her body against mine was something I might never get used to. It fit *so* perfectly.

Natalie released a sigh and snuggled into me. I pressed a kiss to her hair, breathing in her vanilla scent and listening to the way her breathing quickly evened out.

She was gone within minutes, maybe even seconds.

And fuck, so was I.

six months ago

CAMERON

"Why do you keep looking at me like that?" I finally asked, needing to know what was going on in her mind.

Sunny immediately startled like she'd been caught doing something she shouldn't and looked down at her drink.

"I thought maybe if I stared hard enough, I'd be able to tell if you're secretly married," she muttered before taking a sip, and I shook my head with a chuckle.

She was right to be cautious, but no.

"Here," I said, dropping my phone on the bar top. "I'm not married, but you can look through this if you want."

I had absolutely nothing to hide and everything to gain by her trusting me.

Sunny laughed, like I was joking.

I wasn't.

I swiped up on the screen to unlock my phone. "I'm serious, take a look."

"Oh, no." She shook her head, sitting back in her chair like she actually wanted to get as far away from my phone as possible. "I don't need to do that."

"Probably for the best," I sighed and pocketed my phone again.

"You might see my gym progress photos and then realize I was lying when I said I didn't go to the gym this week."

"I knew it." Her lips twitched as she pulled her straw into her mouth, chewing on it. I tried really hard not to stare at how her lips wrapped around it.

"It's the only thing I lied about," I promised.

Sunny rolled her eyes as she tried to repress a grin, but her next words were swallowed up by the sudden roar of music as a live band started up in the back of the bar. I knew from other visits to Mulligan's that they did covers on the weekend, which was fine and all if it wasn't so loud and I didn't have a fine-ass woman I was trying to talk to.

But on the other hand...

"Hey, do you like to dance?"

CHAPTER TWENTY-TWO

cameron

I'D DONE SOME INTERNET stalking on Korey Abrams.

In the name of research.

For the case.

He worked for an architecture firm that had offices in both Boston and Springfield, where he planned to move, and I wanted to know more about the nature of that. Was the move mandatory? Something that his office dictated? Did he have ulterior custody motives when he'd originally requested permission from the court to relocate, or did that only happen after Natalie pushed back and triggered him?

It was too goddamn bad he wasn't trying to move out of state. Too bad his family just happened to live near where he intended to bring Chloe. If either of those things were different, this likely wouldn't even be a case.

Fuck, I'd been *waiting* for this day.

And also dreading it, to a certain extent. Because what did you mean I had to walk into a room that had Korey Abrams in it and *not* immediately punch him in the face? I *badly* wanted to use the same fingers that had made his ex-wife come twice this morning to knock him the fuck out.

But I was only able to knock him out in a professional way. And I supposed that would have to do.

"Mr. Abrams," I said with a nod of greeting when I strode into the conference room at Wilson and Thomas Law. "And Mr. Keller, nice to see you again."

I cleared my throat, trying not to think of the last time I saw this man. I really *shouldn't* be thinking about Natalie's deposition...when I had my hands all over her under the table. Then I might start thinking about the way I had my hands all over Natalie London no less than an hour ago. I might start thinking about the way she sighed my name, like I was the only one who'd ever made her feel that fucking good.

"Mr. Bryant," Korey's lawyer said in return, giving me a tight smile as I unbuttoned my suit jacket and sat across from them at the conference room table, mimicking the way we'd been on Monday with Natalie. Also like Monday, a camera sat between us but faced the opposite way this time, trained on Korey.

I caught him staring at me with a furrowed brow.

"I'm sorry, I don't believe we've met before." He leaned forward with interest, and I couldn't help but note that familiar tone in his voice, the one I'd heard before with other men like him. It was an overly polite cadence that felt forced and fake, a schmoozing quality to it that told me he thought he could win anyone over with a flash of his grin. "Who are you?"

I wanted to laugh in his face. Who the fuck did he think I was?

"Cameron Bryant," I answered. "I'm Dr. London's lawyer."

Korey Abrams was a white man with a sharp jawline, a strong nose that wasn't *too* strong, sullen gray eyes, and a full head of brown hair that would have looked better if it weren't slicked back and exposing his slightly receding hairline. And at the moment, all his features were warping, pulling together in a scrutinizing way. A flash of irritation broke through a carefully curated mask as he flicked his eyes up and down, wandering over me. Assessing me.

"Right," he said, trying to cover up the fact that he was ever confused in the first place. "It's too bad that Jacobs retired and she had to start over again with a new lawyer. How very...disappointing for her."

And how very interesting for him to pretend to care about how the change in legal counsel might affect Natalie. Especially when I suspected he was the only one disappointed with this new arrangement.

Natalie's former lawyer had done a fine job with her previous custody case, but he'd also been a sixty-something man who'd probably do well playing Santa Claus at malls on the weekends if he wanted, and I had a hunch that Korey Abrams would much prefer Natalie to be working with someone like that than with me. I was just self-aware and cocky enough about how I presented to people to know exactly what was going through Korey's head right now.

"Dr. London and I have made quick work of getting to know each other," I said, clearing my throat.

"How nice," Natalie's ex replied, his entire body rigid.

Oh, this was going to be fun.

I'd managed to piss him off, and I hadn't even started questioning him yet.

"Can we begin?" he asked, tapping his finger on the table and mimicking boredom. His attitude had already turned from when I first walked in. "I've got a meeting scheduled this afternoon that I need to make."

"Of course." I opened the folder I'd brought with me, flattening it on the table. "We have a lot of ground to cover today, but we'll see what we can do."

Korey scowled at me. He was trying not to; I could tell. But he couldn't quite control his expression, making it harder for me to control my reaction, too. Getting under this asshole's skin was already so goddamn satisfying.

The court reporter entered the room a second later, on cue. He swore Korey in, and then it was time to get to work.

"Mr. Abrams, who is the primary caretaker for your daughter, Chloe?" I asked.

Korey folded his hands in front of him diplomatically. "Due to the terms of our original custody agreement, Natalie is."

"And you obtain custody of your daughter two weekends per month and a full week during summer and winter break, correct?" He nodded, so I added, "You need to give a verbal response so our court reporter can record your answer."

Korey gave me a stony "Yes."

"Have you ever *not* taken Chloe during one of those designated times?"

He shrugged, like the question wasn't a big deal. "I was traveling over Christmas this past year, so Chloe stayed with her mother."

I knew that already, of course, but I raised a brow for dramatic effect. "For the full week?"

"Yes," he answered, but he sounded a lot less sure of himself that time.

"Any other times that you did not abide by the custody agreement?"

"Just once or twice."

"Which one? Was it once or twice?"

He cleared his throat. "Twice. There were unavoidable work trips."

"Over a weekend?"

He cleared his throat a second time. "Yes."

"And what about prior to your divorce and original custody agreement?" I questioned. "Who was the primary caretaker during your marriage?"

"We split those responsibilities," he said, rather vaguely.

We'd fix that.

"Evenly?"

Korey hesitated. "My wife has always preferred to take the lead in matters involving childcare. And I have obliged her, until now."

I stared at him for a long moment, wondering if he was going to correct himself. When he didn't, I clarified. "You are referring to your *ex*-wife, correct?"

Korey's lips flattened, his annoyance growing.

"Yes."

I nodded, but he continued.

"Sorry." He shifted in his chair, arranging himself in a way meant to convey nonchalance—leaning back, slung arm over the empty chair next to him. But his fingers balled into a fist, giving him away. "Divorce or not, I'll always think of her that way. Old habits and all. You get it."

I hated that I couldn't punch him.

"I don't."

How Natalie had endured this man for so many years? Just the thought alone bothered me so much I had to fight a look of disgust off my face.

"Would you like to discuss the habit that constituted the grounds of your divorce?" I forced myself to ask.

His brows furrowed. "I'm not sure what you mean."

"I'm referring to recurring habits of infidelity."

"Objection," Keller cut in, as I expected. "Relevance."

But, also like I expected, Korey answered anyway. Because, of course, he just had to correct me.

"Recurring? It was only one woman," he said, eyes glittering with a sort of dangerous spark now. Good. My goal today was to crack Korey's facade and show the calculating, narcissistic man beneath the suit. "And no, I don't believe that is necessary to discuss."

"I only bring it up because that woman works at the same company as you, correct?"

"Objection." Keller's voice was harder this time, and I fought a smile. "Relevance."

Korey heeded his lawyer this time but gave me a look like he wanted to know where I was going with this so he could somehow prove me wrong.

"When you say that my client chose to take the lead in childcare prior to your divorce, are you claiming that was a voluntary choice on her behalf?" I asked, continuing regardless of his lack of answer, and Korey muttered a yes. "So it had nothing to do with the extra hours you spent at work as a result of the affair you had with your coworker?"

The glint in Korey's gaze intensified. I watched his fingers curl in and out of that fist and was disappointed when I realized it was probably out of the lens of the camera.

"No," he said, but his tone was icy. "It had nothing to do with that."

I lifted a brow. "You took an oath today to answer truthfully, right?"

Keller aggressively cleared his throat. "Objection, form."

Dragging my gaze to him, I flashed an unimpressed look before turning back to Korey. I didn't *really* need an answer to that one anyway.

"Why have you changed your mind to no longer *oblige* my client regarding childcare responsibilities?" I asked instead.

He gave me a blank look, and I clarified. "Why are you now filing for sole physical custody?"

"I am relocating for work, and sharing custody will be more challenging given the distance. Plus, it is in Chloe's best interests for her to be closer to her grandparents and other family. My schedule at the office is consistent, normal. Unlike Natalie's."

I stiffened at the jab at Natalie but didn't let it deter me from my line of questioning.

"Is your affair partner relocating as well?"

Korey gave a slow nod. "Yes."

"Are the two of you in a relationship?"

The room fell into silence. Korey stared ahead, sort of blank-like, as though he couldn't quite decide what the right answer would be. Which was a fail on his lawyer's part because they should have covered this ahead of time.

Truthfully, if he were trying to move Chloe into a two-"parent" household, it would likely strengthen his case, despite the circumstances of how the relationship started with this other woman.

But Korey said, "Yes...well, it's complicated."

So I moved on. Because it was better for us if we didn't clarify things. Hopefully, the judge would focus more on the "it's complicated" than on the "yes."

"Your work is mandating that you relocate?" I asked.

Again, Korey hesitated. I noticed it, and I was sure a judge would. But he said yes a second later, and then his beady eyes shot to his lawyer, as though he knew he was about to do something he shouldn't. "Look, I simply don't believe that Natalie is able to provide the necessary care for Chloe, given her other responsibilities."

I would be circling back to his work relocation, but right now, we needed to set other things straight.

"And what responsibilities are those?"

"Work responsibilities."

I wished I could have rolled my eyes.

"It has already been determined that my client's work responsibilities have not changed from those she had during your marriage, at which point, according to yourself, she was already taking the lead in the matters involving childcare." I gave him a pointed look, saw Keller opening his mouth out of the corner of my eye, no doubt to object to my statement, and quickly added, "But we're here to discuss you, Mr. Abrams. What do your working hours entail?"

"I work a standard nine-to-five position."

"But with work trips on the weekend," I muttered before quickly launching a question. "Any other unusual or late hours?"

He shrugged. "Occasionally, but I would, of course, prioritize Chloe's needs if she was staying with me full-time."

"And what are Chloe's needs?"

Korey considered me, picking up a coffee cup that had been sitting in front of him and taking a long sip.

Part of me suspected nothing was in there.

"I'm not sure what you mean by that," he said finally.

Of course he wouldn't.

"Can you list some of Chloe's childcare needs that you provide or would provide for?"

"Such as...picking her up from school?"

"Yes," I said, succinct. "That would be one example."

"I don't currently do that, but I would if she were to live with me full-time."

I mean, I should fucking hope so.

"Does the local school district not provide transportation to and from home?"

He frowned. "I am sure they likely do, if Chloe would prefer to take the bus."

"You don't know if they do?"

His frown deepened. "I haven't checked on that specifically yet, no. But there is an excellent private school system that I'd be enrolling Chloe in."

I nodded. "What else?"

"Objection." Keller sounded bored. "Vague."

Yes, Korey certainly had a *vague* idea of his childcare responsibilities.

"Does Chloe participate in any extracurriculars that you've been involved in?" I clarified.

"Yes." Pathetic man seemed smug that he knew the answer for once. "She's learning to ice-skate."

"Where?"

"Bay figure skating club," he answered after an elongated pause.

Ah, close. So close.

"Back Bay Skating," I corrected.

"That's what I said."

I'd been wondering when the gaslighting would begin.

"Would Chloe be able to continue at Back Bay if she were to move with you to Springfield?"

"It's a possibility. If she would prefer that, I could drive her there once a week."

"Is that how often she practices?"

"About that, yeah."

Chloe had practice at least twice a week, but the judge would be provided with that information separately.

"Have you attended her practices? Competitions? Shows?"

"I have."

He was *really* trying to save face, but it wouldn't work.

"How many?"

"A couple practices."

"To clarify, two?"

"Yes."

"When?"

"Once last week and another the week before that."

"So, after you filed for more custody?"

Korey looked like he wanted to snap my neck despite the tight grin on his face. His pale skin had a flush working across it.

"Yes."

For a split second, emotion wormed its way through my professional defense walls, making my heart ache for Chloe. She deserved a father who actually showed up for her. I was thankful she at least had uncles and other family members who did, but damn, this man had failed his daughter in so many ways. And it pissed me the fuck off.

"With the distance, how would you manage it if she had practice more than once a week?"

He crossed his arms over his chest, struggling to maintain the fake nonchalance. "There is a private skating club around Springfield."

"What is it called?"

"I—" Korey's voice cut out. "I...I can't remember at the moment."

Figures.

"What else are you involved in?"

"What else are you curious about?" he shot back.

There were so many things left. He realized that, right? He realized everything that went into being a parent, didn't he?

"Do you typically attend parent–teacher conferences?"

"No, but I would."

A defensive tone snuck into his response, but I didn't need his excuses.

"Just a yes or no is fine," I said before asking, "Do you attend field trips?"

"No."

"Do you attend doctor appointments?"

"No."

"Do you manage Chloe's medical prescriptions?"

"No."

Korey Abrams continued to say no for most of the morning.

And damn if it wasn't satisfying getting to prove how pathetically incompetent he was.

CHAPTER TWENTY-THREE

natalie

 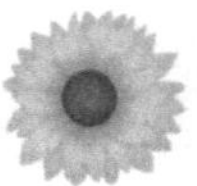 

IT HAD BEEN NEARLY a week since I last talked to Cameron.

He called me after his deposition with Korey to discuss how it went, evaluate further how *my* deposition went, given the results of Korey's, and go over next steps. He hadn't asked me to come into the office. He didn't mention the night we spent together or speak in a way that was even remotely flirtatious. His tone had been even and his cadence patient as I wrapped my head around the details I needed to know. Nothing like how he'd spoken to me while I was splayed out on his bed.

He said the judge might order a mediation to avoid the case going to trial. But he then followed up by saying it was possible the judge would skip it, considering this wasn't our first custody case rodeo, and Korey and I had clearly been unsuccessful with coming to terms on this.

I also suspected Korey didn't *want* to come to terms.

He wanted to play this little game for as long as he could, keeping us tangled in his web.

When Cameron and I hung up, I felt...lost.

And turned on?

Everything he'd said was entirely professional, but just his voice was like a wet dream, especially when it brought back reminders of the other night when he'd called me baby and given me hot little commands like "Suck" while watching me wrap my lips around his cock with a burning, bright gaze.

God, I wanted more.

He'd pushed me to the brink of ruin on Thursday night, so I wasn't surprised when he turned off the lights, wrapped his arms around me, and hadn't initiated sex. I was spent, and I suspected he knew it.

Now, though? Now, I wanted it.

But Cameron hadn't called again, and it had been over a week since we last saw each other.

Was I supposed to be the one who reached out to him? I'd never had a sex arrangement before. I didn't know how it worked, how I was supposed to go about scheduling these...lessons. Or whatever they were. All I knew was that I wanted another one. I'd already learned that my body could apparently come three times in a row, that I was capable of *squirting*, and that I oddly really liked being told what to do. It was a lot to wrap my head around, if I were being honest, but I still wanted *more*.

"Put your helmet on," I said to Chloe. For the fifth time.

The flower-printed helmet was in her hand, but my daughter kept finding other things to do other than actually putting it on. Adjust the seat on her bike, test the brakes, ring the bell on her handlebars.

This girl. I loved her, but damn was she stubborn.

She swung her leg up and over the bike, mounting it.

"Chlo," I said, and she threw me a scowl over her shoulder before I could even finish my sentence.

"I hate my helmet," she whined.

"They save lives," I pointed out. "You know how I know that?"

I'd seen what happened to skulls both when helmets were on and helmets were off, and there was one option that was better than the other.

Chloe was unfazed by my factual rebuttal, still making a disgusted face at her helmet.

"We're not even crossing any major roads," she pouted, but I just pointed at the helmet and then pointed at her head, and she gave in.

"If you want to go shopping for a new one you like better, we can," I offered, the only consolation I could think of. Wearing a helmet was not negotiable, but I'd buy her a new one if she wanted.

Chloe sighed and accepted my olive branch with a mumbled "Yes, please." Then she buckled her straps and started riding down the sidewalk toward the park a few blocks from our house.

I followed behind, keeping her in my line of vision as best as I could. We'd gone to this park countless times, so I wasn't worried. Chloe knew not to get too far ahead of me.

Using the rare few minutes of uninterrupted time, I pulled out my phone and called Ellie.

"Nat!" she answered after the first ring. "You *are* alive."

"Sorry," I groaned, remembering I hadn't responded after she texted me last week. It had been the middle of the shift, and then afterward, I'd been so focused on getting ready to meet Cameron that it completely slipped out of my mind. "Things have been..." I waffled, trying to find the right words. "You know."

"No, I don't. Tell me more."

"Just busy," I said vaguely. "Nothing unusual."

Nothing like climbing into your lawyer's bed or anything.

"Uh-huh."

Unfortunately, I was terrible at delivering lies, and Ellie was excellent at catching them. Not just with me, but everyone.

"Are you still coming next weekend?" I pivoted before she could dig deeper into my life. It wasn't that I didn't want Ellie to know everything that had been going on, but it was really a conversation that would be better in person, glasses of wine in hand.

"I think so," Ellie replied. "Work trip is still on, so...yeah."

I grimaced at the hesitation in her voice.

"I told Noah you would be in town, and he would love if you came," I ventured. "To the party."

"Oh, no," Ellie immediately huffed, and there was a nervous stumbling to her words. "I wouldn't, you know, want to...impose."

"Impose? Ellie, you're practically a part of our family," I said reasonably. Because it was true; she lived down the street from us growing up, and she was always showing up unannounced on our doorstep, infiltrating our family gatherings. And it was never weird, not...before. "Besides, a *lot* of people are going to be there. Friends from college. Some people from Gemma's rink where she works. Some of Noah's *teammates*," I emphasized, and Ellie laughed, already knowing where I was going with that. "You could find yourself a hot football player...and totally avoid Sully if you wanted to."

Her laughter died instantly.

"Who says I care about Sullivan?" she scoffed, and I rolled my eyes.

Despite what either of them said, Ellie and Sully cared an incredible amount about each other. But for some odd reason, they both continued to deny it and live their lives apart.

"We'll figure something out," I promised. "Do you want to stay with me and Chloe?"

"Work booked me in a hotel, otherwise I'd definitely take you up on that so I could spend time with my favorite nine-year-old."

"Mo-om!" Chloe called, and my hackles rose, even though she said it with more of a whiny irritation than alarm. She'd disappeared past the corner I was just turning, and I raced around the bend to find her with her wheel stuck in the slats of a storm drain.

"Speaking of, your favorite nine-year-old has gotten her bike into a little predicament here," I said to Ellie. "Gotta go. Talk more soon?"

"Talk soon," she agreed before hanging up.

Pocketing my phone, I jogged toward Chloe, but before I could reach her, someone else appeared around the opposite corner and ran right up to her side. Someone shirtless, with sweat dripping down their front over rippling muscles. *Abs.*

Jesus Christ, I'd know those abs anywhere. I'd been thinking about them *a lot.*

Gulping, I observed as Cameron popped his earphones out and greeted Chloe with a grin. Then he gripped her handlebars with one large hand and yanked her bike out of the drain, wheel unstuck. The muscles in his arm twisted, and my mouth ran dry.

It wasn't until I heard Chloe's small voice thanking him that I realized I'd stopped dead in my tracks, entranced by the scene in front of me. By Cameron wearing short shorts with a T-shirt hanging from his waistband. By the indents on his hips and his toned thighs. By the way his easy smile shone down on my daughter as he urged her back onto the safety of the sidewalk and then turned around, searching the vicinity.

For me. He was looking for me.

It only took Cameron a few seconds to find me, and then his gaze flared when it met mine. My body responded, heat unraveling in my gut as my brain flashed back to the last time I saw him, when he'd given me a breathless kiss against the door of his apartment, smiling against my lips before we reluctantly walked out the door to his car, but not before a little smack on my ass that I'd been thinking about for a long, *long* time.

Once again, I wondered why he hadn't called me.

He'd enjoyed himself, right?

"It's my favorite mother-daughter duo," Cameron said as I unstuck my feet and walked over to them, repressing the shiver that his smooth voice gave me. He tugged his shirt out of the waistband of his shorts and used it to wipe the sweat from his forehead, and I tried not to stare. But it was challenging, considering the raggedness of his breaths that I wouldn't mind feeling against my skin again, preferably as he fu—

"Hi, Natalie," Cameron said when I still hadn't responded, a little smirk on his face like he knew exactly what I was thinking about.

Goddamn, was I really that easy to read?

"Hi," I answered breathlessly. "I—you—" I flailed my arms in the direction of the park, trying hopelessly to find words and make conversation. "We're going to the playground."

"Ah," Cameron said, and his lips stretched wider. "Over there on Camden?"

"Yup," Chloe interjected.

Now that she had her bike free, she seemed eager to get going on it.

I was also a little eager, both to end this somewhat awkward conversation and to let it drag on forever.

I flicked my gaze over Cameron again. Shameless, I know. But I'd never really seen him *not* wear a suit, and while he knew how to wear the hell out of slacks and a dress shirt, this was an undeniably excellent look for him, too.

"Thanks for helping Chloe with her bike," I said, wishing it didn't sound like I was so...distracted.

Get a grip, Natalie. You've successfully removed portions of someone's skull before to save their life. You can handle talking to a shirtless, handsome man.

"Not a problem," Cameron replied with a wave of his hand. "Chloe's such a champ, I'm sure she could have gotten it herself. But I didn't want her standing in the street."

Chloe nodded as though Cameron was stating facts and she *hadn't* whined my name just a few minutes ago. "I *am* stronger than Luka Stevens, and he's the strongest person in our class."

A laugh slipped through my lips. Not because I didn't believe my daughter might be the strongest person in her class, but because of the matter-of-fact way she said it. "How do you know you're stronger than Luka Stevens?"

Chloe shot me a look, like it had been a ridiculous question. "Arm wrestling match, duh."

"See?" Cameron jabbed his thumb at her. "A champion."

I groaned, immediately thinking of the broken bones I'd

treated. "No more arm-wrestling matches, Chlo. They do not always end pretty, honey."

Her jaw dropped. "But how can I defend my *title*, then?"

Cameron made a noise that I knew was him holding in laughter. He mouthed, "Sorry," when I looked at him before saying, louder, "You'll just forever be undefeated." He clapped a hand on my daughter's shoulder and then switched the subject. "You on summer break yet, Champ?"

"Almost! We just have fun field day on Monday. It's basically optional, but I want to go so I can kick Luka Stevens'—" Chloe cut short at Cameron's raised brow, and I had to press my lips together to keep a straight face.

"Just be careful out there, 'kay?" Cameron said, eyes twinkling. "Your mom's right. Safety first. You need more than strength and speed to be a winner on the field, anyway. You gotta be smart, too. I'm sure your Uncle Noah would agree."

Chloe gave a very serious nod, as though making a mental note.

"I'll ask him this weekend," she said, and I started to worry how intensely she was taking field day.

"Chloe's having a sleepover at Noah's tomorrow," I supplied, struggling to contain my smile. Both at Chloe's energy and at the way Cameron had expertly handled that entire conversation, how he didn't question my parenting stance about arm wrestling and then immediately backtracked to support it before ending the conversation so Chloe didn't continue to argue. *And* she was still happy, which was just an unexpected bonus.

"Yeah, Gemma said we could make a fort again!" Chloe's entire face lit up. "And go to Scoopies! It's my favorite ice cream place."

"That sounds very fun. I *love* forts. And ice cream," Cameron said enthusiastically. Maybe a little too enthusiastically, but I understood as he turned his attention toward me. "And what about you, Mama? Do you have to work?"

I shook my head, ignoring the burst of butterflies at his

sudden, hot attention. And the possible insinuation of his question. "No, actually. Noah and Gemma just felt bad that they haven't had Chloe over since before Delilah was born, so they've been planning this for a while."

Cameron took that in with a slow nod. "So no plans for you, then?"

His eyes trailed over me, and I couldn't breathe.

"No plans," I confirmed.

He was trying hard not to smile as he threw his shirt over his shoulder.

"Maybe it would be a good time for us to review some case notes I have," he said, but his voice was already lower and doing something to my insides.

"That sounds boring," Chloe cut in beneath her breath.

"Very boring," Cameron chuckled before turning his attention back to me. "But your mom is a good...sport. And maybe I could spice it up for her." He raised a knowing brow at the heat rising on my face. "With some tacos?"

"I love tacos," I declared, practically panting.

Oh my God, I needed to get it together.

"Excellent. Tacos tomorrow. At eight." Cameron's short, authoritative voice made my knees weak, and I had to swallow hard. "See you later, Champ," he said to Chloe, raising a flat palm. She jumped up to give him a high five, and then Cameron was off, popping his earphones back in and continuing his run.

I stared after him just long enough to see him look over his shoulder with a smirk.

"Hey, Mom?" Chloe voiced, and there was something about her tone that had me whirling around and dropping to her level so I could see her eyes beneath the helmet visor.

"Yeah, Chlo?"

She chewed on her lip for a second before asking, "Is Cam helping you so I don't have to move away with Dad?"

"He is," I assured her. We'd talked before about how custody worked, in general terms, and she knew what her dad wanted.

Mostly because I'd wanted to check if there was a possibility it was what *she* wanted, even if hearing it would have wrecked me. "He's helping me argue that nothing should change from how it is right now."

Chloe nodded, staying quiet for a moment. "Maybe you should get tacos with him tonight *and* tomorrow night, then."

I sighed, hated that Korey was doing this to her, putting her through this again. While I was happy that she wanted to stay with me, I wasn't happy that she was concerned about it. No child should have to think so much about this sort of thing.

"Don't worry, honey," I assured her. "Cam's been working very hard to figure this out for us. It's going to be okay."

Chloe nodded, but I didn't like the look in her eyes as she took off for the park on her bike, and I needed to remember that whatever happened between Cameron and me...this case and my daughter were the priority here.

Luckily, I still trusted what he told me in his office that day. For some reason, I so *strongly* trusted that he could take care of me in more ways than one, all at the same time.

So hell, I was going to let him do just that.

CHAPTER TWENTY-FOUR

natalie

I DECIDED TO WAIT for Cameron outside.

Early June in Boston deserved to be treasured. The blooming trees, the gentle breezes of summer before the stifling heat rolled in, the people milling about in the evening, heels clicking on the cobblestone.

I took a sip of my wine, hoping it would calm a few of my nerves around seeing Cameron. I felt more jittery than last time. Maybe because I had downtime to think about everything, which didn't happen often. Possibly my expectations were higher, too, since I knew exactly what was in store for me. Or it could be because the teasing scrape of lace against my skin was reminding me what I'd put on beneath my cotton dress.

After dropping Chloe off at Noah's a couple of hours ago, I decided *why not*. Why shouldn't I treat myself to a little shopping spree, pick something up that made me feel sexy and desirable when I put it on? Being a responsible mom didn't mean I couldn't indulge in something that was just for me, right? That was exactly what this whole thing was with Cameron; I might as well play into it.

Now I was wearing lingerie for what felt like the first time in my entire life, feeling a little uncomfortable. Not because I was self-conscious about how I looked—honestly, I'd never felt more confident in something—but because the material cutting into my skin made me squirm with how tight it was. It seemed to be finding dips and curves on my body I didn't know existed and carving into them.

Hopefully, Cameron would peel it off quickly once he got here.

My glass of wine only lasted five more minutes, which aligned perfectly with Cameron's arrival, who strode up to the front of my house at exactly eight o'clock. As promised.

He wore a dress shirt and slacks again, making me wonder if he'd ended up at the office on a Saturday or if that was the only outfit that he owned outside of his short running shorts. Not that it bothered me; he looked so fucking good with his shirtsleeves rolled up, veins twisting across his smooth brown skin as he held a paper bag in one hand.

He stopped short when he realized I was sitting outside, eyes sweeping over me. When he spoke, his voice had a husk to it.

"Next time you want to sit outside at night, call me, and I'll come earlier."

I flicked my eyes up in pretend annoyance. "I'm perfectly safe on my front steps, and it's *barely* dark."

He made a grunting noise but came to sit next to me, settling himself on the concrete stair.

We were quiet for a long moment, the air vibrating with a new frequency now that he was here. Suddenly, my skin also felt stretched too tight beneath the lace, my breathing shallow. The sweet sounds of summer were hidden behind the humming in my veins and the pulse in my throat, which hammered so loudly I wondered if Cameron could hear.

"We should get you a little table and chairs. So you don't have to sit on the ground," he commented thoughtfully, oblivious to my struggles as he pointed to the small cobblestone patio beside my front stoop. The area was slightly overgrown with bushes I'd been planning to trim and a little flower garden I'd been meaning to plant something in. But it was more space than a lot of similar-style homes had outside, so I was grateful for it all the same.

"The ground's not so bad," I replied, even though what he said sounded nice. Maybe one day, I'd get around to it. "I usually sit here because you can see a sliver of the sky through the trees." I pointed above us, and Cameron tipped his head back, following my finger. "And sometimes the stars pop up. Although with all the light pollution in the city, it needs to be a really clear night." Tucking my knees to my chest, I wrapped my arms around them. "I like to sit here when I have a spare second, try to catch a glimpse. Doesn't happen often, though."

"Did you stargaze a lot growing up in Minnesota?" Cam asked, surprising me with the question. We hadn't talked about where I grew up since that night at Mulligan's, but he remembered. Or maybe he knew because of Noah.

"Sometimes," I answered. "My dad worked nights as a security guard, but occasionally, he'd have one off. He'd pile blankets into his pickup truck and drive us out into a field to stare at the sky. He'd tell us stories about them, and Theo, in particular, would eat them up. You could definitely see more stars there, but you also had to contend with the state bird."

"State bird?"

"Mosquitos."

That pulled a chuckle out of him, and he swatted a hand in front of his face where a bug appeared, as if called when it heard its name.

"They can be hard to escape in the summer."

"Yeah," I agreed with a sigh and then pointed to the paper bag in his hands. "What's that?"

"Tacos." He lifted a brow. "Did you think I was kidding about spicing your night up?"

I mimicked his expression. "Are we also working on the case? Because then I might need to change my undergarments."

If I'd misunderstood his intentions about tonight, I was going to be *very* disappointed.

"Don't." A flare of heat crossed Cameron's face as his voice dropped. "The only reason you'd need to change would be to take them off."

Oh, thank goodness.

"I thought you might like having that honor."

Cameron cleared his throat, gripped his knees, and stood.

"Inside."

It was only one word, but it did something to me, reminding me of the short, hot commands he'd given last week when I was in his bed. And Lord, I was desperate to experience that again.

But I was also finding that teasing a stoic man like Cameron Bryant could be a *lot* of fun, too.

My lips cocked to the side. "Are you sure you don't want to wait until the stars peek out? I could tell you some stories."

Cameron didn't miss a beat.

"Is that really what you want right now?" He slung his hand in his pocket and leaned down, speaking in a way that had the hair rising on the back of my neck. Brusque but sensual and smooth at the same time. "I certainly wouldn't mind sitting here with you all night long, Natalie. But did you invite me over so I could stargaze? Or so I could fuck your needy pussy?"

I pressed my lips together, struggling to keep a straight face when he talked like that. "Technically, I think you invited yourself over."

"Oh, you're mouthy tonight." His eyes glinted. "We'll have to fix that."

My stomach flipped, a clear indication that I was in for a treat.

"Inside, Mama," Cameron said, his voice lower and a touch more demanding. And this time, I didn't dare say anything back. I stood on legs that felt like jelly and opened the front door, slipping inside. Cameron followed, and I heard the click of the lock when he turned it behind us.

My footsteps faltered, my breath hiccupping as my stomach hurtled into my throat. It was the anticipation. What it meant to hear him close the door, closing us in together. Alone again.

Cameron's hands shot out, steadying me while gripping my hips. My knees grew weak as he pressed himself into me from behind, his head dipping to my neck.

"You good?" he murmured, lips flirting with my racing pulse point.

Tipping my head, I looked over my shoulder at him. Our eyes connected, tangible, frenzied energy running between us as I nodded, biting down on my lip. Cameron's gaze dropped to my mouth, and he swore beneath his breath. Unable to break away, I reached back, cupping my hand behind his neck.

He knew what I wanted. There was a headiness to his gaze as he watched me.

"Natalie," he rasped. "If I kiss you here, we're never making it up the stairs."

"That's okay," I said with a laugh but forced myself to break away and lead him further into the house, trying to ignore the electric current running through my body.

When I turned to face Cameron fully, he stared me up and down. Then he dropped the paper bag on the coffee table, and it landed with a thud.

"Dinner can wait this time," he said, and it was the first time I'd really noticed a hint of unsteadiness in his tone.

"I'm okay with that, too," I breathed while my fingers toyed with the hem of my shift dress, wondering if I could summon the confidence to take it off. I suspected I could, considering how Cameron's gaze continued to dance over me, staring hungrily, spurring me on. "Do you want to see?"

"Do I want to see?" Cameron repeated, a touch of disbelief in his voice. "As in, do I want to see you take your dress off?"

I nodded, and Cameron shook his head with a rueful smile.

"I must not be doing my job well enough if you honestly have to ask that question."

"Well, I didn't hear from you after last week," I countered, revealing a bit of vulnerability and worry without even really meaning to.

Cameron's grin quickly dipped into a frown. "We talked on Monday."

"About work."

Cameron slipped his hands back into his pockets, seeming to choose his words carefully. "I was trying to give you time and let you set the pace of this. But then I saw you yesterday, and you said you were free, and..."

"And what?"

His expression appeared pained. Desperate. Everything that I'd been experiencing for the last week, making me feel less alone. "And touching you again is all I can think about, Natalie."

His words sank into my bones, and the flood of emotions they elicited dictated my next actions. Peeling my dress over the top of my head, I let it fall to the floor. And then I stood in front of Cameron with nothing on but a red lace bodysuit, vibrant against my pale skin.

"Please touch me," I whispered, and a distinct rumbling came from Cameron's chest. His jaw clenched, and then his fists did, too. I could see them through the fabric of his pants, like he was forcibly holding back, even when I told him not to.

"Has any other man seen you in this before?" he finally asked, taking a measured step toward me.

"No."

"Thank fuck."

The words came out as a grunt as he took two more heavy strides and closed the distance between us. He slid his hands onto my face, and I sighed with relief as he tilted my head back, lowering his own.

"Christ, you're beautiful. And I'm going to touch you *everywhere* tonight, Sunshine," he muttered just before his lips crashed onto mine.

I whimpered my approval as Cameron kissed me hard enough that I was left searching for air. He wasn't holding back, and my body melted at the recognition of his commanding touch, his fierceness. His tongue sought entry into my mouth, and I granted it so he could deepen the kiss. Heat washed over me, settling between my legs.

We stood in my living room, kissing like that. Desperately. Hungrily. Needily. Until standing didn't seem possible anymore. My legs weakened. My body pressed to his, relentlessly trying to get closer, needing more of everything, even as his hands roamed over my curves, fingers sliding beneath the lace bodysuit as he traced the outline of it.

Eventually, Cameron groaned before pulling me down onto the couch, grabbing my hips, and positioning me on his lap. I happily straddled him, my knees sinking into the cushions. And then I wrapped my arms around his neck and let him lead me back to his mouth.

Cameron's hands continued their exploration as we kissed but in more of a frenzied manner, as though he worried I might disappear if he didn't touch all of me fast enough. He ran his hands up and down my sides first and then my back, cupping my ass, squeezing, and tugging me closer to his body, trying to eliminate the space between us.

I gasped when I felt the rough fabric of his pants through the sheer lace between my legs. That and his straining cock behind it, pressing against the apex of my thighs, where I knew I was already wet, likely making a mess. Cameron either didn't know or didn't care, tilting his hips up so that I could get an even better feel of how badly he wanted me, and my breath hitched at the reminder of just how *big* he was. And then I stopped breathing entirely when Cameron's large palms slid up my stomach and covered my breasts, cupping them.

"It's starting to become a problem," he rasped, circling his thumb over the partly visible ring of my nipple.

"What?" I asked, though it was muffled by the moan that broke through my lips when he dragged the pad of his thumb over the tip of my nipple, teasing it. Cameron released a hushed curse when my body responded, growing tight, pebbling beneath his touch.

"How much I fantasize about you." Cameron's reply was almost astounded, like he'd never touched a woman before, even though I knew that wasn't true.

Before I could speak, he bent his head and captured one nipple through the lace, causing me to arch back with a cry. He flicked his tongue out, swirling it around my breast, and I twisted my fingers in the collar of his shirt, needing something to hang on to.

"And now you're wearing this, and I'm so *fucked*, Natalie." His intensity caused a rattling in my bones. "This is all I'm ever going to think about."

Same, I wanted to say. But I couldn't because Cameron was yanking the lace down, exposing my breasts, cupping them in his hands, groaning, and I didn't know how to form words. Only sounds left my lips—pleading, desperate sounds.

"*Oh my God*." Cameron's breath grazed my skin. "Look at you."

"Cameron," I gasped, not knowing how to put into words what I needed.

"Just give me a second. I just need a second to...look at you. Appreciate you."

I nodded, and after several *long* seconds of Cameron doing just that while my heart pounded in my chest, he lowered his head and once again captured a peaked nipple in his mouth, moaning around it. But this time, there was no lace between us, no fabric, and everything felt so new, so hot and wet and sensitive. I threw my head back and closed my eyes, losing myself in the sensations of his lips and tongue and breath.

Cameron spent what seemed like a lifetime exploring my breasts with his mouth, not just kissing, but biting, nipping, lapping. Hushed praises pressed against my raw skin, awed little exclamations about how perfect I was, how good I looked with his hands all over me. I felt like I was barely on Earth, like I might float straight up into the stars, an out-of-body experience. He took his time, almost as though testing my limits, seeing what caused me to whimper and whine. Or, as I was doing now, rock against his hips, desperately seeking friction.

To my despair, Cameron stopped me with a firm hand on my pelvis, fingers digging into my side. "Be good, Natalie."

A sound left my lips at his reminder, both frustrated and undeniably turned on—possibly even more so than last week.

"Such a needy girl tonight," he muttered against my skin. His soft chuckle drove me *wild*. "But I'm not done learning you."

I wanted to complain, but how could I when he continued to give me pleasure like I'd never experienced it before? *God*. His fingers, his lips, his tongue traveled my body, but I felt every touch directly between my legs, like he was stroking me closer and closer to a release. But it was never enough, could never quite get me there.

When Cameron eventually reached between us to undo his belt buckle, my entire body trembled in his lap. I *needed* more.

But then he stilled, and I wanted to cry out in protest. I almost did, until I realized why he'd stopped.

My phone was ringing.

And honestly, I was ready to ignore it, but Cameron was already detangling us, pulling me off him. When I made a little whine, his explanation was incredibly gentle.

"It's Noah," he said, nodding toward my phone on the coffee table.

Shit.

Noah, my brother, who had my daughter staying at his apartment tonight. Right.

I reached to grab the phone before the call went to voicemail, even knowing that I likely sounded breathless when I picked it up.

"Hello?"

"Nat." Noah's panicked voice sent me scrambling to my feet. "I'm so sorry, but I need you to get over here. Chloe's sick."

CHAPTER TWENTY-FIVE

natalie

SHIT, SHIT, SHIT.

Noah assured me that Chloe was *fine*, but I could tell he was worried. Apparently, she threw up after they went to Scoopies, and he thought maybe she'd just overindulged in her ice cream. But then she threw up a second time. And then a third shortly after, and Noah couldn't get her to keep down any fluids. Her temperature was a little high, but nothing alarming. Not yet, anyway.

"I'm sorry," I said while rushing back down the stairs after changing into a T-shirt and shorts. "I'm so sorry we got interrupted like that—"

"Don't be." Cameron shook his head, looking entirely calm and put together. Like his body wasn't vibrating with need like mine was. Like none of this was a big deal, like we hadn't been about to have sex on my couch. "I'll drive."

His keys were in his hand, ready to go.

"You don't need to come," I said, automatic words that I didn't really mean.

"I know I don't." Cameron's voice was as steady as ever, and I hated to admit how much I craved that right now. "But if I handle the driving, then you can focus on Chloe."

That little piece of logic was all I needed to cave.

"Okay." I started out of the front door. "Do you know where Noah—wait, *Noah*." I whirled back around, changing my mind about this entire arrangement. "If you come, then Noah—"

"I'll stay in the car," Cameron replied evenly. He took my elbow and turned me back around, leading me out of the house before he closed the door behind us. "Just give me the directions."

Yeah, okay. Cameron could stay in the car while I ran in to get Chloe. Noah wouldn't need to know. Cameron could drive us back home again, and I could manage the puke bucket because I assumed there'd be a puke bucket.

Everything would be fine.

"It's possible Chloe has already told Noah that we're together working on the case, anyway," he said, continuing to be my voice of reason. We walked to his car and then paused by the passenger door. Cameron leaned forward, pressing a gentle kiss to my forehead that surprised me and caused a flurry of emotion in my chest. A silly reaction, really, considering the things we'd done on my couch less than ten minutes ago. "If Noah sees me, that's what we'll tell him."

I had a lot of other things to say to that. Like how that story might be believable to a nine-year-old, but my brother would see right through it. How I should have considered that Chloe might repeat my plans to Noah in the first place. And how none of that was going to change my mind about letting Cameron drive me to get my daughter. Because he was calm and collected and everything I needed at the moment.

I called Noah from the car, and he assured me that Chloe had been able to hold down a little water since we talked, which was promising. Cameron parked in front of Noah's building, and I ran up to his apartment, where Chloe was wrapped in a blanket on his couch with a bucket by her side, as expected.

Noah assured me he did not want the bucket back.

"I'm sorry, Lo," he said, giving her a hug before leaving. "We'll try this again. I promise."

Chloe made a few noncommittal noises, tucking her head into my stomach.

"You good to get her home?" Noah asked me. "I can come with if you need another set of hands. Gemma's with Delilah."

"We'll be okay," I assured him. "Right, Chlo?"

She nodded, and I said a hasty goodbye, whisking my daughter out the door before she threw up in the entryway of Noah's apartment or he asked too many questions.

"Hi, Chloe," Cam said when we got in the car. His voice was so tender, so gentle, displaying absolutely no irritation or frustration that our night had gotten cut short.

Korey was never this calm in moments of disruption or emergencies. It had bothered me to no end, always having to be the one who kept a level head, who worked through the logistics of a situation and ensured there was an outcome that would keep everyone safe and sound and happy. Well, except Korey. There was no pleasing Korey unless things went precisely the way he wanted them to. He made the littlest inconveniences into the biggest deals, sometimes terrifyingly so, and I didn't miss his raised voice, flailing arms, and blame throwing. Not one fucking bit.

Chloe peeked her head up to look at Cam and squeaked out a greeting before sprawling across the back seat, rather dramatically. I slid in beside her, nudging her to make room for me, which she allowed. Then I stripped off my sweater to cover the seat, wishing I'd asked Noah for a towel or something to put down in the car in case she didn't make it home before another bout of nausea.

"It's okay, Natalie," Cameron said. I looked up to find him shaking his head at what I was doing, fussing over covering his car seats. "Don't worry about it. Just buckle up so we can get the two of you home."

I obeyed, putting my seat belt on and holding the bucket for Chloe as we drove across town, taking note of just how careful

Cameron was with every stop of traffic, making sure the car didn't lurch.

Breathing a sigh of relief when we made it home without any vomiting, I ushered Chloe out of Cameron's car and into the house, covering the couch with an old sheet and putting the bucket in a prime spot. Cam strode to the kitchen and came back a few minutes later, when I was fumbling with the remote, getting frustrated when it wouldn't do what I fucking wanted it to.

Cameron held out his hand, an offer of help that I'd gladly take because I didn't have the patience to find that exact spot where the remote connected to the TV, somewhere behind my stack of crochet needles and Annabeth's cat tower. After I handed it over, Cameron easily turned it on—*annoying*, but I really didn't care at the moment—and found the streaming channel with *Percy Jackson*.

"There you go, Champ," he said, giving Chloe an easy smile, which she attempted to return despite looking a little green.

"Thanks, Cam." She scooted to the edge of the couch, giving a wary glance at the bucket on the floor. "Um, Mom, I think I'm going to—"

She cut off, staring extra hard at the bucket, which I rushed to pluck off the ground and bring closer to her face.

If we could avoid a splash zone, that would be great.

Chloe *didn't* vomit, as I'd been expecting. But she groaned, clutching her stomach, and my chest ached at seeing her like this. She'd been *so* excited to spend the night at Noah's tonight. My poor girl.

"Do you want me to run to the store?" Cameron asked. "I could get some 7UP or Pedialyte. I'm not a doctor, but that's what my mom always gave me. And I didn't see anything like that in your pantry."

"7UP?" Chloe requested weakly, rolling back onto the couch, which told me the wave of nausea must have passed.

I didn't have it in me to say no to her right now, even though I shouldn't let Cameron do me any more favors.

"Does that sound good, honey?"

Chloe nodded, which set Cameron into motion.

"I'll be right back," he said definitively. "Text me any specifics you want."

"Cam, I really appreciate it," I managed to cut in before he got to the door, feeling conflicted. "But you don't want to spend your Saturday night running errands for me."

"You *were* my Saturday night plans, Natalie."

The insinuation of his words wasn't lost on me, nor was the way his gaze burned bright. "But—"

"That doesn't have to change now," he added, leaving me somewhat speechless before he could repeat, "I'll be right back." It was said in a way that harbored no argument. "You can't leave Chloe, so let me go get a few things for you girls. It'll just take a few minutes, and then I can head out, if you want."

Oh, what a dangerous thing to think about—what I wanted.

"Thank you," I whispered.

Cameron nodded, and then he was out the door.

Right before Chloe vomited all over the couch.

Thank God I put down that sheet.

When Cameron returned thirty minutes later, I realized that his idea of *a few things* and my idea of *a few things* were entirely different. He'd bought all the electrolyte drinks the grocery store likely carried, as well as every food item that might fit in the BRAT diet, with the exception of bananas. He must have noticed the overabundance of them in the fruit basket and realized I, at least, had *that* covered.

"There's fresh tacos on the counter," he said after emerging from putting everything away in the kitchen, and my stomach took that inopportune moment to growl. Loudly. Cameron lifted a brow. "Eat them, Natalie. I can sit with Chloe."

I shook my head as I pushed to my feet. Chloe was feeling well enough that she was sitting up, which I knew was likely because she'd just cleared out her stomach a few minutes before. Or what was left in it, anyway. But her temperature was still holding steady, only slightly elevated, and I suspected this was just a stomach virus that needed to run its course.

"That's okay," I assured Cameron. "I'll get to them in a second. Thank you so much."

Cameron narrowed his eyes, like he wasn't sure if he should trust me to take care of myself. But he didn't push it. He just pressed a glass of water into my hands that I hadn't realized he was holding.

"Drink, then," he said before dropping his voice. "You need to stay hydrated, too."

I drank the water, not arguing. Mostly to save me from finding a response.

"Good girl," he muttered, low—so low that I almost hadn't heard him.

I took another long drink, practically draining the glass, and the corner of Cameron's mouth twitched.

"Do you want me to stay?" he asked after a beat of silence where it was just me gulping water, him watching me with fascination, and Percy Jackson talking in the background.

"We're not going to get to any more...case notes tonight. So no, I don't think that's necessary."

Cameron gave a slow nod, seeming to recognize that he'd been dismissed. I didn't mean it to sound like that, but I wanted him to know that staying any longer would shift our predetermined roles. I couldn't ask him to do that. I *shouldn't* ask him to do that. Cameron's expression was mostly unreadable, though, and for some reason, it irked me to no end. What I wouldn't do to get in this man's head, just for a little bit.

"Okay," he agreed. "If you or Chloe need *anything*, text me."

I nodded, but it wasn't good enough for Cameron.

"Promise, Natalie."

"Promise," I whispered. "How much were the groceries? I'll send you some money."

Cameron made a face. "Don't do that."

"But—"

"I don't want your money."

"I'll figure out another way to pay you back, then."

He shook his head at the idea, not even playing into the possibility for an innuendo, like I thought he might. I'd expected to see that twitch of his lips or glint in his eyes, but he actually looked... annoyed. His lips pursed, and then his gaze swept over me, almost like he was analyzing the moment as it stretched on. His body shifted, uncomfortable with standing still but incapable of walking away. It was like he didn't know how to say goodbye without using more than words. Like he wanted to touch me but knew he couldn't.

Touching you again is all I can think about, Natalie.

I'd assumed he'd meant in the context of sex, specifically.

But maybe...

"Night, Sunshine," he breathed, once again low enough that I felt his words more than heard them.

His fingers brushed the inside of my wrist as he walked past me, striding straight to the door. He paused when he reached it, fingers wrapped around the knob.

"Feel better, Champ," he called to Chloe.

And then he was gone, leaving a balloon of emotion in my chest.

six months ago

NATALIE

I actually didn't like to dance.

Well, that wasn't entirely true.

I just wasn't really good at it. Things like rhythm and melody and music escaped me. My brain didn't operate that way, unfortunately. I enjoyed it all, but I couldn't carry a tune or maintain a beat, and did I really want Cam to know that? No, thank you.

But for some reason, when he held out his hand for me to take, I took it.

Hot shivers shot up my arm, radiating from that point of contact. His eyes darkened, like he felt it, too. The mood that surrounded us was flirtatious, fun, but also magnetic and intense. I didn't really know how to describe it but knew it was a dangerous mix. I'd gone down roads I shouldn't have before and regretted it. My past weighed on me heavily, day in and out, and I should really tread carefully.

But when Cam flashed his dimples at me, his smile bright and kind, the music upbeat and inviting, I felt lighter than I had in a really long time.

"I'll dance with you," I answered, and he immediately took note of how I hadn't exactly answered his question.

"You don't have to," he laughed. "It was just an idea."

What a novel concept, not having to do anything I didn't want to

—it wasn't normally something I experienced with other men, my ex in particular. Having choices.

I knew I didn't have to dance. And yet...

"No, I want to," I insisted.

Cam grinned and whisked me out of my seat.

"Then come on, Mama," he murmured, eyes twinkling.

My stomach somersaulted.

Mama.

Being a mom didn't usually make me feel sexy, but when this man said it? It reminded me that that title was the most powerful part of me, and there was nothing wrong with it. In fact, there was everything right about it.

I didn't bother hiding my smile as I followed him to the dance floor.

CHAPTER TWENTY-SIX

cameron

"CAM, MY MAN."

My uncle's booming voice sounded through my car speakers on my way to work, a jarring tug back into reality after my brain had spent the last twenty-four hours tied up in thoughts around Natalie and Chloe: wishing Natalie had let me stay to help, wondering how they were both doing, worrying that Chloe had gotten sicker or Natalie had caught the bug, too.

She didn't text me to ask for anything, not that I was surprised by that. Natalie wasn't used to being with a man who actually helped with things, but I wanted to show her that would never be her reality with me around...even if she wasn't quite ready for that reality yet. I understood why. I understood it went against what we'd agreed upon. But fuck, it hurt to walk away when I could see the stress in her eyes. When all I wanted to do was *help*.

I'd sent one text, asking if Chloe was doing better. Natalie replied, which was something. She said Chloe claimed the 7UP healed her, and then she thanked me again.

I'd barely done anything. She knew that, right? Making sure the two of them had something to eat and drink was the lowest bar in existence.

"What's up, Uncle Tony?" I asked, forcing myself to stop thinking about the London girls.

"Just calling to check in," he said, which I knew was a lie and put me on edge. The minute his name flashed on the screen, a bad feeling sprouted in the pit of my stomach. I loved my uncle, but we didn't usually call each other up out of the blue. There was a reason he was calling, and it likely wasn't good. "How's all that lawyering going?"

I forced a light laugh. "Oh, you know. The usual."

"I heard through the grapevine you might be making partner soon," he said, and I could hear the thick emotion in his voice when he added, "Your dad would have been so fucking proud of you, man. You know that, right?"

"I like to think so," I replied, trying to keep my own emotions in check, considering almost *everything* I'd done in my life had been in honor of him, to live up to his memory. And every day, I wondered what I would do if I failed.

"Pops is proud of you, too," Tony added, and despite my best efforts to remain unemotional during my morning commute, my throat clogged up further at the mention of my grandpa. "He really wanted to come see ya, but I got some bad news."

Yep, here it was. What I'd been waiting for.

I gripped the steering wheel tighter. "What's going on, Tony?"

I needed him to cut to the fucking chase before actual tears formed in my eyes.

"Oh, nothing too bad." Considering my entire family had the tendency to brush bad things under the rug like they were nothing, his words did nothing for my anxiety. "Pops just took a stumble at your mom's last night. Bruised a hip badly, but luckily, nothing's broken."

"Fuck, did you take him in?"

"Of course we took him in," my uncle said with a chuckle. "He's gonna be good, son. But he won't make it to the ball game next week. He can't get around the house great at the moment, let alone Boston. And I should really stick around so his stubborn ass doesn't go and make anything worse. I don't want to put that all on your mom."

A bit of tension relaxed from my shoulders while slight disappointment took its place. I'd been looking forward to having them both in Boston, but all things considered, this was tame news. Tony was right: he shouldn't leave my mom alone with Pops. We'd find another time. I'd offer to come to New York so they wouldn't have to travel. That was likely for the best, anyway.

"We'll reschedule," I said, clearing my throat. "Don't worry about it, Uncle T."

"Knew you'd understand, son," he replied, but I heard a bit of weariness in his voice, and suddenly, I didn't want to wait to find a time to visit.

"Maybe I should come home to help," I offered. "I can move some things around next week and—"

"Nonsense," he cut in gruffly. "You leave us old folks alone and get back to work. You've got a promotion to snatch up. Hey, maybe take some clients to the game, huh? Make the most of it. We'll talk soon, though. 'Kay?"

"Sounds good, Tony," I agreed, still feeling a little guilty as we ended the conversation.

Guilty and stuck on his last words.

Take some clients to the game.

I had two tickets and a sea of clients, many of whom I could really benefit from strengthening our relationship. It could be a chance to show them I was putting in an effort to make them feel important to me and the firm. Tony was right; this would be a great opportunity for that.

But I knew who I wanted to give those two tickets to.

Because I suspected Natalie London would look damn good in a baseball cap.

"Hey, how are things going with the London case?" Daphne asked as soon as I strode into her office, and I couldn't have asked for a better omen that I was making the right call.

Yeah, so *maybe* I wanted to take Natalie and Chloe to the game for personal reasons, but I suspected it was still something that could work in my favor as far as the firm went, too. And the case, if everything went to plan.

"Great," I said, feeling confident in that answer. To put it mildly, Korey had looked incompetent in his deposition. "I wanted to run something by you about that, actually."

Daphne cocked her head to the side, brown corporate bob shifting as if her hair were one solid piece. Her keen, curious eyes stared, inviting me to keep going.

"I have some extra tickets to the Red Caps game next week. I had plans to go with family, but something came up, and I'd like to invite Natalie and Chloe instead. It would give me some more opportunity to get to know Chloe ahead of the trial."

I spoke with Natalie on the phone before this, letting her know that the judge had decided to take their case straight to trial, skipping mediation since Natalie and Korey hadn't been able to come to terms in the past. It was what I'd told her to expect, and she took it in stride, though I sort of wished I could talk to her about it in person. It was better this way, though, to have these professional conversations in ways where I couldn't be tempted to touch her, something that was growing harder and harder to do.

Walking out of Natalie's house Saturday without so much as a hug after I'd planned to spend the entire night *inside* her had just about destroyed me. Of course, I didn't blame her for how everything turned out. While I hadn't been able to stop thinking about how mind-blowing she'd looked on my lap, writhing and needy, I wasn't upset about Noah's interruption. Chloe would always come first. But for Natalie's sake, I wished I could have had the chance to follow through on my promises. And for my sake, I wished I could have kissed her good night.

We'd only had two nights together—not even—and I was already losing my mind. It wasn't exactly a good sign, but I'd never put an end to it, either. I promised Natalie something, and fuck, was I going to deliver. Soon, hopefully.

Of course, I didn't bring *that* topic up on the phone just before this, or the baseball game, not wanting to get ahead of myself. But I had asked if Chloe was continuing to feel better, and Natalie said she was doing good, only bummed that she'd had to miss out on field day at school.

In my mind, it was just another reason to take her to a baseball game. Something to make up for it, right? From what I'd noticed, Chloe seemed to love sports of all kinds.

"I think that's a great idea," Daphne said, brightening at my suggestion.

Thank God.

I probably didn't need to be asking Daphne about this, but I wanted to be *so* aboveboard that no one would think twice. I clearly wasn't afraid of sneaking around with Natalie London, despite what it could mean for my career, but if there was any situation where I didn't have to, I didn't want to.

"I hope you're going to that engagement party this weekend, too," Daphne added, surprising me. "The one Julian and Juniper were talking about." She waved her hand dismissively, like the exact details were lost on her. Or maybe she just didn't want to admit aloud that Noah London was getting engaged. "Continue to foster those client relationships, Bryant."

Well, it was good to know that Daphne supported my integration into the London family dynamics. But honestly, I'd been debating whether I should skip out on the festivities this weekend. It wasn't that I didn't want to celebrate Noah's engagement; I couldn't be happier for him. But spending time with Natalie's entire family while we were both trying to keep each other at arm's length (her more than me)...I wasn't so sure that was a good idea.

But at the same time, I didn't know when else I'd see Natalie next. We didn't have a date for the trial, something I was still waiting on, and while we'd have some work to do ahead of it, everything was still up in the air.

"I'll try to make it," I said, fully knowing that with Daphne's nudging and my desperation to see my favorite single mom again, there wasn't a chance I'd miss it.

CHAPTER TWENTY-SEVEN

cameron

I COULD TELL THE party was already in full swing by the time I pulled up to Noah's new multimillion-dollar home in the Boston suburbs. The sounds of happy chattering, an unrecognizable music genre that I knew was Beau's doing, and joyous laughter swirled in the air, coming from the back of the house.

Wandering through the yard, I spotted Noah first, over by the patio table, wearing an enormous smile, his arm slung around Gemma's shoulders and Delilah strapped to his chest. I didn't miss the sparkle of a new engagement ring on Gemma's finger when she lifted her hand to adjust the little sun hat on Delilah's head. She laughed at something Noah said, pure happiness in the sound, and they both appeared a bit misty-eyed as they stood there together, taking in their surroundings. They had this look like the entire scene before them was too good to be true, and something about it was so *pure* that my heart lurched unexpectedly.

I'd never thought much about marriage before, not in real, concrete terms. I didn't have an *aversion* to the idea, but I'd also never made choices that would lead in that direction. I'd dated casually throughout college, always open with partners about where I stood, that my career path was my priority. I made sure we were compatible in that way, and for the most part, things always worked out.

I figured that one day, once my career was established or maybe once I found the right person, I'd think about relationships differently. That I'd think about marriage...more.

Suffice it to say, I'd thought about marriage more than a few times in the last month.

In general terms, of course.

Two tall men, one much larger than the other, walked up to Noah and Gemma, and based on their size alone, I assumed they were Noah's teammates. Looking closer, I recognized one of them as the Knights' kicker, Phoenix Jones. Not wanting to interrupt their conversation, I scanned the rest of the crowd in the backyard instead, trying to pretend I wasn't looking for one person in particular. A flash of brown hair against the landscape, the exact shade of Natalie's, made my pulse tick faster. But it was Chloe, running across the yard after a golden retriever. Now, I just needed to find her mom.

But after another full sweep of the backyard, I came up empty. Natalie-less.

"She's not here yet."

Fuck me.

Glancing at Julian, who'd made a sudden appearance beside me, I decided not to bother lying.

"Who brought Chloe, then?"

"Her dad did," he answered, and I stiffened at the thought of Korey being here. Luckily, Julian eased my worries a second later. "He dropped her off and left. I guess it's one of his weekends with her, but she begged to come. That's what Blake said when I was talking to him."

As if on cue, the oldest London brother scooped Chloe straight off the ground, sending her into a fit of giggles. The golden retriever jumped into the air after Chloe, standing on her hind legs as though she could save the nine-year-old from her uncle.

I waited until Blake put Chloe back on the ground before looking at Julian.

"Did Blake also say when Natalie was going to show up?"

"Why do you care?" Julian countered, flashing me a grin.

As unhelpful as ever.

I rolled my eyes before spotting Collins.

"You're annoying," I muttered. "Excuse me while I go talk to my sister."

Julian laughed as I strode away from his irritating ass, crossing the lawn to Collins, who brightened as soon as she saw me.

"I didn't know if you'd be here." She beamed as I drew her into a quick hug.

"Well, pretty much all of my favorite people were going to be in one place." I had to raise my voice a little to be heard over the music. "I couldn't exactly miss it."

Seeing Collins made me feel ashamed that I'd even been considering skipping the event.

"Beau will be happy to see you, too," Collins said, pointing behind her to where Beau stood by a makeshift DJ booth. It was a table with two massive speakers sitting on it, almost entirely concealing my brother-in-law. But I could see him enough to know that he was preoccupied with talking to the man who stood next to him—tall, sandy-haired, straight nose, sharp green eyes. There was something oddly familiar about him.

"I would pay you an obscene amount of money if you let me play 'London Bridges.' I promise it's Noah's *favorite* song," the man was saying before pausing to add, "Okay, that's a lie. I don't have an obscene amount of money."

"He has an obscene enough amount on his own," I cut in. "Don't even think about giving him anything."

Beau's head jerked up, his expression morphing into his characteristic easy grin.

"Oh, hey, man. Nice to see you finally show up."

"I'm like..." I checked my watch. "Ten minutes late."

"Okay, no money," the other man said, singularly focused on getting Beau to play some throwback Fergie that I had to imagine haunted anyone with the last name of London in middle school. "Might I offer you my hacking skills?"

Beau laughed, turning back toward him. "Are you *trying* to sabotage this engagement party? Should I also throw in a little 'My Humps,' too?"

"Dude, I am the youngest child out of five," he deadpanned. "I was put on this Earth to annoy the rest of my siblings. Literally no other reason." So *that* was why he seemed familiar—he was one of the London brothers I hadn't met. "Plus, I'll have you know that I made *that*—" He wiggled a finger in the direction of Gemma and Noah, still happily chatting. "—happen. So I think everyone here owes me."

"Not *every* event is about you, Sullivan," a woman's voice said behind me. It was said sort of caustically, without a lot of heat and just a small amount of snark. But Natalie's brother whipped his head around like someone had yelled at him. A flash of stark emotion crossed his face, and then a name I couldn't quite make out fell from his lips like a sigh. The way he stared at whoever was just over my shoulder had me turning in their direction.

But it was another woman who stole all my attention, side-tracking me from their interaction. Natalie stood there, too, looking fucking *stunning* in a coral-colored sundress.

It was unbelievable. That I got to exist in the same place she did for snippets of time.

My mouth ran dry, and my hands twitched, desperate to haul her over my shoulder and take her somewhere no one would find us.

Yep, this was why—this *exact* feeling was why I probably shouldn't have come today. It had been brought to my attention on more than one occasion that I was terrible at masking how much I wanted this woman, and of course, she had to show up looking *radiant*. Like I'd *known* she would.

Natalie smiled at me, giving a little wave of greeting that was altogether too casual for us. In a different world, one where she hadn't walked into my office and I hadn't committed to being her legal representation, one where her ex hadn't hurt her in the way that he had, I'd be sliding my arm around her right now, pulling her into my side.

"Excuse me, *sister*." Natalie startled at the sound of her brother's voice, and I turned back to face him, finding that all the color had drained from his face. His eyes tracked the other woman as she strode away. "I thought you loved me. What the hell?"

"I do love you, Sully." Natalie slipped past me to give her brother a hug, even while he continued to wear a somewhat horrified expression. "But I also love Ellie, and she happened to be in town this weekend, too."

Natalie moved to hug another man who was standing slightly behind Sully. Had he been there the entire time? I hadn't even noticed, but the more I looked at him, the more I realized he looked just like Noah, except even taller and broad-shouldered and with tortoise-shelled glasses sitting on the brim of his nose.

"A goddamn warning would have been nice," Sully muttered, staring across the lawn after the woman who was now crouching next to Chloe.

"If you need to go inside and fix your hair, we'll all cover for you," the quiet brother said, and Sully swung a glare at him.

"What's wrong with my hair?" He ran a hand through his mop of blond hair while wearing a scowl.

"Nothing," Natalie assured him before smacking her other brother on the chest. "Be nice, Theo."

"Ouch." Theo made a show of rubbing his chest, his lips twitching as he cast a warm look at Natalie. "Missed you, too, Nat."

She wrapped herself around his middle, and he threw an arm over her shoulders, hugging his sister to his side and pressing a kiss on top of her head.

"Yeah, be nice, Theo," Sully echoed. "At least I'm capable of *talking* to women instead of just staring at them from the corner."

Theo flushed but held his hands out. "Be my guest. Show me how it's done. I think the love of your life just walked that way." He pointed at Natalie's friend.

"She's not—" Sully broke off with a groan, even as his eyes drifted toward her, too. Then he shook his head and focused on his brother again. "Seriously, though. Please just go talk to her. Put us all out of our misery."

"Julian cuts me off every single time I try. I don't know how he fucking does it," Theo grumbled, and I couldn't withhold a chuckle, causing everyone to look at me.

"Sorry," I muttered. "It's just, that sounds exactly like Julian."

I had to assume they were talking about one of Julian's sisters because that was the only situation I could see Julian interrupting. Besides Gemma, there were four more of them running around here, all with flashes of long, gingery hair.

"Theo, Sully," Natalie said, detaching herself from Theo's side and taking advantage of her brothers' shift in attention to introduce me. "This is Cameron Bryant. He's the lawyer helping with Chloe's custody case, and he works with Julian. Cameron, these are my other brothers."

"The *better* brothers," Sully added beneath his breath before sticking his hand out. "Nice to meet you, man. Thanks for taking care of our girls."

I shook Sully's hand, trying to figure out what to do with the odd sensation that filled my chest at his words.

I *really* liked the idea of taking care of the London girls.

"Anytime. It's nice to meet you both."

"Nice to meet you, Cameron," Theo echoed, also reaching out, and I took his hand. "Please get rid of that weaselly-ass, pathetic man for us."

"Working on it," I assured him, and then both men's attention wandered. I didn't look around to figure out where, exactly, they were staring. Or rather, at whom. But I had a pretty damn good idea.

"Chloe must be feeling better," I said to Natalie, nodding to where her daughter was attempting to climb a tree.

Natalie followed my line of vision and then swore beneath her breath, watching Chloe with careful eyes. "She's going to kill me with stress one day." Her eyes flicked to me, tossing a gentle smile my way. "But yes, she's feeling much better. Thanks again, for everything."

"Of course," I said. "It's too bad she missed field day."

Natalie sighed. "I know, but she had a low-grade fever most of Sunday, and there was no way she should be running around in the hot sun the next day. Chloe doesn't exactly know the concept of 'take it easy.'"

At that exact moment, Chloe jumped off the lowest branch of a tree and rolled over the ground. Natalie grimaced, watching, but Chloe popped back up right away and started running toward the dog again. And then, a second later, back toward the tree.

"Hang on," Natalie said with another heavy exhale. "The last thing I need is her breaking a bone in the middle of an engagement party."

I nodded, watching as Natalie beelined for her daughter, catching her just before she scurried up the tree again.

"So." Another voice appeared at my side, and I didn't need to look to see who it was. "That's still going on, huh?"

"What?"

"The staring at the pretty client, who just happens to be Noah's sister."

I turned my body away from Natalie, forcing myself to face my sister instead. Then I dropped the volume of my voice before responding, even though Natalie's brothers were fully preoccupied with other...things at this point.

"Just between you and me, Lins?"

Collins nodded, her lips stretching. "Of course."

"I think it's going to be going on for a long time." I checked back over my shoulder at Natalie, who had made her way over to Noah and Gemma, Chloe in hand. They were exchanging hugs, smiling, laughing. Natalie's hair shimmered in the wind, and her eyes sparkled in the sun.

Glancing back at Collins, I added, "But she won't always be my client."

I was practically counting down the days until she wasn't.

CHAPTER TWENTY-EIGHT

natalie

HAVING ALL MY FAVORITE people in one place was slightly overwhelming. Tears welled in my lashes when my parents had walked in, both scooping me into a hug before even talking to anyone else.

It had been so long.

I hadn't been at an event with my entire family in *so* long.

Last year, we'd all planned to go to Noah's game together in Minnesota, but there had been an emergency at work, so Gemma took Chloe instead. I'd missed out, again, after so many other times missing out, mostly because of Korey and the way he'd controlled the narrative for years.

He'd tried to do it again today, not wanting to let Chloe come, not at first. I wasn't sure what I would have done. Something illegal, probably, since I refused to beg that man for anything. He relented, luckily, and while I suspected that Noah had called him, I couldn't say for sure. My brother wouldn't admit to anything, but he'd made it very clear that he wanted Chloe to be here.

I was glad he had. Because currently, my brothers were giving Chloe all the attention in the world, making my heart soar. Korey would be here soon, and I was already dreading having to interrupt the fun. But right now? Right now was perfect.

Forever the sportsman, Noah set up a badminton net across the backyard, and all five London men—my dad had jumped in, too—stood surrounding Chloe, feet bare in the grass as they faced off against their opponents, which was all five Briggs sisters, plus Juniper. So six Briggs sisters, essentially.

The Londons were *not* winning.

Every time Theo hit the birdie, he barely tapped it, like he was afraid he'd hurt one of the girls across the net if he actually whacked it properly. But the result was the birdie never making it over the net at all. That, combined with Sully's distraction with Ellie, Chloe's lack of height, and Noah's dazed look of love as he stared at Gemma, meant this match wasn't making it very far.

Smiling at the scene, I walked over to Delaney and tried to ignore Cameron's presence just behind her, where he chatted with Julian and two other guys—Grayson and Bren, other college friends of Noah. Beside them, their wives, Nessa and Madie, were deep in conversation with Cameron's sister, while Ellie had found a friend in Beau, his brother-in-law. I'd overheard them talking animatedly earlier, having an in-depth discussion on why the eagles couldn't just fly Frodo and Sam to Mordor in the first place—a rant I'd heard Ellie give before, on more than one occasion. I was glad she'd found someone who was as passionate about it as she was.

I'd also never seen Sully glare harder at another person before.

Sometimes I just wanted to *shake* him.

"I bet this display is making you rethink the family you married into," I said to Delaney with a laugh.

If *I* was feeling a little overwhelmed, I could only imagine how she felt. This was her first time meeting the entire London crew at once.

"Not at all," Delaney said, shaking her head as she watched the game. Her gaze lingered on Blake, a gentle smile playing on her lips. "This is...beautiful." When she tore herself away from the badminton crew, she looked at me with that same touch of gentleness in her eyes. "How are you?"

"I'm pretty good, actually."

Things had felt...lighter lately.

"Good." She tucked her long, blonde hair behind her ear. "I hope you know that we love having Chloe stay with us. She's always, *always* welcome. If there's anything we can do to impress that upon the court system, please let us know."

"I really appreciate that, Delaney," I said, feeling my throat tighten. "Really. I'll mention it to Cameron."

Delaney glanced over her shoulder at the mention, raising a brow. "Should I tell him right now? He's looking over here."

I turned, finding Cameron's steady gaze on us. Or *me*. As a result, my stomach felt like it was free-falling, drowning in the intensity of his brown gaze. He watched me like it pained him to be as far away from me as he was, and the ache inside me only increased. The attraction between us was so *tangible* sometimes, like a real, living thing, and I didn't think either of us knew what to do about it, nor knew how to handle it.

"Oh, that man is *tortured*," Delaney said under her breath, making me shiver. I hadn't expected her to verbalize it, and there was something about hearing it aloud, the acknowledgment that I wasn't imagining what I was seeing.

"So *now* you can recognize a tortured man," I replied, attempting to take the attention off me and Cameron, to laugh away her comment when really it was tearing me to pieces inside.

Delaney blushed vibrantly as we turned back to the badminton game, and I gave her arm a squeeze. "I'm just teasing, of course. We just all watched Blake pine for you for years and wondered how you never noticed."

She sighed. "Trust me. I wish I had."

Blake turned around then, like he knew we were talking about him. And something about Delaney's expression—likely the pink highlighting her cheeks—made him stride over.

"Are you being nice to my wife, Natalie?" he asked, a faux seriousness on his face.

"She's being very nice," Delaney assured.

Blake smiled, slipping a finger beneath Delaney's chin to tip it up and then pressing a kiss to her lips that only made her blush harder.

"Do you want to play, Lane?" he asked, and she shook her head.

"I like watching," she assured him, and my brother reluctantly returned to the playing field when Chloe called his name.

A second later, my mom appeared, holding Delilah in her arms. "Can't he let her stay the night?"

I didn't have to ask what she was talking about.

"I tried, Mom," I said, knowing I'd have to put an end to Chloe's fun soon and hating it. "But this is his weekend with her, and he didn't have to let her come at all."

I hated that I sounded like I was defending Korey because I wasn't. It was just the facts of the situation.

"He's such a waste of space," my mom muttered, and I snorted at the same time my phone buzzed. I checked it to see a message from the devil himself that he'd just pulled up. *Goddamnit.*

Chloe protested at first, and I couldn't blame her. Once I got her to admit defeat, it took me another five minutes to get her through a line of goodbyes, which were tearful in the case of my parents. She'd also made a lot of new friends today, including all of Gemma's sisters: Janie, Geneivieve, Gianna, and Josie. She gave a high five to Cameron last, and then I couldn't help but notice the way he followed behind as we walked to the front of the house. Blake walked with him, and they were speaking in low tones about something that I couldn't make out.

"Hey, kiddo," Korey said as soon as I opened the car door for Chloe. He glanced at his watch before switching his attention to me, a look of impatience painted on his expression.

"She had a lot of family to say goodbye to," I said. "Since you're taking her away from the party early."

"When will Grandma and Grandpa be back to visit again?" Chloe asked me, soft like she didn't want her dad to hear.

"Soon," I promised her. My parents planned to come for the trial to support me and spend time with Chloe when I was tied up at court. My brothers wouldn't be able to get back here again this summer, though.

"It's almost her bedtime, Natalie," Korey said, voice stern, suddenly the attentive parent.

"When I sleep over at Uncle Noah's, he lets me stay up until nine or ten," Chloe announced, which absolutely *wasn't* going to do what she hoped it would.

"Sounds like a good reason why you shouldn't be sleeping over at Uncle Noah's," Korey said, annoyed, before his eyes caught on something behind me, and his irritation grew fiercer. "What the fuck is he doing here?"

"*Korey*." I glared at him. "We talked about not swearing in front of Chloe."

Korey was too distracted to answer me, though, and I followed his gaze to find Cameron leaning against the house, alone now. He was taking a slow sip from a bottle of beer while he stared straight back at Korey.

Oh my God.

I might have been more concerned about this entire situation if it weren't for the fact that Cameron standing like that was *distracting*. He wore a button-down shirt, as usual, but it was linen. Much more casual, undone at his throat, exposing a bit of his broad chest. His sleeves were pushed up, exposing muscled forearms, and his eyes blazed as he watched us.

"He's friends with Noah," I explained, focusing on Korey again, much to my displeasure.

"Of course you got your brother to get you a new hotshot lawyer," he scoffed. "That explains everything. He paying for it, too?"

"Of course not." I rolled my eyes. "I make more money than you, remember? I can afford my own lawyer."

Korey bristled. "I don't want him hanging around the same places Chloe is. He's a fucking prick."

"*Language.*"

"He's not a prick," Chloe pipped in, sounding confused, and all I could do was grit my teeth together for a second, trying to rein in my frustration.

"We are not having this conversation right now," I said, dropping my voice. I never wanted Chloe to hear us fight. "Cam has been nothing but kind to me and Chloe."

"*Cam?*" Korey repeated, like he disapproved of the nickname. He narrowed his gaze, which darted back to Cameron, and I couldn't help but follow them.

Cameron lifted his beer at Korey, acknowledging the way my ex continued to glare at him while raising a single, questioning brow.

It was a look that said, "*I don't know what your fucking problem is, but I'm not going anywhere.*"

I found it oddly comforting, knowing he was behind me, that I had backup if I really needed it. I also knew I felt that way because Cameron wasn't hotheaded, wasn't someone who might run his mouth at Korey and make things worse. I doubted he'd even step a single foot in our direction unless there was some drastic reason that warranted it, and that was exactly what I needed—knowing I wasn't alone but being supported enough to feel like I could do it alone.

"Fucking prick," Korey repeated under his breath, at least soft enough this time that Chloe likely hadn't heard.

Cameron's lips twitched, like he knew he'd gotten under Korey's skin.

And he liked it.

Ignoring my ex, I focused on saying goodbye to Chloe, giving her a kiss on her head before shutting the car door and watching as they drove away. It wasn't until they were out of sight that I turned on my heel and walked up the driveway toward Cameron.

"I'm starting to wonder what really went down in that deposition," I said, plucking the beer bottle out of his hands and taking a swig. I needed a drink after that interaction.

Cameron watched me with a hooded stare, his eyes focused on my mouth as I swallowed the IPA. Wasn't my usual choice of beer, but I'd take what I could get. When I lowered the bottle and licked my lips, a muscle jumped in my lawyer's jaw.

"We have the entire thing on camera, if you want to watch," he answered after a weighty beat of silence where the summer air seemed to have a pulse.

"I don't really like listening to Korey talk."

"Good thing I don't really let him get a lot of words in."

My lips spread. "No wonder he doesn't like you."

"Feeling's fucking mutual," Cameron grunted, his eyes trailing to the corner where Chloe and Korey had disappeared around. "I don't like it."

I cocked my head to the side. "You don't like what?"

"Chloe going with him."

My heart lurched at his words, leaving me momentarily breathless. I didn't like it, either. In fact, I hated it. But for some reason, I hadn't expected Cameron to vocalize that.

His gaze wandered around the rest of the front yard before he finally looked back at me and lifted his hand, tucking a stray piece of hair behind my ear. "She should be here with your family tonight."

"I know," I whispered, lowering my gaze to stare at the bottle in my hands and the way the beer sloshed against its glass confines.

"Hey." Cameron slipped a finger beneath my chin, raising it so I'd look at him again. It reminded me of what I'd seen Blake do to Delaney, and I wondered for a second if he might kiss me, especially considering how his eyes roamed my face, flicking to my mouth as they did. My heart beat a little faster, but then he said, "I wanted to ask you something."

I mean, of course he wouldn't kiss me. Not standing outside my brother's house. Not where anyone could see us.

Regardless, disappointment threaded through my being.

Our eyes met, a clash of heat, and I gave him a nod to let him know I was listening.

"I have extra tickets to the Caps game on Wednesday night. Plans with my grandpa and uncle fell through. I was wondering if I could take you and Chloe? It's no field day at school, but it's something. I think they might even have root beer floats at the stadium. Or some kind of ice cream, at least."

My lips parted, stunned by his proposal.

That sounded...so nice. I didn't even have to work Wednesday night, and I'd been thinking about what Chloe and I could do that might be special. She'd been such a sports enthusiast lately that I knew she'd love going to a baseball game. And getting to spend time with Cameron was an obvious bonus. For both of us, honestly.

But was it really a good idea?

"Cameron..." I breathed. "That's really sweet, but I don't know."

"Daphne loved the idea," he said, like he'd been waiting to unleash further reasoning on me.

"Your boss?"

He nodded. "I proposed it as client bonding. Strictly professional. Gives me an opportunity to get to know Chloe better." There was a pause before he added, "Of course, she doesn't realize that I've already met Chloe on a number of occasions, but still."

I bit down on a smile but didn't really know what to say. I knew what I *wanted* to say, but...

"If you don't want me spending more time with Chloe, I understand," Cameron offered gently. "But from a professional standpoint, this would be strictly aboveboard. I made sure of it, and we could make sure to tell Chloe exactly what it was so she doesn't get confused."

The way Cameron considered Chloe so carefully with every decision and proposal he made caused my insides to squeeze with a strange mix of emotions. It was so incredibly considerate, but it also made me wonder. Was Cameron so worried about Chloe becoming attached to him because he knew *I* didn't want that? Because he knew I was so worried about spiraling into a new relationship and ultimately causing her more pain if it didn't work out? Or was he worried about it for himself? Did he want to make sure Chloe wouldn't get attached because he had no interest in stepping into a role like that?

I suppose it didn't really matter either way, considering our agreement—the one that didn't go beyond sex. Cameron's motives didn't make a difference, as long as he was following the rules we'd originally laid out, and one baseball game where we were careful about how we acted around each other in front of Chloe wouldn't ruin them.

"I'm sure Chloe would love to go," I said finally. "And I would, too. I'll ask her when she gets home tomorrow."

Cameron's lips split into a genuine smile, his dimples indenting, and I tried to ignore the burst of emotion it caused in my chest.

Just sex—this was *just sex*, I reminded myself for the second time in a matter of minutes. It didn't matter that this man was visibly excited at the idea of taking me and my daughter to a baseball game. It was *still* just sex.

"Excellent," he breathed. "We should probably get back to the party, but first..."

He looked around again, checking for anyone who might have shown up without us realizing it. But the front yard was still empty. I wasn't sure where Blake had wandered off to, but he wasn't anywhere in sight now.

Cameron placed a hand on my hip, giving it a little squeeze as he leaned in. The sudden proximity and heat of his touch that I'd spent *days* thinking about made my breath hitch.

When he spoke, his voice was everything I'd remembered from the other times we'd been this close. Deep. Demanding. A hint of gravel that made flutters erupt low in my belly. "Come home with me tonight. You deserve more than what you got last weekend."

"What do I deserve?" I asked, my voice wispy as desire threaded through me, taking up every part of my being as I thought about what he was saying.

Cameron inched closer, letting his lips graze my ear. "To be fucked, Sunshine. Properly. Repeatedly."

Embarrassingly, a whimper slipped out of me.

But I didn't really care. Not considering how it made Cameron groan and release a hushed "Fuck" before pulling back to wait for a response. He plucked his beer back from my hands, like he needed something to hold onto. Then he took a swig of it, watching me with intent as he swallowed.

Oh, *God*, I wanted to say yes. But I couldn't.

"I'd love to come over...but my friend is in town tonight," I said with a regretful shake of my head. "We made plans—"

"That can be pushed off until brunch tomorrow morning," Ellie cut in, walking out of Noah's front door with a sly grin on her face. "I think I can fend for myself for the night."

"Ellie, no," I insisted, knowing a deep red was coloring my neck and face. Had she heard Cameron's earlier words? "That's not—"

"You're the lawyer," Ellie cut in, sticking her hand out to Cameron. "Aren't you?"

Cameron nodded, his lips pulling into a crooked grin. He'd dropped his hand from where it had been on my hip the moment Ellie walked outside and now raised it to shake Ellie's.

"I knew there was a reason I liked you," she said, and I wanted to melt into the ground. "Ellie Summers. Nice to meet you."

"Cameron Bryant," Cameron replied smoothly. "Same to you."

He looked between the two of us, and if he was bothered that we'd essentially just blown our cover, he didn't act like it.

"I'll leave you two to figure out your plans," he said. "My offer still stands, Natalie."

I nodded, struggling to breathe or formulate words while Cameron pinned me with a long, intense look before walking away.

“That offer involves some horizontal cardio, doesn’t it?” Ellie asked, breaking the tension and making me choke on air as a strangled laugh tried to escape my throat. “Or maybe standing cardio? Upside-down cardio? Experimental cardio?”

When she just stared at me, I threw up my hands.

“All of the above? I don’t know exactly what he has planned, but he’s...talented.”

My cheeks flushed, but Ellie just looked positively delighted by my answer. “I knew he was a man comfortable in his own sexuality.”

“You cannot tell *anyone*, Ellie.”

“Sworn to secrecy,” she promised, pretending to zip her lips shut. And then unzip them again. “But you need to fill me in on the whole secret. I’m not against begging for the details.”

“Can I fill you in over mimosas tomorrow?” I asked, feeling a little guilty at the idea of not spending the rest of the night with her. Even though the sun was already going down, and we both knew we’d probably fall asleep promptly at ten o’clock after one glass of wine.

But Ellie’s face lit up with excitement, pushing my guilt away. “I was hoping you’d say that.”

I laughed and then pulled out my phone, sending Cameron two words.

I’m in.

six months ago

CAMERON

Getting this woman into my arms felt like the single greatest accomplishment of my life, and I tried hard not to think about what that might mean, especially considering the backdrop of where we were.

I hovered my arm around her waist at first, wanting to be careful. There was something about her that told me I needed to—something dark in the back of her gaze, hiding behind all that sunshine.

That was okay with me, though. We all had something, didn't we?

I let her move into my embrace on her own, noting how her steps didn't falter. She was a confident woman, but cautious. Aware. Smart. But also powerless to whatever weird pull there was here, too.

I mean, of course she was. How cruel would it be of the universe to make me this unbelievably desperate to touch her and then her immune to it?

But she wasn't immune to it.

As soon as my hands came in contact with her hips, her body fell into the precise rhythm of mine. Those electrifying eyes lifted, and even in the darkened bar, I saw the spark there. It ignited something inside me, instructing me to pull her closer. Her breath hitched when we collided, her palm flying to my chest, and it took everything in me to keep my hands still, steady. God, they wanted to roam, but it didn't feel like she'd given me free rein yet. Not even when she melted into my hold, letting me dictate our movements.

My hips moved, and her hips moved.

My eyes flicked to her mouth; her eyes flicked to mine.

My breath hit her lips; hers flirted with my entire being.

I was addicted.

And we hadn't even danced an entire song yet.

CHAPTER TWENTY-NINE

natalie

AFTER THE PARTY, I drove Ellie back to her hotel before meeting Cameron at his apartment. He was waiting for me in the lobby, and while he greeted me with a smile when I arrived, he also remained quiet as we walked toward the elevator together. His movements were tight, tense, and I wondered if something might be wrong.

That was, until the elevator doors closed, and he rounded on me, pressing me into the wood-paneled walls, grabbing my chin and planting a hard kiss on my lips that I immediately melted into. Cameron released a husky chuckle against my mouth, like he was amused by how quickly I responded to the feeling of his lips on mine. His fingers wandered up my sides, touching me in an almost frantic way, as though unable to believe he was allowed to put his hands on me again, and I happily wrapped my arms around him in return.

"*Natalie*," he groaned, deepening the kiss until all I could feel was him—his body around me, his lips on my lips, his tongue stroking mine, his breaths tangling in the thick air. Cameron was taking over *everything*, and it was exactly what I wanted, what I needed. "It's been far too fucking long since I've gotten to kiss you."

"It's been a week," I laughed breathlessly, and Cameron shook his head.

"Far too fucking long," he reiterated with a grunt before abruptly pulling away from me. I didn't understand why at first, reeling from the loss of his touch, chasing more of it as he stepped back. But then he started tugging me toward the doors of the elevator, and I realized they had opened.

Cameron walked like he was on a mission, ushering me down the hallway of his apartment, and I could *feel* the acceleration of my heart, racing as fast as Cameron's steps. He led me through his front door and didn't stop walking until we were in his bedroom, making it very clear why we were here. He wasn't disguising this as anything but what it was as he pressed me back up against the wall, tilting my chin up, and dropping his mouth to mine, precisely how I'd been imagining he might when we stood outside Noah's house earlier.

His kiss was softer this time, more curious. He'd gotten the urge out of his system to feel my mouth against his again, and now he wanted to *explore* it. I parted my lips, letting him in, and a full-body sigh came out of Cameron. His hand slipped across my jaw and then kept moving, tangling in my hair, holding me in place so he could kiss me thoroughly, and I didn't mind one bit, not when he kissed me like he'd been *starved* of physical contact.

"Cam," I whimpered when he was unrelenting with his tender pace.

I understood how Cameron operated enough to know by now that he was probably going to drag this out until I wasn't just whimpering but *crying* for more, and I honestly wasn't sure I could handle that tonight. I'd been aching for days, wishing we hadn't been interrupted last week.

Cameron surprised me, though. He broke off from my lips and began unbuckling his belt while stalking across the room, away from me. He opened the bedside table drawer, grabbing a condom from it before he unbuttoned his pants, zipped them down, and pulled out his erection, fisting it.

I stared, jaw dropping with every confident and sure movement he made. Especially when he looked back at me, his gaze meeting mine with blazing intent.

"I need to be inside you," he muttered as he ripped open the condom wrapper.

Comprehending the words he was saying was hard when presented with the sight of him: pants resting low on his hips, hand slowly moving up and down his hard cock as he strode back toward me.

"Do you still want that?" he asked when I was silent, too busy absorbing every detail of this moment.

I nodded, my movements jerky. I was relying on the wall to hold me upright, leaning against it for support.

"Words, Sunshine."

"I want that," I whispered.

Cameron crowded me back against the wall, slipping the condom into my hand.

"Good girl," he praised under his breath, barely audible. "Put that on for me, then."

I looked up at him in somewhat surprise before springing into action, running my fingers up his length in a way that made Cameron shiver. He leaned forward, bracing a palm on the wall behind me, head tilted down to watch me slide the condom over the head of his cock and slowly roll it down.

A hushed curse fell from his lips, and a pleasant flip of my stomach responded.

As soon as I had the condom unrolled to cover him entirely, I looked up at Cameron to find his gaze already trained on me, hawkish, catching every detail, every movement, every breath I took. It should be unsettling, but it was so *comforting* to be seen and not overlooked.

"Has anything changed about what you want? Since we first started this?" he asked, and a million thoughts flooded my mind, ones that involved far too many feelings that I hadn't fully considered yet. But then he added in an even lower voice, "Any requests for how I fuck you tonight?"

My body heated, both in a flush of arousal from his words and embarrassment of the words he *hadn't* said and thought he might.

"No requests," I said, voice just a little shaky. Not with nerves, though. Just with everything else—an overwhelming wave of desire and anticipation. "I trust you'll give me what I need."

Truer words had honestly never been spoken, and Cameron's lips spread with a level of gratification I could almost taste.

"Yes, I fucking will." His gaze flicked over me again. "Take off your underwear, Natalie. I need to make sure you're ready for me."

I was more than ready, but he'd find that out soon.

I kept my eyes on him as I reached down without a second thought, slipping my fingers beneath the hem of my dress and bunching it around my waist in the process. Cameron watched, his eyes never leaving me as I shimmied out of my panties. He put his hand out, and I placed the garment in his palm, trying not to squirm, aware of how my arousal coated the fabric. But Cameron's gaze just glittered knowingly as he pocketed it and leaned forward to brush a gentle kiss across my lips.

"You told me once," he whispered, all while his fingers slid beneath my dress, repeating what I'd just done, trailing up my thigh, leaving goose bumps behind. "That between me and a wall was one of your favorite places to be. I think it's time for me to reinforce that thought."

Gasping as Cameron's fingertips brushed the apex of my thighs, I instinctively parted them for him. He took advantage of that, delving one finger through my slick slit, working his way deeper with every stroke and causing me to swallow a throaty moan.

"God, I missed this." He wore a dazed half-smile on his face. "I fucking dream about how wet this pussy gets."

"Just for you," I admitted on a breathy sigh, and Cameron's eyes lit up.

"Yeah?"

There was something so boyishly charming about how he said it that I hadn't expected him to thrust his fingers inside me a second later. I cried out, body bowing toward him as heat exploded inside me.

"Yeah," I managed to confirm, and Cameron's lips spread into a slow grin as he leisurely drew his fingers out before thrusting them back in. I fought off the urge to close my eyes, drowning beneath the weight of pleasure, before adding, "Korey used to complain I was never wet enough for him."

Cameron's gaze shone now, an almost *threatening* look on his face as he curled his fingers deeper, making me see stars.

When he spoke, there was a brutal gruffness to it.

"That is the one and only time I'll allow you to say his name when I'm inside you, Sunshine."

"I just wanted you to know how much more I—"

My voice vanished as Cameron pulled out of me and brushed his fingers against my clit instead, sending a jolt from my head to my toes. My knees weakened, my entire body softening under the gravity of my want.

"I know," Cameron assured me, speaking the words against my lips with a brazen confidence I found *so* attractive. "That's why I'm letting it slide."

A hot flutter beneath my skin only intensified when Cameron dropped to his knees and peered up at me from the ground, hunger in his eyes. They wandered down my body before focusing on my dress as he pushed it up, gradually exposing my thighs and then my cunt. Cameron stared for a long moment, making my stomach twist and turn pleasantly.

"So beautiful," he said throatily, forcing his gaze back to mine. "You are stunning, and I want you so fucking bad, but first, I need to—" He broke off, shaking his head as his eyes fell back down, tracing every inch of me. That look alone made me tremble.

"Cameron," I whined, and he answered me by leaning forward and burying his face between my thighs. And *God*, the moment his tongue swiped between my legs, sounds raised from my throat, incomprehensible and loud. But Cameron moaned, too, as though he'd been deprived of the taste of me, as though I was the best thing he'd ever had in his mouth before.

He only pulled back to finish his sentence.

"I need to taste you. I just have to taste you, Natalie," he said, voice deep and guttural as his eyes returned to mine and then stayed there while he swiped his tongue across my clit. I tipped my head back with a groan, the intensity of his gaze too strong and overwhelming when combined with the heaviness of the pleasure he was giving me, his tongue stroking between my legs repeatedly. *Holy hell.* My legs weakened further, my knees buckling. Cameron's strong hand wrapped around my waist, holding me steady, but when I was shaking too much to stay upright, he slipped his grip beneath my knee.

"Legs on my shoulders," he said, commanding.

Legs? I wanted to question. *As in both?*

He tossed one where he wanted it, knee bent over his shoulder, allowing him to delve further between my thighs with his tongue. His name left my lips, *again,* and Cameron hummed his delight, making me vibrate from the inside out. My one foot still on the ground barely had a hold on reality as tremors ran up and down my legs.

"Other one, Natalie," Cameron directed and then only gave me a second to adjust to the idea before he was throwing my other leg over his shoulder, too, sweeping me clean off the ground while his mouth continued to do dirty, disastrous things. A shriek escaped me, but then I easily balanced on his strong shoulders, thanks to Cameron's large hand clapping on top of my thigh, holding me in place as he teased my clit with the tip of his tongue. It was all *so much* at once. So much and yet—

"Hold on," he grunted, and I barely had a chance to brace myself before he was moving, *standing* with me on his shoulders. My squeal of surprise morphed into a moan of delight as Cameron swept his tongue back and forth, not stopping for a second as he pinned me against the wall, face between my legs, the scruff along his jawline scraping my skin deliciously, hands flattening on my hips, shoulders holding me in place.

My legs dangled down his back, my fingers curling in his short, soft hair, searching for a grip, and I felt more than heard his husky chuckle, like he was enjoying this situation *immensely*.

"Cameron, I—" I cut off as another wave of intense pleasure washed over me. "*Oh my God*. What are you doing?"

"Isn't it obvious?" he breathed, kissing my inner thigh before blinking up at me. "You're about to come on my face."

"But—" I didn't get more than one syllable out before Cameron's lips were brushing over my clit, making me shudder. "I'm going to—" A groan interrupted me, mine, I think, as he used the tip of his tongue to do delicious things. "*Fall*."

Cameron tightened his grip on my thighs, proving that he wasn't going to let that happen. Then he pulled back and reiterated that with his words. "You know that's not true, Sunshine."

He gave me a sort of chiding look, like he was disappointed that I would even *suggest* he'd let me fall. His eyes stayed trained on mine as he leaned forward and nipped at my inner thigh, love bites meant as reprimands.

"Relax," he instructed. "Let me eat you the way I want to."

Oh my God.

While the idea of relaxing certainly *seemed* like a challenging concept, considering how Cameron had me perched on his shoulders with his face between my legs, as soon as he dove back in, licking and sucking and lavishing my clit with his mouth, I found myself loosening.

Everything in my brain washed away except for the feeling of his tongue pulling pleasure from my body. I forgot where I was, that I was supposed to be holding on, that I was dangling in the air. I forgot about everything that wasn't chasing the high he was giving me, tipping my hips forward. Cameron encouraged it, propelling my movements as I rocked against his face, groaning as my body continued to transform, going from melted bones to a tightened string, ready to snap.

"*Oh my God,*" I moaned, aloud this time, knowing I was about to lose it.

His fingers flexed as a response, a hot, quick squeeze on my hip and leg to tell me that he was there, that he had me. And thank fucking God for that, because when I finally hit my peak, attacked with pleasure *so* intense and acute, I lost all control, my body shaking and slumping against the wall. True to his word, Cameron kept me upright, one hand traveling up my side to keep me from falling while he lessened the strokes with his tongue, carrying me through my orgasm until I was wrung dry.

A devilish grin plastered across his face when he pulled back, and both his hands fell to my ass, smoothing over my cheeks before giving them a little double smack. "That's my girl," he praised, flexing his fingers in a squeeze of appreciation that had me feeling like I was going to melt all over again.

Not only had sex with Korey not been as satisfying as what I'd experienced with Cameron so far, but it was also just not as...*fun*? It wasn't something I had expected; I hadn't expected to have laughter bubbling out of me, like it was now, as I teetered in this weird moment of euphoria.

I closed my eyes, basking in it for a moment, and when I opened them again, Cameron was watching me, a soft smoldering in his gaze.

"I like it when you laugh," he murmured, and then his lips cocked to one side. "But you won't be doing it for long."

Before I could ask what he meant by that, Cameron shifted me off his shoulders, lowering my body to align with his, urging my legs to wrap around his waist instead and pinning me to the wall with his hips. I could feel his cock brush between my thighs, making me squirm, wanting more. Heat flared inside me, reignited by the reminder of why exactly we were here tonight and knowing what was next.

"Yes," I breathed. "More. Please."

"You want more, Mama?" Cameron asked, but his hands instinctively flexed at my plea, a slight tremor running through his body at the idea of *more*.

Biting down on my lip, I nodded.

"You want my cock in that dripping pussy of yours?" he reiterated, a visible tick in his jaw now.

"*Yes*." I rotated my hips to try to feel more of him, to try to make it happen on my own. I managed to brush over the head of his erection and whimpered from the contact. A grumble came from Cameron's chest as he pressed me tighter against the wall, a firm reminder that he called the shots. But still, I pleaded with him. "Please, please, please."

"Be good and stay still for me, then." The huskiness of his voice only made things worse. "You're going to stay still while you take it, Natalie."

It took everything in me to follow Cameron's orders and stop my determined search for more of him, but I did, stilling completely. I even suppressed a shiver when Cameron's rough chuckle hit my skin.

"Oh, you want it bad, don't you?"

I gave the littlest nod, worried that if I moved too much, he wouldn't give me what I wanted.

"I know." He shook his head, like he couldn't quite believe we were here, that we were doing this. "I want it so fucking bad, too. *God*, Sunshine, I—" Cameron broke off when we made contact again—the press of his hips, the slow intrusion of his cock into my body.

He groaned, and there was a flicker of unsteadiness in his eyes, lining his blown pupils, like he wasn't in quite as much control as he was trying to make it seem. "I just want you *so* bad," he repeated, leaning forward until our foreheads were touching and our breaths were mingling as he gradually introduced himself, pushing further and further inside me. "That's it. Good, *so* good."

Cameron was...unlike anything I'd ever felt before. He was

everywhere, stretching me in a way I didn't recognize. I should have expected it, should have known this would happen, but it felt like he was in my *throat*—

"Baby, breathe," he soothed, cutting through my thoughts. "That's only the tip."

Oh.

Oh, of course.

Of course it felt like he was overtaking me, and he was only giving me the *tip*.

He slipped a hand between us, rubbing his thumb over my clit, and my cry of delight got stuck in my throat. But it worked the way he wanted, my body softening at his touch, at the bone-melting pleasure he knew how to deliver.

Cameron took note of the change in my body and thrust upward, burying at least half of his length inside me, leaving me gasping for air because, oh my *God*.

I mean, it *had* to be at least half of him, right?

"Fuck," he groaned, dragging it out to be at least five syllables. "*Natalie*."

Some sort of sound slipped out of me, a garbled, pleasured noise that also sounded a bit pained. It wasn't my fault. Cameron was stretching me in ways I didn't realize were possible. But for that same reason, he was already hitting places inside me that no man had hit before, and I was—*oh*, I was in some sort of tortured heaven.

My fingers curled into the collar of his shirt, both grateful he was wearing it so I had something to hold on to and wishing he didn't have anything on. I wanted to feel his hot skin against mine.

"More," I begged. "I can take it."

I had no idea where that level of confidence came from, considering I already felt like I was being split in two.

"I know you can." Cameron's voice was hoarse as he shook his head, pulling back as though he wanted to watch my face when he destroyed me fully. "God, I can't get over how perfect you are."

And then he buried the rest of his cock inside me.

I screamed, but it was soundless. My eyes rolled up, but then he murmured my name, and I looked to find Cameron with his eyes still on me, a little twist on his lips that told me everything I needed to know. His expression was so cocky, I almost missed how his entire body trembled at first, almost didn't catch how close he was to losing it, too.

But still, he gave me time, waiting.

"God, you take me *so* well," he rasped while letting me adjust to having him *so* deep. And then, when I tightened the grip of my legs around him, tugging him impossibly closer to me, trying to convey with my body what I was simply incapable of saying with words at the moment, Cameron pulled back—only an inch or two —and then thrust upward again.

I truly didn't believe it to be possible, but he seemed to go even deeper with the second rock of his hips, and my lips once again parted, awed. To my surprise, Cameron's eyelids fluttered, like he hadn't imagined any of this was possible, either, and then he began muttering things beneath his breath: how good I felt, how perfect I was, how he couldn't wait to fuck me until I was screaming.

But he didn't *do* that. Not yet. Instead, he pulled away from the wall, remaining inside me as he walked us to the bed in a few quick strides. And then he lowered me to the mattress and didn't waste a second before driving home again.

I made sounds this time. I couldn't help it.

His name flew from my lips, and Cameron dropped his head in a despaired moan, like the pleasure was almost more than he could handle. When he lifted his gaze again, it dragged over me, and then his face twisted with *irritation*?

I understood a second later when he started yanking at my dress, tugging it up and over my head, discarding it on the floor.

Thank *goodness* we were taking our clothes off.

Cameron leaned forward to reach around my back, sliding his hands along the band of my bra to unclasp it, and I fumbled with the buttons on his shirt, needing it off, all while grinding my hips upward, unable to stop chasing the sensation of his cock as it hit deep inside me, stretching me to my very limit.

Pushing Cameron to that limit, too. Or *some* kind of limit. The look on his face was *feral* as he stared down at me.

"Can't get enough of my cock, Natalie?" His husky laugh was heavy with want and tangled in amusement. "Jesus Christ, you were fucking made for me, weren't you?"

I didn't have anything to say to that, knowing fully that he was telling the truth. It did feel that way, like we fit together perfectly, in a way that seemed to be too divine to be a coincidence. It was never this good, this quickly. *Never.*

Cameron helped me discard his shirt while I lifted off the bed to assist him in ridding me of my bra, both our movements frantic. At some point before getting on the bed, he must have dropped his pants to the ground, because after throwing his shirt to the floor, I dragged my fingers down his back, and my hands reached his bare ass. It clenched beneath my touch as he delivered another thrust of his hips.

I choked on air, throwing my head back and my arms above it, luxuriating in the feel of being fucked so deliciously, with Cameron's lips trailing down my neck, nipping at my collarbone, his hands kneading my breasts, fingers plucking at my nipples, all while he moved inside me, repeatedly, perfectly, undeniably good. No, *great.*

"That's it," he encouraged, lifting his head to flash me a cocked smile. "Just lie back like that and let me fuck you good, baby. It's exactly what you deserve."

"Mmm," I hummed, arching my back as he hit me just right.

Cameron's lips curved as he watched, his eyes tracking over me.

Feeling safe under his gaze, I closed my eyes, memorizing the feel of him, moving in and out. Stretching, pulling, obliterating everything I'd known.

"Look at me, Mama." Cameron's voice was both tender and

insistent, and I flicked my gaze back to him, unable *not* to comply. Satisfaction leaked into his even gentler response of "Good girl."

His thrusts picked up, and a whimper crawled from my throat.

"I see you, Natalie," he assured, still speaking in that steely soft tone, and I sucked in, realizing what he was doing, what he was saying. Healing parts of me that Korey had destroyed. "I'm right here with you, and I don't want to be anywhere else. Not when you are the best fucking thing I've ever felt."

My heart, which I'd been keeping as far away from this as possible, tripped over itself, pounding in a beat that wasn't at all steady. Tears pricked the back of my eyelids, and I held my breath, trying to keep it together as I looked for words to respond. My mouth opened. Closed. I should acknowledge him, *this*, but the vulnerability was almost too much, and I shied away from it at the last second.

"Even with the condom on?" I teased through panting breaths. Cameron shook his head like he knew what I was doing, but I didn't let him cut in before I added, "Korey used to hate—"

"*Natalie,*" Cameron interrupted, grit in his voice as he reached down to give my clit a little slap while simultaneously smacking his hips against mine so hard I saw stars. "What the fuck did I say about that man's name coming out of your mouth while I'm inside you?"

I made a mewling sound, because that was all I was capable of in a moment when pleasure was spreading through every inch of me.

"What did I say, baby?" Cameron repeated, his voice softer, more lethal as he delivered another punishing thrust.

"Not to—" The rest of my sentence got swallowed up by a moan as Cameron softened his touch, playing with my clit now.

"Not to what?"

"Say his name," I gasped.

"When?"

"While you're inside me."

He raised a taunting brow. "Who's inside you, Sunshine?"

"You. Are," I panted.

"I sure fucking am," Cameron grunted. "And it is the *best* goddamn thing I've ever felt," he repeated. "Condom or no. Understood?"

I nodded, and Cameron leaned down, bracing himself on the mattress, arms on either side of my shoulders. His pace and movements morphed into something more sensual, lips grazing mine to assure me that beyond anything else, he *cared*. About me. Which made my stomach tighten with a lot more than just the overwhelming bliss and heat and tension.

"So good, Natalie." His rough, broken whispers hit my lips like little kisses. "I just need you to know that you're so good."

For the second time in less than a few minutes, I found myself blinking back tears. What was happening? I hadn't expected this, hadn't expected any of it. I wasn't used to sex being *fun*. I wasn't used to sex being *emotional*. I wasn't used to feeling any way during sex except *used* and *barely* satiated, and Cameron was destroying those ideas, all at once. And I had no idea how to handle it.

"So good," I whispered back because all I could do was repeat Cameron's words, which were true. I might not understand the feelings swirling in my chest, but I also knew that all of it was truly *so good*.

My walls began to tighten, fluttering around his cock with every drive inside me, the rhythm and the pace pushing me to an edge that was both familiar and foreign. The intense, constricting sensation in my core felt so much deeper than I'd ever experienced before, and I grabbed Cameron's shoulders in preparation, feeling like I needed something to hang onto. I couldn't simply *stay still* any longer, and when I started rocking up to meet him, Cameron encouraged it, a pleased expression overtaking his features.

He'd wanted me to hold out until I couldn't anymore and then take everything, and that was exactly what I was doing.

"*Cameron*." I was begging at this point. I needed more from him. I needed everything from him.

And he gave it to me with a growl, slapping his hips against mine—again and again and again until I was panting for air, not even caring if I didn't get it. I'd happily go without the ability to breathe if it just meant reaching the high that I was *so* close to finding.

"*Let go*," Cameron demanded through clenched teeth. "And let me fucking hear you," he added, giving one final push of his cock.

And that was what did it.

It wasn't that I needed his permission, but I *wanted* it. I wanted *him* to want it, I wanted to hear that this was another thing that he cared about—experiencing my pleasure.

To say Cameron cared was likely an understatement.

When I screamed along with my climax, a shaking, crying mess, tears finally releasing and streaming down my face, Cameron didn't take his eyes off me. I could barely see anything, my vision blurring, but I saw him. Saw the way his gaze worshiped me, saw how his jaw clenched, and pupils dilated, and bottom lip slid through his teeth. I heard the way he groaned loudly, enthusiastically, and then let himself go a few seconds afterward.

He tipped his head back, almost like watching me was too much to bear, and he slowed his thrusts, working us both through our orgasms until we were overstimulated, twitching, unable to take any more.

Cameron slid out of me with a regretful look on his face, but then a promise came out of his mouth, almost as though reassuring himself, or maybe both of us, that this wasn't the end. That this was just an intermission.

"That's nowhere near the last time we're doing that tonight," he murmured and then dropped to press a kiss to my forehead and then to my right cheek, wiping away the tears that had fallen on them.

For some odd reason, it felt like the most intimate thing we'd done all night.

"Do we need to talk about these?" he asked, moving to the left cheek to do the same.

I shook my head. Perhaps I should feel embarrassed that I'd cried the first time he fucked me, but surprisingly, I didn't. Cameron spoke in such a matter-of-fact tone, one that harbored no judgment.

"It was...a lot," I said. "In a good way."

He smoothed my hair away from my face and the stickiness on my forehead.

Again, maybe there should be embarrassment, but no.

"As long as it's in a good way."

I didn't know how to tell him that it was in the very best way.

Actually, it was in a way that I wasn't sure I'd ever recover from. A way that felt much too big and overwhelming, considering what we'd agreed upon.

So I just nodded.

"In a very good way." I swallowed hard, my mind spinning. "I just..."

"What?" Cameron breathed when I paused.

"Is it...always that good?" I found myself asking, unable not to. "Have I really—"

I bit down on my lip, unable to get myself to finish the thought, but I suspected he understood.

Even when I'd considered things to be good with Korey and me, it wasn't like that. Nowhere even *close*. Had I really spent a decade misunderstanding what I could expect out of sex?

The pull of Cameron's lips was unreadable.

"No, Sunshine." He continued to smooth my hair, like he didn't know how to stop. "It's not always that good."

Somehow, I had a feeling that was what he was going to say.

CHAPTER THIRTY

natalie

 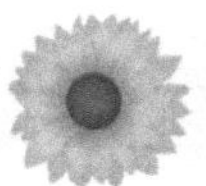 

"NATALIE NOELLE LONDON, I need to know *everything*." Ellie's black hair was thrown into a bun on top of her head, her short, wispy bangs swept to the side, framing a face with a gleaming expression as she plopped down into the seat across from me at the Bellflower Bar. She wore an oversized graphic tee with a black cat on the front that said, *Karma is a Cat.* "How was the cardio?"

I took a long sip of my mimosa before I answered, my face growing hotter by the second. "It was definitely the...*all of the above* option."

"I knew it." Ellie crossed her arms over her chest with a look of triumph. "He looked like a man of many talents."

I sighed into my drink. "Cameron is...amazing."

"Oh?"

Ellie seemed surprised by my response, and I realized how I must have just sounded: wistful and infatuated, like this man had put a spell on me. So unlike me, as evidenced by my best friend's raised brows and twitching smile.

But *last night.*

How was I supposed to act any other way after last night?

As though his first performance of the night hadn't already been mind-blowing, Cameron fucked me two more times. Once in front of the bathroom mirror, taking me from behind while never moving his eyes off me in our reflection. And once more when we were curled up in his bed, a slow, sensual joining of our bodies that once again changed my perception of sex, pushing me to a new limit until we were both gasping and falling asleep within minutes afterward.

He might not have even pulled out.

I should care about that, right?

I hadn't wanted to leave this morning. I'd see him in a few days for that baseball game, assuming Chloe wanted to go, but we'd be back to pretending our relationship was professional, friendly.

We agreed to five lessons, though. That meant two more, right? I'd get two more nights with him but just didn't know when they'd be yet.

"I mean, in bed. He's just amazing in bed." I sat up straighter, tucking my hair behind my ear. "Of course."

"Of course," Ellie repeated slowly. "But you know..."

I shook my head, already knowing where she was going with this.

"Ellie—"

"He won't be your lawyer *forever*, Nat," she cut in, determined as always. "And he seems like a genuinely good guy. I was talking to his brother-in-law for a while last night, Beau? He said Cameron is—"

"Sully hated that, by the way."

It was an asshole move of me to derail her points about Cameron by bringing up my brother and the ex she'd never gotten over. But I also wanted her to know that he'd never gotten over her, either.

Ellie froze.

"What?"

"Sully kept glaring at Beau." I lifted a brow. "Couldn't keep his eyes off wherever you were."

"I know he's your brother, but..." Ellie rolled her eyes, but I saw the flush working its way up her neck. "Sully can go to—"

"What can I get you ladies to eat today?"

It was probably for the best that the waiter interrupted.

Ellie wasn't ready to talk about how she really felt about Sully.

And I wasn't ready to talk about how I really felt about Cameron.

Cameron was all smiles when he picked me and Chloe up for the baseball game. To no one's surprise, Chloe was *very* excited, from the moment I asked her about it to the moment Cameron showed up in front of our house.

And I wasn't sure if her enthusiasm was simply that infectious or if Cameron was truly that happy to be bringing us, but his dimples hadn't disappeared once since we got into his car. Not when we got stuck in traffic near the stadium, or when we had trouble finding parking—driving probably hadn't been a great idea—or when we had to hike a handful of blocks to make it to the entrance, and Chloe whined that her feet hurt.

I'd tried to talk her out of wearing her new sandals, knowing that we might have to walk a lot, but she was insistent. Consequences of your own actions and all that.

"You got this, Champ," Cameron encouraged, flashing her a grin as they strode beside each other on the sidewalk.

"Is it much further?" she asked, screwing her face up when she looked at him, half-blinded by the sun.

Cameron shook his head. "Nah. And I'll make you a deal. If you can make it there, I'll give you a piggyback ride on the way back later. 'Kay?"

Chloe's brows shot up, and she stuck her hand out immediately. "Deal."

Cameron took it with a chuckle, shaking.

"Dad says I'm too heavy for piggyback rides," she added after he dropped her hand, conveniently waiting to add that information until *after* Cameron had already shaken on their deal.

But Cameron just laughed. It was bright and full-bodied and sent an odd sensation careening down my spine.

"Maybe for him," he said, and he did, to his credit, try to contain his grin a *little* bit as he glanced down at Chloe. "But you're not heavier than your mom, are you?"

Chloe seemed confused by that. "No."

"Well, I did have *her* on my shoulders the other day," Cameron said, and I choked on the hot summer air, slapping a hand over my mouth. He shot me an amused look that explicitly said I'd better keep it together. "So I feel pretty confident I can handle a nine-year-old piggyback ride."

"Really?" Chloe looked a little awed by Cameron's strength, and I noticed her sort of eying his muscles in his short-sleeved Red Caps T-shirt, making it even harder to control my facial expression.

Cameron nodded. "Yeah, I was helping her reach something." A slight pause, his glittering eyes darting to me. "On the ceiling."

Oh, I reached something alright. Went straight through the ceiling, actually.

"*You're in trouble,*" I mouthed.

"You felt secure up there, right, Mama?" he asked, ignoring my comment.

I was going to kill him.

I nodded, clearing my throat. "Of course."

"See?" Cameron gave Chloe a warm look. "There you go."

My daughter considered that for a second before checking over her shoulder to ask me, "What was on the ceiling?"

"Just a...spider, honey."

"Ewww." A whole-body shiver worked through her. "Not at our house, right?"

"We took care of the spider. Don't worry, Champ."

"Cam took care of everything," I added and then decidedly *didn't* look at him. I couldn't. I shouldn't.

I wanted to.

"Sure did," he muttered and then cleared his own throat, like he knew we weren't sticking to our own rules very well.

I *so* badly wanted to say fuck the rules, reach out, and I don't know, take his hand? Slip beneath his arm? I had no idea what, exactly. But not touching him felt wrong today.

There were so many reasons that wasn't possible, though. So, we were more careful after that. Once we made it into the stadium, Cameron led the way to our seats, which were somewhere between home and first base, not too many rows up from the field. Chloe should have sat between us; that likely would have been for the best. But I hadn't been thinking when I filed into the row behind him, and now our legs kept brushing and arms bumping, and I was trying *very* hard not to think about the last time we'd been in close contact.

Heat swirled, heavy in the air, both from the summery evening and the proximity of Cameron Bryant. When I glanced over at him, a crooked smile slipped onto his face, like he was enjoying this entire situation far too much, and I didn't know what to make of it. His eyes flicked to the hat on my head, which he'd let me borrow, and his lips parted to say something. But a second later, his smile fell, gaze drifting to something over my shoulder.

"Can I help you?"

Cameron's voice was harsh and hard, and his expression a surprising mix of both as he glared at whoever was behind me. I turned quickly to see a man looking my way from a row in front of us.

"Oh, sorry." The man laughed shakily, clearly unnerved by Cameron's intensity as he ran a hand through short, light brown hair. He looked like he could either be a finance bro in his midtwenties or a college frat boy who was coasting on his dad's credit card. Hard to say for sure. "I was—I just thought I recognized her. Hi."

He gave a little wave to me, and I felt Cameron's body grow stiffer beside me. I noticed his hand out of the corner of my eye, how it moved closer to my leg, flexing, like he wanted to curl his fingers over my thigh.

He didn't, but somehow, I felt the heat of his touch anyway.

I gave the stranger a tight smile. "Hey."

I hoped that would be it, and the man might turn back around, but instead, he doubled down, readjusting his whole body so he could get a better look at me. "Am I sure I don't know you?"

"Yeah," Cameron said flatly. "You're sure."

"*I* don't know you," Chloe muttered beneath her breath as she sank back into her seat, and I had to press my lips together to keep from laughing.

Shaking my head, I cleared my throat. "Sorry, no, I don't think we've met."

I was trying to be at least a *little* polite. But then his eyes dipped to my cleavage instead of focusing on my face, even though the red tank top I had on was relatively modest, and I didn't care so much about being polite anymore. Especially because Cameron immediately noticed and leaned forward in his seat, undoubtedly to say something else. So I cut in, "Hope you enjoy the game."

"You, too." He smiled, but it didn't reach his eyes. And after one more glance my way, he turned back around.

"Weirdo," Chloe muttered.

"*Chloe*," I admonished before glancing at Cameron to find him stewing, his eyes still on the back of the man's head while his jaw clenched and unclenched.

"What's in the bag?" I asked, trying to distract him. I pointed at a plain canvas bag that I'd been wondering about since we got out of the car earlier and he'd swung it over his shoulder.

Cameron released a pent-up sigh and relaxed back into his seat, shrugging. "Just a few things." He put it between his legs and pulled a baseball glove out. "My dad always brought a glove to games for me. I wasn't sure if Chloe would want one. We're in foul ball range, so you never know."

He shrugged again, slightly sheepish and downright adorable. It was the least confident I'd ever seen this man look, and it was all because he wasn't sure if my daughter would be interested in a tradition he'd had with his dad. My lips spread into a smile as I took the glove from him and passed it to Chloe, who immediately responded with a resounding "Cool!" and thrust her hand into it unsuccessfully. Cameron leaned over my lap to try to help her, and I tried not to breathe in his sandalwood cologne too deeply. It swirled around me, reminding me of moments I couldn't think about right now.

"And I brought this for you," he said after spending a few minutes with the glove and returning to his Mary Poppins bag, pulling out the last thing I expected to see: a ball of yarn and crochet hooks.

"Cameron," I laughed. "Why?"

"I know you like to keep your hands busy. I didn't want you getting bored." He smiled, but it was, once again, a little shy. "I can just put it back in the bag if you don't want it. It's not a big deal."

"No, no." I grabbed for the yarn, plopping it in my lap. "As long as you're not embarrassed to be sitting with the strange lady who crochets at a baseball game."

He was quiet, and I looked up from the yarn to see his eyes trained solely on me, his expression suddenly serious.

"I can't imagine ever being embarrassed to be with you."

He had the ability to disarm me so easily it should be concerning. At one point, in that pub in the hours after midnight, it *was* concerning. But now? Now, it was something else.

"This was sweet of you," I said softly. "Thank you."

Cameron nodded, stared at me for a long moment, and then let out a shuddering sigh that I felt in my bones—something that was tangled with longing, the same I felt whenever I looked at him and couldn't touch him.

And the scariest part about it was that it had nothing to do with the want and the yearning I'd felt with him in the bedroom. No, this was a different sort of desire. The desire to just hold someone's hand because you cared about them, because you saw them, because you appreciated them.

"Did you go to a lot of games with your dad?" I asked, needing more of Cameron. I couldn't touch him, but I could worm my way closer to him. Somehow.

"A few times a season," he answered easily. "He was a lawyer, too, so he didn't have a ton of free time, but whenever he could manage it, we would go. Uncle Tony and my grandpa liked to tag along sometimes."

"That's who was supposed to come today?"

He grimaced. "Yeah, Grandpa's recovering from a bit of a fall. He should be okay, though."

"Oh, I'm sorry to hear that." I wrapped my fingers around the ball of yarn, once again resisting the urge to touch him. "I'm sure you miss them."

"I do," he acknowledged. "But I think I'll try to visit home soon. And I'm happy I got to bring you and Chloe. You said once you'd always wanted to bring her to Fenway."

I had said that, hadn't I? And he remembered.

"She's *very* excited," I said, lowering my voice and glancing over to see Chloe on the edge of her seat, watching with fascination at the pre-game warm-ups, glove in hand. I looked back to Cameron to see him watching her, too. A bit of nostalgia swirled in his eyes, like he could see himself in her, and I liked that. He'd just wanted to share this experience with someone who might appreciate it, and Chloe was that person. I was, too, but mostly because it meant I got to spend the evening with them.

"I didn't realize your dad was a lawyer," I said, and Cameron's head swiveled back, eyes finding me again. "Will you tell me more about him?" He gave me a funny stare, and I rushed to add, "You don't have to, of course, if you'd prefer not to."

"No, Sunshine." He absently tucked a strand of my hair behind my ear before seeming to realize what he was doing and dropping his hand. "I'd love to tell you about my dad."

"What was his name?" I asked.

"Elijah." He swallowed. "It's my middle name."

"Is he the reason you went into law?"

He nodded. "It wasn't any kind of pressured thing. There wasn't an expectation, but..."

"You wanted to?"

"I did," he admitted, "though it's...complicated."

"You've listened to me talk a lot, Cameron." I fiddled with the crochet hooks in my hands without taking my attention off him. I didn't know how to look away. "I can be a good listener, too."

Cameron's eyes darted around the field, landing momentarily on Chloe, who was intently watching the big display screen, where an announcer was testing people in the stadium on their lyric knowledge of popular songs. She was giggling at the last person who'd just butchered "Pink Pony Club."

"He was just a really good man," Cameron said finally, looking back at me. "And even though our time together was cut short, being raised by such a loving and successful Black man really shaped me as a child and young adult. It gave me the example I've always tried to follow, both in my personal and professional life. I wasn't the only person who looked up to him, either. He was the kind of guy neighbors called when they needed a hand fixing their fence or getting a ride to the airport. He was a good son. I was young, but I remember how broken he'd seemed when my grandma passed from cancer. His focus was entirely on my grandpa, though. Always making sure he was never alone, bringing him over for dinners multiple times a week. He'd get my uncle to come, too, pulling him out of his grief. And to my mom—"

Cameron broke off, shaking his head.

"My parents were closer than any two people I've known." The corner of Cameron's mouth curved. "They met at a bar."

His eyes were unblinking, not backing down from the way they were looking at me. Looking *through* me, almost. Seeing everything.

My breath hitched.

"Yeah?"

"Yeah." He nodded, lips still tilting with the ghost of a smile. "My mom was behind the counter. It was her parents' place. My dad asked to buy her a drink after her shift, and the rest was history."

"He was as smooth a talker as you, then," I said, suddenly feeling hot—a heat that had nothing to do with the balmy summer evening, the kind of weather that was perfect for a ballgame.

Cameron's grin grew. "You think I'm a smooth talker, Natalie?"

I rolled my eyes, but it was playful. We both knew he was as smooth a talker as they came. "I thought maybe it was from being a lawyer, but now I know it's just genetic."

His smile was full now, as though he liked that—having another tie to his dad.

"I miss him," Cameron said, but there wasn't wistfulness in his voice or sudden grief. Just a simple, profound fact. Not a dip into emotions he kept locked up, but a truth he carried with him day in and day out. "And I know I'm not alone in that. When he died, all I could feel was how heavily everyone took it, aware we lost someone so great. And as I grew up, all I knew was I—" He sighed, huffing a humorless laugh. "It sounds ridiculous."

"You wanted to be great, like him," I put the pieces together for Cameron, and his eyes grew round like he hadn't expected me to *get* it. As if I didn't understand the weight of existing in a family where everyone was so incredibly high achieving and supportive and somehow able to do it all, for *everyone*, making me feel like a failure when sometimes all I could do and be was *Chloe's* all. That some days, I didn't have room for more. "You wanted to be the man that they all lost."

I couldn't help but notice that Cameron hadn't mentioned how his dad had passed. But it also seemed apparent he wanted to talk more about how his dad had lived than how his dad had died, and I didn't want to change that.

"I did, and becoming a lawyer was the best way I knew how," Cameron acknowledged. "Because he was a great lawyer, too. He started in military law because it was how he could fund his education. But that was all before I was born, before he left and branched into family law, working his way to being partner. He cared about the people he worked with. That's what everyone always tells me, anyway.

And that's the kind of lawyer I want to be, too. That kind of man. His shoes are big, though. It's hard to be great in *all* those different ways, getting pulled in a million different directions. He somehow managed to be in so many places, all at the same time, and make it look easy." His eyes shifted to me. "Kind of like you."

"Oh no." I shook my head, immediately brushing that comment off. He had no idea the guilt I carried because of the things I couldn't manage some days. "I don't think I make anything look easy. Because it *isn't*. But you?" This man always made everything seem effortless, how he handled situations and walked around with confidence. "I think you're more like your dad than you realize." When Cameron remained stoic, seemingly unable to find any words to respond to that, I added, "And you know what?"

"What?" he breathed, still looking a little awed, his eyes roaming over my face.

"You're right that there's a million places I could be right now, doing a million things, and I'm sure you probably feel the same.

But for me, I really don't want to be anywhere else but here. I hope you know that."

Cameron stayed quiet for a long moment, his gaze boring into mine, and I worried that maybe I'd said the wrong thing or bared too much. But then his lips cracked into a shy grin.

"Funny," he murmured. "I feel exactly the same way."

I crocheted half a small baseball by the end of the game. I thought it might make up for the fact that Chloe didn't catch a *real* baseball, though she insisted on wearing the glove the entire time anyway. She only took it off when she went to get food with Cameron, after he insisted that she wouldn't be able to hold ice cream with it on her hand. I could tell Chloe wanted to argue that point and attempt to prove him wrong but wanted the ice cream more. Cameron also had a way of saying things that made them sound final, like there would be no *buts*.

I needed to learn his ways.

As promised, he gave her a piggyback ride to the car, including climbing and descending the stairs of the stadium as we exited. He was spoiling her, just a little bit, but I found it really hard to care. Especially when I watched the way her cute face squished onto his shoulder, her eyes fluttering shut with exhaustion. Cameron must have sensed the way her body had melted and shut down as we walked because when we made it to the car, he was gentle with the way he roused her, getting her tucked into the back seat.

The entire thing left me feeling light-headed, giddy, and anxious. Something hopeful and silly bloomed in my chest, something I shouldn't be reading into, something I should put an absolute stop to, but I just *couldn't*. And not only could I *not* get a grip on my emotions, but I also couldn't stop myself from spilling them.

"This felt kinda like a date." The words tumbled out of my mouth when it was just me and Cameron again, standing in my front entryway. It wasn't my fault. He'd done things to my ovaries when he carried my sleeping daughter up the stairs to her room—my daughter, who was truly too old to be carried anywhere—and then looked at me with a crooked grin, dimples on full display.

"I mean, a client date, of course," I tried to amend. "With my daughter tagging along and ketchup stains on my shirt because said daughter put way too many condiments on a hot dog and me spending half the time crocheting like an old lady, but, well..." My voice vanished as Cameron stepped into my space, his lips curving further in amusement. "Never mind."

"You're cute when you ramble," he said, his voice all low and delicious and wonderful. He reached out, sliding his palm onto the side of my face and cupping it while his thumb drifted over my mouth, like he was trying to coax it open again, get me to say more silly things.

Something inside me sighed at his touch, relieved to finally have it again.

"Literally *no one* has ever said that before," I laughed, breathless, feeling like I was riding a high.

"It's true." His eyes dropped to my mouth, seeming to study the way he was caressing it with his fingertip. "And if this felt like a date, then I think that means I get to kiss you good night."

"I know it wasn't a date," I whispered, not wanting him to think I *didn't* know that. I understood exactly where we stood. Even if I was starting to wish that we stood somewhere else.

"Natalie." He shook his head like he didn't care about that, about the specifics. "For the love of God, just let me kiss you before I go."

I barely managed a nod before Cameron dropped his head and brushed a tender kiss across my lips. It was the most tentative kiss he'd ever given me, almost as though he knew that there was something about tonight that was fragile. But even still, after a few moments, he couldn't seem to help but deepen it. His tongue stroked mine. I whimpered. He groaned and then pushed himself back. We couldn't. Not now, not here.

Cameron's mouth hovered over mine even after, though. Separating felt impossible.

"For the record..." His warm breath teased my lips. "A date involving you and your daughter and ketchup stains and crocheting? That's my kind of date."

His words washed over me, making me feel like I was free-falling.

And then he left.

CHAPTER THIRTY-ONE

cameron

THE SENSATION I FELT in my chest when I looked down at my phone while at work and saw that Natalie was calling was undeniable.

I'd been counting down the hours, the minutes, the *seconds* until I saw her again. She was nothing short of incredible, brilliant, beautiful, and I couldn't get enough. The night I'd brought her back to my place? Nothing short of mind-blowing. Even *I* hadn't known sex could be like that.

And the baseball game? Taking Natalie and Chloe to Fenway left me feeling things that I was still processing. Walking out their front door at the end of the night after kissing Natalie had broken a small piece of me...and I think I left it there.

Today, my favorite single mom was supposed to come into the office to keep preparing for the trial, so this phone call was either her telling me that she was running late or early or—

"Cam, hi," she said, her voice frantic from the moment I picked up the phone.

I sat forward in my chair, elbows on my desk.

"Natalie, what's wrong?"

Her voice was half-muffled when she responded, like maybe she was trying to hold the phone to her ear with no hands. "I'm so sorry—fuck, goddamnit." A clattering noise sounded in the background. "Sorry, I—"

"Don't apologize," I interrupted, feeling all my nerve endings tighten. *Something* was wrong. "Just tell me what's going on."

"I can't come in today, I'm so sor—"

"*Natalie.*"

If she apologized one more time, I was going to lose it. If she thought I cared more about her keeping her appointment than *why* she couldn't keep her appointment, I clearly had some things left to prove to her.

"There was an accident on I-93," she said, and for some reason, I stood. As though I could do something about it while in the middle of Boston's financial district. "A massive one. It's all hands on deck at the hospital. I have to go in and—*shit.*"

Dread filled my entire being, taking me back to a moment when I was just a kid, hearing similar words.

"There was an accident. A bad accident, Cam."

I swallowed hard, determined not to let my memories flood my present. Right now, Natalie needed someone who was clear-headed because I could tell she wasn't. She sounded like she was trying to do twelve things at once, and while Natalie was the kind of woman who likely could figure out how to do twelve things at once, it wasn't going too well for her at the moment, making me wish I were there to help.

"But you're okay?" I clarified, my feet taking me back and forth across the length of my office.

"Yes, I'm fine."

Relief trickled down my spine, nonsensical and silly.

Natalie was at home.

She wasn't the one driving. Not the one in the accident.

"I just have to figure out about Chloe." There was a jingle of keys and a slam of a door, and I tightened again, realizing that although she hadn't been driving before, she was about to be. "An incident like this might have a ripple effect across hospital networks, so I don't think I should ask Blake and Delaney. And Noah has mini camps this week, and Gemma's already picking Chloe up from day camp and bringing her to skating afterward, but then Gemma has lessons after Chloe's is done. And she's only just dipping her toes in after maternity leave, so I don't want to put too much on her, but I guess—"

"Natalie, slow down." I didn't like the idea of her getting behind the wheel when her brain was running a mile a minute like this.

"I really don't want to call Korey, but—"

"Do *not* call that man," I interjected, firm. The last thing we needed to do was give Natalie's ex any sort of fuel for his fire before the trial. I took a deep breath and softened my tone before going on. "Skating ends at six, right?"

A shuddering sigh left Natalie's mouth, and, *God*, I wished I were there with her. "Right."

"I'll get Chloe from skating. I'll bring her home, get her dinner, and stay with her as long as needed. Have you changed the code on the back door since I installed it?"

"No."

Something burned in my chest.

"Good."

"Cameron, I really appreciate this," she started and then paused. A car door slammed, more light jingles, and then the dinging of a car with the key in the ignition. "But..."

I'd been waiting for that *but*.

Natalie didn't accept favors without arguing about them first. But this wasn't that for me. A favor. This was something else, something I couldn't fully explain.

"Do you feel uncomfortable with me spending the evening with Chloe?" I asked.

"No, of course not. But—"

"Do you think Chloe would be uncomfortable with me alone at your house?"

Natalie snorted. "Are you kidding me? She's probably going to demand you give her piggyback rides up and down the stairs. She'll be ecstatic."

"Then we're not going to argue about it," I said, once again firm. "I'll take care of Chloe. You go to work, save lives, and get home when you can."

An indistinguishable sound filtered through the speaker, and I stopped pacing, standing still in the middle of my office. My pulse thrummed, loud and insistent in my ear as I waited for Natalie to say something else, anything else.

But eventually, I couldn't take it anymore.

"Sunshine?" I ventured. "Are you okay?"

"Yeah." She released a shaky breath, her voice thick with an emotion I couldn't place. "Yeah, I'm okay. Thank you, Cameron. I—I don't even know what to say."

"Don't say anything. Can you just take a few deep breaths for me before you put the car in drive?"

"Mhm," she hummed. "Yeah. Yeah, good idea."

"Good girl," I said when I heard her inhale, nodding with encouragement, even though I couldn't see her and she couldn't see me.

Maybe I should change that. I *needed* to change that.

"I wanna see you. Just for a sec, okay?"

Since we were on a time crunch, I didn't wait for her response before I switched the call to video. She could choose not to accept it if she wanted to. But she didn't do that, and within seconds, I had a visual of Natalie sitting in her car, looking as gorgeous as ever. Her hair was pulled back, giving a clear view of her face. Of the way she was biting her lip anxiously and wiping beneath her lash line. Of her vibrant green eyes as they sought mine and her pinkened, pretty cheeks.

"Hey, baby."

She flashed me a weak smile, but her gaze sparkled at the soft tone I used. At my words.

"Hi, Cam," she whispered.

"You good?" I wouldn't blame her if she wasn't, not in a

million years. Fuck, *I* wasn't good right now, even if I'd pretend to be for her sake. I needed this moment just as badly. "Should we take another deep breath together?"

When she nodded, I nodded, and then she breathed in, and I breathed in, a feeling of syncopation, even though we weren't even in the same room.

I wanted *so* badly to be in the same room.

I'd never longed to hold someone like this before. Never been this desperate to wrap my arms around another person's shoulders or lift them into my arms. My hands itched to grab hers, and it killed me that I couldn't.

"I'm good," she said after a few moments of breathing, and I was so fucking relieved to hear that she *sounded* like she was good. Natalie's voice held steady, in control. There was squareness in the way she looked at me now, like she was ready to face things head-on, ready to tackle whatever lay ahead of her. And thank God for that. Because I couldn't even begin to imagine what she might deal with today. "I've got this."

"I know you do, Sunshine. You're so fucking amazing and talented." Her eyes rounded at the reassurance, letting it fill her. "Did you eat something before getting in the car? Hydrate?"

She nodded and picked up a half-eaten sandwich of some kind, a bag of some veggies, and a bottle of water to show me. It wasn't much, but it was something.

"That's my girl. Do you need me to bring you anything else? Chloe and I could deliver dinner later."

"No, I've got more food in my bag. This is just for now." She visibly swallowed before adding, "But thank you. I owe you."

All I could do was shake my head.

If we had more time, I'd explain to her that there was nothing about this that was transactional. That I cared about her far more than I should, and I'd always be there if she or Chloe needed me. That there was very little she could do to *keep* me from being there for her or Chloe.

One day, she'd figure it out.

Well, one day, I'd make *sure* she figured it out.

But I knew I had to continue my course. Slow, steady, and dependable. That was all I could be and do right now.

"Drive safe for me, okay?" I said, and she nodded. Even that little bit of reassurance from her made me feel better. And yet, unease still swirled in my gut, the same feeling I always got whenever I saw accidents on the news or heard of fatal crashes that brought me back to the worst moments of my life. "Could you..." I cleared my throat, realizing how hoarse I sounded. "I know you're about to be really busy, but can you please just text me when you get to work?"

"I can do that," she agreed, voice breathy.

Fifteen minutes later, I got a text from Natalie that she'd made it to SCMC.

And the tension in my stomach finally began to melt.

"Sorry, Champ. Not gonna happen. Those stairs were not built for piggyback rides."

I chuckled at the image in front of me: Chloe with her hands on her hips, standing at the bottom of the narrow, hundred-year-old steps in Natalie's townhouse.

"It's just that my legs are so *weak* from skating all night. I don't think I can make it to my room to change for dinner."

Chloe pretended to wilt against the railing, even as the corner of her lips tweaked in a secret smile.

I told Chloe we could either order pizza or walk to the grocery store around the block to make homemade pizza. Surprisingly, she picked the latter. And then asked if we could also pick up root beer and ice cream while we were there, which I suspected explained the dinner decision.

But now, suddenly, her legs weren't operating.

"Do I need to tell Gemma she's working you too hard?" I asked, flashing her a look of pretend concern. "Call your mom and tell her your legs stopped moving?"

"No!" Chloe's eyes grew wide as she straightened. "No, you know what? I think I'm good, actually."

"Oh, thank *goodness*," I laughed as I watched Chloe start bounding up the stairs. "I'd hate to stress your mom out any more than she already is."

Chloe flew around the corner at the top of her stairs, disappearing into her bedroom, and I waited in the living room for her to change and come back down, tossing my briefcase on the couch.

I'd gone right from work to the rink, and to her credit, Gemma didn't even bat an eye when I said I was there to pick Chloe up. I suspected Natalie had told her, but if Gemma thought it was weird, she didn't say anything. She just smiled when Chloe popped off the bleacher and jumped to reach my high-five greeting.

This was the last thing I expected to be doing tonight, and I still had a pile of work waiting for me after Chloe went to bed, but I couldn't imagine being anywhere else, doing anything else.

I could tell myself that I was here so that Natalie didn't have to call Korey, so we could keep our upper hand in the custody trial, that by being here, I was helping my case at work. But all of that would be a lie.

I was here because I wanted to be here. I was here because having to leave after the baseball game the other night had twisted something in my chest, and not even just because I'd wanted to take Natalie to bed and return to my favorite place between her thighs. I was here because nothing else really mattered if Natalie and Chloe weren't safe and happy and cared for.

"Okay, ready!" Chloe announced as she bounced back down the stairs, wearing jean shorts and a shirt that read *Back Bay*

Skating Star. She slipped on a pair of sandals before bounding out the front door without even waiting for me.

I would be lucky if I ever had as much energy as this child.

With a peek outside, I found Chloe sitting on the stoop, told her to stay there, and then locked up the house, exiting through the back before going to meet her in the front. She popped up right away, flashing me with a bright, excited grin that dimmed a little as she went down each step toward the sidewalk.

I was about to ask what was wrong when she cocked her head to the side and looked at me. "You said Mom was stressed?"

The question caught me off guard; it had been a good ten minutes since I said that.

"It's always a little stressful when things pop up unexpectedly, you know? Your mom has a big job to do and lives to save." I studied her for a second before deciding to add, "One time, my parents were in a car accident, and someone just like *your* mom saved *my* mom's life."

My dad's injuries might have been too extensive, but because of surgeons like Natalie, I still had my mom. And I was grateful for that every goddamn day.

I smiled reassuringly at Chloe, hoping to wipe the worry off her face while also being realistic. Chloe was old enough to understand some semblance of the truth. "Being a superhero is a lot of work, but your mom is really good at it."

"Wow." Chloe grinned at that, softer than usual, a tenderness in the gaze that matched her mother's. "She is kind of like a superhero, isn't she?"

"She sure is, Champ."

"Maybe we should get her something at the store," Chloe said, giving me a funny little side-eye. "Like flowers."

"Flowers sound like a great idea," I said, ignoring the curious way that Chloe was looking at me, like she was putting things together in her mind that I should really be dispelling. But I couldn't turn down the idea of doing something for Natalie, not after the stress on her face earlier.

"Yeah?"

Chloe looked a little too excited about the idea of flowers, but I just nodded.

"Yeah, I think I have the perfect ones in mind."

"Hey, Cam?"

"Chloe?"

"Is your mom okay now?"

My throat tightened. "My mom is great, kiddo. That was many years ago."

"Oh, good." Chloe surprised me, looking visibly relieved. "Should we get her flowers, too?"

I chuckled. "She lives in New York. But next time I visit her, I'll be sure to bring her some flowers."

Chloe gave an emphatic nod, as if she approved.

"Perfect."

And that was exactly how it felt.

CHAPTER THIRTY-TWO

cameron

CHLOE AND I HAD a busy evening. After a trip to the store, we threw together our scratch pizzas, and Chloe had asked if we could dye the crust blue—a nod to Percy Jackson, whose mom always made blue food for him, his favorite color. I couldn't exactly say no to that, so after a quick look in the cupboards and procuring some food dye, we made homemade pizzas with blue crust.

While they were in the oven, we went back to the front patio and planted a row of sunflower seeds in the empty garden bed. And since Chloe had been slightly appalled in the store when I told her how long it would take before any flowers might actually *appear* from the seeds, we also arranged some fresh cut sunflowers in a vase, placing them on the counter for Natalie when she got home.

"She'll like those," Chloe said decidedly as I slid a slice of pizza onto a plate for her. It was a little misshapen because the dough hadn't quite cooperated with me the way I'd hoped—probably because of the dye—but it tasted good, and who really cared what shape the pizza was in, anyway?

"I think so," I agreed. "Your mom has always seemed very... sunny to me."

Chloe cocked her head in thought. "Lately, she has been."

I hesitated before handing Chloe a napkin, noting how the sauce burst from the edges of her mouth when she took a bite of the pizza.

I dove into my own slice, trying to withhold the question that wanted to claw its way out of my throat. But it wasn't my place to dive into Natalie's past by using her daughter.

"Maybe it's because you call her Sunshine," Chloe added, causing me to freeze again. "I think she likes that."

Fuck.

I should really clarify something here. Natalie would *want* me to clarify things with Chloe so she didn't get the wrong idea and end up getting hurt. Even if *I'd* rather live in a world where hope lived, too. Chloe and I could be hopeful together.

In another world, at another time, maybe.

"Chloe, you know I really like your mom," I started tentatively. "But we're not—"

"I *know*," Chloe cut me off, adding five extra syllables to the word through her groan. She said it in a way that made me think this was a repeat conversation for her. That maybe Natalie had already had this talk. "But *why*? You just said you like her. And she says she likes you."

My lips twitched as I tried to control my reaction to that.

They'd definitely had this conversation before, and while I *knew* that meant that Natalie and I needed to be more careful around Chloe, it also warmed parts of me that I'd recently learned existed.

"Because there are rules about that," I said, giving her a factual answer. "Since I'm her lawyer."

Chloe pouted into her pizza for a moment before flashing a look filled with curiosity. "But you *do* like her?"

I nodded with a gentle smile. "Of course I do. I like her. I like you. I like your whole family, Chloe."

She narrowed her eyes at me, perceptive enough to know that

I was avoiding *fully* answering her question, but she dropped the topic.

I got Chloe to bed by nine, and honestly, I wasn't sure if that was normal for her. But even if it was a little later than usual, it was summer, and Chloe said she didn't have day camp tomorrow. I wondered how that might work with Natalie's schedule, especially depending on how long she got stuck at the hospital, but if I needed to take a day off to help, I'd take a day off. Or Chloe might even like to take a little trip to Gardner Law.

I didn't hear from Natalie for most of the night. I got one response from her around ten, after I'd sent an update that Chloe had gone to bed and all was well. She said that it was still going to be a while, that she was so sorry. I told her not to worry, knowing that she probably was. I was fully prepared to camp out on her living room couch tonight.

But to my surprise, Natalie walked in the door a little after one in the morning, wearing a vacant expression that terrified me more than any tears might. It wiped away all the relief that I felt just from seeing her make it home again.

I stood from where I'd been hunched over paperwork at the kitchen island and took a tentative step toward her. She looked skittish.

"You're awake," she said with a dumbfounded look. "I should have told you. I—you could have slept."

"I know," I assured her. "But I had some things I had to finish up. And I was waiting...in case you got home."

Like hell would I have been able to sleep before she made it back to me and Chloe.

Natalie nodded. She stared down at her feet, like she didn't know how to move them.

"Why don't you sit down, Natalie?" I offered, using the softest voice I could muster, walking around the island to grab her electric kettle from the corner of the kitchen. Natalie watched me, unmoving, while I filled it up and turned it on. Just like I had the first night I was here after one of her shifts.

Tonight was different, though. *She* was different, more broken, and I could barely handle seeing it. Especially when I started toward her as the kettle began heating, and she took a step back.

I felt a cracking sensation just behind my sternum.

It took everything in me, but I retreated, moving instead through the kitchen to find the tea packets and a mug.

"I already gave Annabeth her nighttime treats," I said. "She came looking for them earlier, and I couldn't say no. She didn't get more than two, though. I promise."

Natalie was silent. A glance over my shoulder told me she was processing, her eyes glazed over, her head nodding.

"Thank you," she whispered after a second. She'd still been holding her bags but slowly lowered them to the ground, plopping them by her feet. She stepped over them, slipped her shoes off, and then quietly padded to the barstools at the island, sliding onto one of them.

She froze, sending me into a panic until I realized she'd spotted the flowers on the counter. Her lips parted as she stared at them, almost like she'd never seen flowers sitting in a vase in her kitchen before, like it was an entirely new concept.

"Chloe wanted to get those for you," I murmured, trying to focus on making tea but continuing to get sidetracked by Natalie—everything about her. She reached out, brushing her fingertips over the petals of a flower. When her eyes flicked to mine, they were watery.

"Chloe wanted to get these for me?"

I nodded and dunked a tea bag into the steaming mug before handing it to her.

"Chloe wanted to get me flowers?" she repeated.

"Yeah." My lips stretched in a smile. "She did."

"She picked out...sunflowers?" she asked, and the corners of my mouth tilted further, my grin growing.

I suspected she knew the answer to that question, but she

seemed desperate for a response. So I just shook my head and said, "No, Sunshine. She didn't pick them out."

Natalie swallowed hard at my response, her eyes glistening.

"I love them," she breathed, studying the flowers a moment longer before dropping her gaze to her tea. She blew on it, took a tentative sip, and then looked back to me. "Thank you."

I smiled at her and thought about mentioning the sunflower seeds we'd planted but decided to let Chloe do it. I might have decided on the kind of flower, but the idea had been Chloe's. And she deserved to have a part in the surprise.

Busying myself with preparing coffee for the next morning, I gave Natalie space as she drank her tea. Every sip seemed to be bringing more life back into her, but her demeanor was still shuttered. A wall that didn't usually exist between us stood erect, and I wanted to give it a chance to fall before I had to knock it down. Because I refused to let Natalie suffer alone tonight.

When the tea was gone, the coffee was prepped, and Natalie's head was drooping lower and lower, I gently urged, "Let's get you upstairs."

Natalie nodded, and I thought she might let me help her, but then she abruptly stood, though a bit unsteady on her feet, wincing.

She was sore. Of course she was sore. That was probably the first time she'd sat down since she left the house over sixteen hours ago.

"I got it." She waved me away. "You should go home and get some rest. I'm really sorry, I should have said that a half hour ago."

Not a chance.

"I wouldn't have gone a half hour ago, and I don't plan on going now."

Her lips pressed into a line. "I appreciate you babysitting Chloe, but you don't—you don't need to babysit me. I'm okay."

Ignoring the pang in my chest, I considered her. "*Are* you?"

She was making it hard for me to believe that was true.

Natalie didn't answer the question. And when she spoke, she looked at the ceiling, like she couldn't bear to look at me. "I've been dealing with terrible nights and terrible shifts for years on my own, Cameron."

And that thought alone broke my fucking heart. Did she not realize that?

I took a deep breath, trying to keep myself steady for her. "I know you're capable of spending tonight on your own. I know you can take care of yourself. But is that what you *want*?"

If I went home right now, I'd spend the entire night worrying about her while trying not to get sucked back into my own grief. But if she insisted that I leave, I would. Because this had never been the plan, and I was well aware of it. Natalie knew it, too, and I suspected she was struggling with that.

Natalie was still blinking at the ceiling.

The plan can change, baby. Let's change the plan. Let me be here for you.

When she didn't respond, I couldn't take it any longer. "I don't want to leave you like this, Natalie," I said, my voice low, grave, pleading. "Please don't push me away."

Her face crumpled as she lowered it again. "I'm not—I'm sorry, Cameron. It's just today was—" She broke off with a choked sob, pressing her hand to her mouth, and I moved in closer, wanting, *needing* for her to let me hold her.

"I know," I acknowledged, while gently circling my arms around her, giving her the opportunity to move away if she didn't want this. But she leaned in, seeking my touch. Thank *God*. "I know what it was, and I don't want to leave you alone right now." *I* didn't want to be alone right now. Selfishly, I needed her just as much as I felt like she needed me. "Let me stay. Let me get you to bed."

At that, Natalie wordlessly nodded. And then her entire body crumpled in my arms, and I caught her. Finally. Relief hit me like a freight train, making me realize just how badly it would have hurt to walk away. But she wasn't making me. Thank *fuck* she wasn't making me.

Scooping her off her feet, I brought Natalie to her bedroom. She cried softly into my shoulder, creating a heartache I didn't fully understand. I'd never wanted to fix something so badly before without knowing how. All I could think to do was follow the routine that she'd once told me, take her through the movements she usually did after work, and hope that provided some sort of comfort.

I walked Natalie into her en suite bathroom and lowered her to sit on the countertop. Murmuring a few words of encouragement, I pressed a kiss to the top of her head and spun to turn on the shower. The spraying water splashed loudly against white subway tiles, drowning out Natalie's soft sniffles. When I faced her again, she had her head leaning against the wall as she stared at her feet, and the blank look on her face frightened me more than I ever could have imagined.

"Natalie," I breathed, afraid that if I spoke too loudly, it might spook her.

She lifted her gaze, meeting my eyes, and I immediately felt better. I needed her eyes on me, needed to know she was there, that she hadn't retreated somewhere I couldn't follow. Brushing her hair out of her face, I pushed my fingers into her thick honey strands, massaging gently, and her whole body sighed.

"Do you want to talk about it?" I asked.

She shook her head, squeezing her eyes shut in a way that squeezed my heart, too.

"Do you want me to leave so you can shower? I can wait in your room."

She shook her head again.

"Do you want me to help you?"

A nod.

Good. Yes.

Natalie's features twisted a little, like she hated that she needed help right now, and I didn't want her to feel that way. So I jumped right in, dropping my hands to the hem of her shirt as I pressed more reassuring kisses to her face.

"Arms up," I directed softly, and Natalie raised her hands above her head, letting me pull her shirt up and over. Then she let me unclasp her bra, dropping it to the ground as she stood, shimmying out of her pants.

"Good girl," I encouraged, dropping my hands to her bare skin, massaging my thumbs into her hip bones for a moment as we stood face-to-face. Natalie wiped at her tears, trying to get rid of them as she looked up at me, a pleading expression on her face. What did she want? I would do anything, give her anything that I could, that I had.

I cupped her face. "Words, baby."

"You?" she asked, her voice threadbare as her hands dropped to the buttons on my shirt, starting to undo them with shaky fingers.

"You want me to get in with you?"

She nodded, and I took over for her, unbuttoning my shirt and stripping out of it, along with the rest of my clothes. As soon as I was done, Natalie put her arms up, hooking them around my neck, and I lifted her into my arms without hesitation, cupping my hands beneath her bottom as I walked her to the shower, slipping behind the curtain.

It wasn't a very large space, and we hardly both fit beneath the spray, but steam rose into the air, and that, along with the flare of body heat as we wrapped around each other, kept us warm. *Hot.*

I put Natalie back down, letting her slide to her feet again. It was slightly torturous, the way her naked, wet body slithered down mine. But I wanted to free my hands so I could take care of her the way she deserved.

"Head back for me," I rasped, and Natalie obeyed, letting the water coat her hair and stream down her back. I slicked my hands over her head, pushing the wetness into her strands and away from her face before looking around the tiny shower for shampoo.

When I found it, I deposited a small dollop in my palm and then turned back to Natalie. "Can I?"

She nodded and twisted in my arms so I could reach better. I took my time, massaging the shampoo into her scalp. Natalie tipped her head back, handing me full control as the water sprayed over us.

I'd never washed anyone's hair before, and I wanted to get it right.

It felt really important to get it right.

So I made sure her entire head was sudsy before I rinsed it off, slowly washing the soap away, and the day. Then I repeated the process with her conditioner, pulling it through her hair and rinsing it off. A little moan slipped out of Natalie as my fingers worked, a massage that I hoped was gentle and thorough. It was hard to tell what kind of moan it was, though, if it had to do with my probing touch or if it was something more desperate.

"Natalie. Baby." I wrapped an arm around her waist, tentatively pulling her against my chest. Her weight sagged in relief, like she'd been waiting for that, and I held on to her tighter. She dropped her head back, tipping it onto my shoulder, her face tilting up toward mine. Her eyes were closed, her expression slightly pained. I brushed my lips over her hairline, whispering against wet, dewy skin. "I'm not sure what exactly happened tonight, but I need you to know that you are the most brilliant woman I know. Brilliant and beautiful and strong."

She exhaled, and I felt the heaviness of it. "I don't feel remotely strong right now, Cameron."

I drew a lazy circle around her belly button with my thumb, feeling the way her body relaxed beneath my touch, just how I'd been hoping. "Right now, you don't need to be. That's why I'm here."

Natalie's eyes opened, blinking rapidly at first, either batting away the shower water or her tears, I couldn't tell. But then her green gaze met mine in a moment of breathlessness. She lifted her arm, circling around my neck. Holding on. Her fingertips scraped my skin, a graze, yet it felt like she was digging into me, hooking something inside me. Holding on.

She tipped her chin further, making it clear what she wanted.

And how was I ever supposed to say no?

The kiss was achingly deep, like we were trying to reach the place that we felt tethered, a reassurance that it was there. That *we* were here, in the same place. It ignited something in me I wasn't used to, that went beyond the skin-crawling want, the disastrous need to have her. Something that felt raw and untouched by anyone but Natalie.

"Sunshine," I breathed against her lips, forcing myself to pull back, to retreat from feelings that were so big there wasn't space for them here, not right now. Not when Natalie's feelings were the priority and mine were a mess. And that meant not getting swept up in a kiss I couldn't control.

But she blinked up at me like all she wanted was *more*. More of me, more of my touch, more of this, of us. So I asked, "Will you let me wash the rest of you?"

She nodded, pulling her bottom lip between her teeth and testing my restraint.

That mouth—*fuck*.

I regretfully dragged my gaze from Natalie's, if only to find the body wash. But as soon as I had what I needed, my eyes found hers again. They were still watching me, inspecting every inch of my face. She felt calmer, like my kiss had taken some of her grief or heartache or whatever she was feeling.

Maybe that was why it had felt like that. Because we were sharing parts of ourselves that didn't have words yet, the emotions she didn't know how to say aloud tonight.

Natalie's lips parted when my hands slid back onto her skin, washing the plane of her stomach. The faintest whimper escaped them, and my heart hammered in my chest, my pulse racing as I worked my palm over her body, sculpting it to her form. I stayed in safe areas, washing her back, her sides, her arms, but when Natalie gave me a heated look over her shoulder and the tiniest nod, I wandered beneath her breasts and then over them, cupping her in my hands. Natalie arched her back, pushing into my touch, asking for more. And God, I wanted to give her everything.

"Cameron."

My name left her mouth on a plea, and it nearly broke me. Natalie squirmed in my arms, pushing her ass into my cock, which had been rock hard since the moment I'd pressed her naked body against mine. I'd just been ignoring it—*trying* to ignore it—hoping she would, too.

She wasn't, not anymore.

Her breathing was ragged, her stare blazing, her fingertips begging as they dug into my skin.

My hand dipped between her legs, and she gasped. Her pupils dilated, ringed with something unnamed.

"*Please*, Cameron."

I shuddered at the sound of her desperation.

"What do you want?" I choked. "What do you need? I'll give you anything."

"You," she whispered.

I swallowed hard, slipping my hand from between her legs, letting it wander to her hip, gripping hard. It was all I could do to keep myself together until I knew exactly what she meant by that.

"How do you want me, Natalie?" I dipped my head, finding her ear. "I need you to be explicit. Because I'll happily wrap you in a towel and hold you all night long if that's what you need right now. We can talk or not talk. We can start a movie. I can watch you crochet until you can't keep your eyes open. Or I can fuck you, but you have to tell me."

I saw her lick her lips before letting words through them that destroyed me. "Please fuck me. I need—I need to feel—" She broke off, unable or unwilling to say it. "Please fuck me."

I closed my eyes, breathing in. Breathing out.

Her words echoed in my brain, bouncing off the walls.

Natalie made an eager sound, her body slipping against mine in a way that was so utterly erotic. She turned in my arms, her hands dragging down my front, fingers exploring the muscled V that led to my pelvis. My cock brushed her stomach.

"Cameron?"

Opening my eyes, I found hers. They were bright, eager, needy. But they were also *wanting*. Not hungry—*starving*. She was looking at me like maybe she didn't just need to be fucked; she needed *me* to be the one to do it.

I hoped to hell that was true.

I understood I'd offered myself up, said I'd give her anything I could. And while I didn't regret that, I also *hoped* she felt the way I did right now. I didn't simply need a release, didn't want to lose myself in just anyone. It was her, all her. I needed *Natalie*. This was so much more than sex for the sake of sex, and all I could do was cross my fingers that there was a distinction for her, too.

It really *felt* like there was, and that was what I would hold on to until I knew for sure. Because now was not the right time to ask. I'd just have to trust.

"I'm here," I promised, eyes fluttering as Natalie boldly wrapped a hand around my cock, pumping it up and down. Heat unraveled at the base of my spine before traveling up it. God, the things she could do to me. It was unparalleled, *nothing* like anything I'd felt before. She had no idea how fast she could take me to the brink, so I grabbed her wrist, stilling her. "Fuck, Sunshine. Slow down."

Natalie pressed herself closer, her wet tits sliding against my chest. I groaned, and she lifted onto her tiptoes, dragging her body up mine as she reached to kiss my neck, scraping her teeth over my collarbone. Her puffs of air grazed my skin, and I felt her shake her head. "I can't. Please."

Jesus fucking Christ.

"Condom," I grunted, but Natalie continued to shake her head.

"I don't care. I don't need it. Just—" She moaned as I rocked my hips into her.

"You do care," I reminded her. "You told me you cared that first night, Natalie. It's okay, baby. I'll be inside you soon."

Before she could argue, I turned off the shower, scooped her into my arms, and walked us into the bedroom, snatching a few towels on my way.

If what Natalie needed from me tonight was to forget and to feel and to get lost in something that wasn't her own mind, then that was what I was going to give her. And hell, I was going to get lost in her, too.

CHAPTER THIRTY-THREE

cameron

"YOU HAVE TO BE quiet, Sunshine." I stared down at Natalie, who was panting, sprawled out across her bedsheets, looking dewy and gorgeous. A goddamn goddess. "Can you do that?"

She bit her bottom lip, nodding. Her eyes were focused on my hands and the way I was rolling the condom over my cock, which was aching, pulsing for her.

Once it was in place, I slid my palms onto her thighs, spreading them further apart. Natalie glistened for me, her arousal apparent even from here, and my cock throbbed harder.

But I also felt my want in so many other places tonight than just there. My entire body pulsed with a desire like I'd never known.

Placing a knee on the end of the bed, I hovered over Natalie, watching her chest rise and fall in anticipation, appreciating the way her breasts rocked and her nipples peaked. The pretty flush that I always saw on her face covered her entire body, evidence of the way she wanted me.

It almost wasn't fair that she existed, nearly unbelievable that there was someone out there like her, someone I was so attracted and attached to that it almost hurt to look at her. Because what happened if I ever *lost* her?

Losing people was something I couldn't help but think about, all the time, but the idea of losing Natalie? Simply unthinkable, unbearable.

I couldn't lose her.

I couldn't lose this.

But tonight wasn't about what I needed; it was about what *she* needed.

I lowered my voice to a barely audible pitch, one only meant for her. "Put a pillow under your lower back." Natalie gave me a funny look but obeyed. My lips twitched. I fucking loved showing her ways to heighten her pleasure in the bedroom, but I had to try hard not to think about whether she would take those things and use them with someone else. Because *fuck that.*

I swallowed hard, forcing those thoughts away and focusing on Natalie. Right now, she was *mine.* She was about to come around *my* cock while being held in *my* arms, and it was going to be *so* fucking good because everything with this woman was. It didn't matter what would happen in the future or had happened in the past. Nothing mattered right now but this moment.

Sliding a finger between her legs, I studied how Natalie's eyes expanded—relief twisting with need, that feeling of getting what you'd been waiting for. I dove further into her wet pussy, dipping my finger deeper until I was inside her, where I goddamn belonged. Natalie gasped, and it was loud—*too* loud.

"*Natalie,*" I reprimanded, harsh in the way I knew she liked.

"I'm sorry," she panted, squirming against my touch, seeking more of it. "I can't help it. It's so—"

"You *can,*" I insisted, thrusting again and enjoying the way her body bowed off the bed. "And you *will.*"

Natalie pressed her lips together, desperately attempting to cut off any sounds, but her whimper still slipped through when I added a second finger.

"Baby, do you want to be fucked or not? Because if you're this loud with just my fingers, how will you handle my cock?"

Natalie's eyes widened, realizing I might be serious.

I wasn't serious. I'd find a way to fuck her, to keep her quiet.

"Yes," she pleaded, canting her hips into the air as I withdrew my fingers. "Please, Cam. I can handle it."

She could handle anything. My beautiful, brilliant girl.

"So pretty when you beg," I said, my voice muffled by a trembling in it I couldn't conceal. How had I become so lucky that I got to have her like this? "But you don't have to. Not with me. Never with me."

The irony of our dynamic was that she could say jump, and I'd say how high. She had me wrapped around her pretty little finger, and I wasn't sure she even realized it.

"I know," she breathed, comfort visibly coating her features when I dropped onto the bed, leaning over her. "But I can't wait."

"Stop telling me things you can't do," I warned. "When I know you can do fucking anything."

For some reason, that made tears sparkle in her eyes, and I shook my head, dropping to brush a kiss over her lips. I didn't want her to cry. I just wanted her to know that she was so goddamn breathtaking and incredible. She had no *idea* just how incredible she was.

She sighed my name against my lips, and I deepened the kiss.

"Oh, *God*." A desperate moan slipped out of me as her tongue tangled with mine. Fuck, it was dangerous kissing her tonight. It felt like there was too much on the line. Too much at risk.

Natalie circled her arms around my neck, pulling me closer until there wasn't any space between us—none at all. Her chest pressed against mine, and I could feel the rapid pace of her heart, thumping, burrowing into me. Heat trickled down my spine, so intense and urgent that I didn't know what to do besides pull back just enough so I could drag my cock through her soaked cunt, aligning us just right.

"Yes," Natalie panted, a quiet plea into the night.

"That's it, baby," I encouraged between harsh breaths. "Stay quiet for me. Just like that while I fuck you."

"Mhm," she hummed, wiggling beneath me.

I used a hand to stay her movements, fingertips pressing into her hip bone. Every little jerk of her body threatened to send me into overdrive too soon.

I took my time teasing her with the tip of my dick, letting it drag against her clit, wanting to see if she could follow through with her promise. But Natalie moaned, loudly, throwing her head back and squeezing her eyes shut in a moment of pleasure.

God, how I loved giving her that. I loved seeing the way she responded to me, how her body molded and moved when I directed it. I loved how much she matched me, our dynamics perfectly in sync.

But as much as I loved all of that, I didn't love that she wasn't listening to me.

"Natalie. Why aren't you doing what I asked?" I growled, stilling.

She didn't like that, her body arching beneath mine, attempting to get more from me.

"I—" She stopped herself before she said that she couldn't help it, knowing better. "Cameron, I—"

"Do you need help?"

Natalie nodded without hesitation, and I slipped my hand over her mouth, pressing down just enough to smother her cries. Then I rocked my hips, letting the head of my cock graze her clit again, making us both moan—Natalie into the palm of my hand and me into the press of my lips.

Her eyes flickered shut momentarily, and when she opened them again, they flared, glistening with renewed sparks.

Oh, she *liked* that. She liked handing even more control to me, maybe even needed it. My girl didn't have to do anything. I would do it all, everything. She just had to lie there and take it—every single ounce of pleasure I planned to deliver.

"Yeah?" I checked, rocking against her again, giving her

another small taste of my cock. Natalie's cries were louder that time, but they echoed in her mouth, unable to escape. When they tapered off, I lifted my palm, letting her answer.

"Yes," she agreed, enthused, her eyes alight with wonder. "But Cameron, I—"

She broke off when I shifted, not on purpose this time, but Natalie and I both felt the repercussions of it, our bodies simultaneously tightening with the simple brushes of contact. And she must have thought it was intentional because she whined, "Don't tease me tonight. I need—I want—"

"I'll give you exactly what you fucking want," I cut in and covered her mouth with my palm again before readjusting and thrusting my tip inside her. "Because I know, baby."

God, *being inside her*. There was absolutely nothing better, and I knew Natalie agreed. She gasped—I didn't so much hear it, but I felt it. My hand suctioned to her mouth. Her eyes widened, almost like she'd forgotten how good we were together, how big I felt inside her.

"More, Sunshine?" I checked, holding my breath in anticipation, throbbing in need until Natalie nodded. "That's my girl."

I sank in further, swallowing my own groan when Natalie's walls fluttered around me. Her eyes rolled before finding mine, a visual check-in. Her body shook, pulsing, ready to break.

But not fucking yet.

"You can't come until you take all of me," I said, keeping my voice low, a strained command. "And you *will* take all of me, Natalie. Understood?"

Her eyes glittered because we both knew she could handle it, that she *wanted* it. I lifted my palm from her mouth, just long enough for her to say, "*Yes*," before I clamped my hand back down and thrust all the way inside her.

Natalie's muffled cries and tight heat were almost enough to put me over the edge. Oh, *hell*. Her gaze shone, staring up at me, staring *through* me. I felt her everywhere, wrapping around my bones and sinking beneath my skin.

"Good *fucking* girl." I released a muted groan. "You're such a good girl for me."

Natalie nodded and wiggled her hips, like she wanted to *keep* being my good girl. So eager, so beautiful, so perfect. Unable to help myself, I lowered my mouth to her neck, kissing a path up it, needing to feel her speeding pulse beneath my lips. It raced, impatient and wild, and I soaked it in, loving every fucking second.

When my lips found her ear, I tugged on her earlobe with my teeth, feeling the inward tug of her breath against my palm.

"You wanted to be fucked," I said, a rough whisper against the shell of her ear. "So I'm going to fuck you good now. Are you ready?"

She whimpered. I felt the vibrations of it, followed by the trembling of her body, and the tilting of her hips. Finally, a nod.

"Good. If you want me to stop for any reason, bite my hand."

She nodded again, and then I nodded.

"Practice that for me, baby."

Natalie's teeth scraped my palm. She couldn't get enough skin between her teeth to do any damage, but I felt the bite, no mistaking it, and that was what we needed.

I centered myself over her again, giving a tilted smile. "Good job, Sunshine."

And then I withdrew a few inches before slamming inside Natalie's cunt, harder this time, watching how her eyes grew and her head tossed back against the bed, her wet hair drenching the pristine, white pillowcases.

None of that mattered right now. The only thing that mattered was Natalie and making her feel alive and perfect and loved.

"So good," I moaned, a low admission pressed against her forehead. The arch of her back from the pillow meant I was hitting even deeper than ever before, so deep that I felt Natalie quake with already mounting pressure. "So, *so* good."

And then I did it again, driving my hips against hers, seeing how far I could bury myself inside her.

Natalie's cries bounced against my hand, and I thrust again.

Slow, but steady and hard, reaching. Perfect strokes, over and over again, making her climb higher and higher. She was panting against my palm, and suddenly, I wanted to feel it. I *needed* to feel her breaths and how what I was doing to her affected them.

"Control yourself, Mama," I rasped, my one warning before I slid my hand from her mouth. Natalie's gasp was so distinct, her pupils blown as she bit down on her lip, like she wasn't sure she could handle staying quiet. But when I grazed my lips over hers, parting them again, she tilted her chin, chasing my mouth.

My ragged, desperate breaths mixed with hers. Staying quiet seemed impossible, but there was also something erotic about it, something intoxicating about how the only sounds in the room were the quiet slap of my hips hitting hers and our hot and heavy breathing.

Natalie's eyes were wild as they searched mine. She wrapped her arms around my neck, tugging me closer. My forehead hit hers, and then we were right there—together. Bodies writhing, muscles constricting, orgasms building.

"*Cameron*," she whined breathlessly, and I knew hers was here. That she couldn't hold back anymore, and I slammed my hand back over her mouth *just* in time.

I watched in awe as evidence of Natalie's climax washed over her face, her release seeming to liberate her. I felt as she tightened all around me and then melted, breaking down into pieces that I made an internal promise to put back together again.

Beautiful and brilliant. As always.

My hand slid away after she crested, and then I used the opportunity to kiss her through my own turning point, thrusting only twice more before exploding, unraveling, spiraling, lost in the feel of Natalie London.

We slowed. Her hands began to wander, drifting down my back and then back up, spreading over my shoulders and then onto my chest. She flattened a palm directly over my heart, and I kissed her harder, almost afraid to let the moment die.

I wasn't sure how many minutes passed before I finally gave in and let my mouth slide from hers, dragging it down the column of her throat, the dip of her collarbone, the swell of her breasts, lower and lower until I'd slipped out of her and was kneeling at the end of the bed again.

"Let me clean you up." I pressed a kiss to her cunt, making Natalie gasp. And then I dove in further, dragging my tongue through her pussy and licking off the arousal that coated her inner thighs. Natalie's soft groans propelled me, making it hard to stop, and I flipped her over onto her stomach so her sounds could be smothered in a pillow when I lifted her hips and dragged my tongue from her pussy further back, spreading her perfect cheeks so I could explore other parts of her. I couldn't fucking help it. Letting her, *this*, go was becoming more impossible each and every time.

Natalie tensed at the swipe of my tongue and then softened, releasing a sound that made me hard all over again.

I pulled back with a tilted grin. "Can I tell you a secret?" I asked softly, and Natalie nodded, squirming as I replaced my mouth with my fingers, finding her tight little asshole and experimenting with light pressure, watching her closely for a reaction. Her lips parted, her eyes rolled. *Good.* "I'd really like to fuck you here, Natalie."

She nodded again, a barely audible "Mhm" coming from her lips.

"Not now," I added, and she almost looked...disappointed. "Next time, maybe."

"Next time," she repeated, and then she closed her eyes like she wanted to imagine it.

"Have you done that before?"

She shook her head without opening her eyes. "Have you?"

"Only with men."

Natalie lifted her lids, finding me, and maybe I was seeing

things I wanted to be there, but Natalie looked at me almost *possessively*, as though she liked that she'd be the first woman I'd experience that with.

God, she had no fucking clue, did she? How it felt for me when we were together? She stood alone in every experience. Every single one. No one felt like she did. No one was her.

Suddenly, I had to tell her.

"Natalie...I hope you know that everything we do feels new. Everything we do feels like my first time. With anyone."

I took a step away after that because, based on the marveling way Natalie stared at me, I'd said too much.

Walking to the bathroom, I disposed of the condom and took a few steadying breaths. When I returned, I found Natalie curled up beneath the comforter, snuggled into the bed. To my immense relief, she wore a contented smile, and she even crooked a finger, which was all it took to convince me to slip beneath the covers with her.

I lay on my back, throwing an arm out, and Natalie snuck beneath it, exactly how I'd been hoping she would. Tucking her into my side, I dropped a kiss on her forehead, and Natalie exhaled, a rush of emotions leaving her body.

"Thank you." She nuzzled further into my neck, whispers of gratitude on repeat. "Everything feels new to me, too. I'm guessing you already knew that, but still...thank you, Cameron. Not just for tonight, but for all of it."

Fuck, I wished she'd stop thanking me like it was a favor. Like I didn't spend every waking moment thinking about her—the things we'd done together, what we'd do next.

"Natalie..." I blew a breath out between my teeth, similar to her. "You are unreal. All of it is unreal."

She burrowed deeper into my side. I let her, drawing her close beneath the blankets and brushing a hand over damp hair that would probably be tangled and messy tomorrow. Natalie didn't seem to care, and I sure as hell didn't, either. I loved this side of her, the stripped-down one. Mostly because I suspected not many, if anyone, got to see it.

But I did.

And I'd never take that for fucking granted.

"When do you have to go back to the hospital?" I asked.

Another heavy exhale. "In the morning."

I nodded, half expecting that answer.

"I just came home to shower and get a few hours of sleep before going back," she added. "I texted Gemma to see if there was any way that Chloe could hang out with her in the morning. She does have skating in the afternoon anyway."

"Or she could come to the office with me," I offered with a shrug, without even really thinking about it. "And then I could take her to skating."

Natalie twisted her head, looking at me with wide eyes. "Cameron—"

"Ask Chloe in the morning what she'd rather do. If she wants to come with me, she absolutely can. Text me, and I'll swing by before work to get her."

When Natalie just blinked at me in response, I spread my fingers into her hair, gently massaging her scalp like I had in the shower, encouraging her to put her head back down. Seeming too exhausted to fight it, Natalie snuggled back into my side.

"I'll wait until you fall asleep, and then I'll sneak out, okay?"

She wrapped herself around me tighter. And then the smallest confession: "I don't want you to. I don't want you to go."

Fuck me.

"I don't want to, either," I promised. I really, *really* didn't want to leave. "But you know I have to, Sunshine." I paused, debating whether I should say what was on the tip of my tongue. But responsibility won over, and I admitted, "Chloe...she suspects. She knows I'm obsessed with you. I'm not good enough at hiding it."

"I know. I'm not, either." Natalie's gaze flicked to mine, still expansive and searching. "I wish..."

The end of the sentence hung in the air, lingering.

Finish the sentence, baby. What do you wish?

She didn't say anything else, though.

So I just said, "I wish, too."

Fingers crossed we were wishing for the same damn things.

The room was still after that. Natalie sank further into my embrace, a gradual, quiet trust fall. Her breathing evened out, and I thought she'd fallen asleep, but then she spoke, almost startling me.

"Hey, Cameron?"

I glanced down at her. She hadn't opened her eyes, still had her face nestled, her breath fanning my skin in both a delicious and comforting way.

"Natalie?"

"You're a really, *really* good man." She sighed, her voice reducing to a barely there murmur. "And for what it's worth, I think your dad would be so very proud of who you are."

My breath caught in my throat. I closed my eyes, tipping my head back against the headboard of Natalie's bed.

"You know, he died in a car accident," I admitted, voice raw. I didn't love talking about the specifics, but I wanted her to know this. "And...I've never once blamed the doctors who did everything they could to save him. Because it was never going to be possible, not with how my dad swerved the car, so he got the brunt of the impact instead of his wife. And, more importantly, because they were the same team who did everything they could to save my mom. And I still have her because of them."

I felt Natalie lift her head to look at me.

"Cameron." She choked on my name, and I opened my eyes, finding her watery ones looking back at me.

"You are amazing, Natalie," I insisted. "And while I might not know what happened tonight, I need you to know that I owe the world to surgeons like you. The entire goddamn world. Okay?"

She swallowed hard and then nodded.

My entire goddamn world.

Fuck.

"Come here," I said gruffly, and Natalie dropped back to her place in my arms.

"I'm *so* sorry," she whispered, and I shook my head. She didn't need to apologize for anything.

"Just let me hold you," I said, knowing it sounded like I was begging. Pleading for more pieces of her than maybe she was ready to give. "You go to sleep and just let me hold you."

"I..." Her hesitant voice made my chest hurt. "I don't know if I want to. I think I'd rather stay with you, stay awake for you."

Oh, my sweet girl.

I wanted her to stay with me, too. But maybe another night.

"You need to sleep," I insisted, knowing she needed it. "Sleep, Sunshine."

And then she did.

CHAPTER THIRTY-FOUR

natalie

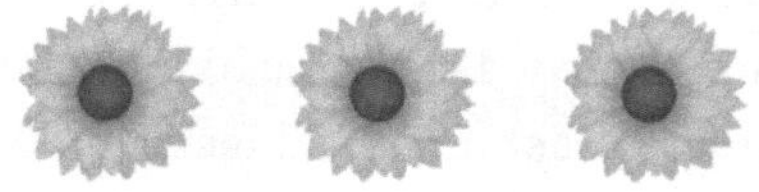

I WOKE THE NEXT morning alone. It was something that I was used to, of course. I woke up alone during my marriage to Korey. I woke up alone after the divorce. I'd been waking up alone for years.

But this morning, I *ached* with loneliness for the first time in a long time.

I didn't mind being a single mom. There were many parts of it that I loved—the freedom, the bond between Chloe and me, just two girls against the world.

So I knew I didn't wake up feeling lonely for any other reason than that Cameron wasn't here with me.

I'd fallen asleep in his arms, and I woke to an empty bed. And after all the tenderness, care, attention he'd given me last night, finding myself here without it was suddenly gutting me.

I knew what he'd said was right; I didn't *need* him. I would have managed through the night without him. But I also knew that I would have woken up this morning feeling a hell of a lot more broken if he hadn't been here to put my pieces back together again.

Yesterday was one of the most traumatic shifts I'd ever worked.

Dealing with trauma was my job. It was, quite literally, part of the job title. And there was a part of me that had grown desensitized to it over the years. Not necessarily a good thing, but it was the truth, and it took a lot to break me. Blood, broken bones, burns—I'd seen it all.

But last night...there was just *so* much. It wasn't one devastating injury; it was a never-ending cycle of them. It wasn't over, either. Today, I had to be ready to dive right back into it all.

And while, sure, there was an ache of loneliness this morning, if I *hadn't* had Cameron last night, I'd feel even worse waking up. He'd known what I needed, and he didn't hesitate in giving it to me, even after I tried to push him away downstairs.

And then there was the shower. The sex. The kisses in my hair. His words before I fell asleep, the ones I'd badly needed to hear.

I'd had no idea about the accident with his parents. And now that I did, I was so glad I trusted my gut and let him stay. Because I think he needed it, too. Inadvertently hurting Cameron would have only made all this worse; it was something I *never* wanted to do.

Last night felt like proof that our relationship was shifting—crossing a line, moving from a place with distinct boundaries and rules to something lawless and without borders. And I didn't know what to do about it.

"Mom?"

Chloe's quiet voice broke through my thoughts. She cracked the door open, her movements soft and tentative—something I was sure was very hard for her.

"I'm here, honey," I said, rolling to the edge of my bed before remembering I was naked. So I rushed to add, "Just give me one second, okay?"

Chloe paused, and I searched the ottoman at the foot of the bed frantically. I remembered throwing my robe on it when rushing to leave the house yesterday.

Finding and slipping it on, I went to meet my daughter by the door, opening it wider. She smiled at me, again with an odd, slight hesitation. I suspected she knew that I was going to tell her I had to go back to work, and she wasn't looking forward to it. But I gave her an encouraging grin anyway and ushered her down the stairs for breakfast. Chloe peered around the living room at the bottom of the steps, clear curiosity in her gaze.

"Where's Cameron?"

"Oh, he left last night, sweetie. After I got home."

And after a shower, sex, and cuddling. My insides flipped at the memories. I'd never been treated like that before. When I locked myself in the bathroom to cry after shifts while married to Korey, he'd never once come to check on me. He let me grieve alone, whereas Cameron wouldn't even allow the possibility. I had a feeling that if I locked him out, he'd break down the door to get in.

"Oh."

Chloe nodded, but clear disappointment swirled on her face. Which caused me to blurt, "He wondered if maybe you wanted to go to work with him today, though." Chloe's eyes—no, her *entire* face—lit up. "I have to go back to the hospital, but if you wanted—"

"Yes!"

"It might be a little boring. You know that, right?" I said, making sure she understood what she was getting into. "Cameron has an important job with a lot of things to get done, and he might not have time to hang out with you much."

I wanted Chloe to slow her thought process a little bit, think about this, but it was likely a lost cause. Just like I was. *I* should slow down. *I* should be thinking more about how excited Chloe was to spend time with Cameron, how she'd been looking for him this morning, how Cameron had said last night that she was suspicious, and *shit*. Yeah, we were both going down roads that might lead to hurt, which was exactly what I hadn't wanted.

But it was too late for that today. I'd already dangled the opportunity in front of her, and I couldn't take it away now.

"I'll bring my book!" Chloe announced, rushing upstairs to

get it, I was sure. "And my tablet!" She was still shouting when she made it to the top of the stairs. "And my own snacks!"

I laughed, shaking my head, wishing my heart felt a little less like it was going to explode.

It had happened, hadn't it?

Chloe was attached.

I was attached.

But I couldn't *quite* get myself to feel bad about it. Couldn't *quite* get myself to believe that doom was really on the horizon, even if logic might say it was.

Instead, when I picked up my phone to text Cameron about taking my daughter to work, all I could feel was that lingering dose of hope.

Too bad it wouldn't last for long.

"We need to talk."

It was the first thing Gemma said to me when she opened the door later that night, when I arrived at her and Noah's apartment to pick up Chloe after skating. My brother and his fiancée were still making the slow transition to the new house in the suburbs —a good thing for me that they hadn't entirely relocated yet.

"What's going on?"

I frowned, taking in Gemma's huddled posture, the quick glance over her shoulder as she let me inside. Anxiety made a swift arrival, sinking in my gut.

"I don't want Chloe to hear," she said, and that sinking feeling only worsened. "Noah's with the girls on the couch."

"Gemma, what's wrong?"

I needed her to tell me before I lost it. It had been another long, intense day at the hospital, and I wasn't sure I could handle any more trauma tonight.

"I'm sure you're incredibly tired, and I wish I didn't have to bring this up right now, but you need to know." She took a deep breath, scaring the living shit out of me while giving me a sympathetic, caring look. "Korey came to skating tonight."

"Oh, *God*," I muttered, rubbing my forehead in preparation for whatever else Gemma was about to say. Because I was sure there was more. "He's trying to suck up and look like he actually cares about his daughter before the trial."

Gemma nodded, agreeing. "Chloe was...mostly happy to see him," she added. "She seemed a little worried he was taking her home with him. The first thing she said was, 'I thought I was going home with Gemma.' Korey didn't like that."

My stomach tightened, keenly aware of just how much that probably bothered my ex.

"But as soon as I cleared things up for her, she was fine," Gemma said.

I nodded. Okay, that was good.

Except I could tell Gemma wasn't done.

"And then Korey asked about her day," she continued hesitantly. "And Chloe was maybe a little *too* excited to spill everything. Specifically, about Cameron. And going to the firm with him. And last night, when he babysat her."

Oh, *shit.*

I leaned against the wall, suddenly feeling a little faint. I had no doubt Korey would try to use this information in ways I didn't even want to think about.

"Why don't you come in?" Gemma asked gently, noting my reaction. "Sit down for a little bit. Can I get you anything?"

"No, no," I assured her. "I'm okay. Really. It's just..." I sighed, shaking my head. "There was an emergency yesterday at work, and Cameron offered to help, and then he offered again today, and Chloe was *so* excited. She really likes him, and—" I broke off with a groan.

And I *really like him.*

Gemma nodded, understanding. "She told Korey that, too. How much she likes Cameron."

"Shit," I cursed under my breath. "How did Korey react?"

She winced, which wasn't a good sign. "Not great. He wasn't *mean* to Chloe or anything, but he was asking her all these questions about Cameron, and I could tell by his expression that he wasn't happy, and I'm just worried for you and the case and Cameron's promotion."

"I—Cameron's promotion?"

Gemma cocked her head to the side. "Yeah, Noah told me a bit ago that he's hoping to make junior partner soon. I figured he might have told you since you've been working so closely. I guess his chances are really good, as long as..." She trailed off when she saw my expression, the blood draining from my face. "Nat?"

Why the hell wouldn't he tell me that? Why would Cameron *not* mention how close he was to a promotion when we were doing things that could very much *cost* him that promotion?

Oh my God. I was going to cost him a promotion, wasn't I? Korey was going to do something that would cost Cameron everything, his dreams of following in his dad's footsteps, and all because he wanted to help me and Chloe. All because he was a better man than Korey ever was.

"I just—" I shook my head, still reeling with that information. "I just didn't know."

"I'm sure it's fine." Gemma was quick to reassure me, but I wasn't so easily convinced. My stomach roiled with guilt, hot and heavy in my gut. "I mean, you haven't done anything *wrong*. He's just been helping out a bit, right?"

I bit down on my lip, flashed her a shaky grin, and said, "Right."

"Oh." Gemma stared, blue eyes wandering my face and taking in every inch of it. She saw the guilt, I was sure of it, especially when her eyes popped a little wider. "*Oh*."

I grimaced and tried to wave away her clear worry. "We're not *dating* or anything."

What we had been doing might be worse than that, though. At least where his job was concerned.

Gemma gave me a look. "Kind of like how Noah and I weren't *dating* for months?"

"Yeah, maybe like that." I huffed a humorless laugh, remembering how obvious it had been to me that my brother was a lost cause for his friend's sister. How Noah had claimed to be helping with her pregnancy just because he wanted to be a good *roommate*. How he'd come to Chloe's skating practices and pace around the edge of the rink with worry, watching his niece's pregnant coach. How the two of them would steal glances at each other when they thought no one was looking.

All of that had been happening when they were supposedly just *friends*—with benefits, I'd learned—but it had been clear to me from the start that it was so much more than that.

Maybe, just maybe, Cameron and I could be so much more than that, too.

But now, with Korey involved...

Fuck, everything was a mess, wasn't it?

Gemma laughed, but it was warm and soothing. She squeezed my arm. "Starting things in secret isn't always a bad thing, you know. It's a little bubble of time when everything belongs to just the two of you. Everything will work out, even if the bubble pops. And Korey doesn't know anything for certain, right? *I* didn't even realize. I mean, I suspected *something* when Cameron started showing up at the rink, and it was hard to miss the way he was looking at you at our engagement party, but..." She trailed off and flashed a gentle, compassionate smile and, with the tiniest whisper, added, "I'm happy for you."

"Don't be," I said, shaking my head. "Not yet. We might not—it's not totally like that, even." Gemma flashed me a look of disbelief, but she didn't get it. "And there's still so much at risk and—"

"Everything will work out," Gemma reinforced.

And God, I'd never wanted to believe someone more.

I didn't really know what to do with all the information she had given me or the feelings swirling in my gut, but I knew one thing that would help. That wouldn't make it worse.

And even though I hated to do it, I knew it had to be done.

six months ago

NATALIE

I was starting to think that this man could read my mind.

He moved to the beat of something inside me, something that I wasn't used to people seeing, hearing, feeling.

It made my entire body pulsate, like a beacon that he was drawn to. A moth to a flame, yet there wasn't a bone inside me that wanted to let this die. His hot breath fanned the curve of my neck as he dropped his head. His lips flirted with my pulse point as he muttered, "Just checking that you're real."

"You should check again," I encouraged and then threw an arm up, wrapping it around his neck and holding his head there, letting him press open-mouthed kisses down my throat, leaving me panting.

"Oh, fuck." His moan was guttural, coming from somewhere deep inside him, and it did things deep inside me, too. "Has anyone ever told you you're perfect?"

All I did was hum in response, thinking about those words.

They made something twist inside me, a distinct turn from the road I'd been cruising down, thanks to a few drinks and the heat of Cam's touch.

"Come with me?" he breathed, phrased like a demand I could refuse, if I wanted.

But I didn't want to.

I wanted to go with him—anywhere.

And as he pulled me into the back hallway of the bar and pressed me up against the wall in a way that was both delicious and heart-stopping, I realized that was the problem, wasn't it?

There wasn't a bone in my body that wanted to let this moment die, but there were thoughts swirling in my brain that wondered if I should.

Because it had only been a few hours, a few drinks, a few words exchanged, and I knew.

I knew I was already at risk.

CHAPTER THIRTY-FIVE

cameron

"NO LITTLE VISITORS TODAY?" Daphne asked, poking her head into my office.

"Not today."

I hadn't been entirely sure how Daphne would react to Chloe's coming to work with me yesterday, but she'd *loved* it. She viewed it as me going the extra mile for my client, even though we both knew it was bordering on unprofessional. Luckily, Daphne's obsession with the Londons trumped that.

Chloe had been a little celebrity yesterday. She'd bounced back and forth between my office and the Briggses', depending on what we had going on. Most of the time, she spent reading her book or doodling on her tablet. We deemed one of my pens on my desk to be *Riptide*—Percy Jackson's sword that appeared as a disposable ballpoint pen when in its dormant form. Chloe used a permanent marker to scribble "Anaklusmos" on its side, and I'd smiled to myself.

Overall, it really hadn't been a problem at all. If she'd been a more challenging guest, Daphne might have felt differently. But as it stood, she'd been thrilled.

"That little girl adores you," Daphne cooed, which sounded a little strange coming out of her mouth when I was so used to the commanding, authoritative tone she usually used. But I nodded, trying to ignore the lump in my throat.

"She's a sweet kid," I said, attempting to sound as bland as possible. "The Londons are a great family. My sister went to college with Noah, so I've known them for a long time."

There. That sounded neutral, right?

Not like I was completely obsessed with my client and had grown attached to her daughter, too.

Not like I had a text sitting on my phone from that same client that was destroying me inside every time I looked at it.

SUNNY: I think we need to end this, Cameron.
Can we talk later?

I'd been staring at the text message from Natalie all morning, wishing my heart didn't feel so constricted.

End this.

End *what*?

Daphne flashed me a polite smile and then disappeared from my doorway, which was good.

I needed to return to torturing myself by staring at Natalie's message.

Did she want me to *end* the way I couldn't stop thinking about her? *End* how I felt about her? Did she want me to *end* caring for Chloe? *End* the way we were sneaking into each other's beds at night?

She needed to tell me what we were ending because it was driving me wild. Mostly because I was afraid she was going to say all of the above. And while I'd always known that there might come a time where she cut me off, I didn't expect it to be so soon, not before we even finished our arrangement. And I certainly hadn't expected it to be after the last night we spent together.

But then again, Natalie never asked for the things I'd been giving her.

She hadn't asked for flowers or baseball dates. She hadn't

asked for someone to make her tea after late-night shifts or wash her hair. And while I knew she was appreciative of the things I'd done for her and Chloe because she'd made a point to tell me on more than one occasion, they still weren't things she asked for. She'd wanted a guy who could treat her right in the bedroom, not a guy who could treat her right everywhere else, too.

Was this her finally realizing that it was all too much? Too soon? I'd pushed too far, crossed a boundary I shouldn't have, and now I was going to regret it.

Fuck, I was *already* regretting it. Because whatever she meant by that text, I didn't like it. As far as Natalie London was concerned, I didn't want to end a single goddamn thing.

I wanted *all* of it.

My phone lit up, and for a second, I thought Natalie might be calling. But it wasn't her. Of course not.

It was my mom, calling back about visiting this upcoming weekend, I was sure.

"Hey, Mom," I said, answering.

"Oh, hi!" She sounded almost surprised that I'd answered, making me think there were more times than I realized that she called and I didn't pick up. "I hope I'm not catching you at a bad time."

"Always have time for you, Mom," I promised.

"Oh, shush," she muttered. "I know you're busy. My busy boy."

I pursed my lips, not liking how her default was to brush me off. "Not too busy to come home this weekend, though. Maybe go with you and Pops to the Summerfest Street Parade if he's up for it?"

"Oh, Cam." The dip in her tone made me frown. "You know we'd love to see you, but we don't want to take you away from Boston. You have so much going on, and we're fine. You know that, right? We're *good* here."

I wasn't shocked she was doing this. In the past, I probably would have listened to her. I *had* listened to her when she gave this speech now and again because, yeah, life was busy, and I'd been putting all my eggs in one basket, thinking my career trajectory was the one way I could be as great as my dad, as successful as him.

"I know you're okay, Mom," I acknowledged. "But it's been a while since I've been home, and I miss you all."

"Oh." Something about what I'd said made her perk up, but not necessarily in the way I'd been hoping. "Oh, well, you know we miss you, too." A pause sat heavy between us. "Is everything *okay*, Cam? Is work okay?"

"Work's good," I assured her. Busy as fuck, as usual. But that would never change. And I didn't want to waste all the other good parts of life. "There are just..." I released a sigh, one filled with pent-up emotions. "There are other things I want to start prioritizing outside of work, I think."

"Yeah?"

"Yeah."

Definitely.

"Does this mean you're *finally* going to start dating?"

This time when my mom spoke, she sounded hopeful. And honestly, I needed that right now, when I still wanted to be hopeful, too.

"I..." I trailed off, unsure how to answer that, especially considering Natalie's text that still sat on my phone, unanswered. "I'd like to, but we'll see."

There was only one person I was interested in dating. So if she wasn't *also* interested in it, then no, I probably wasn't going to start dating.

"Hmm." I could *hear* the wheels turning in my mom's head. "You met someone at Mulligan's not that long ago, right? Whatever happened to them?"

She *would* hit the nail on the head.

"What was their name again?" she went on, musing more to herself than me. "I can't remember."

"Natalie," I said with a laugh, pinching the bridge of my nose and tipping my head back as I let the truth wash over me. "And I think I'm in deep with her, Mom."

I was heading out of the office later that day when Julian called after me, halting me in my tracks when I heard the tension in his voice.

"Cam, hold up."

My friend's blue eyes were extra vibrant when I turned around in the Gardner Law lobby, putting me on edge.

"What's up?"

He did a quick look around us before he spoke, further stretching my nerves to their breaking point. "You're going to meet with Korey Abrams' lawyer, right?"

Answering with a nod, I looked at my watch to check the time. I had about twenty minutes to get to Wilson and Thomas, but it wasn't far. It was my last meeting of the day, the one that I was least looking forward to, especially because I'd much rather go straight home and call Natalie, get to the bottom of whatever the fuck she wanted to end.

But earlier this week, Korey's lawyer had reached out about meeting before the trial. They wanted to present some kind of custody agreement, and I suspected it was because they knew that sole physical custody was a leap they weren't going to make happen in trial.

Korey might have some things on his side—a more consistent work schedule, a supposed partner to help with childcare, and proximity to grandparents with his move—but Chloe had roots here, in Boston. There was extended family here, too. Sure, maybe they weren't retired, maybe they didn't have the flexibility of Korey's parents, but they were here. They'd proven to be a good support system, even if Natalie did need a lot of help. And Natalie had more than proven herself. Korey and Keller knew this. She'd shown that she had always been the involved parent, that she'd always prioritized Chloe.

Natalie hadn't been able to fit the meeting into her schedule this week—we hadn't even been able to reschedule our meeting from the day she'd gotten called into the hospital—so she told me to go ahead without her, and I could fill her in on what they wanted later.

"I was talking to Gemma, and she said that Korey came to skating practice last night," Julian continued, and I stood straighter, brows furrowing. I didn't like the direction this was going one fucking bit.

"Asshole's trying to make himself look better, huh?"

Julian nodded, but it was in an impatient sort of way, like he hadn't actually made his point yet.

"Chloe mentioned you," he said, causing dread to creep into my veins. It flowed straight to my heart. "To Korey. A lot, I guess. Like about her coming to the office yesterday."

"*Fuck.*"

"Yeah." Julian drew out the word. "I wanted to make sure you had a heads-up before your meeting."

"Thanks, man," I said with a sigh, shaking my head in irritation.

I didn't blame Chloe, of course. I hadn't even thought to say anything to the nine-year-old about her dad. It wasn't really my place, and she saw her dad so infrequently I didn't even consider it would be an issue. But I should have expected that he might try to show up more, especially with the trial looming, and I just knew that he was about to make this meeting even harder than it had to be.

"Need backup?" Julian offered, but I waved him off.

"I can handle that asshole," I assured him. "It's fine. He doesn't have proof of anything."

Julian tilted his head to the side, a crooked grin sliding onto his face. "He doesn't have proof of what?"

Shit, I hadn't meant for that to slip out.

I inhaled. Exhaled. Leveled Julian with a look. His eyes dazzled as he raised a brow. I gave a resigned nod. His smirk grew while giving a shake of his head, a little disappointed but a little knowing, like he understood what it was to give into something inevitable. I mean, I was pretty sure he'd crossed lines in this office with Juniper, but that still wasn't as bad as me, as this. Juniper was a colleague, not a client.

He patted me on the shoulder, giving it a squeeze.

"*Nothing*," I said then, aloud—a word that contradicted our entire former exchange.

Because that was what Julian needed to know: nothing. If, God forbid, my relationship with Natalie somehow came to light and Korey managed to find real, tangible proof, I needed Julian to have plausible deniability.

Julian laughed and then dropped his hand.

"Go get rid of Korey's ass so you can put this behind you and get your girl," he muttered under his breath and then let me go.

His words of encouragement were pretty much the only thing keeping me sane as I made my way through the startlingly hot Boston streets to Wilson and Thomas, especially since I wasn't even sure if Natalie *wanted* to be my girl after the text she sent this morn—*wait*.

Did Natalie know that Chloe had talked to Korey about me? About us? Because if she did...that just might explain everything. I *hoped* it explained everything. And I hoped she knew she couldn't push me away that easily, not just to appease her manipulative ex.

With that possibility in mind, my steps were lighter as I made my way to the same conference room where we'd held Korey's deposition. The ex-husband in question wasn't there yet when I walked in, but his lawyer was. I gave Mr. Keller a curt greeting, which he returned as I rounded the table to sit across from him.

"My client will be here soon, but we'd like to propose a new custody agreement ahead of trial."

"Sure," I replied with a nod, having expected that. It felt a bit like a waste of time since I was sure Natalie would have no interest in going for whatever split arrangement they'd concocted. But oh well. "Let's—"

"Wait a *fucking* minute."

Korey Abrams burst through the doors of the conference room in the most overdramatic fashion I had ever seen—arms swinging, suit jacket flying open, eyes flaring. He seethed, and all of that glaring attention was going straight to me.

"We're not doing *anything* until we talk about what this man has been doing."

Korey leaned over the table, jabbing a finger at me. His lawyer looked between the two of us, clearly unaware of his client's concerns. Too bad, honestly, because maybe he could have warned Korey that this was going to go nowhere. Could have saved us some fucking time.

"I'm afraid I don't know what you're talking about," I said flatly.

"Don't give me that shit." Korey straightened, putting his hands on his hips. His voice lowered to a degree that might be threatening, if I could ever be threatened by a man this small. "I want you to stay the fuck away from my daughter and the hell away from my wife," he hissed.

I gritted my teeth, if only because he kept conveniently forgetting that he'd lost the privilege of calling Natalie that a long time ago.

"I am representing your *ex*-wife in your custody trial, Mr. Abrams," I intoned, doing my best to sound bored by his intimidation. "Our collaboration is necessary for the case."

"Your collaboration," he repeated, huffing a humorless laugh beneath his breath. "Your *collaboration*. So that's what we're calling it, huh?"

"Mr. Abrams—"

Mr. Keller attempted to cut in, but Korey turned to him and spat, "This man has been parading around with *my* family. Taking them to baseball games, bringing my daughter to a *law firm*, babysitting her so Natalie can spend all her fucking time at work, as usual."

I folded my hands on the table in front of me. "Mr. Abrams, as I know Natalie told you at her brother's house, I am a friend of the family. I have been for many years. And it is important for me to foster good relationships with my clients, which is all I have been doing."

"*Good relationships*," Korey sputtered, and I could tell from the wild glaze coating his eyes as they swung back to me that he was spiraling. *Shit*. "You're fucking my wife, aren't you?"

No.

I'm fucking your ex-wife, Abrams.

Before I even got a chance to respond to his allegation, Korey looked back to his lawyer, thrust a finger at me, and proclaimed, "He's *fucking* my wife. Aren't there some goddamn rules against that?"

Mr. Keller looked increasingly out of his depth, so much so that it might be humorous if I wasn't counting on him to keep his client in check. "Yes, there are very serious rules about that." He gave me a pointed look, a raised brow, and I glared back, stony-faced. "If there were to be a confirmed relationship."

"And there is *not*," I said, my voice dropping like an anvil. "We have established that I am simply a friend of the family. To which there are no rules against."

"You're fucking lying," Korey argued, huffing in a way that was a tad worrying, health-wise.

I shook my head.

I wasn't lying. Omitting the truth, but whatever. I wasn't under oath. And hopefully, Keller wouldn't figure out an avenue to put me under oath.

"There is no proof otherwise, Mr. Abrams," I said, spreading my hands out as if to welcome any proof—which I knew he didn't have. "So I suggest you let your jealousy and anger about what you've lost go, and let us proceed."

Okay, *fine*, so I shouldn't have provoked him further. But he was making it *so* very hard not to.

Korey seemed speechless for a moment, and then there were a few incoherent babbles before he shook his head, putting his foot in the ground. "There's no way in hell that's going to happen."

"Mr. Abrams," Keller tried again, and this time, he actually managed to get his client's attention. "Why don't you have a seat so we can...sort this out?"

A muscle twitched in Korey's jaw, but he sat, flopping into a chair in a dramatized fashion, as usual. I tried hard to remain expressionless at the entire scene, though it proved to be more of a challenge than I liked to admit.

Sure, my job was on the line here. But ultimately, Korey and I both knew he had no proof that I'd been doing exactly what he accused me of doing. And it was hard not to be at least a little smug about it.

But all of that faded when Keller asked, "What is it that you would like to happen here, Mr. Abrams?"

And Korey gave a flatlined look across the table to say, "I want this asshole thrown off the case."

My entire body tightened at the thought.

For some reason, I hadn't expected him to say that, and the idea of not being Natalie's lawyer anymore, of not pushing through to the end of the case...it felt unfathomable. It could jeopardize the progress I'd made toward becoming partner and the good standing I had in the firm. It could imply guilt, that I *had* been carrying on a secret relationship with Natalie. But mostly, it could mean not getting to be the one who stood by her side when we won this thing.

Out of everything, that was the most inconceivable thought. That was what weighed the heaviest on my conscience.

Natalie.

Just, *Natalie.*

"That would be up to my client to decide," I said with a shrug, faking nonchalance.

Korey scoffed, irritated, because he knew what Natalie's response to that would be. And wasn't that just a little bit satisfying? That he knew she'd pick me?

I tried to control the twitch of my lips.

"Gardner Law has other talented lawyers, and it is within her right to request a new one," I added. "But that decision is up to her."

Korey pressed his lips together, folding arms over his chest. And even though he didn't push it further, I knew I had another reason I needed to call Natalie tonight.

And I wasn't looking forward to any of it.

Somehow, Keller got Korey to focus on the task at hand, and we were able to move on with the meeting, although not without consistent glaring across the table on the man-child's part.

Their proposition still involved Natalie giving up a lot of time with Chloe, and I knew she'd never go for it. But I promised to present the proposition to my client and then left Wilson and Thomas Law, my stomach sinking with every step.

Without Korey breathing down my neck, I didn't have to pretend that his accusations and finger-pointing weren't eating me up inside. Not because I gave a shit about what he thought about me, but because I could readily admit that he *could* be dangerous. He didn't have a lot left to lose here, and desperate men went to desperate measures to regain their slipping control. He could very well threaten what Natalie and I had built—with the case and in our personal lives. And I didn't know what the hell to do about it.

This case was far from over. There were still a number of weeks before the trial, hearings scheduled prior to it, and then the possibility that it could take days to weeks for the judge to decide on a ruling. That was a lot of time for Korey to dig deeper into our lives, a lot of time for shit to go sideways.

But giving up Natalie? In any capacity?

Fuck, I didn't know how the hell I was supposed to do that at this point. Letting someone else take the case had always felt like a nonnegotiable, but now? Now that it meant I might have to give up Natalie for weeks, if not months? Right when it felt like we were at a tipping point?

I was afraid something had to give, but I shook my head, knowing I was getting ahead of myself. The last thing I heard from Natalie was *I think we should end this.* Before anything else, I needed to figure out what the hell she meant by that. And if she really thought it would be that easy to simply walk away.

It wouldn't be. It would involve severing something inside both of us, the pull that kept drawing us back together time and time again.

She could deny her feelings all she wanted, but I knew they were there. Maybe they weren't as intense or all-consuming as mine, but they existed. They were in the depth of her eyes when she looked at me the other night, the softness of her voice, the trust of her weight as it sank into me, knowing I'd take care of her. And I'd wait as long as I fucking had to until she realized what was right in front of us.

Yeah, maybe she hadn't asked for this, for the direction our relationship had turned. But it *had* turned, and I wasn't sure I could let her run away out of fear again. Not this time.

I just needed her to stay long enough for us to figure this out.

I needed her to trust that I'd figure this out.

I'd do *anything* to figure this out.

CHAPTER THIRTY-SIX

natalie

MY STOMACH SANK WHEN I saw Cameron's name flash up on the screen, the opposite reaction I usually had to anything involving him. I'd been dreading this conversation all day. He hadn't even responded to my text, leaving me to wonder what he was thinking, if he was mad. Leaving me to wonder if he would call.

But now, he was.

Of course he was.

Because when had I ever asked him for something and Cameron hadn't delivered?

"Hello?" I answered, tentative.

"Hey, baby," he responded, and just like that, all my defense walls were knocked down.

He didn't sound mad. Not at all, actually. His voice had notes of exhaustion and stress, but also determination. He didn't sound like he was ready to give up whatever this was, whatever we were.

"I'm sorry it got late," he added. "I got held up with some work stuff."

I cleared my throat, trying to keep the emotion out of it. "It's okay."

"Where are you?"

"In bed," I said honestly. I'd been trying to keep my eyes open in hopes that he would call or text me back. It had been another strenuous day at SCMC, but I'd needed to hear from him.

"Mm," he hummed, like he was imagining it. Remembering it. Being together last night, the things we'd done, said. It sent shivers running through me. I could feel the ghost of his touch running up my body, parting my thighs, pressing over my mouth.

Focus. *Focus.*

"Did you see my text?" I ventured, because I was starting to think maybe he hadn't. Otherwise, he wouldn't be acting so normal.

And that was the achingly sad truth of it all, wasn't it? How badly I wanted this to be our normal? How badly I wanted a reality where he'd call me at the end of a long day, his husky voice in my ear saying, "Hey, baby," when I picked up the phone.

We'd talk about mundane things like the weather and the little idiosyncrasies of our lives. He'd ask me about Chloe because he so evidently cared about her, and I'd tell him, fill him in on everything that he'd missed since the last time we talked. Like if Annabeth had terrorized my brothers that day or if Chloe had learned anything new at skating. He'd ask me if I'd eaten enough, and I'd ask him if he watched any baseball before bed. He'd tell me if he'd been reading anything new from Juniper's little work library, and I'd giggle at his answer. Maybe he'd whisper dirty words in my ear, or maybe he wouldn't. Because our relationship would be more than that. We'd be more than that.

But we couldn't be that, not right now.

"I did," Cameron said so nonchalantly that it left me wondering if we were talking about the same text. "I saw you think we should end things."

You think.

Oh, God, he was going to fight for this, for us, wasn't he?

That was something I hadn't expected, though I maybe should have. It was just that Cameron was usually so respectful, so good at abiding by the boundaries I put in place. I assumed that if I told him we were done, he'd walk away without a second thought.

"I just have one question to ask you about that, Sunshine," he continued, and I sank further into my bed, trying to hide from the inevitability of this conversation and the slight pain that lingered in his words.

"What?" I squeaked out.

"Did you send me that because Korey found out that I've been spending time with you and Chloe, or did you send that because you really want to end this?"

I sucked in, surprised that he'd both known and seen right through me, and Cameron went on.

"Yeah, I started to wonder, you know? Why would she send me something like that after just last night begging me not to leave? And then today, I had that meeting with Korey and his lawyer—" I sat up in bed, slapping a hand over my mouth so I wouldn't interrupt him. But *shit.* "And it went exactly how you could probably guess it went."

"Oh my God," I gasped. "I completely forgot that was today. Cameron, I'm so sorry. If I had remembered, I would have called you this morning to—"

"It's okay," he cut in, all suave and unbothered as usual. "It's all going to be okay, Natalie. Just answer the question, please. Did you send that text because you're worried about Korey? Or do you want to reevaluate our relationship and arrangement for another reason? If you do...it's alright. I just need to know."

His voice strained to get the last part out, letting me know that no, it wouldn't be alright. But, like I originally assumed, he'd respect boundaries if I put them in place.

I released a breath, loud enough that Cameron could likely hear the whoosh of air attacking the phone speaker.

"I sent it because of Korey," I admitted before rushing to add, "I'm *worried*, Cameron. About you, about the case. Why didn't you tell me that you were up for a promotion?"

"Ah," he sighed, sounding a little disappointed. But not necessarily in me. "How'd you find out about that?"

"Gemma, from Noah." I sighed, too, staring up at my ceiling fan, watching it go round and round. A heat wave had hit Boston this week, and even inside, the air felt thick and sticky, making worry and anxiety cling to me like a second skin. "She told me about Korey showing up at skating and mentioned your promotion because she had the same worries. And I felt foolish that I hadn't known. Cameron, I don't want you to jeopardize advancing your career over this. That's amazing that you're so close to taking that step at your firm."

"Oh, baby." Cameron gave a husky chuckle, something that made my insides tingle. "If what we've been doing is discovered, with proof, it's not just the opportunity of junior partner that I'd be losing. There's a chance I could be disbarred."

"You'd be—" My jaw dropped, my breath leaving my body. I sat up straight in bed. "What? Cameron, *no*."

How selfish could I be? Why had I not thought to look into it myself, research the consequences of what we'd been doing? I'd foolishly assumed that since Cameron had been so confident about it, so unworried and sure and everything Cameron normally was, that it wasn't anything *quite* so serious. I'd known it wouldn't be good, but I hadn't realized it would be so terribly bad, either.

"I—I—" I couldn't even form words, my brain spinning too fast, my stomach sinking rapidly, falling into a pit of guilt. I clutched my abdomen out of the possibility I was going to be sick. "We can't do this," I gasped, somehow finding my voice. "You could lose your ability to practice law? After everything you've worked towards, following in your dad's footsteps? Oh my God, Cam." I choked on the dense, humid air. "We shouldn't have—*I* shouldn't have—"

"*Hey*," he cut in, his voice sharp enough that it cut straight through my panic and hit me square in the chest. "Breathe, Mama. Take a deep breath."

I listened. Because when Cameron told me to do something, I knew it would make me feel better. It always did.

My breathing grew easier, though only marginally. I closed my eyes, forcing air in and out of my lungs. I could hear Cameron breathing, too. And then his calm voice as he encouraged me. "That's it. Just breathe, Sunshine. I wish I was there to hold you, but you're doing a good job. I can tell. Take another one for me?"

I nodded, even though he couldn't see me, and funneled more air into my body, which helped to slow the rapid pace of my pulse.

"Good girl," Cameron murmured, even gentler. "None of that now. I knew what I was doing, and I chose to do it. None of this is on you. Got it?"

I heard him, and I understood what he was saying, but I couldn't just let this go. "But Cam—"

"Everything will be fine," he assured me, and I just had no idea how he possessed just *so* much confidence all the time. "I didn't tell you because I knew you would react like this. And Natalie—" He broke off, releasing a resigned sigh. Like whatever he was about to say was a truth he couldn't avoid, even if he wanted to. He dropped his voice, so it hit deep. "Natalie, I *wanted* you. I still do. You have no—"

He cut himself off again, making me feel like I was dangling on the edge of something. He liked to do that, didn't he?

"Is there any chance you can come into the office tomorrow?" he asked instead of finishing his other sentence. "There are a few things regarding the case I'd like to go over." He paused before adding, "Pertaining to my meeting with Korey today."

I was tentative to reply. "Okay."

"If tomorrow doesn't work for you, we can find another time," he offered, hearing my hesitation.

"No, it's just..." I swallowed. "You're making me *nervous*, Cam. I'm so nervous about this entire thing. Can you just tell me whatever it is now?"

"Don't be," he insisted. His voice was tender and self-assured, everything I needed in order to believe him. "You don't have to worry about a damn thing, Sunshine. But I'd like to...see you in person when we talk about this. Do you want me to come over tonight?"

I flung myself back in bed, biting my lip as I contemplated that. I badly wanted Cameron here. I missed his touch, his calming presence, his steadying words. But I was exhausted, and he was exhausted, and most importantly, we needed to be careful now. More careful than we have been.

"That's okay," I breathed. "But I do...miss you."

"Oh, *fuck.*" The curse seemed to slip out of him, like he hadn't expected me to say that, to speak with such raw honesty. But he also couldn't seem to wait to follow my lead. "I miss you, too. I've been thinking about you all fucking day, Natalie."

Flutters erupted in my stomach at the idea that he might think about me just as much as I thought about him. But I also suspected I knew the reason I was on his mind, and it probably wasn't a good one.

"I'm sorry if I worried you," I said, my voice quiet, full of guilt. "With the text."

"Worry?" Cameron huffed a humorless laugh, and then his voice descended into something gruff, gravelly. Hurt leaked through his words. "Baby, I was in agony."

A hot sensation expanded, pressing against the walls of my chest.

Agony.

It was exactly how I'd felt all day, too. The thought of being apart from him and cutting short the relationship that had begun to blossom was nothing short of *agony.*

"I'm sorry," I repeated, a whisper of regret.

"It's okay," he assured me, no longer sounding quite so pained. Instead, something else was in his voice, something I couldn't quite place. "It made me realize something. We can talk about it tomorrow, alright? I know you had another long day at work."

"Yeah, yeah, I did." I paused, knowing I should say good night, let us both hang up and go to sleep. But the achiness from this morning returned, and I couldn't get myself to put down the phone. Not yet. "Hey, Cam?"

"Hm?"

"Can we talk a little bit before bed, though? Just about...whatever. Not work or this." I shrugged. "I don't know."

There was silence from the other end of the phone, and I started to feel silly. Until his voice broke through, and he sounded so content, so *happy*, that I just wanted to bottle up the sound of his voice and keep it forever.

"I would love to talk before bed," he said. "What'd you have for dinner, Sunshine?"

I turned onto my side and smiled into my pillow.

And then I told Cameron about my day.

And then asked him about his.

And fell asleep with my phone pressed to my ear.

CHAPTER THIRTY-SEVEN

cameron

NATALIE HAD GONE QUIET. Her gentle breaths were the only thing coming through the speaker, but I couldn't get myself to hang up.

It was soothing to me, to hear that she was sleeping peacefully.

It was all I wanted for Natalie—peace. Happiness. Some fucking rest.

I needed to pick whichever path gave her the most of that. Because right now, all I could do was replay the panic in her voice, the guilt, the worry.

I knew it was multifaceted. Worry for me, worry for Chloe, worry for whatever Korey might do next. Jealousy was a dangerous emotion, and she knew him better than anyone—knew what he might be capable of.

Fuck, I didn't want her to worry. I'd never meant to complicate things for her, and that was exactly what I'd done. I needed to *un*complicate it, needed to detangle the web. But it felt impossible when I was so unbelievably tied up in her.

Lying flat on my back, I stared up at the ceiling, Natalie's soft sighs in my ear.

I thought about Korey—the man responsible for all of this.

Natalie clearly didn't *want* to break things off between us. But she probably thought that if we did, I could continue as her lawyer.

It wasn't like Korey would know we broke it off, though. It wasn't like he'd somehow be satisfied by the change in our relationship if he didn't know it happened. He didn't know *anything* had happened, but I could tell he was stuck on it. Would *stay* stuck on it. Chloe might report that I was around less if he saw her again, but I certainly wasn't going to count on that or involve a nine-year-old in this. Protecting Chloe from his manipulation was what this was all about in the first place.

Korey was losing, and he knew it. That much was evident by the way they'd tried to draft a new custody agreement. And a losing man fought harder than a winning man.

Shit. I hated to admit it, but it was possible that the best strategy in this was to make Korey feel like he was winning.

Which meant doing the thing I should have done from the very beginning but I was too selfish to consider. The thing my ego hadn't let me even think about.

Of all the things I could lose, though, my pride was what I cared least about at the moment.

Closing my eyes, I let Natalie's deep breathing wash over me.

She said she missed me, and it had taken everything in me not to sprint to her.

She said she missed me, and I realized I couldn't live without her. I realized that there was now someone—no, *two* someones—in this world I just couldn't even think about giving up.

No matter the cost.

CHAPTER THIRTY-EIGHT

natalie

CAMERON STOOD WHEN I walked into his office the next day, flashing me a professional smile. There was a hard-to-miss twinkle in his eyes that calmed my overwrought nerves.

"Ah, Dr. London, thank you so much for coming in."

I shut the door behind me before sinking into one of the chairs across from his desk and raising a brow, giving him a once-over. He wore his usual clean-cut suit, tailored so perfectly to his fit physique, and it was really hard not to have a hot flash in reaction to his presence.

God, I missed him, and it had only been thirty-six hours or so.

"Dr. London?" I echoed, clearing my throat.

Cameron's eyes shone brighter, but he shrugged. "I'm just practicing."

"Practicing?"

"Acting like I've never been inside you before."

I nearly choked on my own tongue. "*Cameron.*"

On instinct, I looked over my shoulder, double-checking that the door was firmly closed and no one could overhear us. It was, but the small window lining the door taunted me, reminding me that we weren't entirely alone. That anyone could walk by and look into his office. When I turned back around, Cameron was standing in front of his desk, leaning back against it.

He was so close, barely two feet away. And my body was vibrating with the need to get even closer. It felt weird walking into a room where he was and *not* sliding straight into his arms.

How the hell were we going to do this?

Especially when Cameron wore that cocky little smirk on his face, confidence shining through. Which did put me somewhat at ease. He wore an expression like he didn't plan on anything bad happening—as though he could control the world.

"No one's going to hear anything, Sunshine," he said, reaffirming my thoughts. His voice was gentle now, just another thing that soothed me.

He stared at me for a long moment, his hands flexing like he also struggled with the urge to close the distance between us. Possibly like it was killing him not to. Eventually, he crossed both arms over his chest and inhaled deeply. A muttered curse slipped through his lips a moment later.

"What?" I asked.

"Nothing." He was looking at me like he didn't know what to do about my existence. "It's just my office is going to smell like you for the rest of the day, and it's going to torture me."

"I'm...sorry?"

A laugh fell out of his mouth, bright and colorful, changing his entire demeanor. "Never apologize for the way you affect other people by just being you, Natalie."

My heart clenched, letting those words wrap around it and squeeze tight. The way Cameron managed to touch me while not even putting his hands on me blew me away every time. I gave him a shaky smile, and he returned it, allowing me a few seconds to sink into his warm, brown gaze before bringing me back to reality, sharp and swift.

"Korey wants me off your case."

I jolted. "*What?*"

He nodded, calm as ever. "He doesn't like that I'm spending time with Chloe, and he accused us of...having a relationship."

"Having a relationship?" I echoed.

A muscle in Cameron's jaw jumped. "His exact words were that I was 'fucking his wife.'"

My jaw dropped. I'd known Korey would jump to conclusions, but he was usually more, I don't know, underhanded in his accusations. Which told me he was clearly losing it—all that control he'd been trying to hold on to, it was slipping out of his grasp, and he was losing it.

"I denied it, of course," Cameron said, dropping his voice. "I'm fucking his *ex*-wife."

Of course Cam was madder about that distinction than anything else, and despite the circumstances, I found myself fighting a grin.

"But Korey wouldn't stop pushing the matter. He wants me off the case."

Off the case.

The words bounced around my brain, and I struggled to believe them.

I wasn't sure I'd ever hated Korey more than I did at this moment.

"Oh my God." I sank lower in my chair, feeling sick to my stomach.

I should have been more careful, should have told Cameron no all the times I'd given in and said yes, should have put more boundaries in place until after the case was over, especially where Chloe was involved.

But it was so hard to regret nights like the baseball game, where Chloe had gotten to experience something that she never really had with her own father. It was hard to regret her spending time with a man whom I was starting to hope might be a permanent figure in her life.

Now, though...

"He can't do that, can he? Force you off the case?"

Cameron shook his head, and a bit of relief slipped into my bloodstream.

"No, he can't. And I don't think he has any proof of anything because if he did, he would have said something yesterday. I know he's calculating and manipulative, but he lost control during that meeting. And trust me, he has nothing."

"Okay." I nodded, taking all that information in and agreeing. It certainly didn't *sound* like Korey was his usual self. This sounded more like the version of my ex when I'd told him we were getting divorced—the spiraling, accusatory version. "Good. That's...good."

Cameron mimicked me, also nodding. "It is. But I would bet he's going to try to find proof now."

My stomach sank again. Because I knew Cameron was right about that, too. "So, we *should* end things. At least until the case is over."

Our conversation on the phone last night had made me think that we were going to find a way around that, but Cameron's expression told me that maybe I'd been holding on to false hope or misinterpreted his confidence.

But I understood. Completely. If something happened to Cameron's career because of me, I wasn't sure what I'd do.

Cameron remained silent for a long moment, biting the inside of his cheek. And then finally, he said, "Natalie, it could be months yet."

Months.

"We're still weeks out from the trial date, and the court calendar is tight, so if there's any rescheduling, if Korey and his lawyer try something to buy more time, it could get pushed another month back. And once the trial is over, it's possible we might get a decision that day, but it might also be days or weeks. I..." He paused, shaking his head. Cameron looked as tortured as I felt. "If we don't give Korey what he wants, he's going to keep digging until he finds *something* to feel like he has the upper hand again. I don't like the idea of waiting for the other shoe to drop. And I like the idea of doing that waiting without you even less."

"What are you saying?" I whispered, afraid of what his answer was.

Cameron's sigh was so heavy I felt it weighing me down, too. "That I think I should step away from this case."

I'd seen it coming from his expression, but my body revolted at the idea. Firstly, of giving Korey *anything* he wanted, and secondly, of not having Cameron as my attorney—at making him give away something he'd been working on for weeks now. "Cameron. That's—" God, it was such a struggle to believe he was even suggesting this. "But wouldn't that look...but how would that affect—"

"It wouldn't affect the case at all," he said stoically. "A judge's main concern would be that nothing is delayed with the trial, and I would work overtime to catch your new representation up so that doesn't happen."

"My new representation?" I repeated, feeling another surge of disbelief. He was serious, wasn't he? "Who would that even be?"

Selfishly, I didn't *want* new representation.

"My suggestion would be Juniper Briggs," he answered, and while I didn't like that he'd clearly thought about this, the idea of Juniper taking over did put me a little at ease. "She also has a great background in family law, is a phenomenal lawyer, and we could still work closely together to make sure all the bases for the trial are covered. I'd still help to take care of things behind the scenes. Also, I suspect Korey is a raging misogynist and would somehow think he has the upper hand if I let Juniper take my place. Until she wiped the floor with him, that is."

I couldn't argue with any of the points he was making. They were all very good points, and I knew he was likely right about all of them. But there was something he had yet to touch on, something equally important.

"Okay, yes, all true, but..." I sat forward in my chair, clutching the arms on it. "But what about *you*?"

Cameron frowned, brows drawn together. "Me?"

"You told me after my deposition that your boss had her eyes on this case. That it might look bad if—"

"Since the pressure is coming from Korey, she'll understand why I'm doing it," he cut in, trying to reassure me. "Sure, she might be a little disappointed, and maybe it will set me back a few steps from junior partner, but Natalie—" He cut off, rubbing his jaw for a second before giving me a defeated look and saying, "I don't fucking care."

"What?" So much of what he was saying was *so* hard to wrap my brain around. "What do you mean you don't care? I *know* how important your job is to you."

Cameron simply shrugged like he was lost to the truth of the matter, lost to what he was about to say.

"Not as important to me as you are."

I stared at him, feeling my pulse in my throat, making it hard to swallow. Or breathe. Or think. He couldn't...*mean* that. Could he?

The corners of Cameron's mouth turned down, and his eyes grew sympathetic as he watched my reaction. Sighing, he shook his head.

"Natalie. Baby." He crouched to his knees in front of me, meeting me at eye level. "Come on. You must realize by now."

"Realize?"

Cameron gave me a look. "Sunshine."

He looked disappointed in me, and I tried to puzzle together *why*.

"What?" I whispered.

He reached out, brushing hair out of my face before cupping my cheek. "You have to know how much I care for you. How I feel about you?"

My heartbeat roared in my ears at his words, like my body refused to let me ignore how it raced. And I didn't want to. I closed my eyes, listening to it while pressing into the palm of

Cameron's hand, feeding off his touch. It hadn't been very long, but I missed it so much.

I'd suspected how he felt, but I hadn't known. Cameron had this way about him where he was *so* very responsible, so very *good*. And I knew he took pride in being that way, being a man who was there for everyone, in the way that he wanted to take after his dad.

So while *yes*, there were signs, and *yes*, there were moments when I felt, in my bones, that we were so much more than we were pretending to be, I hadn't *known*. Not for sure.

"This isn't what you wanted." Cameron's deep voice broke through my thoughts, and I opened to find him staring intently at me. "I realize that. I know you wanted someone to fuck you, and you never asked for someone to fall for you, but..." He shrugged, like there was nothing he could do about it.

"Cameron," I choked out, not sure what to do with the emotions building inside me. I placed my hand over his on my cheek, feeling some desperate need to cling to his touch. It was what we'd been using to communicate for so long, and I'd been relying on it instead of words to convey how I felt about him.

And he understood, nodding. He always, somehow, understood.

He'd talk for us right now. Until I could, until I was ready.

"I know you didn't want to dive back into a relationship that moved too quickly," he acknowledged. "But Natalie, if you let me...I'd like to move really slow with you. I'd like to move at whatever pace you want, just so long as I get to be with you. And I don't really want to wait months to do that, but the only way that'll work is if I'm no longer your lawyer."

That hope that had been bubbling in my chest for the last week suddenly expanded, ready to burst right out of me and live out in the open, finally.

"You want that?" I breathed.

"Oh, baby." Cameron's lips spread in a gentle but unavoidable smile. Like the thought alone of being together threatened all his restraint. "I want it so fucking bad. You have no idea."

A tingle ran down my spine and spread, making me feel like I was sitting on pins and needles. Like maybe I should get up and dance instead.

"I really wanted to end this custody case by your side," he continued, brushing his thumb back and forth over my cheekbone. "It kills me to give up the opportunity to personally crush Korey in court. But I like the idea of being by your side in a different way much, much more. If you'll let me."

"Cameron, I..." I shook my head, flailing as I tried to piece together my thoughts. He'd jumbled them all up with his words. So many perfect, heart-stopping words. "I don't know what to say."

The corner of his mouth went up and down, like he was nervous and wasn't sure what emotions to convey. But Cameron was never nervous, and I suddenly realized how crucial it was that I reassure him, that I do a better job of *finding* what to say.

"I like you," I managed, a threadbare whisper. It wasn't beautiful prose or well thought out, but it was the truth. "*A lot*, Cameron. In a really big, scary way."

Cameron used his other hand to cup my other cheek, and I realized tears had leaked from my eyes when he brushed something away beneath them. He gave me an encouraging smile, his eyes roving over me like he was afraid I might vanish or that I'd take my words back. He stared at me like he was struggling to believe that I'd said that, and maybe he understood why I'd been so speechless, too. Why finding words was hard when you heard ones you never expected.

Finally, he said, "I like you in a really big, scary way, too."

I swallowed before confessing, "I have since that first night. At Mulligan's." He nodded, like he knew. "I've always just been... scared. And I'm sorry."

"You don't need to apologize for that." Cameron dropped his hands and then leaned back again, like he suddenly remembered we were still in his office. "It killed me when you ran away, but I understood." His lips twisted wryly. "Didn't stop me from thinking about you every fucking day, though."

"I'm sorry," I repeated.

I thought about him, too. So much.

"Stop," he muttered, giving me a look I didn't dare disobey. "No more apologies, Sunshine."

"Okay," I said, because it was all I could think to say.

Cameron stood, leaning against his desk again, this time resting on his palms, which he planted on either side of his hips. I found myself roving my gaze over him, wondering how this man truly existed and how eager I suddenly was to make him mine.

When my slow perusal made it to his face, I got trapped in his hot gaze. He raised a brow, like he knew what I was thinking.

I felt feverish, with the warmth spreading over my cheeks.

"I'm going home this weekend," he said after a moment, clearing his throat. "To see my family. Why don't you take a few days to think about the case and everything else, okay? We can talk on Monday, maybe?"

"Sure, I'd like that."

I didn't really like it. I wanted to confirm everything with him right now, draw lines to make things incredibly clear after so many weeks of the lines feeling blurred. In my gut, I knew he was right. About everything he'd said regarding Korey and the case and how awful it would be to pretend like we didn't mean anything to each other. I knew he was also right that I should take the time to think everything through. It was the smart thing. And I promised myself that I'd do the smart things this time around.

"Maybe I could take you out to dinner? To chat about it or just...because," Cameron ventured, chewing on his bottom lip. "If you want."

Oh, nervous Cameron was adorable. It made me want to *squeal*.

I flashed him a shy grin. "Like a date?"

A shrug. "That's up to you, baby."

I nodded, and Cameron's smile grew more confident again.

"Dinner on Monday," I said. "Yes."

God, I couldn't even get a full sentence out.

"I'll leave it up to you if you want Chloe to come," he offered. "She's welcome."

What was he *doing* to me?

"Chloe would love to come," I said honestly. If she knew I was getting dinner with Cameron, she'd beg for an invite. However, there were other realities that came with that. And I needed him to know that. "But you know...if we start dating, Chloe will likely begin to ask really intrusive questions."

Cameron didn't even blink, that was how unsurprised he was. "I would expect nothing less from her."

I cocked a brow. Did he *really* know what he was getting himself into?

"She's going to want to know about things like babies—"

"I like babies."

"—and marriage and—"

"I'd happily take your last name."

"Cameron," I scolded, laughter bubbling out of me. I just couldn't remember the last time I'd been *so* happy, even while there was so much up in the air. "I'm being *serious*."

His grin was full now. "So am I." He leaned forward, and I could tell he wanted to reach out, wanted to touch me again, if just by the way his fingers flexed on the top of his desk. His voice dropped to a pitch that was throaty and thick, and I basked in it as he said, "I've been trying my best to act nonchalant, Natalie. Like I don't want to punch the lights out of every man who looks at you a little too long, like that asshat at the baseball game. But it's just that, an act. There's nothing fucking casual about the way I feel for you or the way I want to keep you to myself. I want you to be mine, and *God*, I want everyone to know it."

I was lost for words, in awe of what he'd admitted.

And Cameron immediately misinterpreted my stunned expression for panic.

"When you're ready, of course." He dropped back to a crouch in front of me, gripping the arm of my chair. "Because we're not going to go off my timeline or Chloe's. We'll move at your speed, Natalie. Always your speed."

"It's okay, Cameron," I reassured him. "I...want everything you're saying, too." He stared, seeming shocked by my response, while I cocked my head to the side, considering the full picture. "Does moving slow mean we'd have to stop..." I raised a brow, checking behind me again to look out the small window. For a moment, I'd forgotten we were still here, sitting in Cameron's office. Back where it all started.

When I looked back at Cameron, he was fighting a grin.

"Having sex?" he finished for me. I nodded, and he said, "If that's what you want."

I shook my head because *no*, it was *not* what I wanted, and Cameron's laugh coated me in the most wonderful feeling in the world.

"Glad we're on the same page," he murmured before pushing to his feet and offering me a hand. "Would you like to maybe talk to Juniper? Before you decide for sure what you'd like to do?"

I released a breath. "Yeah, that sounds good. If she's available."

Cameron's fingers closed around mine, holding it tight, and I realized then how much he'd been like a lifeline to me these last months. An anchor in this stormy season. And the idea of getting to weather other seasons with him was just a treasure. Something I couldn't quite yet fathom.

"Okay. Let's go, Sunshine," he said, making me really, truly believe the thought he kept putting in my head every time he called me that.

Sunny days were ahead.

They might even be here right now.

CHAPTER THIRTY-NINE

cameron

"SO, YOUR MOM SAYS there's a someone."

I laughed at the way he said it. Everyone in my family was always so very cognizant of not assuming the gender of who I was dating, my eighty-year-old grandfather included. It was a little thing, really, but it went a long way in making me feel accepted by my family as a bisexual man. They'd only *ever* made me feel accepted, ever since I came out during my undergrad years in college, and I knew how lucky I was to know they'd welcome anyone I brought home to meet them. I also knew how much they would love Natalie, and I hoped to hell one day I could bring her here.

"There's a woman, yes," I said with a smile.

I didn't know how not to smile when I talked about Natalie, especially when I thought about our conversation at the office on Friday and how I got to see her tomorrow.

It wasn't entirely clear if it would be for a date or just dinner. Natalie was spending the weekend thinking about how she wanted to proceed with the trial, but I had a feeling in my bones that I wasn't going to be her lawyer by the time I saw her tomorrow night. Which shouldn't make me as happy as it did.

"Well..." Pops waved his hand, like he wanted me to get on with it. "Come on, then. Tell me about her."

I laughed again, crossing one leg over the other. We sat on the porch of my mom's house, which was a lot less rickety after I spent the morning fixing some of the floorboards. It overlooked her blooming flower gardens, and my eyes kept drifting to the sunflowers, rising higher than the rest of the plants. I'd already asked her for tips on growing them, thinking of the seeds Chloe and I had planted.

"She's a mom," I said because I knew it was one of Natalie's favorite roles, closely followed by, "And a trauma surgeon."

"Oh, ho," Pops chuckled. "A woman as smart as that, and she still agreed to go out with *you*?" He slapped his leg, like no one had ever made a funnier joke. The wrinkles around the corner of his eyes deepened as he looked at me, grinning.

"Look, it's still new," I acknowledged, putting my hands up in defense. "She might still come to her senses."

"No, no." He batted that idea away and then looked out at the quiet street, lined with older, maintained homes. My family lived in upstate New York, on the outskirts of the city. They'd found a little slice of peace here, and I always forgot just *how* peaceful it was until I came home and sank into it. "I was just joking, kid. She picked you *because* she's so smart. That's the real truth, eh?"

"She is very smart," I agreed with a grin. "And she's a great mom. I took her and her nine-year-old daughter, Chloe, to the game."

Pops gave me a side-eye. Because despite his age and his bruised hip, absolutely nothing got past this man. "I thought Tony said you were gonna take a client."

I side-eyed him back.

He cracked a smile, shaking his head.

"You never did let anything get in your way, did you?" A laugh wheezed out of him, and he tipped back in his cushioned rocker. "That was always something I admired about you. Something you and your dad had in common."

"Well," I sighed. "It does get a little tricky when the two things you want more than anything get in each other's way, but..." I shrugged. "I'm hoping by tomorrow, she'll be someone else's client. And I don't regret picking her."

"And you shouldn't!" Pops exclaimed, more explosive than I would have expected. He jabbed a finger at me. "Jobs come and go. But the people you love? Nothing replaces them. Nothing, Cam. So if that's how you feel..."

His brown gaze misted over as he looked at me, and tears prickled the back of my own eyes.

Yeah, that was really how I felt—like nothing could replace Natalie or Chloe in my life. And it was the truth, what I'd said. I hadn't regretted making the decision to prioritize them *once*, but hearing my grandfather reinforce what I'd felt so prominently in my gut? And seeing the fierceness in his gaze as he did? Fuck, I'd needed that.

I'd looked up to him my entire life. All I ever wanted to do was make this man proud, and there'd still been a small part of me that worried I might be letting him down with the way I'd handled everything. But here he was, telling me that wasn't true at all.

"What?" he prompted, when I cleared my throat but still hadn't said anything.

I shook my head. "It just seems foolish now."

He frowned. "What's foolish?"

"That I really thought you'd want me to prioritize making partner so I could follow in Dad's footsteps."

"Oh, kid." He pursed his lips, like he couldn't believe he had to say this aloud. Disappointed in a different way than I'd expected. "Your dad, my son, he was more than a good lawyer."

"I know that."

I knew that all too well, but being a lawyer was the one thing I'd always felt like I could maybe do as well as him. *Maybe*.

"And so are you," Pops added. "But you're also more than just his son. You shouldn't stick to a path just because someone else left it unfinished. No one expects you to do that."

I was quiet for a long moment, letting words sink in that I'd *really* needed to hear. I could almost feel the weight sliding from my shoulders, disappearing from sight. My chest ached, a sudden grief in knowing Pops was right; Dad's path was always going to be unfinished. And there was nothing I could do about it.

Nothing I did would change that.

And while that thought destroyed me, it also freed me.

"I think I know that, too," I finally said, my voice hoarse. "At least now, I do."

"Good." Pops nodded. He settled his hands on his round belly, like it was his own little table. "So that's where you met this girl?"

A grin split onto my face, and I was suddenly bursting inside, feeling renewed and so damn hopeful about where things were headed. Because I'd known from the very beginning that Natalie was someone so fucking special. And I finally got to tell someone why.

"No, actually. Get this." I turned, wanting to see his expression when I told him. "I met her at Mulligan's."

Pops' face lit up, his eyes sparkling.

I was born in California because my parents had moved there for work and spent some years out west. But my roots were here, on the East Coast. My grandfather had lived here in New York his whole life. It was where he raised my dad and my uncle with my grandmother. And my mom was from Boston. She used to live not too far away from where Noah and Gemma's apartment was, in Back Bay, and it was part of the reason I'd looked into Boston law schools before ultimately landing my job at Gardner. My mom had met my dad when he was in Boston visiting a friend from college, a story Pops knew well.

"Mulligan's," he repeated under his breath, an amused chuckle following it. He got more comfortable in his chair, tipping his head back on the patio cushions. "Yeah. You just let me know when the wedding is, 'kay?"

My chest felt like it might burst wide open at the thought, even as I reminded myself what I promised Natalie—that we'd take this as slow as she wanted.

"Will do, Pops."

He shook his head. "Why the hell did you ever agree to represent her in the first place?"

"I've been asking myself that question a lot lately," I admitted. "I should have known that this would always be the outcome. But she's a little skittish, you know? I don't think she would have taken a chance on me if it seemed like too much of a sure thing. I think the fact that we couldn't be together—not really—was her safety blanket of sorts. And given her past, I don't blame her."

"Mmm," Pops hummed. "Everything has a way of working out the way it's supposed to, doesn't it?"

"It does," I said, hoping I could speak it into existence.

Everything would work out.

CHAPTER FORTY

cameron

WHEN I ARRIVED AT Natalie's the next day, she opened the door before I even walked up the steps, giving me a shy smile. I gave her a bold one back because I was so fucking done hiding how I felt whenever I saw this woman.

That caused her grin to widen. She waited for me on the top stair, the door closing behind her, and I skipped a few to get up to her, stepping into her arms when she opened them for me.

God yes.

This. This was what I'd been craving.

Natalie locked her hands around my neck, pressing herself closer, and I took that as a sign that I was allowed to swoop in for a kiss, brushing one against her mouth. Heat sparked, unraveling inside me. I'd wanted to do this on Friday *so* badly. I hated not being able to kiss her freely, and her lips curved beneath mine, as though she'd been feeling and thinking the same things as me.

"Yeah?" I questioned, needing to hear from her mouth that this was the direction we were heading. The one where I got to kiss her whenever I wanted. Outside of confirming our plans for this evening, I hadn't heard from her all day, making me anxious about her decision for the case. Although I'd hate pausing our relationship, it would be *fine* if she decided she didn't want to switch representation. But we'd have to be incredibly careful moving forward. And kissing in front of her house probably didn't fall under that definition.

"Yeah," she breathed before lifting on her toes to kiss me again.

And fuck if I didn't want to kiss her back. I'd never wanted anything more in the world, actually.

But I needed to *know*.

"What'd you decide about the case, Sunshine?" I breathed against her lips. "Can you tell me where we stand before I lose my mind?"

"Oh." Natalie pulled back, her cheeks tinting pink. "Right. You're fired." She winked at me, and I'd never once been happier to hear those words or see her smiling face.

Relief trickled down my back, making me feel like I was melting on her front steps. I had to put a hand on her door frame to steady myself before I pressed my forehead to hers, murmuring, "Say it again."

"What?" she laughed. "You're fired?"

"Mm yeah, it's the hottest fucking thing you've ever said."

Natalie batted her lashes, dropped her voice, and then repeated slowly, "You're. Fired."

"Thank fucking God, Natalie," I groaned before capturing her mouth, kissing her hard and fast before trailing my lips to her jaw and her throat and eventually back up to her lips.

"I talked to Juniper more this morning," Natalie added, and I tried to ignore the way her breaths were slightly labored, her cheeks becoming even rosier when I looked down, forcing some space between us. Her hands drifted to my chest, one palm resting over my heart. "And I told her that I'd fill you in. I'd meant to lead with that when you got here, but then I saw you and..." She drifted off with a shrug.

"Trust me, I get it," I assured her with a sigh. "But I needed to know for sure what tonight was."

Natalie dropped her arms and took a step back, leaning

against her front door. She hesitated before giving me a hopeful look. "If you're still okay with the idea of dates including my nine-year-old daughter, I'd like it to be that? A date, I mean."

She sounded a little tentative, a little unsure, and I knew I still had some work to do to prove to her that I'd take *any* kind of date—as long as it was with her.

"I'm *so* fucking okay with that."

"Great." A heavy breath fell from her lips. "I don't know what you had in mind, but there's this sandwich place over by our favorite park. It's a nice night, and I was thinking we could walk there?" She bit her bottom lip, blinking up at me with a bit of uncertainty. "I know it's nothing special, but—"

"That sounds *very* special," I cut in. "And I love that idea, but only if you let me buy."

"Oh, you don't have to—"

"Is this a date or not, Natalie?"

She rolled her eyes, but her still-pink cheeks gave her away. "It's a date."

"Damn right it is," I muttered, leaning forward to drop a kiss on the top of her head.

"How was your weekend?" she asked when I straightened again. "Is your grandfather doing better?"

"He is." Well enough to give me shit for most of the weekend. "And it was great to see everyone. Missed you, though."

"I missed you, too," she whispered. Our eyes caught, and I sank into her green ones, momentarily getting lost to the pull of them. The pull of her. Until she brought me back to reality, asking, "Hey, before we leave...can you talk to Chloe?"

"Of course, I'll talk to Chloe," I said, my brows pulling together. "Is everything okay?"

Natalie nodded, grabbing the door handle and twisting to let us inside. "Yeah, she's just a little bummed and wants to talk to you."

Concern and confusion wrapped around me, but I followed Natalie into the house without any more questions. We found

Chloe sitting on the couch, slumped in the corner of it. She looked up when she noticed me standing there and then focused back down on her hands, which were resting on the orange cat curled in her lap.

"Hi, Cam," she said, soft and shy as I sat next to her on the couch.

Natalie squeezed Chloe's shoulder and then disappeared into the kitchen, but not before giving me a little glance, one that meant the world. Like she was trusting me to handle this—whatever *this* was—on my own.

"What's up, Champ?"

Chloe's eyes skirted over to me when I spoke, doe-eyed and a little withdrawn, a look I'd honestly never seen on her before.

"Everything okay?" I added.

"I just..." Chloe drifted off, repositioning in a way that had Annabeth jumping off her lap. But when she settled into place again, she was a few inches closer to me. "Are you mad at me?"

She peeked up like she was afraid of my answer.

"Mad at you?" I echoed with disbelief. "Chloe, why would I be mad at you?"

Her face screwed up. "Because I told Dad about you, and then he got mad. I don't know *why* he got mad, but I guess I shouldn't have told him about going to the law gardener and the baseball game and stuff."

My heart squeezed, even while I tried not to chuckle at what I was pretty sure was a mispronunciation of Gardner. "Oh, sweetheart. No, of course I'm not upset with you about that."

Chloe dared to look hopeful. "Really? But Mom says you're not her lawyer anymore, and I feel like it's all my fault."

"It's *not* your fault," I insisted. "And I'm *not* mad. Okay?"

Natalie firing me was the best part of my day, but I understood why Chloe might be confused about that.

"Okay." She gave a little nod, but doubt still lingered.

I sighed, debating the right course of action on this, debating what to say that would help Chloe wrap her head around what had happened in a way that wouldn't demonize the one real father she did have. While I certainly didn't like the man, it would never be my place to try to push him out of Chloe's life if she wanted him there or frame him in a way that created a wedge in their relationship.

"There are some things you should know, Chloe," I said after a beat of silence.

She cocked her head to the side, her eyes still round. "What?"

"First of all, because I was your mom's lawyer, your dad's automatically not going to like me very much." She needed to know Korey's reaction wasn't her fault, not one bit. That man didn't like me from the start. "It was my job to ask him some uncomfortable questions, and that might mean he's not my biggest fan. Does that make sense?"

She pressed her lips together, seeming to think hard on it before saying, "I guess so."

I nodded. "Second of all, your mom and I decided together that it would be best that she get a new lawyer. Your dad didn't make us do that, okay? So nothing's your fault."

She released a sigh that was too heavy for a nine-year-old, making my chest hurt. "Okay. I guess...I guess that's good."

"You've met Juniper, right?" I gave Chloe an encouraging smile, and she nodded. "She's going to be your mom's new lawyer."

"I like Juniper," Chloe said, but her voice was still distant. "She has pretty dresses."

"Yes, she does," I agreed. "Is something else still bugging you, Champ?"

She shrugged, not answering aloud, so I gave her some time. Annabeth jumped back onto her lap, and she pet her absent-mindedly.

"But if you're not mom's lawyer...does that mean you won't be around anymore?" she asked eventually—so quiet I almost couldn't hear her.

Oh, this kid. She'd wormed her way into my heart in ways I never imagined possible.

"I'm here tonight, aren't I?" I said, grinning through the emotion in my throat.

Chloe gave a slow nod.

"I'm hoping to be around a lot, Chloe," I said, a little more seriously. I wanted to tell her just *how much* I planned to be around but knew that would contradict the promise I'd made to Natalie about going slow. So I just added, "Would you like that?"

Her nod was more eager this time. "Yes."

"Good. That makes me happy." Happy and achy and maybe a tiny bit terrified, knowing that this tiny human was counting on me. But mostly happy. So *fucking* happy. "You ready to head to the park?"

She perked up a little, but I could tell there was still something on the tip of her tongue. I just never expected it to be "Can I give you a hug?"

I held my arms out, chuckling as Chloe immediately dove into them.

"Yeah, Chloe," I promised her. "I'm always here for a good hug."

Chloe bounced up off the couch a moment later, her usual energy mostly restored.

And then I took my sunshine girl and her spirited daughter to get sandwiches in the park.

To no one's surprise, we stopped to get ice cream on the way home and ate it on their front stoop, attempting to look up at the stars through the small clearing of tree branches above.

It was admittedly hard to see very many, and the setting sun brought a swarm of bugs with it, chasing us inside.

But that was okay.

I told Natalie there'd be other chances to see the stars.

Other dates.

So many other dates to come.

CHAPTER FORTY-ONE

natalie

  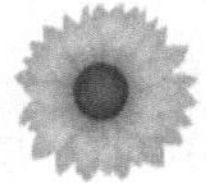

Hi

It's your dearest sister, here with another babysitting request.

I'm sorry. It's not for a few weeks.

BLAKE: Nat, you know we never care. Did you pick up an extra shift?

No, actually…I'm trying to plan a date?

NOAH: Why did you say it like a question? Are you not sure it's a date or you're not sure it's happening?

No, I'm pretty sure it's a date. And I'm pretty sure it's happening.

I have just been corrected that it is absolutely a date and it's definitely happening.

BLAKE: Not for a few weeks, huh? I don't suppose that has anything to do with a certain trial being over in a couple weeks…

It might.

NOAH: And I don't suppose that means your date is with your lawyer...

Actually, no.

BLAKE: No?

No, I have a new lawyer.

NOAH: Cameron ditched you???

He did not *ditch* me, Noah. But Korey was causing problems. We both thought it was for the best.

BLAKE: When the fuck is Korey not causing problems.

NOAH: Who is your lawyer now, then?

Juniper.

NOAH: Oh, well, RIP to all Korey's hopes and dreams then.

BLAKE: Will Juniper's destruction of your pathetic ex-husband be recorded? Or better yet, can I come watch?

The next couple of weeks were tense as we prepared for the trial, and while I couldn't deny that I was stressed and worried and, well, sometimes downright terrified of what might happen with Chloe's custody, there were also pockets of time where I felt so incredibly happy and at peace.

The first thing I realized after firing Cameron was just how much he had been holding back.

With his touches, his words, his thoughtful actions.

If I'd thought he was attentive and supportive before, it was nothing to how he treated me now that we'd redefined our relationship. I felt like a spoiled-rotten princess, even though nothing Cameron had done for me cost him much more than time and consideration. On nights when I wasn't at the hospital, he often came over and cooked dinner with Chloe and me. Sometimes while meals sat in the oven, he'd take Chloe to the park, and I sat in the kitchen with a glass of wine, a moment to put my feet up without feeling guilty. Cameron encouraged me to spend time on myself, rediscover things I enjoyed. I read a book, went on a run, took a bath—all for the first time in years.

It felt like a partnership. It felt like I finally had someone who I could lean on, who was willing to split responsibilities and share the load, even when it wasn't his load to share. I tried to reciprocate when I could. I often packed Cameron lunches for work and made sure to carve out time for the things I knew he liked. We'd started watching baseball at our house after dinner, and Chloe eagerly took on the task of learning all the players' names and numbers while I curled up with my crochet hooks. Cameron would quiz her over root beer floats, and then she'd fall asleep before the end of the final inning.

That was when I got kisses.

I'd urge Chloe to her room, and then Cameron would press me down into the couch and kiss me until I was breathless, murmuring all the things he wanted to do to me in bed later while I begged him to do them right then and there.

We moved slowly, but likely not as slow as we could have.

And I was more than okay with that.

Falling wasn't all that scary, not when you knew the person standing beside you would catch you at the end of the day.

Therapy helped, too. I expected my therapist to tell me to take it easy, to proceed into a new relationship with an abundance of caution, but she hadn't. She told me to put a little more trust in myself and everything that I had learned—and unlearned—since escaping Korey's emotional manipulation. She reminded me that I *knew* the signs now. We talked about what those signs were. We talked about how Cameron had none of them.

We ended up not waiting until after the trial to have our first official date night. It preceded it by a few days, but Cameron wanted to give me a night to take my mind off everything, and it worked.

He wasn't my lawyer any longer; we *could* go on a date. We just hadn't wanted to do anything too publicly right after switching representation and cause any further suspicion or speculation that there had been something carrying on while we were still professionally tied. And we didn't want Korey to know, of course. He'd know eventually, but for now, it was still better if he didn't.

Korey had acted incredibly smug about the change in representation, like he'd already won by getting Cameron fired. While I hated that, it also assured me that he was less likely to keep digging. His ego had been restored. He thought we were behind, that Juniper wouldn't be able to pull things together fast enough for the trial. He was full steam ahead, pressing to get this over with now because he thought he had the upper hand. And while it was still possible he might still try to pull something, at least now if something *did* happen, I could tell him that I was free to date whoever I liked. There were no rules anymore. None at all.

Chloe was with Blake and Delaney tonight, who were taking her on a little road trip to get dinner with Delaney's brother, Bryan. There was some chatter that Bryan might move to Boston soon, so it would be good for Chloe to get a chance to meet him. Blake and Delaney had been researching different independent-living opportunities for Bryan, who was a young adult who had Down syndrome. Ultimately, though, they said moving away from Delaney's slightly estranged parents was up to him, so Chloe declared she was going to try to convince Bryan that living in Boston was the *best*, and he should definitely move.

My daughter was always looking to build our family out, as big as she could. But I was just happy she was excited about tonight and staying over at Blake and Delaney's. It took a weight off my shoulder, lessened the guilt I had about spending an evening where I *could* be with my daughter to instead go out with the hottest, kindest man I'd ever met.

Adjusting the bodice of my corset top, I was wondering if I'd tied it a bit too tight when Cameron knocked on the door. He hadn't told me where we were going and insisted I could wear whatever I felt best in. And this was that. I'd paired the top with a flirty skirt, wanting something that felt different. Because tonight, *I* felt different.

When I opened the door, Cameron froze. Every part of his body remained still while his eyes worked over me, seeming to meticulously take notes. Then he released a barely audible curse and tipped his head back, staring at the sky and giving me the opportunity to drink him in. He'd dressed casually, at least in Cameron's standards. His usual work attire was replaced by an unbuttoned, olive-colored linen shirt. It draped open, and the white fabric beneath it clung to the contours of his chest, leaving me staring.

"Cameron. Baby," I said, saying his name the way he did mine sometimes. "You look really nice."

Cameron lowered his gaze again, his eyes flaring. His voice was tight as he spoke.

"Come out here."

"What?"

He ran a hand down his face and slipped his knuckle into his mouth, biting it before answering. "I need you to come out here, because if I go in there, we'll never leave."

Something skipped a beat inside me. Maybe more than one beat, actually.

I cocked my head to the side. "Why's that?"

He released a weathered sigh, his voice sinking to a new depth. "Because you have no idea how badly I want to hear you call me baby while my hands are up that tiny skirt of yours."

"I think we can make that happen," I said, stepping out my front door with a little extra bounce in my step. "Later."

Cameron made some kind of discernible noise while I turned

to close and lock the door behind me. When I spun to face him again, he framed my waist with his large hands. "You are so stunning," he breathed, sounding husky and warm. "My sunny girl blinded me for a moment."

"Oh, stop," I laughed, trying to push him off.

But he wouldn't let me go.

"No," he said simply. "You know better than that. You know you can't push me away that easily, Natalie."

I stared at him, knowing he was right. I did know that.

"I'm not going to stop," he went on. "Not for a long time. My girl's always gonna know exactly how gorgeous she is."

"Is that what I am?" I pulled my bottom lip between my teeth in thought, and Cameron's gaze flicked to my mouth. "Your girl?"

I really liked the sound of that.

"Mmm." Cameron shook his head, oddly a little disappointed in the question. And then I understood why. "If you're really asking me that, then I have some work to do tonight, don't I?" He raised a brow. "Let's go."

Taking my hand, Cameron led me down the steps. But before we could make it to his car, something caught my eye out of my peripheral vision.

Were plants *growing* in my garden?

I dropped Cameron's hand, getting sidetracked as I walked across the tiny patio. "What's that?"

Cameron was silent for a moment, and then, when he seemed to figure out what I was talking about, said, "Oh, Chloe didn't tell you about that?"

I frowned, staring at the little sprouts in the soil. "Tell me about what?"

"We planted flowers that night you were at the hospital."

Turning, I stared at him. "You planted flowers?"

He nodded, looking amused at my shocked expression. "Sunflowers, baby."

God, the things he could do to my pulse with just a couple of words.

"The flowers were Chloe's idea," Cameron added, just like he did with the sunflowers in the vase that night. But I knew better than to believe he hadn't played a part.

"She has a sudden thing for sunflowers, huh?"

He shrugged, the corner of his mouth twitching as he held his hand out, and I walked back to him, taking it. "Do you like them? I'm sorry if you had another idea for that patch of soil."

I had to swallow past the lump in my throat before I could answer. "I love them. I've been meaning to plant something there for a while. I can't wait to watch them grow."

Cameron gave me a warm look. "Me too."

We walked to his car, and he opened the door for me—always a gentleman, it would seem. Although he also wore this crooked smile that told me he had plans for tonight that would make me rethink whether that was true.

"Where are we going to eat?" I asked as I slid into the front seat of his car, itching for more details.

"Somewhere...unexpected."

"Oh?"

That caught my interest, but I had to wait while Cameron shut my door and walked around to get into the driver's seat. He took his time buckling his seat belt and then looked pointedly my way, waiting for me to do the same. I reached back to grab it.

"I really have no interest in taking you somewhere I'd have to share you with other people," he finally answered, taking the buckle out of my hands and clicking it in place for me before resting his hand on my thigh, adding heat to an already warm day. "I knew you were going to look as amazing as you do, and I'm fucking tired of keeping my hands off you in public, Natalie." Cameron slid his hand to my knee, giving it a little squeeze.

It reminded me of how he'd touched me under the table during my deposition, both keeping me grounded and sending my body into overdrive.

He was doing the same thing right now.

"Oh," I repeated, feeling flustered.

"Unless you'd prefer I keep my hands to myself?" he asked, casting a speculative glance my way.

He started to loosen the grip he had on my knee, and I immediately placed my own hand on top of his, stopping him.

"I didn't say that," I said, breathless. My entire body flushed hot, and I wondered if Cameron could feel the heat radiating off my skin, beneath his touch.

His lips quirked to the side, his dimples making an appearance. "That's what I thought."

So smug, but I didn't even care.

"That's one of the best parts about this." I smiled at him while he pulled out of his parking spot, and like he could sense my smile, his grin grew bigger, too.

"What is, baby?"

"That we don't have to hold back or pretend that this isn't...something."

He chuckled darkly in that way that made all my hairs stand on end. "Oh, it's something, alright."

Cameron slid his hand further up my leg while driving one-handed, not taking his eyes off the road, and I struggled to form coherent thoughts, let alone sentences.

"But you should know not everything has changed," he added. "The rules are the same, Natalie."

He gave my inner thigh a little pat, like a command to open further, and I obeyed without thinking.

"The rules?" I gasped when I felt his fingertips tracing a path upward. "Like that you're in charge?"

Cameron shook his head. "First of all, I'm only in charge when you want me to be. Understood?"

I glanced over at him. "You mean, in the bedroom?"

He drew lazy circles on my inner thigh, drifting his touch back toward my knee and then back up again, making me squirm.

"I mean anywhere or anytime you need me to be," Cameron answered, as calmly as ever. "Whenever you want, I've got you."

I stared at the road in front of us, blinking.

I've got you.

What a strange concept.

"But even then, you can tell me no," Cameron added. "That's the rule I want you to know. That you can always tell me no. Us being together, *this*—" He squeezed my thigh again, as though to make sure I was listening. "—doesn't mean you can't."

I shook my head because the thought of that seemed foreign to me. "I've never wanted to tell you no, Cameron."

"I know," he acknowledged, his tone patient and honest. Like it was just a simple truth that I'd always wanted him, in every scenario. "But I want this for the long haul, baby. And one day, you might want to tell me no. And I'm trusting you to do that." When I continued to stare at him, slightly mystified by this entire conversation and where it was coming from, Cameron lowered his voice. "I know you did things with that man you didn't want to, and that's never you and me, got it? That's *never* you and me."

Emotion rammed into me like a freight train, his words colliding in my brain and finally making sense. Because he was right. Korey never physically forced me to do things I didn't want to, but he emotionally manipulated me into it, making me think that maybe if I did what he wanted, I'd finally feel some semblance of love.

It never worked, never made me feel any different. And finally, I learned to say no. And I said it a lot, finally ending with the resounding no that ended our marriage.

Cameron was right. Him and me? We were different than that. So very, very different. And I had no problem promising him that. I'd found my voice, and he only ever encouraged me to use it.

I cleared my throat. "I'll say no, Cameron. I promise."

"Yeah?" he checked, glancing over at me with a glittering gaze that made my pulse triple in rate as I nodded in response. His hand then slowly slid back up my inner thigh, teasing as it inched higher. "So if I wanted to pull your skirt up and play with this pussy in traffic, what would you say?"

I didn't look away from him when I answered, "Nothing."

Cameron's hand flexed on my thigh, a low groan coming out of him.

And I couldn't help but smirk. "You couldn't wait until later?"

"No," he admitted, and the hoarseness in his voice made me believe him. "What about our entire relationship has given you the impression that I'm good at resisting you, Natalie London? I risked my entire career just for a taste of you."

"I think you got more than a taste," I laughed, ignoring that little twinge of guilt that I still felt whenever I thought of what could have gone wrong. Instead, I focused on my current flood of feelings, brought on by his wandering touch. I canted my hips, wanting, *needing* more of it. "And I'm no better."

I had no idea how to resist him, either. Not now, in the middle of traffic, and not before, in a conference room at Gardner Law.

"Mm," Cameron hummed, sounding satisfied. "You love when my hands are between these thighs, don't you?"

He hooked a finger beneath the hem of my underwear, and I sucked in, clutching the door handle.

"Among other things," I said after getting a hold of myself.

"*Fuck.*"

Cameron readjusted his grip on the steering wheel, and all I could do was stare at the veins in his hand as the fingers on his other one tugged my underwear to one side.

I was panting now, heart racing, palms sweating. Cameron's body seemed just as tense, and it was deeply gratifying to know that I had the ability to affect him—this normally calm, cool, collected man—as much as he affected me.

Shifting in my seat, I tried to spread my legs wider, give him better access, because *oh my God*, I needed it. I needed him to actually touch me instead of ghosting his fingers over my slit.

"Natalie." Cameron's voice was hard, and I was glued to it. "Who's allowed to touch this pussy besides you?"

He swiped two fingers between my legs, letting them drift over my clit, and I released a whimper.

Again. I needed him to do it *again*.

But he stopped, fingers hovering until I answered him.

"My boyfriend," I answered breathily. "Only my boyfriend."

"God, baby." Cameron made a guttural noise, his entire body reacting to that. We hadn't used titles yet, but I knew it was only because he was waiting for me to be ready. And I was so much more than ready for this to officially be everything that it was. He rewarded me, his fingers making another pass through my pussy. "And who's that?"

I squirmed when he stopped again, waiting for my answer.

"*You.*"

"Fuck right it's me," Cameron growled and then gave me what I wanted, thrusting inside me and causing a gasp to fly from my lips. And then his thumb grazed my clit, moving in tiny flicks, and I nearly lost it, gripping the handle on the door harder and flinging my head back, eyes squeezed shut because it was just *so* good.

"So fucking glad we both know now that you're mine," he rasped, slowly working his fingers in and out of me. "And this pussy is mine. Isn't that right?"

I barely managed a nod, and Cameron curled his fingers, hitting a spot inside me that felt like a reward but was really a reprimand.

"Yes," I cried. "*Yes*, Cameron. Baby."

"Oh, hell," he groaned, and I saw him shake his head out of the corner of my eye. "You have no fucking idea what it does to me to hear you say my name like that."

I moaned, the only feasible response when he was playing with my pussy so expertly. Somewhere in my consciousness, I realized that other cars were all around us, that even though no one would really be able to *see* anything, it was conceivable that we weren't being discreet. But God, it only heightened the experience. And it was almost like Cameron was reminding me that the thrill of us wasn't over. That he was going to continue to show me what sex could be like, but *only* with him.

"Yes, be loud for me, Natalie," he encouraged, even as I felt the car round a corner. My eyes flicked over, watching him expertly turn the wheel with one hand while he continued to work me over with the other. "We've had to be so quiet lately. Are you going to let me hear you tonight?"

I nodded.

"Good girl," he murmured as he pulled into a parking lot I didn't recognize. "I can't wait."

And then he slipped his fingers from inside me, readjusted my underwear so it was back in place, and pulled my skirt back down.

I stared at him, in a mix of horror and arousal, as he flashed me a playful smirk and sucked his fingers clean.

"Ready?" he asked, as though he hadn't just fingered me to *almost* completion.

"I— But—" I wiggled in my seat, crossing one leg over the other to try to appease the ache between my thighs.

"Oh, I'm sorry." His grin was practically diabolical. "Did you want to come?"

I pressed my lips together, trying not to let a little whine of disappointment slip out of me.

It was no use.

Cameron's eyes blazed bright, feral in the way they worked over me.

"Well, *I* want you to sit on my face, Sunshine, but sometimes we have to wait for the things we want." He licked his lips like he was imagining it and then opened his car door. "Come on, baby."

And because following Cameron Bryant was the easiest thing in the world, I stepped out of the car and took his hand.

CHAPTER FORTY-TWO

natalie

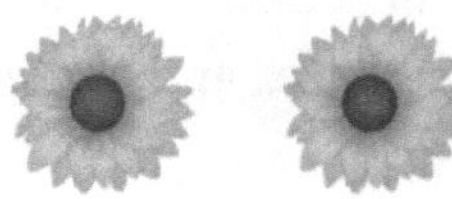

CAMERON LED ME TOWARD a building that was boxy and nondescript, and it wasn't until we got closer to the doors that I realized I'd been here before.

"Are we at the—"

I cut off, because there was no way, right?

But Cameron smoothly finished for me. "Planetarium?" He gave me a sideways glance that glowed with excitement. "Of course we are."

I was still reeling from what had happened in the car, and now *this*?

Speechless, I followed him inside, where it was all but empty except for us. Cameron directed me to an auditorium that boasted a domed ceiling, sprinkled with lights. *Stars*. We walked past the rows of plush seats, down to the middle of the room, where blankets were laid on the ground, along with boxes of some kind of takeout food, drinks, and cushions.

I stared at the display, completely lost for words.

He'd rented out a *planetarium* for our first date?

"I wanted to give you the stars without the bugs," he said, turning toward me and shucking his hands in his pockets, looking a bit sheepish. It was my favorite look of his, a reminder that even though Cameron always acted like he had everything put together, this was all new for him, too. And we were both just doing our best, hoping for the best.

My heart swelled in my chest, pressing against my sternum.

"One day, I'll find a truck, load you and Chloe up in it, and take my girls somewhere out of the city to stargaze the way your dad took you when you were younger, but until then..." Cameron drifted off, his eyes roaming across the starry ceiling, and I shook my head in disbelief.

My girls.

I had no idea how to put into words what his thoughtfulness meant to me. I was constantly in *awe*.

"Natalie?"

The tone of Cameron's voice made me realize that I'd been staring at him with my hand over my mouth and tears in my eyes. My whole body vibrated, both because of the edge he'd left me on in the car and the emotions bouncing around inside me. He could probably *see* the way I shook. "Are you okay?"

I nodded, dropping my hand to reveal the smile beneath it, and Cameron chuckled, opening his arms and moving toward me.

"Come here, Mama," he murmured, and I gladly stepped into his arms.

"It's just the nicest thing anyone has ever done for me," I admitted. "And what you said about stargazing with Chloe—" My throat closed for a second, words getting stuck in it. "She'd really like that."

"I'd really like it, too," he said, voice gentle, like he knew I was moments from breaking. He pulled me down onto the blanket, tucking me between his legs and dragging me back against his chest. Then he reached around to unbox the food: sandwiches with thick, decadent bread, colorful fruit, and gourmet snacks. He brought a strawberry up for me to take a bite, and I leaned forward, happy to do so.

The room was dimly lit, dark enough so we could see the stars but enough light so we could see our food. It settled a sort of peace over me. In the background, soft music played, the gentle strumming of guitars and familiar melodies flowing from a hidden speaker.

"You know, I think about the things I'd like to do with the two of you all the time," Cameron said after a long pause. His lips pressed to the column of my throat while I chewed, lingering in a way that made me feel flushed. "But only when you're ready. And Chloe, too."

"Chloe?"

Had he *met* my daughter? She couldn't be more excited every time Cameron walked in the door in the evenings. Or when she staggered downstairs in the morning to find that he was still there, making her breakfast in the kitchen.

I felt Cameron's shoulder move in a shrug.

"Maybe she doesn't want someone new to play dad yet." He hesitated and then added, "I've been thinking about it a lot recently, what I would have done if my mom had brought home someone new when I was younger. She never did, but I think I would have been happy, especially for her. Although I suppose it would have depended on who he was, you know? If he treated her right."

I nodded, appreciating the way he was thinking about this so thoroughly. Always considerate, always reflective. "Chloe sees the way you treat me. She sees how *good* you treat me, and I just know that one day, when she's older, it will help her know what she should expect from a partner. And I think even now..." I looked over my shoulder and realized the way Cameron was hanging on my every word. "I think I haven't seen my daughter as happy as she is in a long time."

"Yeah?"

The corner of Cameron's mouth slid up at that, but he looked away from me, focusing on grabbing a grape and popping it into his mouth. Once again, acting shy.

"Yeah, Cameron," I insisted, and his arm tightened around me, pulling me close.

I'd never been happier to be so entirely cocooned in his arms. No more hesitation, no more holding back.

"I don't think she minds you playing dad one bit," I continued, curling my legs beneath my bottom, inching further into his embrace. "I hope that's what *you* want, though."

Cameron released a little laugh, like the thought of him *not* wanting it was humorous.

"Do you think Chloe would like a beach vacation?" he asked instead of answering me. His voice grew rough, emotion clear in it. "Maybe we could do a long weekend on the Cape? After the trial?" I opened my mouth to respond, but before I could, he added, "Also, I'd very much like a copy of her skating schedule. Like the competitions or shows or anything outside her normal practices, since I already know when those are."

"I—yes." A laugh bubbled out of me. "Yes, to both. She would love a beach vacation." I paused, let my voice lower and soften a degree as I thought about the picture of Cameron and his family in his office. "I'd love to go to the Cape with you."

"Yeah?"

I nodded, and his lips pressed to the top of my head before he lowered his face next to mine. There was a pregnant pause and then a quiet admission against my ear.

"I'm trying not to get ahead of myself, but I'm really excited. I think I could be a good dad. If you ever wanted me to be and Chloe was okay with having another one. I had a really great role model, after all."

I tipped my head back, needing to see his face. Stars shimmered above his head like a halo, and his eyes were just as bright as the constellations, just as clearly telling a story.

God, I'd fallen so hard for this man.

But I couldn't help the tiniest thread of doubt for the future weave through my mind.

"I know you'd be amazing at it, Cameron. But what if...what if we don't get a chance to do those things. What if Korey—"

"Not going to happen," Cameron said, voice hard. "If, God

forbid, this week doesn't go the way we hope, I won't stop fighting, Natalie. We'll appeal, we'll keep pushing, we'll make it happen. You trust me, right?"

"With everything I am."

"I made a promise to you, and I still plan on keeping it, okay?"

"Okay," I breathed, already more at ease.

Cameron dropped a hard kiss to my lips and then pulled back to stare at me, his mouth opening and closing like he wanted to say something else. His eyes had a tortured quality to them, like it was killing him to keep it inside. My breath hitched, and words bubbled onto the tip of my own tongue, too.

But then, he swallowed and murmured, "I want you to eat before getting too distracted."

Practical as always.

I tried to ignore the odd swirl of disappointment that vanished quickly anyway.

We spent the better part of the next hour eating and laughing before Cameron packed all the food up, and we landed on our backs, staring up at the skies. I pointed out the constellations I knew the names of, and Cameron listened, peppering me with questions about them, which I admittedly didn't know a lot of the answers to.

"When's the last time you've been home?" he asked after a moment of silence with only mellow notes of music lingering between us. "I know your parents are coming to support you for the trial, but maybe you'd like to visit Minnesota sometime, too."

"It's been a long time, so I'd really like that." It was something that had been on my mind for a while. "Maybe sometime this fall? We could try to line it up with one of Noah's games, and I could show you around where I grew up."

Cameron's grin spread. "Oh, do I get to come?"

"Oh, I mean, I guess—"

One single finger pressed over my mouth to shut me up.

"I'd love to come," he said, tracing the edges of my lips in a hypnotized sort of way. "Not a day goes by that I don't want to learn more about you."

Cameron dropped his hand, and I had to clear my throat before I was able to talk.

"I hope you know I feel the same about you," I replied. "It's distracting, how much I think about you. How I want to know more about you. Your family. Everything."

"Well." Cameron let out a surprisingly unsteady sigh. "Did you know that my mom's family is actually from Boston?"

"Really?"

He nodded. "Yeah, she was an only child, so I don't have much extended family on her side. But sometimes, when I'm missing being home, I like to go to the bar that my grandparents used to own, before they passed. The one my mom worked at when she was younger. Where she met my dad."

I tipped my head back so I could see him better and found Cameron already looking down at me, some unnamed emotion swimming in his gaze.

"It's in Boston?" I asked, feeling a little breathless without really knowing why. "The bar they met at?"

Cameron nodded, but it was slow. He brushed a hand over my hair, gently playing with it.

"Where is it? We should go."

The corner of his mouth twitched.

"Oh, Sunny."

My brows furrowed. "What?"

"We already have, baby." He smiled at me again, but this time, it was more in his eyes than anywhere else. "We already have."

CHAPTER FORTY-THREE

cameron

"HEY, CAMERON?"

Natalie had been relatively quiet on our ride back to her house. I could tell she was contemplative, but I knew her silence wasn't bad. She looked more relaxed and at ease than I'd seen her in a long time, and her voice sounded assured, like whatever she was about to say or ask me was something she felt confident about.

"Yeah, Sunshine?"

I drove through the alleyway in the back of her town house, where I normally parked if I was spending the night. Finding my usual spot, I stopped the car and turned to face her.

Natalie pulled her bottom lip through her teeth as she turned my way, too, looking me up and down, and I had a feeling she was about to fuck with my thin restraint.

Did she think it only affected *her* when I edged her? That I didn't feel just as deprived?

"Can I make one request for tonight?" she asked, surprising me.

"You mean for when I take you inside and fuck you?"

There was still just enough light in the sky for me to see Natalie's cheeks tinge pink.

"Yeah," she said, faint but not shy. Not anymore. "For that."

"Anything."

I enjoyed taking a more dominant role in the bedroom, but mostly because I loved seeing the trust in Natalie's gaze when she followed my directions. I loved knowing I could provide her a sense of comfort, moments in time where she didn't have to think, and her pleasure was the entire focus. I loved giving that to her. And watching her take it, too. Watching her take whatever I decided to do, however I decided to make her come, turned me the fuck on.

But I had no problem if she wanted to dictate more of what happened when we were together.

"I'm bringing it up now instead of in the moment because I want you to know that I mean it," Natalie rushed on. "I understand why you insisted last time, considering my...emotional state and what I'd requested before, but this time—"

"Natalie," I cut in because it wasn't adding up in my brain what she was talking about.

"Sorry." She sucked in. "I'd just—I'd like you to fuck me without a condom." She swallowed and added, "Using one was a safety measure for me. A security blanket. But I already feel so safe with you, Cameron. And I don't feel like I need that anymore. But it's up to you, and if that's something you're okay with."

If I was *okay* with that?

Her words were squeezing my heart. *And* my dick, making it feel like it was going to explode. The chance to feel *all* of Natalie London with no barriers?

When I remained speechless, Natalie went on to add, "I'm still on birth control, of course, and—"

I shook my head and stepped out of the car.

I hadn't meant to hesitate when she made her request; I'd just been stunned. And I didn't want her to misunderstand. So I walked around to Natalie's side of the car and opened her door when she still hadn't. She looked up at me like an adorable deer in the headlights.

Jerking my head toward the back door, I directed, "Inside, Mama."

"Oh." Her mouth formed a perfect O as she blinked at me, and then she scrambled to her feet.

Walking with quick, impatient strides with Natalie on my heels, I went to the door, punching in the digits on the lock to let us inside. My blood had been running hot all evening long, ever since I saw Natalie wearing that tight little outfit when I picked her up, but *now*? Now, I fucking needed her. Immediately.

The door swung open, and I reached for Natalie's hand, pulling her inside the house. She flew into me with a gasp, and I grabbed her hips to steady her while walking us back into the kitchen, the door shutting with a bang behind her. An adorable, happy sound slipped out of Natalie, and my heart thumped wildly.

Fuck, did I love this woman. I loved her intelligence, her kindness, her passion. And I loved being here, in this home with her. I loved that she'd welcomed me into it, despite her past and the trauma she'd experienced the last time she let a man in. She didn't have to give me a chance, and it was a goddamn privilege that she had. I knew what it meant that I was in her kitchen right now, and I wanted to *stay*. With her. And Chloe. I wanted to stay so fucking bad and build a life here, in this house. Marriage, babies, I wanted the whole damn thing with Natalie London.

And even though I couldn't say all of this, not yet, not when I'd promised to follow her timeline, and it was still so soon, only our first official date...I wanted a little bit of it tonight. And I suspected she did, too. She'd been so vulnerable earlier, so reassuring that she wanted me to be here, even if she wasn't quite ready to say words that were on the tip of both of our tongues.

And that was okay. Maybe tonight, we could just play make-believe. Maybe we could just lean into it, let her see how it tasted without risking anything yet.

"You don't have to reassure me that you're on birth control, Natalie," I said lowly, continuing to walk her back until she bumped into one side of the kitchen island. “In fact, what if tonight we just...pretended?”

She blinked, confused. “Pretended?”

“That you’re not.”

“That I’m not?”

“On birth control.” I used my grip on her hips to pick her up and slide her onto the countertop. She gasped in surprise, but her eyes glowed, tracking my words. “And what if we pretended that I’m not just *playing* dad?” I wedged myself between her legs and tried to control my grin when she automatically spread her thighs for me, letting me in. “Hm, Natalie? Just for tonight, what if we pretended that that’s exactly what I am.”

Natalie’s breath hitched, but it was hard to say if it had more to do with my proposition or the way I was trailing my fingers up and down her sides. Or maybe it was the press of my erection between her legs when I pulled her to the edge of the countertop.

Her chest heaved as I lowered my head, grazing my lips over hers in a ghost of a kiss.

“I think I’d like to play house with you, Mama,” I breathed and then held my breath, waiting for her to say something.

I didn’t have to wait long.

“Yes, please.” Natalie licked her lips, wetting them and teasing mine in the process. “As long as playing house involves you fucking me in our kitchen.”

Oh, she was going to get fucked, alright.

“On our countertops?”

“Mhm,” Natalie hummed, leaning on her palms and tipping her head back to allow me better access. I trailed my lips down her neck, licking at her pulse point, feeling the racing pace of it beneath my mouth.

“You’d like that, baby?”

“Yes,” she sighed, sounding so fucking contented by the idea of it all that a growl emitted from my chest, and within seconds, my hands were sliding beneath her skirt, finding the band of her underwear, hooking my fingers in it.

"Lift your hips for me, then, Sunshine."

Natalie did, and I yanked her underwear down her legs before stuffing them in my pocket. We wouldn't be needing those tonight.

Natalie watched me, her gaze seductive, confident. "Am I ever going to get those back?" She raised a brow, casting a glance at my pants. "That's not the first pair of underwear you've slipped into your pocket, never to be seen again."

She remembered that, did she?

Guilty.

My hands found her thighs again, palming them. And then I raised a brow back and dropped my voice. "What else am I supposed to wrap around my cock when I'm at home, thinking about you, and you're not there?"

Natalie's gaze gleamed, flaring at my insinuation. "Do you really do that?"

"Do you want me to send you a picture next time?" I asked, leaning in to whisper kisses over her mouth.

"Uh-huh." Her warm breath hit my lips, sending a shiver through me, making me groan.

Fuck, I needed her.

Natalie tipped her chin in anticipation of my kiss at exactly the right moment, once again proving our connection. My mouth slanted over hers hungrily, ready to devour. Holy shit, I wanted to taste and touch and tease every inch of this woman, and Natalie was just as ready for that. She moaned and pushed herself up, kissing me harder, wanting the same thing I did. My name came out of her mouth, a little whine that was *so* fucking satisfying. Hearing her desperation was like music to my ears, a reassurance that I wasn't alone here in my want.

We both wanted the same things. Some of it was big and scary and momentous, but some of it was as simple as breathing. Some of it was just the need to feel her body against mine, to feel the perfect way we fit together again.

"Natalie." Her name sounded harsh coming from my lips, but

the desire was unrelenting, almost painful at this point, and I didn't have it in me to tone anything down. I knew she'd understand. "Your top. Off. Now."

"What?" Natalie faked a gasp when I started yanking at the ties in the back. "You don't like it?"

"I like it too much," I assured her, my voice low and taut. "I like how it fits your body like a fucking glove because *God*, do I love your body. I like just about everything about it except how goddamn—" I grunted, ripping the laces far enough apart that there was enough give for her to slip it over her head. "Hard it is to get *off*."

Natalie huffed a laugh. "Looks like you managed."

"Almost." I gripped the hem of the top. "Arms up."

Natalie sat straighter and put her arms in the air, letting me slide the corset over her head. I threw it to the floor, where it would likely stay for the rest of the night.

The hottest and most infuriating piece of clothing I'd ever encountered.

I turned back to Natalie to find her leaning back on her hands again, watching me with a hooded gaze. She was naked except for the skirt around her waist, and I didn't know how to stop staring. Her honey-colored hair was curled in soft waves tonight, flowing over her shoulders, stopping just past her collarbone. Her arms had a warm glow to them from the summer sun, but her breasts were pale, pretty, pink and her nipples puckered, waiting for my mouth.

I'd never been this hard in my entire life. But it wasn't just my cock that pulsed wildly; it was my entire body. I felt the vibrations of my desire in every single nerve ending when I looked at her.

And I needed to do something about it. *Now*.

"Don't move," I ordered as I began discarding my own clothes, tossing my shirt to the ground and unbuttoning my pants. "Stay right there, just like that."

I felt panicked, like I couldn't get to her fast enough.

"I don't plan on going anywhere, Cameron," she said, seeming a little entertained at how flustered I was.

I didn't usually *get* flustered, but this was something else, this entire thing. And the way Natalie looked, sitting there on top of the counter in a kitchen that held some sort of magic and comfort in it, a place that wrapped around me with warmth in the same way she did...it was all so perfect. *She* was perfect.

"You're so fucking beautiful, Natalie." I shook my head, wishing I had more words, *better* words. "You're so unbelievable, and I just—"

Love you.

I just love you, Sunshine. And I don't know what to fucking do about it.

"Cam, I—" She choked on her words, same as me. "So are you. Come here," she whispered, seeming to have sensed the shift in me. Her eyes were pleading and soulful as I stepped back between her legs. Natalie reached forward as we slid together again, our lips connecting in a hot, drugging kiss. She helped me push my pants and briefs to the ground, her hand finding my cock, which throbbed as she worked her fingers around it. I moaned into her mouth, eyes drifting shut while momentarily losing myself to the push and pull of her strokes.

So good. It was all *so* good.

"Natalie," I breathed, dragging my lips away from her mouth so I could taste the rest of her. I trailed them down the column of her throat to her chest, sucking and nipping at her soft skin. Call me possessive, but I wanted her to wake up tomorrow, look in the mirror, and see just how much I'd made her mine tonight.

"I'm right here," she promised, her breath hiccupping when I sucked her nipple into my mouth, tugging on it with my lips.

"I know." Groaning, I dropped my head to her chest as her grip tightened around my cock. *Fuck.* I couldn't wait any longer.

Pushing her skirt up around her hips, I exposed her pretty, glistening cunt at the same time Natalie ran her thumb over my tip, swirling precum on her finger. I jolted, releasing a string of expletives and fisting the fabric of Natalie's skirt, needing something to hold on to.

A satisfied smugness played across her features, and I decided then and there that I hadn't teased her enough tonight.

Sweeping my fingers down her body, I brushed over her clit, making Natalie's entire body twitch and her smile fade. Her lips pressed together, barely concealing her moans when I made a second pass over her clit and then settled in to circle it with my thumb, mimicking what she'd been doing over the head of my cock.

"I need to be inside you, baby. Please. *Please* let me inside you," I begged in a rasp. Natalie groaned, her eagerness apparent, and I trembled while nodding at how her fingers were still wrapped around my cock. "Bring me closer, 'kay? That's it. Guide me inside so I can feel you."

Natalie gave a little tug that had me seeing stars and then aligned my erection just right, until I was nudging inside her sweet, wet pussy.

I choked out a low curse. Natalie sucked in and released her grip, leaning back onto her palms again and spreading her legs wider. She looked down her gorgeous body, watching with parted lips as I inched in deeper.

"It's so..." she started and then stopped, her jaw dropping further when I delivered another thrust, burying half my length inside her. *Fuck*, the way she wrapped around me. The heat of her body, the sensation of her walls squeezing me so divinely. It was going to fucking *destroy* me.

But not before I figured out what she was about to say.

"It's so what, baby?"

Natalie chewed on her bottom lip, still staring at the way I was filling her, making me absolutely *throb* while she did, and I realized this might be the first time she'd seen it. Seen how perfectly we looked when we fit together.

"You like the way your cunt looks when it's stuffed with my cock, don't you?" I muttered, trying to control the corner of my mouth from sliding into a crooked grin. But I lost the battle, fully smirking as I studied her expression. "Is that what you were going to say?"

Natalie pressed her lips together, looking up at me beneath sooty lashes. "Maybe."

"Maybe?" I echoed. "Should I stop?"

We didn't do maybes here.

"Don't stop," Natalie hurried to protest when I began pulling back. "Please."

That was more like it.

"Then I'm going to ask you again," I said, knowing she could hear the soft warning in my tone. "And this time, you need to answer with 'Yes, Daddy' if you want to be fucked like a good girl, got it?"

Natalie's greedy little nod made me *feral*.

I leaned forward, gradually sliding inside her as I dropped my lips to hers, wanting to make sure she didn't just hear my question but *felt* it, too. Lowering my voice to a husky whisper, I repeated, "You like the way your cunt looks when it's stuffed with my cock, don't you?"

Natalie bit down on my bottom lip, tugging it into her mouth for a breathless moment before answering me with a velvety murmur I wanted to *drown* in. "Yes, Daddy."

"That's what I *fucking* thought," I groaned and then thrust the rest of the way into Natalie's sweet pussy. Electrifying pleasure warped my vision, forcing me to momentarily still as I took in the reality of being surrounded by her tight, wet heat. A sharp cry left Natalie's lips when I bottomed out inside her, but it quickly evolved into a moan of pleasure as she adjusted to the feel of me, so fucking deep inside her. When my vision cleared, I looked down at her, at us, and nearly lost it. "You look *so* good when you're full of me, baby."

Natalie nodded and lifted her ass from the counter, asking for friction. So I gripped her hips, forcing her back down and keeping her in place before I gave what she was looking for, pulling back to slam inside her again. Natalie took all of me, tipping her head back with another moan of appreciation, and I *finally* let loose.

"*Yes*," she cried. "Yes, that's—"

Her words vanished, her jaw dropping, but I understood.

"I know, Sunshine." I thrust again, harder. "I know what it is. I know you want all of me."

She whimpered, nodding as I picked up my pace. Her eyes were on the ceiling, her mouth open, hot little sounds falling out of it as I fucked her.

"I want all of you, too," I promised. "I want everything, baby."

Every. Fucking. Thing.

"*Cameron*," she gasped, eyes rolling back further when I twisted my arms beneath her legs and tugged her hips further over the edge of the counter, bringing them up to meet the drive of my hips. Her bare feet dangled over my forearms, and I fucking loved being tangled in her.

"I'm right here," I reminded her. "Give me your eyes, Mama."

I needed to see her.

I needed *her* to see *me*.

Natalie's gaze slid to mine instantly, connecting like a puzzle piece sliding into place. I saw her breath catch in her throat, and I knew it was because of whatever she saw on my expression.

"You're so fucking perfect," I panted between thrusts, the thoughts that kept repeating in my mind on a loop. "*So* beautiful, Natalie. You are—everything."

Not unlike the first time we fucked, Natalie's eyes grew watery. They were wide windows to her soul—a soul I cherished with all my heart. And this time when I stared down at her, seeing her for everything that she was, I knew she was seeing me back, too. I knew she was seeing everything clearly. Maybe even for the very first time.

"Cameron, I—*please*." She broke off, seeming unable to get her words out the way she wanted to. But I didn't need her words right now. I just needed this, her.

"Shh, I know."

Natalie's eyes softened while her jaw tightened, her body moving rhythmically against mine, and I knew she was already close.

And goddamnit, so was I.

"Natalie," I rasped, needing to make one thing exponentially clear. "You're going to take my cum for me. Okay? You're going to let me fill this needy pussy like it's mine."

She nodded. And then blew my fucking mind when she breathed, "Because it is."

"*Yes.*" God, what was she doing to me? "And just when you thought you couldn't be any more full, I'm going to give you more. Understood?"

Her head bobbed, eyes rolling as I snapped my hips hard against her, but it wasn't clear enough for me.

"Yeah, Sunshine? That what you want?"

"*Yes.*" Her gaze burned as it locked on me. Her green eyes were round, begging me to understand the things she couldn't say.

The only thing we were pretending tonight was that we both didn't know the truth. But that was okay with me. As long as I had her and she kept looking at me like she was right now.

"That's what I'll give you, then, baby." My voice was hoarse, threatening to give out under the weight of such pure pleasure. "But I need you to be a good girl and come for me. Can you do that?"

Releasing one of Natalie's hips, I brought my hand between us instead, rubbing her clit with my thumb as I continued to work in and out of her. Natalie made a sharp, needy noise in response, telling me to keep going. I did, and her brows scrunched together, telling me she was even closer to her release. She always had that adorable look of concentration right before she let go, almost as though she didn't want to miss it.

As if she ever could with me.

Sure enough, Natalie's entire body bowed off the counter a second later as a breathy scream fell from her lips, her eyes squeezing shut and her fingers flexing across the granite countertops. A series of trembling waves worked through her body, and I absorbed it all, almost tipping over my own edge when her walls tightened around me, suctioning my cock deliciously.

"That's it," I encouraged. "That's my girl."

She pressed her lips together, like she was trying to contain just how much she was feeling, but she nodded. She knew she was my girl. No one else's but *mine*.

That thought alone sent me reeling, pleasure cresting as I tipped my head back with a cry and spilled into her. I drove into her once, twice more, wanting her to take all of it, and she did. Fuck, she did. When I lowered my gaze, it was to find Natalie watching me with glistening eyes, bright and alive. I breathed her name, and she nodded, a wordless communication passing between us.

Because that was...yeah. Something unparalleled, something that went beyond fantasy.

I slipped out slowly, enjoying how Natalie's body twitched with overstimulation. She looked just as good with me pulling out, my cum dripping from her body, as she did with me thrusting in. Possibly even better. It was jaw-droppingly hot, and I stared, rubbing my jaw with one hand, wondering what the hell to do with the feeling of possession coursing through me.

The only thing I could think to do was swipe my fingers between her legs, gathering my cum and promptly pushing it back inside her.

Natalie gasped, her eyes flying wide, even while her lips barely contained a grin.

"You like that, baby?" I murmured, my fingers stilled deep inside her. "You like it when I breed this pussy?"

She nodded without hesitating, and I swore beneath my breath.

"I'm going to become addicted to this," I warned her as I withdrew my fingers and sucked them into my mouth, our combined tastes dancing on my tongue, only securing the addiction I knew was on the horizon. "It's going to become a problem, Natalie."

"I don't know," she laughed, her heated gaze locked on my mouth. "It sounds like a good problem to have. It *feels* like a good problem to have."

I shook my head. "I'm so fucking glad you agree."

Natalie's eyes wandered up to mine and then latched on, keeping a simmering eye contact as we both worked to catch our breath and wrap our heads around what just happened.

"I'm not going anywhere, Natalie," I found myself saying. "Which means, whatever happens this week...I will be here. Fighting for you. And Chloe. Fighting for *this* life. Okay?"

Natalie continued to hold my gaze while she took a shaky breath. Tears lined her lashes, but they didn't fall. Eventually, she nodded.

After a long moment, I circled my arms around her, cupping her bottom. "Can I take you to bed, Sunshine?"

"Yeah, Cameron." After a long exhale, she flashed me the sweetest smile in the world. It shone so fucking bright. "I think our bed is calling our name."

CHAPTER FORTY-FOUR

cameron

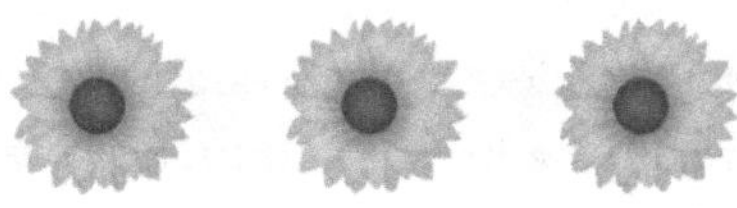

I'D SPENT COUNTLESS HOURS in a courtroom, but none of them had made me feel the way I did now.

I had all the faith in the world in Juniper—I never would have stepped aside if I didn't—but that didn't mean that I didn't feel a little powerless and a lot restless, standing at the back of the room.

This was our third consecutive day here. Blake and Delaney had been called as witnesses yesterday and then stayed to support Natalie in the gallery. Today, they'd switched with Gemma and Noah—who'd watched Chloe yesterday—so they could be brought forward to the stand.

Korey's lawyer pressed Noah the hardest. They questioned his fame and character and ability to be the support system Natalie claimed he was. Noah kept his cool, like he promised me he would when we talked last week. He told me he was used to getting grilled by the press and media, but I'd been a little worried it would be different when the topic of conversation was his family. But he did well. I suspected it pissed Juniper off more than Noah, based on the fire in her words when it was her turn.

My eyes drifted over Natalie's parents in the gallery, sitting next to Ellie. They'd all flown in for the trial, even though there wasn't much they could do except just...be here. But sometimes that was all that mattered. Anne London had her hand in Natalie's best friend's while they sat stoically in the benches. I couldn't see their faces from where I was standing, but I could see the tension in their shoulders.

I felt it, too. Everything had gone how I imagined it would, for the most part. But God, I needed this to be done for Natalie's sake. I could see how exhausted and stressed she was. Not many people would notice. Her shoulders were straight, her chin up. But her eyes told me she needed a break, and fuck if it wasn't killing me. The trial likely could have wrapped up yesterday. I'd been *hoping* we were going to, but at least we were getting a ruling today. The judge was on a recess at the moment and would be coming back shortly.

Well, hopefully shortly. But as long as we didn't have to wait days or weeks for a decision, I didn't fucking care.

I physically couldn't imagine it at this point, letting Chloe leave with Korey. To *live* with him? There was no way in fucking hell. I could barely stomach the idea of letting her go with him for his normal visitation weekends. Chloe belonged with Natalie and me. In Boston, with the rest of her family. Not a dad who only used her as a tool, a pawn in a game of chess.

I had so many plans for the three of us. A *lifetime* of plans for my girls, my family.

The bailiff cleared their throat, and I stood straighter. They called for us to all rise, and people shuffled to their feet as Judge Anderson entered the room again.

Fuck, this was it.

My eyes drifted to Natalie, and at the same moment, she glanced over her shoulder. Our eyes met, and I gave her an encouraging smile. *This is it, Sunshine. After this, it'll all be over.*

She breathed in. Breathed out. I could tell she didn't want to look away from me, terrified of facing a reality that might not be what we'd worked for. But I gave her a nod, and she straightened her shoulders, twisting back to the front of the courtroom anyway, strong as ever as she gave all her attention to the judge.

I kept all my attention on her. We waited with bated breath as Judge Anderson began an oral reading of the ruling, and I just couldn't take my eyes off Natalie. Which meant I got to see everything I felt reflected in her—the shift of her body, the breath whooshing out of her, the loosening of her shoulders, the relief in her posture as it was all brought to a conclusion.

Natalie would maintain sole physical custody of Chloe.

Chloe was staying with Natalie.

Chloe was staying with *us*.

And I couldn't keep the smile off my fucking face, even while I could barely believe that it had been announced, that this was *over*.

Fuck, I was so goddamn relieved to have this finally draw to a close. And *so* unbelievably happy for Natalie. And Chloe, because I knew this was what she'd wanted, too.

She wouldn't have to move schools or find a new skating club. She wouldn't have to be separated from the extended family who'd actually *been* there for her. She wouldn't have to move back in with a man who had been an apathetic loser toward her his entire life.

As Judge Anderson stopped speaking, I was moving. I hadn't wanted to risk agitating Korey before things were final. I'd kept to the background, letting Juniper do her job expertly, like I'd known she would. I hated not being directly beside Natalie, but if I had been the one fighting for her, it would have been so hard to stay professional at this point. I wouldn't have been able to keep my hand from finding hers and giving it a squeeze. My eyes would have constantly tracked her movements instead of staying focused on the task at hand. I probably would have called her Sunshine in front of the entire court. Kissed the top of her head as I sat down. Wrapped my hand around the curve of her thigh beneath the table. In the last month, I'd lost the ability to pretend around her, and I didn't really know how to go back.

And now, I got to march to the front of the courtroom and catch Natalie in my arms when she turned and met me in the aisle, a mixed expression of exhaustion and elation dancing across her features.

"*Cameron.*" She choked out my name, crumpling a little despite the smile stretching over that beautiful face.

"See?" I whispered over the top of her head. "I told you everything was going to be okay."

She nodded, like she'd known, too. But knowing it would happen and finally having it happen were different, and we both knew that.

Relief was a drug I could get high on at this point.

Natalie pulled back, wiping at her eyes. Behind her, I noticed Korey. He stood alone, looking as angry as ever. I'd seen parents lose custody battles before. I'd seen their defeated, sad expressions, the ones that told me that they'd really wanted their kids. And maybe they hadn't made the best choices in life and needed to do things differently before they could make that happen. Or maybe they really *had* deserved a chance, but the case simply hadn't gone the way they wanted.

Korey bore no resemblance to those parents.

His reaction had nothing to do with the love of his daughter or the desire to be a good parent.

The look on his face was one of indignation and rage—emotions that stemmed from his ego being wounded as he watched his control over Natalie and Chloe snap.

And then he had to watch me throw an arm around his ex-wife's shoulders before tossing one final wink his way, and I was pretty sure that was the nail in his proverbial coffin, considering how his gaze flared and his face turned a whole new shade of red.

I hoped he understood it was a "thank you." Because without him throwing me off this case, I wouldn't be sleeping in Natalie's bed more than I was sleeping in my own.

Korey's face twisted in outrage, but we both knew he couldn't do a damn thing about it anymore. I turned, gently guiding

Natalie in the opposite direction of her ex-husband and letting him stare at our backs as we walked away, stepping through the large, imposing double doors of the courtroom.

I heard Juniper's little tsk behind me.

"I saw that, Bryant," she muttered.

"Do you know how exhausting it is to always be the bigger person, St. James?" I asked over my shoulder.

She gave me a look back that I knew had nothing to do with Korey and everything to do with my slipup of her name.

"*Briggs*, sorry," I laughed.

Juniper tossed her long brown hair over her shoulder and smiled, the look of a lawyer who knew they'd just crushed it in court. Her heels clicked against marble as we walked into the atrium outside the courtroom.

Natalie slipped from beneath my arm, attacking Juniper with a hug that was warmly returned. "Thank you *so* much. I don't know how I'll ever repay you."

Juniper shook her head. "We all love Chloe so much, Natalie. No one wanted to see her leave Boston, and now she doesn't have to."

"Juniper." A voice cleared behind me, and I glanced back to see Noah, flanked by Gemma, Julian, Ellie, and Natalie's parents. "I hope you know that I am your *biggest* fan," Noah said, his grin wide.

Julian scoffed next to him. "The fuck you are," he grunted, but his lips were also tilted in a smile as he bent over, brushing a kiss over the top of Juniper's head and muttering, "Me haces tan orgulloso, Juni baby."

A blush worked its way to Juniper's cheeks, but she let Julian pull her into him. His hand came to rest on her stomach, smoothing over it protectively. We'd recently learned that Juniper was pregnant with twins, which meant Julian spent a lot more time glaring at, well, basically anyone who dared to get too close to his wife. I heard him check in with her beneath his breath, switching to English to ask her if she needed anything. She tipped her head up, making it hard to hear her response, and I looked back to Natalie.

She was releasing a long breath, shaking the nerves out of her hands as she looked around at the circle of smiling people. Noah and Gemma simultaneously pulled her into their arms, followed by her parents, and I slipped away to the back of the crowd.

I'd already gotten my hug, and if I wrapped my arms around her again, I was worried our new relationship would detract from the moment. I didn't know what she'd told her parents about me or if she was ready to introduce us. We'd met at Noah's engagement party, but I hadn't been Natalie's boyfriend then. I hadn't been the man who hoped to be in her and Chloe's life for a long fucking time. Preferably forever.

It was a lot for her today. I knew it was a lot, and I didn't want to add any more to it. I was happy enough to step back and watch the joy on Natalie's face, appreciate the spark in her eyes and the wonder in her voice, like she couldn't believe she was finally *free*. Gratitude and love radiated from her, and my heart filled to a brim I hadn't even known existed. I hadn't realized I could feel any more for her than I already had, but *God*. I loved everything about this woman. How the hell I'd managed not to tell her yet was beyond me.

Her eyes connected with mine, and for a moment, the world stopped spinning. Time slowed, and everything faded to a blur. And the only solid, sure thing in the world was her. Us.

"Thank you," she mouthed, eyes shining.

I smiled at her, gave the littlest nod.

Her body shifted, almost like there was a gravitational pull yanking her toward me, even as her eyes flicked around, landing on my face and then around her family's, unable to decide where she wanted to be. I didn't want her to have to pick.

I jerked my head to the door and mouthed that I'd be outside. And because I didn't want her to argue or feel bad, I turned and walked away before she could say anything, heading toward the courthouse doors.

Stepping out into the soggy August air, I released a sigh filled with pent-up energy and walked down the brick sidewalk, the reddish cobblestone uneven beneath my feet. But I only got a handful of strides away from the front door when I heard the heavy footsteps of someone following me.

I knew who it was before I even turned around. I could just sense it in the energy he brought with him wherever he went.

"Hey, asshole!" he called, accusations in his tone as I turned to find him charging toward me, and fuck if I wasn't somewhat grateful for it. Because it meant I got to put my hand out to stop him, grabbing him by the front of his shirt and slamming his back against the side of the courthouse.

Shit, that felt good. I'd been waiting to do that for a long fucking time. Waiting to watch the alarm and uncertainty fly onto his face as he realized who the fuck he was actually dealing with here.

"Do not even think about it," I growled before he could say a damn thing. I leaned in, letting him know how unbelievably serious I was. "You fucked up, Abrams. You lost them, and it's no one's fault but your own. You never deserved them. *Never*. And if you even think about going after my girls one more time, I will fucking *end* you. You think I haven't been looking into you? You think I don't know about all the little things your architectural firm is doing?" I raised a menacing brow. "Stay the fuck away from Natalie and Chloe, understood?"

Korey blinked, in shock.

"*Understood*?" I repeated.

I didn't have time for this.

He nodded but then muttered, "Fuck you."

I smirked. The only one fucking me was his ex-wife, and man, wasn't that the best goddamn truth.

A click of heels sounded on the pavement, and I looked over my shoulder to see Natalie running out of the courthouse after us. Fuck.

Releasing Korey, I pushed him in the opposite direction of

Natalie. "Get the hell out of here. Don't even dare to look at her, Abrams."

Korey glared for a moment, and then his gaze swung to the right, like he was going to directly defy me, so I took a threatening step forward. And that was all it took for him to spin on his heel in a huff and disappear down the street.

I turned back around just in time for Natalie to barrel into me, fueled by the momentum of the downward-sloping path and uneven Boston sidewalks. She pushed me up against the courthouse's brick wall, flattening her hands to my chest in an attempt to stop herself, practically knocking the wind out of me in the process. But I didn't mind. Not when her body was pressed against mine and I got to wrap my arms around her.

"What was that?" she breathed. "Is everything okay?"

I held her closer. "Everything is okay, Sunshine. He wanted to have some words. I made him do the listening instead."

Natalie raised a brow, and a mix of emotions passed over her face, like she couldn't decide if she was worried or turned on.

"Everything is fine," I assured her. "You won, baby. *We* won."

"We did," she agreed, sounding awed by that fact. Her eyes roamed over me, taking me in.

"What are you doing out here?" I asked.

"What am *I* doing?" she repeated. A smile broke onto her face, pure and beautiful. She wound her hands up my front, hooking them together behind my neck. "What are *you* doing? Why did you leave?"

"Because this is your moment, Natalie." I cupped her face. "With your family. I wanted to give you space."

She shook her head. "I don't want space."

"I can see that," I chuckled, considering she hadn't stepped back, still anchored to my front while my back pressed against the courthouse wall. "You know, I can see why you like this position so much. It's very nice."

Her lips twitched, but she was still looking at me expectantly. So I added, "I promised you slow, so that's what I'm trying to give you. I'm here for you, but I don't have to meet your parents right this second if that's too much all at one time."

"It's not too much." She said it so quickly my heart skipped a little. "You said this is my moment. With my family. But Cameron, that's you. This was *our* win for *our* family. And I think...I think you might actually be going *too* slow for me."

Her eyes were round, getting bigger by the moment, like she was realizing just how true that was right as she was saying it.

"Yeah?"

My breath hitched, my joy bubbling out of me.

It was everything I'd ever wanted to hear. The best thing in the world.

She nodded, leaning into me as though her body could do the talking. No more barriers, she was saying. No more walls. Nothing between us.

"Well, thank you for telling me," I murmured, struggling to contain my happiness. "I will have *no* problem speeding things up a bit."

"That sounds nice." She beamed, flooring me with her enthusiasm. "And I'd really like to introduce you to my parents, if you're up for it. I've told them about you."

"I'd love to meet your parents," I said easily. "I've told my family about you, too."

"Yeah?" She pressed her lips together, like that made her happy to think about.

"Yeah, of course." I smoothed a hand up her back and then down, sneaking my fingers beneath the hem of her blazer and the blouse beneath so I could touch her bare skin. "My Pops wants us to keep him in the loop about a wedding date."

Her irises bloomed, like greenery coming up to breathe in early spring, and I wasn't sure if it was because of what I'd said or the skin-to-skin contact. So I stilled, backtracking on both.

"Did I swing too far in the other direction?"

Natalie came out of her shock and giggled. "No, actually."

God, the pure elation that was radiating from her today was the best thing I'd ever seen.

"No?" I checked and then resumed the gentle way I was trailing my fingers along her lower back.

"No." She smiled and cocked her head to the side, giving me a thoughtful look. Like she was trying to memorize me. This. "Hey, Cam?"

"Yeah, Sunshine?"

She pushed up onto her toes, as though she needed to be closer to me, like she was telling a secret. "I think I love you."

I was wrong before.

This was the best thing I'd ever heard or seen.

This expression on Natalie's face, right now, as she breathed those words.

Holy hell, my heart might not make it through today.

"Oh, Natalie baby." I laughed because I couldn't even begin to contain my relief at getting to say the next words aloud. The ones I'd been thinking about for what felt like forever. The ones I'd been holding my tongue so I wouldn't say them aloud too soon. "I *know* I love you. God, I love you so fucking much."

An adorable, joyful sound spilled from Natalie's lips, too, and I couldn't help but drop my hands and scoop her off her feet, spinning us around so I pinned her back against the wall. She hung on to me, arms still locked around my neck as she tipped her face to look at me. I lowered my gaze, our foreheads touching, our breath mingling, and I was about to kiss her when she whispered, "I know I love you, too. I don't know why I said that."

I shook my head. I knew she did. I knew it was just taking her longer to trust the truth and our reality. And whether she was ready to admit it or not had never affected the way I felt about her.

"It doesn't matter either way," I said honestly and then brushed my lips over hers, unable not to. "I couldn't get myself to stop falling deeper in love with you if I tried. I just keep falling, and I can't stop, Natalie. You mean the world to me, and I just want to get this right. I'm so goddamn determined to get this right. For you and for Chloe."

"Cameron, you got it right," she assured me and then mimicked me, kissing the corner of my mouth lightly and then nipping on my bottom lip. "You *always* get it right. And I *love* you, okay? I feel it more and more every single day. I knew I was at risk of falling for you from the moment we met. That's the truth, and that's what I ran from that night. But I don't want to run from it anymore. It's still big and scary, but it's also the most comforting thing in the world, the way I love you. The way you love me."

"Oh my God, Natalie," I groaned before kissing her hard. I didn't know what else to do. I didn't know how to comprehend what she'd just said without bursting, so I did the only thing I could think of and kissed her the way I always wanted to from the moment I met her.

For me, the risk had been different.

I'd felt everything that was at stake that night, too. In the bar. But only because I knew she was moments from slipping through my fingers. I saw it in her gaze, saw the panic spreading across her face.

But then she showed up in my office, and I'd felt it so deep in my bones. Because I knew I'd do anything for her. Even if it meant risking everything I'd worked for. Because the biggest risk of all had always been what it was at the start: losing her.

Natalie whimpered my name against my lips, and I forced myself to pull back, knowing if I didn't soon, I'd lose the ability to stop altogether.

"I love you," I reiterated, brushing the tip of my nose against hers.

"So you said," she laughed softly.

"And I'll keep saying it." Over and over again, until my lungs gave out. "Let's go find your family before they find us, yeah?"

Natalie sighed, like she didn't want this moment to end, and as much as I could appreciate that, I also knew we had the rest of our lives to talk about us. Because that was the sort of long haul I was in for.

I put her down, letting her feet flatten on the cobblestone before lacing our fingers together. Natalie led the charge this time, leading me back toward the doors of the courthouse, and I was more than happy to follow.

"After this, can we go find Chloe?" she asked over her shoulder. "Blake and Delaney said they're at the park by our house. I want to tell her the good news."

"Of course, we can."

"Together?" she questioned, and my heart squeezed.

"I'd love that." I gripped her hand tighter. "If you're sure."

Natalie whipped open the door to the courthouse with her other hand and then paused, making sure our eyes connected. There was that same sizzling connection, the one I felt the first time I looked at her, but there was also something deeper now. A knot in my chest that tightened with every movement she made, every word she said. It tied us together in the most beautiful way.

"I'm *so* sure."

CHAPTER FORTY-FIVE

natalie

Three months later

"SURPRISE!"

Chloe's voice was the loudest as we cheered. She bounced on her toes beside me as Cameron took one step in the door, only to take two steps back, blown away by the crowd gathered near the entrance of Mulligan's, ready to celebrate him. Shock painted his expression, which quickly bloomed into something pure and wholesome—a joy so real I could breathe it in from across the room.

"What's this?" he laughed, his eyes wandering the people in front of him until they landed on me. I couldn't help a giggle from escaping me as he shook his head, knowing this was my doing.

"What's this, Sunshine?" he repeated, but it was softer this time, and my heart leapt into my throat.

I felt my feet moving, unable to stay away from him, and Cameron opened his arms. I dove into them with another laugh, and he looked down at me, radiating warmth.

"Congratulations on your promotion, baby," I whispered, and Cameron's eyes grew a little wider. A sheen covered them as he stared at me, like he couldn't really believe any of this.

But I could.

I'd always known that if Cameron set out to achieve something, he would make it happen.

It took him a little longer to make junior partner than I think he originally wanted, but he'd never once complained. Daphne had been a little disappointed with the turn in the custody case but had also understood, given the pressure from Korey. Cameron hadn't faced any real pushback or consequences, and Daphne seemed mostly supportive of our relationship, though I don't think she realized *when* our relationship started. I doubted Cameron would lie if she ever asked directly, but so far, it hadn't happened.

Overall, it took a handful of months after the case and many long days at the office before he was offered what he wanted, but finally, he'd gotten there.

Junior partner—the youngest at the firm.

He'd tried to downplay it, but I knew it was a big deal for him. I *knew* that even though he told me that his priorities had shifted, that he wanted to put more focus on his family and the beginning of our family, that this moment was still huge to him. It was a way he was connected with his dad, and the occasion deserved to be celebrated.

"We're so happy for you!"

Cameron's mom rushed forward next, and I tried to pull back from his side to let him greet her, but Cameron held me tighter, pulling me into his side and not letting go. But he looked toward her, grinning, surprised and happy to see her here.

"Thank you, Mom." He draped his free arm around her, enveloping her on his other side and tilting his head so it rested on top of hers. I saw his eyes wander to the rest of the crowd, who had gone back to chatting, milling around the bar and high-top tables in Mulligan's. Behind them, a large sign hung on the back wall that Chloe had made, her loopy handwriting spelling out "*Congratulations*" and "*Gardener Law is lucky to have you*" with drawings of sunflowers sprouting from the bottom.

I didn't have the heart to tell her that she'd spelled the name of his law firm wrong, and I thought it sort of fit anyway.

Gardner was one of the reasons Cameron had planted himself here in Boston, why he'd grown as a professional and as a human until I'd been lucky enough for him to bloom into my life.

And the other reason...what had drawn Cameron to this city and brought us together the first time? It was this place right here: Mulligan's.

I'd rented it out for the afternoon and evening; I thought it'd be nice to have the place to ourselves. I'd also wanted Chloe to be involved today and knew that likely wouldn't be appropriate with other patrons around. Cameron's mom, Mia, was friendly with the owners who had taken over after her parents, and they were more than happy to let us have the bar tonight, so much so that they tried to let us have it for free. But I wasn't going to let that happen. It was my way of giving back to them. For being the place that introduced me to Cameron. A place where I'd felt *alive* for the first time in so very long.

"I can't believe..." Cameron trailed off as he took everyone in —from Julian and Juniper laughing with my brothers to his grandfather and uncle studying the baseball game on the huge wall-mounted TV, Chloe between them, watching with just as much intensity. "You're here," he finished finally. "That you all came, that you're all here."

"We wouldn't miss it for the world," his mom gushed. "When Natalie proposed the idea, I don't even think I let her finish her sentence before saying yes."

"It's true," I laughed.

Mia had been *so* enthusiastic when I'd called about the idea.

Although, to be honest, since I first met her at a family baseball outing a couple of months ago, there hadn't been a time where she hadn't been enthusiastic. Mia was so lovely, so excited to welcome Chloe and me into their family folds.

But I was pretty sure today was extra special for her, too. I'd seen the wistfulness in her gaze when she'd looked around Mulligan's after first arriving. There was a sparkle in her gaze, a flush rising over fair, freckled skin. Memories danced over her face, so apparent that I had to look away, feeling like I was intruding on a private moment.

I felt Cameron's gaze fall on me again and grinned up at him, feeling a little watery, like my emotions lived too close to the surface today.

"You've got such a special girl," his mom was saying as Cameron stared down at me, just...looking. And all I could do was look back. "*Two* special girls," his mom amended as Chloe's bright laughter rang throughout the room.

Out of the corner of my eye, I saw Noah standing with his arms across his chest, lips twitching with reluctant amusement. Beside him, the devious crinkle in the corner of Pops' eye made me suspect that Cameron's grandfather just roasted my brother about something.

"I sure do," Cameron breathed, and I rolled my bottom lip into my mouth, slightly sheepish. "So fucking special."

I was still getting used to being with a man who didn't shy away from public affection or declarations. A man who was loath to take his hands off me, really no matter where we were, as evidenced by the way he still had me pressed into his side.

Mia drifted away. I heard her saying something to Pops that made me think she was playfully chastising him, but I couldn't get myself to look away from Cameron to see what, exactly, was going on.

"Thank you for this." Cameron's eyes dropped to my lips a second before his mouth did, landing a tender kiss that seemed to travel, making its way to my ear where he whispered, "I'll give you a proper thank-you later tonight, yeah?"

My breath hitched as I tried to fight the burst of heat inside me, and I had to clear my throat before I was able to respond.

"I can't wait," I said, my husky voice betraying me. Cameron pulled back, unnamed intensity swirling in his expression. "I'm so proud of you. We all are."

Cameron's eyes fluttered shut at my words, and he leaned forward, pressing a kiss to my forehead this time. "Fuck, you make me *so* happy."

"I could say the same thing about you."

So happy.

I hadn't known happiness like this existed.

Every day, I felt lucky to experience it. What a privilege it was to not only have that emotion sprinkled in with all the others that life brought, but to have it feel so *present*.

Cameron brushed the tip of his nose along my hairline, inhaling as he murmured, "And here I thought you told me to meet you at Mulligan's because you wanted to celebrate it being a year since the first time we shared a drink here."

I tipped my head back so I could meet his warm gaze.

"I think we can celebrate that, too." I grinned. "As long as you're okay with sharing that drink with others this time."

"I'm definitely okay with that." Cameron's lips curved, too. "Having our family together, *here*? I couldn't be more grateful for this." Something danced in his gaze as his voice dropped. "I'll get you to myself later."

My cheeks heated. "Yes, you will."

"Come on, Sunny." Grabbing my hand, he led me toward the bar, where a single bartender was working. We sidled up to it, Cameron's large hand palming the small of my back as he looked at me. "What do you want, baby?"

While I thought on it, Cameron glanced at the bartender, saying, "Whatever it is she wants, I'm paying for it."

The familiar words caused a laugh to bubble up inside me.

A year ago, I had been so uncertain about letting anyone crash into my life again, to tear down the walls that I'd so carefully constructed.

And now, instead of building walls, I was building roots. A life.

And I wasn't at all afraid to share it.

A sense of calm washed over me before I replied.

"I think I'll have whatever he's having."

epilogue

Two months later

NATALIE

"I THINK THE FENWAY one should be in the middle." My daughter stood in the center of the living room, one hand on a hip and one hand stroking her chin thoughtfully. "It's arguably the best one."

"Arguably." Cameron adjusted his framed stadium posters at Chloe's suggestion, holding them up against the wall so she could judge their location. "You're starting to sound like a lawyer, kiddo."

I shook my head, peeking down at my hands and the crocheted version of Winnie I was making for Delilah's first birthday. "Between you and Blake, she's going to know more big words than she knows what to do with."

Chloe gave me a look over her shoulder. "You say that like it's a bad thing. I'm almost in middle school, Mom."

I could barely believe that, honestly. Couldn't believe she was already ten years old. A whole decade of being my daughter, of doing life together.

"Middle school next year, college the one after at the rate you're learning."

Chloe shrugged. "Works for me."

"Nu-uh." Cameron stuck a nail in his mouth to hold it while he adjusted the wall hanging, getting it positioned just right. We were filling the townhome with some of his things, and I couldn't love it more, having him all around me. "No growing up too fast allowed in this house."

"Moved in two days ago, and already making rules, huh?" I teased.

Cameron's eyes cut to me, amused and happy.

"He's allowed to make *some* rules, Mom," Chloe said as she crashed onto the couch. Annabeth jumped on her lap, and she began absently petting her. "Just as long as he leaves my ice cream alone."

"I would never dream of touching your ice cream, Champ."

Chloe beamed, pleased. She leaned toward me, dropping her voice in a conspiratorial whisper. "I like this."

She didn't have to explain what she meant.

Chloe's last day of elementary school

CAMERON

"I really hate leaving you when you're not feeling well," I whispered against Natalie's temple. It was a little warm, but nothing too concerning.

She shook her head. "It's just a stomach bug. I'm sure it'll get better soon, but I don't think I can manage standing on that hot field all day."

"No, of course not." I pressed a kiss to her skin.

Her eyes fluttered shut, her head sinking deeper into the pillow. “I feel bad making you do it, though.”

I shook my head. “I don’t mind going to field day for you. Chloe and I will have fun. I just need you to promise to text me if you start feeling worse.”

Natalie nodded. “Promise.”

“Okay, Sunshine. I love you.”

“I love you, too.” A small smile lingered on her lips. “Thank you.”

“Of course, baby.” I turned off the lamp next to our bed, wanting her to get some more rest. Then I made my way to the door, gently shutting it behind me before I went downstairs to find Chloe waiting for me, water bottle in hand and hair in the high ponytail I’d helped her with before going back upstairs to say goodbye to Natalie.

A pretty good ponytail, if I do say so myself. Every time I did Chloe’s hair, I got a little better at it.

“Ready, kiddo?”

“Ready!”

To my relief, she hadn’t been too disappointed when I’d told her I was stepping in for her mom at field day. Actually, though I could tell she felt bad that Natalie was sick, Chloe seemed excited that I was coming.

Hopping off the kitchen barstool, Chloe sped out the door, and I followed her out to the car.

It was a short drive to her school, and after we parked, Chloe led me to the back of it, where there was a playground and a field. A crowd was gathering at the edge of it, and I heard Chloe mutter to me, “Luka Stevens beat us here.”

I couldn’t help a laugh from escaping. “We’ll beat him on the field, Champ.”

She made a satisfied noise in her throat and then grabbed my hand, tugging me across the black pavement. Sun beat down on us, the early heat of June present in the air despite it being early morning.

"Chloe!" Her teacher, Mrs. Hanson, brightened when she saw us walking up. "So glad you could make it." She looked to me. "Good to see you again, Mr. Bryant."

I smiled at her. "Same to you." I'd gone with Natalie to Chloe's last parent-teacher conference and met Chloe's teacher then. She'd been nothing but kind and welcoming over the last year. "Natalie's sick today, so I hope it's okay that I came to help out instead."

"Oh, of course it is. We'll miss her, of course, but always happy to have any kind of support."

She looked more than a little relieved to have more adults here, and I couldn't blame her, considering the growing group of fifth graders behind her, which Chloe dragged me toward. Two girls gravitated toward us, who I thought I recognized from pictures of Chloe's last field trip. She waved at them excitedly.

"Chloeee!" one of them squealed, while the other one looked at me curiously, which Chloe caught.

"This is Cam," she said matter-of-factly. "He's my...sorta dad."

Warmth blossomed in my chest, threatening to take over as Chloe's friends giggled. My favorite ten-year-old looked back at me, a little sheepish, as if not sure if I was okay with that title.

But I was so okay with it. The idea of being a dad, or even just a sorta dad, filled me with so much pride. And the thought of being *her* dad? I fucking loved it. And I loved that she was starting to think of me that way.

And I wanted her to know that.

Later, after we were both dripping in sweat from running around all day and dragging our feet back to the car, I said to Chloe, "I like being your sorta dad, Champ. I like it a lot."

She glanced my way, squinting from the sun. "Yeah?"

I nodded and then cleared my throat. It felt thick. "You can call me that whenever you want. But I wouldn't mind just being your dad, too."

"You wouldn't?"

"No." My chest felt tight. "I'd really like that, actually. But I know you already have a dad, so if you want, we could come up with a different name for me, too."

"Hmm." She pressed her lips together in thought. "I can have two dads, can't I? Percy Jackson does."

I laughed, happiness floating out of me. "You sure can."

One summer after

NATALIE

"Three," I called across the beach.

My daughter crouched down, ready to dive headfirst into the sparkling Cape Cod waters. "This time, you're going *down*," she threatened.

"Two!"

Cameron laughed, lining up next to her. Salt water ran in rivulets down his muscled body, his swimsuit plastered to thick thighs, dripping from their last race. He'd won that one. "Did you just threaten to drown me, Chloe?"

She just shrugged.

"One!"

My two loves splashed into the water simultaneously, taking off across the length of the beach in front of our rental cottage. I sank my toes deeper into the sand and watched, smiling to myself as Cameron stopped every few feet to look over at Chloe and make sure she hadn't fallen too far behind. She was a strong swimmer, but just the stretch and power of his body meant he pulled ahead with every stroke. With every sport they played together, he liked to make sure she won some and lost some. Keep it balanced.

This time, Chloe made it past the line they drew in the sand on shore and jumped up, raising her fists above her head in a victory stance.

Cameron pulled up behind her, shaking the water out of his

face and pretending to act winded and defeated, slapping a hand to his broad, bare chest. "What a champ," he said with a smile. "As usual."

He was such a beautiful man. How had I gotten so lucky?

Crouching in the water, he turned his back toward Chloe, who immediately jumped onto it, wrapping one arm around his neck while raising the other in a pumping motion as they took a little victory lap.

"I think it's your mom's turn," Cameron announced, turning toward me and flashing dimples he knew I'd have a hard time saying no to. "You think you can beat her, Champ?"

"Oh, yeah," Chloe said, waving a hand like that was no big deal.

Rude.

"What do you think, Mama?" Cameron called.

"I think it's pretty comfy here on the sand!" I called back, sinking lower in my beach chair.

"Come on, Mom!" Chloe encouraged, sliding off Cameron's back.

Cameron raised a brow at me. "Do I need to come get you, Sunshine?"

Sighing dramatically, I nodded. "I think you might."

His warm, brown gaze heated me from the inside out as he emerged from the water, all wet and perfectly sculpted. I tried not to stare too hard; after all, my daughter was *right* there. But Cameron clocked my wandering gaze immediately, smirking as he marched through the sand.

"Careful there, Mama," he murmured as he approached, sun bright across his face. His eyes roamed over me appreciatively. "There are consequences for looking at me like that. Especially when you're sitting there in that hot little swimsuit, looking absolutely *edible.*"

"Consequences?" My lips twisted. "I was hoping you'd say that."

Cameron shook his head, husky laughter filling the air.

And then *I* was in the air, getting thrown over his shoulder as he charged back toward the water, my daughter cheering in the background.

I'd never been more happy to dive deep into something.

Afterward, when the sun had begun to go down and Cameron had built a fire on the beach, I strolled along the water's edge, listening to the crackle and pop filling the summer air and appreciating the scene. Chloe was curled into a cocoon of blankets on the sand, Cameron's old copy of *The Lightning Thief* in her hands. When I'd warned her to be careful with it, Cameron had shrugged the idea off.

"I like the idea that the pages are well-loved," he'd said earlier, voice casual.

Now, he spoke again. But he sounded a little more tentative, catching my attention from across the beach.

"Hey, Chloe?"

I pulled my cardigan around me tighter and traced a line in the sand with my toes.

My daughter perked up. "Yeah?"

"You know I love you and your mom a lot, right?"

"I know."

I liked the way she didn't hesitate.

"What would you think if I asked your mom to marry me?"

Chloe giggled uncharacteristically, and I froze, my heart flying into my throat.

"Ugh, *finally*," she answered. "That's what I would think." And then it was quiet except for the thumping in my chest, which I suspected could be heard all the way across the ocean. A few beats later, Chloe's curious voice interrupted the stillness. "But if Mom becomes a Bryant...can I, too? I don't know why I have my dad's last name if I never see him."

"You know, I was thinking we could all be Londons. I made a promise once that I'd never take your mom away from her family in any way. And I think that includes her name. Would you want to be a London, Chlo?"

"Yeah, I do." Her confession was quiet, barely audible, but it tore me up inside. "Especially if you're going to be."

"I'll see what I can do, 'kay?"

"That means you'll take care of it, doesn't it?"

"Yeah, Champ. That means I'll take care of it."

The next fall

NATALIE

Cameron burst through the door at home, carrying the most sunflowers I had ever seen at one time...ever.

"Do you think this is enough?"

"Do I think that's *enough*?" I echoed, choking on an incredulous laugh.

"Yeah." He gave me a serious look, like he was really concerned. "There's a few more in the car. And I suppose we could cut the ones on the front patio if we really need more—"

"No." I shook my head. "Uh-uh. No cutting the ones on the patio. Those are *my* sunflowers."

Cameron's lips twitched as he put the pile of flowers down on the counter. They seemed to spread everywhere, taking up the entire room.

"I will not touch them, then," he assured me and then closed the distance between us, sweeping me into his arms with surprising quickness. "God, I can't wait. I feel like I've been waiting for so long."

I tipped my head back to look at him, say something maybe, but Cameron took advantage of the opportunity to cover my lips with his, sinking us into a deep, toe-curling kiss. Heat bloomed, brighter and hotter than ever before, and I gripped his shoulders, hanging on. I knew he'd carry me through this weekend. And then the rest of our lives.

"You've been very patient," I whispered against his lips when we finally broke apart. "Thank you for that. I love you, like, an unbelievable amount."

"I love you so fucking much," he groaned in response. "I would have waited lifetimes to marry you, Natalie London. *Lifetimes.*"

"Only two more days. I promise."

"Two more days," he sighed, dropping his forehead to mine. "Two more days until I get to see my beautiful bride walk down the aisle."

"With the biggest bouquet of sunflowers anyone has ever seen," I laughed.

"Exactly." Cameron pressed his mouth to mine again, lingering slightly. "What should we do until then?"

There were a million tasks on my to-do list to prepare for the wedding weekend, but we had about thirty minutes until Chloe came home from school, and the house was calm. It was the last bit of quiet we'd probably have for days to come. And I didn't want to do anything but—

Cameron picked me clean off my feet, reading my mind.

"I've made an executive decision," he grunted, "I want to fuck my fiancée one more time."

"One more time?" I asked breathlessly. "And then what? Will my husband take over?"

"Yeah, baby." Cameron's heavy footsteps sounded against the creaky stairs. "He will. He's gonna take care of you for the rest of your life, don't you worry about that."

I wasn't the least bit worried.

Thirteen years later

CAMERON

"Are we *really* sure he's good enough for you?"

"*Yeah*, Dad." Chloe rolled her eyes at me, but there was no mistaking the nervous, jittery smile on her face. “We’re sure. And even if we weren’t, do you really think *now* is a good time to bring it up?”

I raised a brow. “Better than in ten minutes from now, when it’s too late.”

Chloe shook her head, huffing a laugh before she turned her attention to her dress, fluffing the white fabric around her ankles.

God, where had the time gone?

My throat tightened, and I nudged her with my elbow. She looked up, those green eyes bright and wide, reminding me of her mother’s. Her whole face had traces of her mom in it, her beauty and her brilliance.

“You know I’m kidding, right?”

Her lips tugged to one side. “I know you’re kidding.”

“I just don’t think *anyone* is good enough for you.”

“I know you think that, too.”

“I’m a big fan of Oliver,” I said, wanting to make sure we were clear on that.

Chloe nodded, a slight sheen in her eyes now. “I wouldn’t be marrying him if you weren’t.”

My throat squeezed, threatening to close on itself. “He let your twelve-year-old brother be a groomsman. That really sealed the deal for me.”

Chloe laughed, twirling her bouquet in her hand. It was a summery yellow mix of blooms, but there were sunflowers in it.

She grew up with them.

“Eli looks really cute in his tuxedo,” she said, standing on her tiptoes to look at the front of the crowd, where her brother stood with her future husband.

“He’s happy to be included,” I said, also sneaking a peek at my son. His dark brown hair was brushed out of his face—a rarity. I could tell he was nervous to be standing up there, but also trying to keep his cool. Like he didn’t want anyone to know how excited he was. He smiled at someone in the audience, his dimples popping, and then he chanced a glance at Oliver, who stood anxiously waiting for us. For Chloe.

I looked back at the bride to find her cocking her head to the side, watching me. Her long golden-brown hair was perfectly curled, flowing over her shoulders with a sparkling pin holding it back on one side. "We'll always be around for him, Dad." She pressed her lips together before adding, "I don't know if I ever said this to you, but...thanks for giving me the one thing I always wanted."

I reached out, grabbing her free hand and giving it a squeeze. "A sibling?"

"Well, yeah, but—" Her smile was soft. Mature. Calm now, the anxiety dimming. "I love Eli, but I was going to say a dad. Someone who I know will always take care of things. Who will always take care of Mom. I remember how she was before...before you. It's fuzzy, but I remember. And I know how she is now."

I pulled Chloe in for a hug this time, trying to be cognizant of the wedding dress and bridal bouquet, but truthfully not really giving a damn. "I care about your mom and you so fucking much, Chlo. And I always will."

"I know," she whispered into my chest. "I'm gonna keep London, you know. You worked so hard for me to be Chloe London, so I'm gonna keep it. Oliver's okay with that, and it's what I want. To be like Mom, and Eli, and you. Even though I love Oliver so much, too."

I never imagined that my heart had the capacity to feel this goddamn full, and I clutched Chloe tighter, even as the music that was our cue began to play.

"As long as that's what you want," I said, feeling like all my vital organs might burst out of my chest.

"It is," Chloe confirmed and then pulled away, holding out her hand.

I inhaled, steadying myself, and took it. "You ready, Champ?"

She nodded, an excited gleam on her face. "So ready, Dad."

We only took one step down the aisle before my gaze found

Natalie, standing at the end of the front row of guests, looking stunning. It had been thirteen years since she'd walked down the aisle to me, sunflowers in her hand, honey hair framing her gorgeous face, and now here we were again. Her watery eyes brimmed with overflowing emotion as they flicked between Chloe and me. So much love, so much pride. God, I adored this woman and the life we'd created. More and more every single day.

When we reached where she stood, Chloe and I paused, as was planned, and I leaned forward, brushing a kiss on Natalie's wet cheek.

"It started with just the two of you, and that's the way it should end, too," I murmured.

Natalie swallowed hard, her emerald eyes brimming with tears as she switched places with me, giving Chloe a hug and then taking her arm. They stared at each other for a long moment without saying anything, and then finally, Natalie's eyes found their way back to me.

Like they always did.

"No, Cam." Her smile made me feel like I was floating. Anytime she looked at me, really. "It's just the beginning, didn't you know? There's still so much more left to come."

And as usual, she was right.

THE END

acknowledgments

I HAVE A DEEP love for this story. I've never written anything that is quite like it before, and that meant that it needed a little extra love and care to get right. It also needed (read: *I* needed) a little extra support, and I have an entire village of people to thank for being a part of the team who got me to the finish line.

To Nate, I'm so lucky to be with a partner who shows up for me in every way - including carrying an endless number of boxes of books at events and when they show up on our doorstep! Thank you for making space for my dreams in your life.

To Caitlin, you've been my number one sounding board for years (like, decades) when it comes to all things books, and I'm so grateful for you! Thank you for being the best personal assistant and best friend.

To Deidre and Alyssa, who have read this book more times than anyone else, I don't know how you're not sick of it and me yet, but thank you so much for your feedback, expertise, and everything you do for me!

My alpha readers, Kelsey and Hanna, you are my rocks! Thank you for sticking through all the messy parts of my first draft with me. Your input and willingness to listen to my rambling thoughts is invaluable.

To the most amazing crew of beta readers: Belinda, Nikki, Emma, Madison, Reilly, and Stephanie. I'm so lucky to have you all on my team for another release. Your feedback was so instrumental to bringing this book to life - thank you!

To my sensitivity readers: Aliyah, Leah, Ari, Savanna, Lo, Jackie, Taylin, Elisha, Kayla, and Kayla. I'm profoundly grateful for the time you took in reading Natalie and Cameron's book and providing context to the story that I might not have had otherwise. Your feedback was truly so important, and I couldn't have crafted this story without you.

To my agent, Rebeka, thank you for believing in me and these stories! I appreciate our partnership so much, and I can't wait to continue it.

Sandra, thank you for being so reliable and someone I can trust with all my projects. I appreciate your editing expertise so much - thank you!

To Alie, thank you for bringing Cameron & Natalie to life in your art! You are always the biggest joy to work with.

To Cassie, Sierra, & Simran, who are content queens and have helped to keep my socials going so I could focus more on what I really enjoy: writing! Thank you endlessly.

To Ruby, I wrote in my last acknowledgments that I can't wait to hug you IRL soon, and that still hasn't happened...so I REALLY think we need to do something about that! Thank you for putting up with me for so many years and always being there for me, from the very beginning! It is a joy to navigate the writing world together.

To my fellow authors and friends in the book community, I'm so honored to experience this space with you and to interact with you all. I'm so lucky to get to be a part of such a thriving community. Thank you for making this job the best!

To my friends and co-workers who have been nothing but supportive as I transition into my new author era, I appreciate you endlessly. Even if some of you are terrible at keeping my double life a secret, I love and appreciate you all the same.

To my readers, you mean the world to me! Some of you have been here since the beginning, and I can't thank you enough. And to those who have just joined me, thank you for being here! I couldn't do this without your support. Thank you, thank you, thank you.

And to my family, of course. Your support will always mean the world to me because I know not everyone is that lucky. Thank you for always cheering me on, no matter what I do!

about the author

AMELIE RHYS is a romance author with a love for writing swoony stories packed with tension and heat. When she's not daydreaming about fictional characters, Amelie loves to travel new places (so she can write about them) and find new coffee shops and bookstores (so she can curl up and read in them). Amelie also likes spending time at the lake with her family. She lives in Minnesota with her husband and her dog.

Books by Amelie Rhys
Alive at Night
Awake at Dawn
Attached at Heart
Already At Risk

www.ingramcontent.com/pod-product-compliance
Lightning Source LLC
Chambersburg PA
CBHW020002120726
47903CB00004B/1093